D0973928

MIDNIGHT'S KISS

Thea Harrison

BERKLEY SENSATION, NEW YORK

THE BERKLEY PUBLISHING GROUP
Published by the Penguin Group
Penguin Group (USA) LLC
375 Hudson Street, New York, New York 10014

USA • Canada • UK • Ireland • Australia • New Zealand • India • South Africa • China

penguin.com

A Penguin Random House Company

MIDNIGHT'S KISS

A Berkley Sensation Book / published by arrangement with the author

Copyright © 2015 by Teddy Harrison.
Excerpt from *Shadow's End* by Thea Harrison copyright © 2015 by Teddy Harrison.
Penguin supports copyright. Copyright fuels creativity, encourages diverse voices,
promotes free speech, and creates a vibrant culture. Thank you for buying an authorized
edition of this book and for complying with copyright laws by not reproducing, scanning,
or distributing any part of it in any form without permission. You are supporting writers
and allowing Penguin to continue to publish books for every reader.

Berkley Sensation Books are published by The Berkley Publishing Group.
BERKLEY SENSATION® is a registered trademark of Penguin Group (USA) LLC.
The "B" design is a trademark of Penguin Group (USA) LLC.

For information, address: The Berkley Publishing Group,
a division of Penguin Group (USA) LLC,
375 Hudson Street, New York, New York 10014.

ISBN: 978-0-425-27438-5

PUBLISHING HISTORY
Berkley Sensation mass-market edition / May 2015

PRINTED IN THE UNITED STATES OF AMERICA

10 9 8 7 6 5 4 3 2 1

Cover art by Tony Mauro.
Cover design by George Long.
Interior text design by Tiffany Estreicher.

To my author friends who are so patient, understanding and supportive, even when I get that crazed deadline look in my eyes. You know who you are. Thanks for being there.

≡ ONE ≡

Something happened to Julian as he stood in the San Francisco alleyway, looking down at his progeny and longtime friend.

Xavier lay curled on his side on the ambulance stretcher, the lines of his poison-wracked body rigid. Blood was everywhere—the stretcher, the concrete underneath. It had poured like a river out of him and had run in a thin red line down the gutter. The EMTs had had to drain out the poison and infuse him with as much fresh, untainted blood as quickly as they could.

Julian didn't know what it was, the thing that had happened to him. He wasn't like Xavier. He wasn't especially introspective or philosophical. He was most comfortable with taking action.

Whatever it was, his reaction ran deep. It felt like something essential had broken inside him.

His patience, maybe.

Yeah, that was pretty much broken all to hell and back.

Xavier gazed up at him, his young-looking face drawn with pain. His eyes still leaked crimson at the corners. While he had passed the danger point, or "magic hour" as the EMTs called it, the brodifacoum would make every joint and muscle in his body ache for the next three weeks, as his immune system worked to rid itself of any remnant of the poison.

Mindful of that, Julian kept his hand gentle as he touched Xavier's shoulder, when all he really wanted to do was grab the other man and clench him in a bear hug.

No, he wasn't ready to live in a world without Xavier in it. For too many decades to count, Xavier had been his Jiminy Cricket and the one example Julian could always look to whenever he wondered what it meant to be a fine man.

He spared a quick glance for Tess, the human woman who hovered so protectively near Xavier's dark head. When Julian had first seen Tess at the Vampyre's Ball, she had been rigid with terror and antipathy. Now as she gazed at Xavier, her expression was filled with so much love, Julian felt as if he was witnessing something naked and profound.

Cynically, he wondered just how long that would last. Weeks, or months?

Even if her feelings lasted for a few years, what concerned him most was that Xavier looked at Tess with the same expression.

Xavier didn't fall in love lightly or as a passing fancy. He would not stop loving Tess after a few fleeting years, and she had made no secret of the fact that she had serious issues with Vampyres.

However, any potential outcome of their liaison was an issue to be confronted on another day. Right now, Tess looked more than happy to look after Xavier, which was all that mattered, because Julian had a traitor to hunt down, and he needed to focus all his attention on the task.

And he planned on enjoying every minute of it.

Justine, the woman behind the assassination attempt, was an old, Powerful Vampyre and a member of the Nightkind council. For years, Justine had been undermining him, quietly and sometimes not so quietly sabotaging all of his attempts to genuinely unite the council members. Trying to kill Xavier was just her latest gambit—but this time, with her attacking a

Nightkind government official, Julian was fiercely glad she had finally gone too far.

This time, he thought, I'm going to destroy you, and every one of your co-conspirators, even if they sit on the Nightkind council too.

It was time for him to clean house, and if his hands got a little dirty in the process, why then, so be it. The Roman politician and philosopher Cicero, who had lived and died two hundred years before Julian, had once said, "Laws are silent in times of war."

If that was true, so too was Julian's threadbare, incomplete conscience.

As he strode toward his black Jaguar, he ran through the names of the twelve who sat on the council. Of all the members, he trusted Dominic the most.

The other Vampyre had been a Norman lord under William the Conqueror, and had run one of the most successful mercenary companies in Europe during the Middle Ages.

He was calculating, calm in a crisis, and along with another council member, Marged, he was also the most neutral of all the council members. Unlike Marged, whose main abilities lay in commerce, Dominic knew how to respond when situations escalated to violence.

Pulling out his cell phone, Julian dialed Dominic's number.

Just when he thought the call would roll to voicemail, the ringing stopped and Dominic's deep baritone voice sounded. "Good evening, Julian."

"Where are you?" Julian asked.

Despite his terseness, the other Vampyre's voice remained courteous and neutral. "At home. Why?"

Sliding into the driver's seat of his car, Julian did some quick calculations. Dominic's estate lay in Napa Valley, a couple of hours' drive away, but the other Vampyre had a helicopter and could make the trip to Evenfall much quicker if necessary. That, however, was assuming Dominic would be willing and able to drop everything and come at a moment's notice.

Starting his car, Julian headed for his house in Nob Hill. While the great, hulking Norman-style castle Evenfall was the Nightkind King's official residence, it lay in Marin County across the Golden Gate Bridge. For the sake of convenience, Julian also owned a house in the city, a nineteenth-century mansion that was located not far from Xavier's own townhome.

As he negotiated through the heavy traffic around the site of the attack, Julian told the other man, "Justine tried to have Xavier assassinated tonight."

A brief, intense silence took over the other end of the connection. Then Dominic said, "Tried?"

"He survived, along with one of his attendants, but he'll be incapacitated for a few weeks." Julian's voice turned savage. "It was brodifacoum poisoning."

The other Vampyre drew in a breath, the quiet, telltale reaction as strong as a curse. "Do you have proof that it was Justine who tried to kill him?"

Dominic's neutral tone was beginning to grate on Julian. He growled, "Don't tell me you don't believe what I'm saying."

"Not at all," Dominic said. "I'm trying to ascertain what you know, and whether or not you have enough to take to the council."

Fuck the council.

Julian caught himself up before he said it aloud. Instead, he replied between his teeth, "I have two surviving witnesses."

Dominic said, "I realize you're very angry. If someone tried to murder one of my progeny, I would be too, but think for a minute. While Xavier's integrity is well known, the council won't accept testimony from either him or his attendant. Attendants can be spelled into believing something is true when it isn't, and as your progeny, Xavier would have to say anything you compelled him to."

The fact that Dominic's cool reasoning was correct made Julian even angrier. He snapped, "Goddammit."

"All I'm trying to point out is that you're going to need

more than just their stories," Dominic told him. "But never mind that for now—what actually happened?"

Julian yanked his unruly emotions back under control. "Justine bribed one of Xavier's attendants in order to get him into the city. If everyone had been killed in the attack, there wouldn't have been any witnesses at all. Xavier nearly did die. If his one surviving attendant hadn't known what needed to be done when he'd been poisoned and taken such quick action, he *would* have died."

"Where's Justine now?"

"I don't know. That's what I need to find out." Julian pulled in front of the black wrought iron gates to his house and keyed in the security code. As the gate swung open, he told the other man, "Maybe going after Xavier was an end play for Justine. She's certainly held a grudge against him for long enough. But maybe assassinating him was just the first step in a broader agenda, and maybe Justine wasn't the only Vampyre involved. I need to track her down, and I need for you to get to Evenfall as quickly as you can to keep things stable while I'm gone."

If Xavier had been killed, his loss would have indisputably weakened Julian's political position even further. Setting aside the friendship factor, not only would Julian have lost his staunchest supporter in the Nightkind government, but he would have also lost his spymaster and most reliable source of information.

Dominic said, "I need some time to wrap up some personal matters, but I can be in Evenfall by tomorrow evening. Will that be soon enough?"

"Yes. I'll be in touch when I know something."

"Be smart, Julian. Use your head. Justine has allies. Whether or not you find her, just make sure you bring back proof that you can take in front of the whole council, enough so that even her allies would have to back down. That way, if nothing else, you can see that she's discredited and removed from office."

"I hear what you're saying," Julian said. Finally, for the

first time in their conversation, he achieved a semblance of equanimity.

He did, in fact, hear exactly what Dominic was saying—and not saying. Dominic knew very well Julian had no intention of bringing Justine back to Evenfall, and he was warning him to get all his ducks in a row. It was sound advice.

With a punch of a thumb, Julian disconnected the call. As soon as the gate opened wide, he gunned his car down the short, curving driveway and braked in front of the huge, sprawling mansion.

The building had a hint of European flair. Built out of golden limestone, it had tall, stately windows trimmed in black iron. Alerted by the house security system, Gregoire, Julian's majordomo, opened the double front doors and stood waiting attentively, his intelligent, plain features impassive.

As Julian jogged up the front steps, he was already dialing another number.

Evenfall's IT administrator, Gavin, answered on the first ring. "Yes, sir?"

Julian nodded at Gregoire as he swept past. He said to Gavin, "I want Evenfall on a total information lockdown within the next ten minutes—five if you can manage it. No Internet, no cell phone reception. The only lines of communication I want open are the dedicated phone lines under our control. Got it?"

"Yes, sir." Gavin sounded somber and unsettled. "But I have to warn you, I might not be able to make the lockdown total."

"What do you mean?" Julian raced up the stairs to his suite.

"These days, a lot of people have independent Internet access with hotspots in their cell phones," Gavin said. "I don't have any control over shutting those down. Evenfall is a big place, but I can see about putting out enough interference to scramble their signals."

"Do that until you receive further instructions from either me, Xavier or Dominic." He disconnected and dialed his head of security, Yolanthe. When she answered, he told her, "Two things. I'm putting Evenfall on a lockdown. Until further notice, nobody is allowed to enter the castle walls or leave, except for Dominic, who will be arriving tomorrow evening."

"Very good," Yolanthe said. Unlike Gavin, she sounded calm to the point of sleepy. "And the other thing?"

"I want a strike team to meet me here in the city," he told her. "Keep it lean and mean, no more than ten fighters. Get them here as soon as you can."

That woke her up. Sounding very alert, she said, "We'll grab a chopper and be with you in twenty minutes."

"Good enough."

Twenty minutes. Thinking quickly, Julian did some math.

It had taken him fifteen minutes to navigate through city traffic to get to the house from the alley where Xavier had almost died. Before that, Julian had spent some time on the scene, waiting to hear if Xavier would survive and questioning various officials who had been first responders. And it had also taken him time to get to San Francisco from Marin County.

How long ago had he kicked Justine out of Evenfall?

Even though the Nightkind political season was over for the year, Justine had been insisting upon reconvening the council. She had claimed that Xavier had exceeded his authority when he had made this year's trade agreements with the Light Fae heir Melisande.

As always when Julian's thoughts turned to Melly, a hard knot of old pain and anger tightened in his chest.

She had once meant the world to him, and the affair they had begun so lightly in defiance of all convention had quickly turned into something much more serious. The kind of serious where a man started thinking of ways to change his life in order to be with the woman he cared about.

At least it had for him. Clearly it hadn't for her, or she would never have betrayed him with the Elven heir Ferion.

The whole thing had happened decades ago, in the 1990s, and time wasn't the only thing that had moved on. Melly and Ferion's affair hadn't lasted either. Just recently, Ferion had become the Elven lord of his demesne, while Melly still lived the carefree life of a rich, jet-setting single.

Virtually everyone had gotten on with their lives, except for him. Some part of him still remained frozen in that terrible moment of realization when he had stared at the photos of Melly and Ferion together.

Now, every time he saw her photo online or in the papers, he snarled and snapped like a wounded tiger at anyone who had the misfortune to be in the vicinity. He couldn't even summon a pretense of indifference. Whenever he was forced to be in the same room as Melly, any attempt at conversation quickly devolved into a shouting match.

Their troubled dynamic made it even more difficult to understand why Melly's mother, Tatiana, had sent Melly to conduct this year's trade negotiations with the Nightkind— unless Xavier was right, and Justine had been behind that ploy too. Julian and Melly had flamed out as usual, and none of the trade agreements had been approved until Xavier had stepped in and talked to Melly personally.

When Justine had tried to claim the agreements weren't valid, Xavier had outmaneuvered her once again by recording Julian and Melly in verbal agreement with each other. Julian had confronted Justine with the recording, and she had left Evenfall just after sunset.

Now Julian reexamined things in a different light.

With the Nightkind political season over, the council had already met and disbanded for the year. Had Justine been looking for an excuse to get the council together one more time?

If they had reconvened upon her insistence, and the assassination attempt against Xavier had been successful, what would have been her next move—an assassination attempt against Julian?

And who would have made it with her?

Julian had a sense of time trickling away from him. The more time that passed, the more time Justine had to figure out her next moves. Even as she had left Evenfall hours ago, she would have been thinking ahead and rerouting any plans she had laid in place.

By now she had to know the attempt against Xavier's life had failed, so she would be rerouting again.

I have questions for you, Justine, he thought savagely. Many questions.

What are you doing now?

Upstairs in his suite, he washed and changed quickly, donning black fatigues, boots, and a T-shirt. When he was finished, he jogged downstairs and called for Gregoire, who appeared again almost immediately.

He told the human, "I'm here for only a short while, and I don't know when I'll be back in the city. Evenfall is on lockdown. You need to keep the house here on lockdown too. Don't allow anybody on the property, except for Xavier or Yolanthe."

"Of course," Gregoire said. "Do you need to feed before you leave?"

Julian shook his head. Then he paused to look into the other man's eyes. While he did not encourage the kind of familiarity in his household that some other Vampyres did, Gregoire had been with him for almost forty years, quietly and unassumingly going about his tasks, and somehow always managing to ensure that everything was exactly the way that Julian wished.

He put his hand on the other man's shoulder. "No, but thank you for thinking of it. Look after yourself and the others. I would be—most displeased if something happened to you."

Gregoire smiled and somehow managed to look worried at the same time. "I will, sir. Please look after yourself as well."

Over the normal sounds of the city at night, Julian could hear the steady chopping of an approaching helicopter. Yolanthe's strike team was almost here. He left Gregoire and strode into his study, where he went to a weapons cabinet that was tastefully concealed behind a walnut panel. By the time he had armed himself, the helicopter had landed on the helipad on the grounds behind the detached garage.

Yolanthe met him at the rear door.

Standing at five foot ten, Yolanthe was tall for a woman, but not unusually so. She had a lean, muscled body and panther-quick reflexes. Her strong-boned, olive brown features were classic Greek, and she wore her sleek black hair cut short in a no-nonsense style that hugged her shapely skull.

Julian had met Yolanthe when he had been a young Vampyre and still a general in the Roman army. They had been on opposite sides of a small, nasty border war.

With the weight of superior numbers on Julian's side, the war hadn't lasted long. Impressed with Yolanthe's fighting skills and intelligent tactical ability, he had successfully recruited her, then several years later had turned her. She was one of his first progeny.

He told her, "We're not staying."

She fell into step beside him. Together they made their way quickly to the military helicopter waiting on the helipad. She asked, "Where are we headed, and what's our mission?"

Julian leaped into the helicopter, glancing around and nodding at the nine familiar faces inside. He was unsurprised to find who Yolanthe had picked for the mission—all of the fighters present had served him for a long time. He knew them well, and trusted them.

As Yolanthe joined him, he told the team, "Justine tried to kill Xavier, but she didn't succeed. He's survived and he's going to recover. He was also able to tell me what had happened. We're going to take control of her estate. I doubt she'll be there, but I'm hoping we'll find some clues about where she's gone. Expect extreme resistance."

"Understood, sir." Yolanthe touched the pilot on the shoulder. "We'll need to set down a good quarter of a mile away and jog in, so we can get an element of surprise. Let's go."

As the whine of the chopper blades increased, Julian took a seat. Justine's home lay south of the Bay, along the border of Silicon Valley, just outside of a small, upscale town called Los Gatos. By car, the trip would take over an hour. By air, they would be able to get there much sooner.

Justine's estate was located some distance outside of the town, her land adjacent to Sanborn County Park. In an area populated with multimillion-dollar homes, her property was a lavish one by anyone's standards. An elder Vampyre with a well-established wealth, she kept a household of over a hundred attendants, all of whom would have received some degree of weapons training.

As they grew closer, his muscles tightened in anticipation. The pilot set the helicopter in a picturesque, open clearing and powered down. Yolanthe handed Julian a headset, which he donned. While telepathy was by far the stealthiest method of communication, for most creatures it was only possible to telepathize within a range of a few feet, and it was useless for group communications.

He stepped out of the helicopter. The spring night air felt cool and damp against his skin. As soon as the other fighters hit the ground, they began to run.

A high security fence surrounded the estate, but that was no real obstacle for Vampyres. As Julian drew near, he put on a burst of power and speed, and launched into the air to clear the top of the fence by a good yard. He paused until all the others had joined him, then the team fanned out and stalked toward the mansion.

His sharp gaze scanned the area as they grew close, and he knew Yolanthe and the others were doing the same, looking for potential traps or security pitfalls. The scene looked perfectly domestic and peaceful.

A sense of disquiet stirred.

Julian didn't bother to use his headset. Yolanthe was in charge of her team, and she would be the one to issue them orders. He told her telepathically, *Something's not right. We need to slow down.*

She responded immediately, whispering into her mic, "Everybody, hold up."

The team came to a halt. Julian studied the huge, sprawling mansion. Every interior light blazed, yet as he strained to listen, the house was completely silent. He could hear nothing. No music, or television. No sounds, anywhere in the area, until he grew convinced the property was deserted.

He muttered to Yolanthe, *I don't like this.*

I don't either. While she had straightened from her crouch, her expression remained hard and wary.

Keep your team here. He headed for the house.

She whispered a quick set of orders and raced to fall into step beside him. That hadn't been exactly what he had meant, but other than throwing her an irritated glance, he said nothing and they continued the rest of the way together.

They came to the house at an angle and slightly to the rear, so that after they rounded a landscaped copse, the entire back of the building came into view.

A door stood open. Light streamed out, throwing a rectangle of illumination on the well-tended lawn.

Abandoning his cautious stance, he strode up to the doorway, Yolanthe at his heels. Stepping inside, he came into a large, luxurious kitchen.

Three people, two women and a man, lay in pools of crimson on the floor around a butcher-block island. Their throats had been cut. He recognized one of the women. She had been Justine's latest lover, the beautiful woman Justine had kept on a leash at the Vampyre's Ball. Now the dead woman's pale features wore a bewildered expression.

He exchanged a sharp, frowning glance with Yolanthe, then moved into the hall. Throughout the ground level, he found more bodies, many more. A larger group was gathered in a family-style rec room. Those had been shot, each one double tapped with professional efficiency, a bullet to the heart and a bullet to the head.

Son of a bitch.

He stood staring at them, until Yolanthe stepped into the room. She swore softly when she caught sight of the group.

Only then did he turn away. His gaze fell to a small, telltale pile of dust, all of what typically remained of a Vampyre after they had been killed.

After walking through a few more rooms, he stopped and pinched his nose. A tension headache began to squeeze the back of his skull.

He had been right. There was nobody in the house—nobody left alive.

"There aren't any signs of struggle," Yolanthe said.

He said softly, "An outside attacker didn't commit these murders. Either these people had died willingly, or Justine had spelled them into compliance. Either way, she slaughtered her entire household."

Justine had known he would come here. Of course she had. She had realized that as soon as she heard that Xavier had survived. And she had made quite sure that nobody would be able to tell Julian anything.

His voice turned gravelly with the force of his emotion, he said, "You might as well call in the rest of the team. Have them search the other buildings, just in case. Let me know what the body count is when you're done."

The other Vampyre looked grim, her complexion pale. "Yes, sir."

While Yolanthe's team searched the property, Julian walked through the silent house. When he came to a darkened office, he flipped on the light and went to sit at the desk. A forensics team would scour everything in the room, including any files, but for now, he turned on a desktop computer and watched as it powered up.

The welcome screen appeared, with a prompt to set up the computer. It had been wiped and reset to the factory default.

Leaving the office, he walked upstairs and looked through the stylish rooms. Standing in Justine's bedroom, he closed his eyes and inhaled the scent of expensive perfume.

What was she doing now? Where was she headed next?

If he didn't find her in the next twenty four hours, his search could very well become lengthy. He could freeze her assets, at least those he could find. But Justine was not the kind of person to keep all of her assets in easily accessible places. No Vampyre of any age would. Long-term survival was often based on a wide diversity of resources.

So, she would have money. And as Dominic had pointed out, she had allies. While she might have slaughtered her household, she wouldn't give up on her lifestyle in the Nightkind demesne so easily.

She had history here, and political aspirations. She had grudges.

"Ninety-two," Yolanthe said from the doorway. She sounded

furious. "What kind of monster kills ninety-two of her own people?"

The question was so clearly rhetorical, he didn't bother to answer. Instead, he opened his eyes and said, "When news of what happened here gets out, let's hope she loses a few friends over it." He turned to the doorway. "We need a forensics team out here. Also, the computer in the office has been set to the factory default, but maybe Gavin will know some electronic voodoo that can recover data."

Yolanthe nodded. "It's four o'clock, and daybreak will be soon. I'll get a human team out to go over the property. We can take the computer with us."

He nodded. "Let's get out of here."

The flight back to Evenfall was silent and grim. Julian watched out the window as the eastern sky lightened with pre-dawn. After landing, as he strode into the castle, angry Vampyres tried to besiege him with questions about Internet access and when they could leave.

In an instant, Yolanthe's team surrounded him, fangs out and snarling a warning.

The complaints cut off abruptly. Shocked and staring, the other Vampyres fell back.

One of the team split off from the rest to take the computer to Gavin. Yolanthe stayed in the group that maintained a secure perimeter around Julian as he strode to his suite. Once he gained access to his rooms, he gave orders that he was not to be disturbed, and he got to work.

On a lockdown, only two dedicated lines were left open. One of them went to Gavin in the IT headquarters, and the other fed into Julian's suite.

Gavin had also set up a program on Julian's computer that kept a running total of who was in residence at Evenfall, including council members. At any given time, usually when the council was in session, Evenfall could potentially have up to three hundred souls.

Julian checked it quickly. One hundred and eighty-nine people were locked in, including two council members, Annis and Leopold. He couldn't remember the business that had brought them to Evenfall, and it didn't matter—they wouldn't be leaving anytime soon. Right now, they were two less council members he had to worry about.

The icon for his email inbox indicated he had nearly a thousand messages. He ignored those as well. What he focused on instead was composing a letter to the human governor of California.

The demesnes of the Elder Races overlaid human states and governments. Humans were governed by human law, and those of the Elder Races were subject to the laws of their demesnes. The borders that separated them were invisible ones of race and community.

The global unifier was commerce. Sales taxes were split, and the taxes on income went to the relevant agency, either Elder Races or human. For the most part, the two different realms coexisted well enough.

Sometimes they didn't, especially when the clashes of one spilled into the physical space of the other.

This would be one of those times.

As soon as the letter was finished, Julian put it in the body of an email and hit send. Afterward, he sent copies of the letter to local human officials.

When he had finished, he went to the doors that led to the hall, opened them and told Yolanthe, "See that the media room is ready, and let any press we have in Evenfall know that I'll be making an official statement in a half an hour."

Speculation shifted in her dark eyes, but all she said was, "Yes, sir."

He strode into his bedroom to change into a uniform, not parade dress, which was reserved for more ceremonial occasions, but somber black. Then he left the suite and, surrounded by his guards, he strode to the media room in the IT headquarters. More people had gathered in the large communal spaces and hall, but this time, no one attempted to stop or talk to him. Instead they watched him and his guards in tense silence.

Fifteen minutes later, in the media room, they were ready to shoot. Julian looked into the cameras. "Over the last twelve hours, there have been two significant attacks against Nightkind government officials, resulting in multiple casualties. The death count is now well over a hundred."

At least it was, when you counted all the attackers who had died going up against Xavier and Tess. He said, "Significantly, most of those who died were humans."

As he paused, no one made a sound, although everyone in the room stirred, including his guards. While technically, he spoke the truth—most of those in Justine's household had been human—once humans became part of a Vampyre's household, they were considered to be part of the Nightkind demesne.

Still, their deaths would have a hell of an emotional punch. The massacre signified a massive betrayal of the trust Julian had worked so hard to build between the Vampyres and the human population, and Julian was not above twisting the literal truth to his advantage whenever necessary.

Deliberately, he continued. "These terrible crimes must be answered. As King, I am placing the Nightkind demesne under martial law, effective immediately. From sundown today, any Nightkind creature found more than a quarter of a mile away from its domicile of residence will be subject to the severest penalty by law, up to and including death. Martial law is an extreme measure, to be used only in cases of emergency. The Nightkind demesne is presently in just that kind of emergency. People of the Nightkind demesne, the movement restrictions are for your protection, as we search for the criminals who initiated the attacks and we take every necessary step to make sure that another attack doesn't happen."

For a brief moment, he hesitated. The temptation to call Justine out in public grew so strong he had to clench his muscles against giving in to it. Publicly identifying her as the person responsible for so many deaths would be even more effective at stopping her movements than implementing martial law, but without acceptable proof to back up his claim, he knew the entire Nightkind council would turn against him.

None of them, not even Dominic, would tolerate an unsubstantiated attack against one of their own. The resulting backlash would end up hurting Julian's ability to hunt for Justine far more than it would help. He needed to gather proof first, the kind of proof that the council would accept.

His frustration boiled over. For the first time in his speech, he let his fury show in his clenched features and burning gaze. He felt his fangs descend and let them show in an expression of naked aggression. "Rest assured," he said softly, "we have no higher priority than this. We will hunt down those who are responsible, and they will be brought to justice. I won't be taking questions today. That will be all."

The room erupted into noise. Ignoring the shouted questions, he left the room. Yolanthe and the other guards fell into place around him.

This time, he headed into the secure part of the IT area. Gavin left his workstation to meet him.

Without preamble, Julian said, "You saw the statement?"

"Yes, sir." The younger Vampyre's eyes were wide and worried.

"I won't be able to justify keeping the demesne under martial law for long," he said. "It will help to have the human population outraged, so we might be able to get a few weeks. If Justine is still in the demesne—and even if she isn't—it will make it harder for her, and anyone else working with her, to maneuver. In the meantime, we need to speed up the search."

"I've frozen her assets," Gavin told him. "At least those that I could find. You must know she'll have hidden assets. Cash deposits, offshore accounts."

Julian looked at him from under lowered eyebrows. "Of course."

"I've programmed some searches to see what I can find."

"Just do the best you can." He moved on to the next thing. "What about the computer? Were you able to get any information from that?"

"No. I'm sorry." Looking frustrated, Gavin rubbed the back of his head. "I'm going to try a few more things, but I don't think I'll be able to retrieve anything. Sometimes you can actually recover files after a factory reset, but I think she used another program to make sure the hard drive was wiped clean."

"Understood."

If she had gone to the trouble of making sure the hard drive was completely wiped, why hadn't she simply destroyed the computer? Had she done it to taunt him?

Scowling, Julian turned away and headed back to his suite. He had a million and one things to do before Dominic arrived that evening. After that, he would be free to go after Justine personally.

Even if he had managed to cripple Justine's movements—at least for now—she had already crippled him by taking Xavier out of commission. He needed to get eyes on each of the council members, especially Darius, but aside from the two held in Evenfall, the others would be scattered all over Northern California.

Again, he got the sense of time slipping away from him. He spent the rest of the afternoon and evening working with Yolanthe to deploy handpicked soldiers to each council member's home. Twice he talked to Xavier. While the other man was clearly tired, he was more than willing to help. He had a handful of people he could send out on reconnaissance as well.

By the time Dominic arrived late that evening, Julian had a plan in place. Those who were deployed would report their findings to Xavier, who would then contact Julian with anything newsworthy that looked suspicious. Julian would follow up the leads in person. The search would be brutally meticulous, but that was often how wars were won—by gathering painstaking intelligence and winning one battle at a time.

Meeting with Dominic strained his patience. Yolanthe's team was rested and waiting for him. He forced himself to be thorough as he went over final details, while the part of him that had broken strained to be on the move.

If Dominic had been born in modern times, he might have been the star quarterback for his college team. Standing six foot four, the other Vampyre was broad shouldered and lean hipped, his powerful frame perfectly suited to wearing heavy armor and waging war atop a horse.

He had icy blue eyes and blond hair, and the kind of looks that made him a favorite with the opposite sex, while his handsome face bore a scar from temple to jawline that gave him an aura of danger. The danger was very real, but not so much the romance. Dominic was one of the most coldly pragmatic men Julian had ever met.

At the end of the meeting, Dominic asked, "How's the search going?"

While Julian was willing to share administrative details about Evenfall, he had no intention of talking about the hunt for Justine. All he said was, "We'll get her—and anyone else who is working with her."

Speculation shifted in Dominic's icy gaze, but he nodded. "Fair enough."

Julian's phone rang. Not his cell phone—thanks to Gavin's efforts, that wouldn't work until he left Evenfall. The phone in his office rang, on one of the two dedicated lines in the castle.

Very few people had that number. Quickly he strode into the other room to check the caller ID.

His eyebrows rose. The incoming call was from Tatiana, the Light Fae Queen in Los Angeles.

Reflexively, he checked the time. It was almost three o'clock in the morning.

He could think of no good reason for Tatiana to be calling him at three in the morning. Tatiana had hated him ever since he had broken off his affair with Melly.

He let the call roll to voicemail. After he listened to what she had to say, he would decide when he would get back to her.

Almost immediately, the phone rang again. Instead of leaving a voicemail message, Tatiana had called back.

Unease ran cold fingers down his spine. This time, he answered the call. "Tatiana, you might have seen in the news that I'm in the middle of something urgent right now."

The Light Fae Queen's voice sounded in his ear. Usually she was the epitome of elegance and iron, but this time the iron sounded rusted and strained. "So am I. Julian, I need for you to come as quickly as you can."

What the fuck?

His stomach clenched. "What's the matter? What's wrong?"

"I can't tell you that," said Tatiana in measured tones that spoke of extreme control. "You know as well as I do that phone conversations might not be secure."

His mind flashed to the one possible reason Tatiana might have for calling him. He demanded, "Has something happened to Melly?"

The possibility was inconceivable. Melly was so vibrant, so young, just a few hundred years old. An array of images flashed through his mind, each worse than the one before. Melly, in a car accident—Melly in the hospital, badly injured . . . or dead.

That last thought caused dread to wash over him in a sick, cold wave.

"All I can say is, please, for the love of all the gods, can we put our differences aside just this once? Will you come to help me?"

In an instant, he abandoned the one thing that had consumed him for the last forty-eight hours. He had already set his plan in motion. Yolanthe could take it over and spearhead the search for Justine.

He told her, "I'll be there as soon as I can."

≡ TWO ≡

"Come on, Melly, will you wake up already?" someone demanded. An impatient woman, with a familiar voice. "Hell's bells, I didn't realize I compelled you to go down that hard. Sometimes I don't know my own strength."

Melly had been having the strangest dream.

The first part had been awesome. She dreamed she was skiing, whipping along the downhill slope so fast she could hear the wind whistle in her ears. Gods, she loved that rush.

Something snagged her left ski, and she lost all control. The world flipped as she tumbled head over heels. Ow. Ow. Ow.

Then with the sneaky suddenness that dreams could sometimes have, the scene shifted and she landed in a sprawl in the living room of her small Malibu house. Through the open archway that led to her bedroom, she saw Julian lying in her bed.

The tangled sheets had fallen around his hips. She knew from memory every muscled bulge and hollow of his broad, scarred chest. Her heart started to pound as she stared at him. It'd been so long since they'd been together, so very long.

Could it be possible for skin to feel hungry? Her skin ached for the sensation of his rough, callused fingers.

His white-flecked dark hair tousled, he watched her with wolflike eyes. "Pick up your damn phone, will you?" he snapped.

He was such a killjoy. Furiously, she threw her phone at him, and he blurred to catch it. As she watched, Julian crushed the phone in one hand.

"Okay," the director said. (Who was directing this film? Squinting, she tried to look past the bright set lights.) "We need just one more thing before we call it a wrap. Come on, Melly— give us one of your awesome screams. Wake up and don't hold back, just let 'er rip."

Obligingly, she tried to open her mouth to belt out a good one, but she still had her skiing helmet on with the chin guard strapped tight. Somebody had added a mouthpiece to it, and the whole thing was actually kind of making it hard to breathe.

As she struggled to get her hands free so she could tear off the mouthpiece, she discovered that she was wrapped in a straitjacket. . . .

That couldn't be right. They had finished the film with the straitjacket years ago.

What the hell?

Her eyes popped open.

Someone was carrying her over his shoulder, fireman-style. His body held a small frisson of Power that she identified immediately as Vampyre. Her head bobbed upside down. She had pinned her long, curly hair into a loose chignon, and it had slipped sideways over one ear. Strong, bouncing beams of light illuminated a rough stony hallway.

Not a hallway. A tunnel.

She was gagged, and her wrists and ankles were tied.

Panic struck. She erupted into wild struggles.

She almost managed to flip out of the strange male's hold, but, swearing, he hoisted her into a more secure position and wrapped his arms around her thighs.

Someone bent over her and smacked her over the ear so hard her head rang. "Behave."

Craning her neck, she stared up at a beautiful, young-looking woman with auburn hair. A very familiar woman, and a very old Vampyre, one of the most Powerful in the Nightkind demesne. Justine.

The wrongness of the situation rocketed around Melly's mind. She had gone skiing, and had just returned to her Malibu home to get ready for her next shoot, when she remembered Justine had shown up on her doorstep. After that—nothing.

While she couldn't talk physically, she could telepathically. *Justine*, she said tensely. *What the fuck are you doing?*

Justine petted her head then removed the gag. "There, there," said the Vampyre. "Everything will probably be okay."

Everything will *probably* be okay?

"What are you talking about!" Melly's head ached, and she struggled to think past it.

There was no way she could have been prepared for this, none.

When she went out in public, she was usually attended by a guard or two, but her Malibu home was in a gated community with a good security system. Other actors and celebrities lived in the community, and normally, Melly felt perfectly safe there.

Normally, she would never have imagined someone like *Justine* would kidnap her. Justine had been on friendly terms with Melly's mother, Tatiana, the Light Fae Queen, for a very long time, and she had made friendly overtures to Melly for years.

Justine straightened and said to the man, "Put her in this one."

Melly looked around wildly as the man carried her into a cell, an honest-to-goodness dungeon-y cell that had been hewn out of rock with metal bars and a door fitted across the opening.

The man dumped her unceremoniously on the floor with

such force, her hair slipped half out of its knot. She felt a couple of hairpins slide down her neck and drop into her top.

Breathing heavily, Melly almost planted her foot in the Vampyre's face. She could have done it. She was fast enough, angry enough, and she'd certainly had her own fair share of training. Tatiana had insisted both her daughters learn self-defense.

But while she might be able to kick the shit out of Vampyre Guy, she knew she was no match for Justine, who leaned against the open cell door, watching. And she still hoped to get somewhere by talking.

"Justine," she said. "I don't know what's going on, or why you felt compelled to kidnap me, but if we go to my mom and we just talk it over, I'm sure we can figure out how to fix things."

Justine smiled at her. "Look at you," the Vampyre said. "Pretty and well meaning, and stupid as a poodle. I've always had a soft spot for you, Melly, but some things can't get fixed by running to your mom for help."

Melly angled out her jaw as both fury and worry deepened. Well first, Justine was just plain wrong, because her mom was the most formidable woman Melly had ever met.

But with Justine kidnapping Melly and refusing to talk to Tatiana, this was bad, really bad. She said between her teeth, "What did you do?"

"I took a gamble and it didn't go so well. So, now I'm taking another gamble." The Vampyre met Melly's gaze. "We're going to find out if Julian has any lingering feelings for you. I'm thinking he might, and if he does, how far will he go to see that you're safe? Would he even trade himself for you?" As Justine smiled, a tip of her descended fangs showed between her red lips.

Melly's stomach clenched. Justine had slipped some kind of leash, and if she felt she needed leverage against Julian, something terrible had happened in the Nightkind demesne. "You're going to be sadly disappointed," she said bitterly. "What Julian and I shared ended a long time ago."

"We'll see. Sometimes old feelings refuse to die." Justine told Vampyre Guy, "Strip those pins out of her hair, and pat her down to make sure she doesn't have anything in her pockets. When you're done, untie her."

Obediently, Vampyre Guy yanked his hands through Melly's long curls, pulling out hairpins. He was none too gentle about it, and tears sprang to her eyes at the pain in her scalp. When he was finished, he ran his hands down every inch of her body, untied her wrists and legs, straightened and stepped out of the cell.

Justine reached inside to set a jug of water and a package on the floor. "Here's enough food and water for a day, along with a small LED flashlight. The batteries aren't going to last you a full twenty-four hours, so I would use it sparingly, if I were you. Someone will bring you more food and water tomorrow, most likely. Hang tight—we'll know soon enough what Julian will do."

Most likely.

Most likely bring more food and water.

Melly's breath shook in her throat. Which meant Justine was fully prepared to cut ties and abandon her if things didn't go her way.

Taking her lantern, Justine shut the door of the cell and locked it with a key. "'Bye, darling."

Fuck you. Darling.

Melly didn't have a very aggressive personality, but she was pretty sure she could murder Justine's ass if she got half the chance.

The light faded gradually as Justine and Vampyre Guy left. Before it disappeared completely, she lunged for the packet Justine had left on the floor, located the flashlight and turned it on and off several times to test it.

It worked. The beam of light was small and thin, but it was infinitely better than the intense, complete darkness.

She forced herself to turn it off. Then, in the darkness, she wrapped her arms around herself, shaking.

After a while, stirring, she whispered, "Poodles are smart."

Twisting, she groped down the back of her neck until her fingers connected with what she was searching for. Snagging it, she pulled out the hairpins that had slipped down her top earlier.

Poodles could also bite when someone least expected it.

Gripping the pins tightly between thumb and forefinger and navigating from memory, she made her way across the cell until her outstretched hands collided with cold steel bars. Then she felt her way to the cell door and ran her fingers along the heavy, square metal that contained the lock. Most likely, it was a pin and tumbler lock, which was the most common type of lock in the world.

If so, she needed two pieces of metal in order to pick it. Luckily, she had hairpins and she knew how to use them. Using her teeth, she stripped off the little pieces of rubber on the ends of the pins. After she tucked one hairpin into her pocket, she bent the other one back and forth until it broke into two pieces.

Taking the first piece, she bent one end just enough so that it could be used as a pick. When she was satisfied with the result, she bent the other end to use as a handle. The last modification she made was to take the second piece and bend it into the correct shape so that she could use it as the lever.

The sensitive tips of her fingers found the keyhole. After she inserted her makeshift lever, she slipped in her pick. As she worked on the lock, her mind darted frantically from thought to thought.

Cold emanated from the rough rock that surrounded her. It penetrated the soles of her stylish ballet flats and ankle-length linen slacks, and raised goose bumps on the skin of her arms that were left bare by a matching sleeveless shirt. She had dressed for warm weather on the beach, not spelunking.

The chill suggested she was pretty deeply underground, but underground where? If she were being held on Justine's estate, why would Justine bother to stash her underground in a cell?

It would have made much more sense if Justine had hedged her bets and kept Melly in a more or less comfortable state, perhaps locked up somewhere in Justine's mansion and close at hand, so that Justine could get to her quickly and easily if she needed to change her course of action.

But whatever had happened to turn Justine rogue, Julian was somehow involved, so maybe Justine couldn't go back to her home. That had a ring of truth to it. Melly was willing to bet she wasn't anywhere near Justine's estate.

No, she was somewhere else, somewhere secret enough that Justine believed neither Julian nor any of his people would locate her. And since Melly had been knocked unconscious, she had no memory of the kind of journey it had taken to bring her to this place. She could literally be almost anywhere.

She ran a mental check on herself. Her hands were shaking, but that was from nerves and shock more than anything else. As a Light Fae, Melly healed fast, but her leg and hip still ached fiercely from the downhill tumble she took when she had been on her weekend ski trip. She was hungry and thirsty, but not so much that it had become urgent. Rather, she felt more or less like she did whenever she'd had such a busy day, she forgot to eat.

Also, there was the flashlight. It meant she wasn't in an Other land, where magic was enhanced and modern technology didn't work.

Logically that would mean she was no more than a day's journey away from Malibu, but the trick was, how had they traveled? If Justine had put her on a plane, a day's journey could mean that she was on the other side of the continent, somewhere on the East Coast.

Her shoulders sagged. Deduction could only get her so far. She wouldn't be able to figure out where she was until she got aboveground and could have a look around.

Her mind darted to more hopeful thoughts. If she had been gone from home a day or so, someone would have noticed her absence by now.

She ran over the timeline. She had been coming home from her ski trip when Justine had kidnapped her. She had arrived in Malibu in the early evening, and she had been scheduled to be on set the next morning to start shooting a new movie.

Melly always showed up for work on time. It was a point

of pride to her that she didn't trade on her status in the Light Fae demesne. If anything, she worked harder than anybody else in order to be taken seriously as a professional.

She knew to a fraction of an inch how much acting talent she had—or didn't have. She might not star in any Oscar-winning films, but she liked her career, had fun with it and made a lot of money, and those who worked with her knew she was as reliable as clockwork.

When she hadn't shown up for work, events would have been set in motion. Her mother Tatiana was not just the Light Fae Queen. She was also head of Northern Lights, the movie studio where Melly's latest movie was being shot, and Melly was her heir.

As soon as Melly's absence had been noted, and someone had checked out her little Malibu beach house and found her gone, the situation would have rocketed to Def Con 1. Sniffling, she thought of the Queen's extreme displeasure that even now must be hanging over Los Angeles like a nuclear mushroom cloud.

Because if her mama ain't happy, ain't nobody happy.

Then there was Melly's younger twin, Bailey. She and Bailey had always had a sixth sense about how each other fared. Even though Bailey lived and worked in Jamaica, she could very well have known something was wrong with Melly before morning had ever come.

"I bet you knew, didn't you, Bailey?" she whispered, holding the thought close like huddling in a comforting blanket. "And you called Mom. Maybe you even got her out of bed."

Then her mind, traitorous bitch that it was, slipped to Julian.

She thought of how their reunion might be, after he rescued her from Justine's clutches. He would run toward her, his rough, hard features and wolflike eyes alight with emotion and concern.

Her imagination put them in a sunlit, open field strewn with wildflowers. (She tried to picture Julian in a flowing white poet's shirt, black pants and black boots, but she couldn't get his ancient, scarred cowboy boots out of her head. Plus, Julian was about as poetic as a bull mastiff, so she gave up on that image almost immediately.)

She would run toward him too, arms outstretched, and as he snatched her close and lowered his head to take her mouth, the camera could zoom in for a close-up. . . .

Oops, wait a minute, she forgot. Vampyre. Cut the scene.

He would run toward her over a moonlit, open field strewn with wildflowers. . . .

That wouldn't film very well. Nobody would see the wildflowers in the moonlight. Besides, filming a running scene at night over a rough, open field was a good way to trip and break a leg.

And Julian wouldn't haul her close for one of those deep, soul-destroying kisses he knew how to do so well. More likely he would yell at her for some stupid thing or other, because that's all he did these days.

The back of her nose prickled and she blinked rapidly as her eyes dampened. Damn her stupid eyes. She must be allergic to some kind of mold in this gods-forsaken pit.

She wasn't going to think about Julian anymore, or how he might respond to Justine's ultimatum. As heir to the Light Fae demesne, she knew better than to hope he might act out of some kind of sentimentality. He was the Nightkind King. Even if he had any lingering feelings for her, other than anger, he couldn't afford to give in to kidnappers' demands.

Damn, the lock was a stiff son of a bitch. She could feel the ends of her makeshift lock pick catching on the interior mechanism, but the hairpin was made out of soft, cheap metal. She had already bent it out of shape, and it kept trying to bend further. And the darkness was so absolute, it was starting to get to her.

Since she was rescuing herself, she didn't need to worry so much about conserving the flashlight's batteries. Flipping the switch, she took a moment to survey her cell. It was rough and bare, except for a cheap-looking, collapsible cot with a thin foam mattress, and a folded, green wool army blanket. There was also what looked to be a hole in the floor in one corner. Was that some kind of primitive latrine?

Grimacing, she turned back to the door, took the end of the flashlight between her teeth and worked carefully at the lock.

There it was. She felt it catch through her fingers. The mechanism gave way to the gentle pressure she exerted, and the lock turned. Halle-fucking-lujah.

Blowing out a heartfelt sigh, she kissed the pieces of her lucky hairpin and tucked them with the second hairpin, in the pocket of her pants. Then she collected the jug of water and packet of food. She might be miles from anywhere and facing a stiff hike, and she would need to eat and drink soon.

Stepping out of the cell, she ran the flashlight's thin beam of light around the immediate area. As she did so, she realized there was more than one cell. With a sense of dread, she counted a total of four barred doors, although she was relieved to see the other cells were empty, their doors standing open. Two of the cells had thick manacles chained to the walls. To her left, the roughly hewn tunnel simply ended a few feet beyond the small cellblock.

These four cells were the end destination. But why carve them so deeply into the earth that not even a hint of light penetrated? What kind of creatures had Justine held captive down here?

Vampyres. She trapped Vampyres.

Shuddering, Melly turned her back on the cells and started down the tunnel. The going was a bit trickier than she had anticipated. The rocky floor felt rough and uneven under her thin-soled flats, and she had to keep the flashlight trained on the ground so she could see where to put her feet. She couldn't afford to add a sprained ankle to her other injuries.

After leaving the cellblock, she quickly reached the end of the tunnel, where she found another barred door that opened into another corridor. Like the other empty cells, this door was unlocked, propped open with a fist-sized rock.

Choosing to go left or right in the new corridor had no

meaning to her, so she shrugged and went right. As she ran into a fork in the hulking rock, she chose right again, and soon her tunnel intersected yet another corridor.

This time she decided to stay with the tunnel she was already in. Disturbed at how large the tunnel system appeared to be, she kept count of her choices—two rights and across—in case she reached another dead end and needed to backtrack.

After going so long where the only sounds she heard were the ones she made, her sensitive ears picked up a distant . . . something.

What was that? It sounded like a shuffling, or a scraping sound. Cocking her head, she tried to identify it, but she couldn't imagine what would make such a noise.

The sound seemed to grow louder as she went, or maybe she drew closer to it. It was definitely shuffling. Or scraping. Or both?

And there was light up ahead. To be sure, she turned off her flashlight and saw that the darkness up ahead was broken by some kind of illumination that seemed to flicker. As her eyes adjusted, she moved forward cautiously. At the same time, a whiff of air stirred down the tunnel, bringing with it a stench that made her grimace. It smelled like garbage, or meat that had gone bad.

The flickering light up ahead grew stronger, and after a few more steps, her tunnel ended at a massive, cave-like room.

The light came from several torches, set into old, iron sconces.

The shuffling, scraping sounds came from a mass of creatures that were crouched in the middle of the cave. They were . . . they were . . .

For a moment her mind refused to process what she was seeing. Her heart knew better, though, and it kicked into an accelerated rhythm.

The crouching creatures were human shaped and dressed in filthy-looking, ragged clothes. As she sucked in a breath of the stinking air, a few of the creatures lifted their heads to look at her. Their eyes flashed red in the torchlight, and their mouths were dark with what looked like blood.

One of them sniffed at the air, its lips peeled back from long fangs that glinted a wicked white in the torchlight. She caught a glimpse of the supine forms the creatures surrounded. One of the unmoving bodies wore jeans and sneakers. Another wore a pencil-thin skirt and a single high-heeled pump, the other foot sadly bare.

"Oohhh," Melly whispered. "Shit."

As more of the creatures turned to look at her and sniff the air, they let out a collective sigh. "*Aaaaahhhh.*"

One stood upright and took a step toward her.

Whirling, she flicked on her flashlight and ran.

Panic lent her wings. From behind, she heard growls and snarling, and the sounds of many feet hitting the hard, cold floor, as the group of creatures gave chase.

Creatures. Vampyres.

Only they were Vampyres like Melly had never seen before. Stripped of civilized courtesies, cleanliness or manners, they were bestial and feral.

Forget the rough floor, or going carefully.

If you fall, you're dead, Melly. So don't you fucking fall.

The beam of light from the flashlight she clenched in one fist flashed wildly. Her breath sawed in her throat, and the abused muscles in her injured leg flared with pain as she pushed her body as hard as she could.

Across the corridor. Left at the fork. Then left again. They sounded closer. How close were they? She didn't dare look behind her. It would slow her down.

There, up ahead, was the barred door at the opening of the cellblock tunnel, propped open with the rock. She leaped at it.

Wonder of wonders, she still had the jug of water and packet of food under one arm. Taking the end of the small flashlight between her teeth, she grabbed the door and hauled it shut with a loud clang. As she did so, she caught a glimpse of the horde just yards away. Please gods, let the closed door buy her a few more seconds.

Whirling, she pelted down the tunnel and lunged into her cell. All the cell doors opened inward. Letting the water and food fall where it would, she slammed the door shut, yanked out her makeshift lock pick and with shaking fingers dug into the lock.

Please please please please.

Out of the corner of her eye, she could just barely see down to the tunnel's end. The feral Vampyres clawed the tunnel gate open and raced toward her.

She gave the pick in the lock a final, desperate twist. Even as the tumbler inside the lock turned, the piece of hairpin bent.

Sobbing, she threw herself backward as the Vampyres reached her cell and tried to snatch her through the bars. Claws raked down her left forearm, and she stumbled and fell. Jarred from her teeth, the flashlight bounced along the floor. The thin, cold beam of light flashed over fangs, arms straining toward her between the bars of the cell door, and bloody, distorted faces.

There were so many of them. Dozens, well over a hundred.

Over the sound of the Vampyre's snarling, she became aware of the high, almost inaudible whimpering sound she made as she tried to catch her breath, and she made herself stop. Rolling stiffly onto her hands and knees, she gathered together the water jug, the food packet, and the flashlight.

She had dropped the bent piece of hairpin, but she didn't bother to look for it. It had fallen somewhere too close to the cell door and those deadly, groping hands. If the Vampyres wandered off, she could look for it then and see if it was salvageable.

Clutching her meager possessions, she scooted backward until her shoulder blades connected to the wall opposite the cell door. Then she slid along the wall sideways until she reached a corner. It didn't give her any more distance or safety from the Vampyres, but she needed to brace herself against the steadiness of the two walls.

After she set down her supplies, she crawled over to the cot, grabbed one end and dragged it to her corner. It was probably made from aluminum, and it was as lightweight and flimsy as it looked. It bounced along the floor until she reached her corner again.

She flashed the light over the Vampyres still straining to reach her. Unlike the cheap cot, the cell door was strong and heavy, and it held solid against their combined weight.

Halle-fucking-lujah.

She grabbed the scratchy, wool blanket and wrapped it around her shoulders. Upending the cot onto its side, she pulled it close until the ends connected with the walls of her corner, and she sat inside the triangle it made.

Childish? Possibly. Certainly it didn't serve any better purpose other than giving her the thinnest of fragile psychological barriers to hide behind, but hey, it had been a truly rotten night, and right now she would take any positives she could lay her hands on.

Patting the edge of the cot, she took several deep breaths. Then she turned off her flashlight. It was even more important to conserve the batteries as much as possible now.

She did end up getting an answer to one question. Now she knew where she was.

For decades, she had heard stories of the tunnels that ran underneath San Francisco. In the 1990s, when she and Julian had been at the hottest part of their scorching affair, Julian had taken Nightkind troops to burn out a nest of them that had gathered below the city. Melly had spent a sleepless night, aching for him to return.

Vampyres turned feral when they fed often enough from drug-addicted humans. She would have thought that fact alone would be all the detriment they needed to keep from doing it, but as Julian had told her, human problems didn't just vanish when one became a Vampyre.

If they were an alcoholic or a drug addict as a human, they still had those cravings as a Vampyre, only then neither alcohol nor drugs had any direct effect. Not only did Vampyres need human blood for sustenance, they needed blood as a carrying agent.

They could only get drunk from feeding from humans

who were inebriated, and they could only get high from humans who were high. And Julian never could keep the tunnels completely clear. The ferals always came back eventually.

Melly was in the tunnels, somewhere underneath San Francisco.

The feral Vampyres kept making incoherent, snarling noises and trying to get to her through the cell door for a very long time. She pulled one corner of the blanket over her head.

Rocking, she whispered, "Mom's going to be so pissed when she finds out."

She huddled in on herself, until the warmth from the rough blanket took away the chill of shock that had set in. Then she turned on the light again and inspected her packet of food.

Food, ha. Her lip curled. Someone had picked up a few random items at a gas station. There were a couple of packets of jerky, a bag of mixed nuts and a couple of candy bars. Still, it was calories and better than nothing. She would have been really worried about her relative worth if they hadn't given her any food at all.

Opening a packet of jerky, she chewed each bite slowly and thoroughly, sucking every bit of taste and satisfaction she could out of it. While it didn't fill the gnawing hole in her belly, at least it was something. While she had a terrible sweet tooth and wanted one of the candy bars badly, Justine's words echoed in her mind.

Most likely bring more food and water.

She didn't dare eat anything else, because she had no idea how long she needed to make what she had last. Firmly, she set aside the food and opened her bottle of water to drink only what she felt she absolutely needed.

After that, she got to work again.

Inspecting her cot, she found the mechanics of it were simple. It folded in the middle and sat on four legs that were hinged so they could be folded against the bottom of the frame. After studying the legs, she narrowed her eyes at the Vampyres still straining at the bars of her cage.

Taking hold of one of the legs, she bent it against the hinge, back and forth, until the hinge broke. Hefting the aluminum piece, she stood and walked over to the bars to stand just outside the reach of those grasping hands. As she walked up and down in front of the Vampyres, she watched and waited . . .

Until there. That one.

Moving fast, she darted forward to snatch the wrist of one of the Vampyres and yank on it as hard as she could.

Snarling, the Vampyre's body slammed against the bars of the cage.

In that same moment, Melly struck, stabbing her makeshift stake into the Vampyre's chest. It wasn't easy. The cot leg didn't have a sharp enough point, so she had to throw her weight into driving the tip through the Vampyre's chest wall. If she had been less fit or a human woman, she might not have been able to do it.

As it was, she felt the tip break through the hard chest plate and slide into the soft flesh underneath. The sensation made her stomach roil.

Heart pounding, she threw herself backward before any of the others could grab hold of her, while the Vampyre she staked shuddered and collapsed into dust.

Shivering and breathing hard, Melly looked at all the others. They watched her in return, red eyes glowing in the beam of her flashlight.

One down.

⇒ THREE ⇐

The first rosy blush of sunrise was beginning to peek over rolling hills when Julian arrived at the Light Fae Queen's palatial home in west Bel Air. Another quintessential California residence, her mansion was elegant, old Hollywood.

He knew from memory the open-style entertaining rooms that graced the ground floor, with French doors that opened to extensive manicured gardens filled with flowerbeds surrounding an immense swimming pool. Tatiana loved to entertain, and she had volunteered to host many political functions over the last ninety years.

Yolanthe had tried to insist upon accompanying him, but he had vetoed that idea. He wanted her to stay on point on the search for Justine, so he took a few of his personal guards instead.

He had flown into LAX on the Nightkind government jet. The town car that Tatiana had reserved for him was specifically modified for Vampyres' use, with dark, treated windows that blocked out harmful UV rays.

As soon as the car slowed to a stop in front of the Queen's residence, his guards donned the protective gear that all

Vampyres needed to wear if they chose to go out during the daytime—clothes made of material that specifically blocked UV light and that covered every inch of their bodies, leather gloves, hoods to cover their faces and heads, and dark glasses. The effect was sinister, but unavoidable.

Unprotected, their movements and actions would soon be severely hampered by daylight, so the guards were following standard procedure, but Julian was under no such edict. Since it was a short distance from the town car to the house, and the sun had not yet crested over the eastern hills, he didn't bother to don full protective gear. Instead, he grabbed a cloak in one hand and made for the wide, double front doors. His guards fell into step on either side of him.

Before Julian had a chance to knock, two Light Fae guards opened the doors, dressed in their signature blue and tan uniforms. They had clearly been watching for his arrival.

One guard led him toward the rear of the house, to a large, familiar family-style living room.

In the doorway, Julian jerked a halt. "There has to be somewhere else I can wait."

"Sir," said the Light Fae guard. "This is the safest room for you. It faces west and won't get any direct sunlight until late afternoon."

"I know that," Julian said shortly.

"Do you want me to escort you to another room anyway?" The guard's handsome features were puzzled.

His expression grim, Julian gestured to his own guards to remain in the hall as he stepped inside and glanced around. Very little had changed about the room since he had last been in it.

Wrestling with unruly emotions, he told the other male, "Never mind. This will do."

The guard asked, "Do you require refreshment, sir?"

Surprised, he raised one eyebrow. "Are you offering to donate?"

The guard's face remained studiously polite. "If it is necessary. Sir."

It was highly unusual for the Light Fae, or any of the other Elder Races, to offer to feed a Vampyre. The general assumption was that a Vampyre met his needs through his household. By having one of her guards offer him sustenance, Tatiana was making a huge concession in light of his abrupt trip.

The guard did not look enthusiastic at the prospect of letting Julian feed from him, but at least he didn't appear revolted. Julian said dryly, "Thank you, no. Where is the Queen?"

"She will be with you as soon as she is able. I'll let her know you've arrived. If you will just wait here, sir."

"Of course."

Once the Light Fae guard had left and shut the door behind him, Julian turned to confront the empty room.

There, in the corner by the French doors, was where it had all begun.

He fell into memories of the past.

It was the Festival of the Masque, and Tatiana had thrown another massive party. The number of guests was easily over a thousand, as people from all races and demesnes attended. Some wore simple masks and others donned elaborate finery. Fauns chased sylphs, while devils leered, and angels flirted.

Late into the evening, almost everybody was drunk except for Julian when he went looking for a quiet spot. Bored and contemplating leaving, he stepped into the family room.

That night, the French doors were propped open, letting in the cool breeze. A masked woman stood alone beside the drawn, cream-colored curtains, looking out at the revelry.

He knew who she was immediately, of course, but still he had to pause to admire the spectacle she made. Her white, floor-length halter dress accentuated every spectacular inch of her golden, curvy body. Her long, thick hair had been crimped into tight curls that swept off her forehead and cascaded about her shapely shoulders and down her hourglass back like a lion's mane.

When she looked at him, her eyes gleamed behind a golden cat mask.

"Let me guess," he said, as he strolled toward her. In an

effort to hide how the sight of her affected him, he strove to sound lazy, disinterested. "You're the goddess of love, Inanna."

One corner of her full lips lifted. Gods, she had a sexy mouth, made perfectly for fitting around a man's erection.

"Well, duh," Melly said cheerfully. "I am a very drunken goddess of love. Hello, Julian. Such a shame you Vampyres can't fully appreciate champagne. Mommy spent a fortune on the good stuff for tonight."

"We can fully appreciate many wonderful things about champagne," Julian told her as he stopped by her side. "The scent, the taste. How intoxicating the effects of champagne can be as it courses through the blood of a beautiful woman." Taking her hand, he raised it to his lips. At the last moment, he turned it so that he could press his lips to the velvet skin at her inner wrist.

"Mmmn." The throaty sound she made shot straight to his cock. "You're a sexy beast, your majesty."

"I'm a bastard, and you know it." Parting his lips as they pressed against her skin, he licked her lightly. "I've never made any pretense about being anything else."

When he lifted his head, he found her smiling at him. "Yes, I do know. It's one of the things that makes you sexy *and* a beast." She lifted her wrist to him again. "Here, have a sip of champagne on me."

Carefully, he wrapped his fingers around her slender hand, while he met and held her gaze. "Your mother wouldn't approve," he said. By then he had dropped all attempts at indifference, and his lowered voice turned gravelly and soft.

She lowered one eyelid in a wink. "What Mommy doesn't know won't hurt her, will it? Besides, isn't it half the fun when you do something you know you shouldn't?"

He came closer, until the tips of her breasts brushed against the jacket of his black tux. "Indeed, it is," he said. "Very well, just a nip."

The heat that came off of her body was exhilarating. She grinned at him, and he gave her a lazy, crooked smile in return.

As he lowered his head again, he noticed that her nipples

had come erect underneath the expensive white silk halter. He lost his smile as his cock hardened further and his fangs sprang out.

Gods, he just knew she was going to taste *so damn good. . . .*

A noise from out in the hall broke the hold those vivid memories had over him and hurtled him back to the present.

Jerking away from the spot where he had first tasted Melly, he swallowed hard as he struggled to get himself under control.

Any hint of her scent had vanished from the room. Now it smelled of beeswax and lemon furniture polish. How long had it been since Melly was here? Did she ever think of him when she stood in this place?

As he roamed the spacious, elegantly decorated room, his mind filled with other images. This time, instead of memories from the past, his imagination created one nightmare scenario after another. Most of the scenarios focused on images of Melly badly injured, or worse, dead.

One part of him knew he was being irrational. When he forced himself to think logically, he knew Tatiana would not have asked for his help if Melly were already dead. He doubted that he would have warranted even a phone call from her. The only way he would have heard about Melly's death would have been through official channels.

In fact, it was entirely possible that Tatiana had asked for his help for any number of urgent reasons that had nothing to do with Melly. Yet he had never heard Tatiana sound quite so emotional, so . . . needy as she had when she had called him.

Something had struck her hard in the gut, and he knew of only one thing that could cause her to respond in such a way, and that was if one of her beloved daughters were in some kind of peril.

From the front of the house came the sounds of conversation and approaching footsteps. Moments later, the same Light Fae guard that had escorted him into the room ushered in two males.

Julian stopped in his pacing to stare at the new arrivals.

He knew the other men well, if not deeply, for both of them were fixtures in the inter-demesne political landscape, and Julian often conversed with them at political functions.

The first male was Soren, a first-generation Djinn and the head of the Elder tribunal. While Djinn were beings of spirit and almost unimaginable Power, they often took physical form when interacting with other creatures. From what Julian understood, they could assume any physical form they chose. A Djinn could appear to be male or female, human or animal, or any creature of the Elder Races, but most often they chose to manifest as a single figure, as if that particular form was the clearest expression of their identity.

Soren's physical form was that of a tall, broad-shouldered man, with craggy features, white hair, and the piercing, diamond-like gaze that all Djinn shared. He held such concentrated Power that it took an effort for Julian to look directly at him.

The second male was from the Wyr demesne in New York. Dragos Cuelebre, Lord of the Wyr, had sent his First sentinel, Graydon. A gryphon in his Wyr form, Graydon was a massive figure, easily the largest of all seven of the Wyr sentinels, who were famous throughout the world for their superlative fighting skills.

Graydon was also one of the first generation of the Elder Races. Born at the beginning of the world, he carried an intense aura of Power just as Soren did, but whereas Soren's Power felt sharp and clear, like a piercing white light, Graydon's felt warmer and golden, like a hot summer evening.

Normally Graydon's rough, weather-beaten features wore a mild, good-humored expression, but now, his gray eyes held a sober, sharp look.

Julian's sense of dread increased. He had thought he was being irrational, but the arrival of the other two males escalated the unknown issue to something more extreme than he had been capable of imagining.

Graydon crossed the room to shake hands. "Julian," the other man said. "I caught your press conference yesterday about the attacks. How has the search been going?"

"It's early in the investigation," replied Julian. "But we've got a search protocol laid out. We'll catch who's responsible."

With a keen gaze, Graydon searched his expression. "You said you had over a hundred dead, and most of the casualties were human?"

"Yes." Unwilling to talk details, he braced himself to field off more questions.

But Graydon surprised him, as the other man shook his head. "That's unacceptable. I'm sure you have plenty of resources at your disposal for the search, but I want you to know Dragos is prepared to send you Wyr trackers, if you think you'll need them."

Julian had been in battle mode and coping with adversarial issues for so long, the simple offer of help caught him off guard. Surprised, he said slowly, "Thank you. I don't have an answer for you right now, but I appreciate the offer very much."

"Just say the word, and I'll send a team." Graydon paused. "I guess you being here is too much for coincidence. Did Tatiana ask you for help too?"

"Yes." Julian looked from Graydon to Soren. "Do either of you have any idea what this is about?"

The Djinn shook his head. "I was going to ask you the same thing. The only thing we know is that Tatiana asked me to bring Graydon here as soon as I could."

Graydon walked over to the large windows, his gaze roaming over the placid scene outside. "We would have arrived sooner, except I can rarely get away at a moment's notice these days."

Julian nodded. Recently, at the Sentinel Games in January, Graydon had assumed the duties of First sentinel, and as a result, his workload had to have increased exponentially.

He said, "I guess Tatiana will tell us why we're here as soon as she can."

On impulse, he pulled out his cell phone, scrolled to Melly's contact information and punched the call button. He wasn't expecting much. When he had recently tried to call her about the blasted trade agreements, she hadn't answered his phone calls or messages. Still, he felt the need to try.

The phone call didn't ring but rolled over immediately to voicemail, which meant nothing other than Melly's phone was turned off. For all he knew, she was busy consulting with her mother over whatever crisis the Light Fae demesne faced. As Tatiana's heir, Melly would undoubtedly be involved to some extent.

Not bothering to leave a message, he disconnected the call, all too aware of Soren's piercing, curious gaze lingering on him.

While the other two men talked quietly, Julian moved to the far side of the large room. His nerves were jumping with tension, and making even the pretense of polite conversation was beyond him. Closing his eyes, he let himself go completely still as only a Vampyre could do, while in reality, his muscles were so tight, he felt ready to lash out at a moment's notice.

It's been over twenty years since she betrayed me, he thought. I shouldn't care this much. I shouldn't care at all.

The fact that he did made him feel trapped and angry, and for one reason or another, he had been feeling that way for far too damn long.

For almost two hundred years, he had held steady against his sire Carling's increasingly erratic behavior and contradictory commands. What had once been an affectionate, respectful business arrangement had turned sour, then descended to bitterness and finally outright hostility, while he fought to hold the Nightkind demesne together despite the several selfish, predatory bastards who sat on the council.

Born a Roman slave, he had won his freedom in the arena as a gladiator. Then he had fought his way to the position of general in Emperor Hadrian's army. And then he had fought some more, for years upon years. War, in one form or another, was all he had ever known.

When Carling had offered him the unimaginatively long life and the Power of a Vampyre, he had leapt at the opportunity. After all, he'd had one master or another his whole life. Becoming eternally subject to Carling as his sire had seemed easy.

But it was a hell of a lot easier to talk about living through eternity than it was to actually live through an endless parade of years. Decades. Centuries.

Millennia.

No human soul can fully understand that long of a life. Looking back, he wasn't sure when everything had become so intolerable. He had seen over two thousand years pass, and he had borne so many yokes around his neck and engaged in so many struggles for so long, he felt like a pit bull at the end of his leash.

You breed a dog to fight then set him to fight for long enough, after a while that's all he knows. He'll fight and he'll fight, until eventually somebody comes along and puts him down.

After what felt like an interminable wait, everything seemed to happen at once.

Some distance away in the house, rapid footsteps sounded on the stairs.

Two pairs of footsteps, and both of them were light and quick enough to be feminine.

The tight band around Julian's chest began to ease. Opening his eyes, he drew in a breath and turned to face the door. Graydon and Soren evidently heard the people approaching, for they turned as well.

The door opened. Tatiana strode in, followed by her younger daughter Bailey, Melisande's twin.

Bailey was so like Melly, and yet not. They both had the same tall frame, with long, muscled limbs and voluptuous curves, the same rich, golden brown skin, green eyes, elegantly pointed ears and curly, blond hair. They even had somewhat the same angular features, and by some trick of nature, many of the same gestures.

For the barest moment, Julian's eyes refused to accept what he was seeing. The first thing he thought was, oh, she cut her hair.

But, no.

It was Bailey who had a short, tousled hairstyle and dressed like a fighter, wearing jeans, a tan T-shirt and a gun in a belt holster, Bailey who looked at him with undisguised antipathy on her drawn, tired face.

This time when the dread returned, it slammed an invisible fist into his solar plexus.

He forced his attention away from Bailey and focused on Tatiana.

The Light Fae Queen looked as elegant as ever. Her golden hair was pinned at the back of her head in an intricate style that set off her graceful head and neck. She wore a nude-colored suit and matching high-heeled shoes. The outfit was at once both conservative and subtly shocking. Her makeup was immaculate, and her composure appeared to be superb, all of which made the raw expression in her bloodshot eyes hit like another blow.

Without preamble, Tatiana said, "I can't express how much it means to me that you were each willing to come and help without even knowing the nature of our crisis."

"What's wrong, Tatiana?" Soren asked.

Taking a deep breath, she visibly braced herself. "My daughter Melisande is missing. We discovered it early this morning."

Julian stood immobile as her words sank in.

Without seeming to move quickly, somehow Soren was across the room and standing in front of Tatiana, who looked up at him with naked pain and fear in her eyes.

The Djinn took both her hands and said in a voice more gentle than Julian had ever heard from him before, "Tell us everything you know."

Bailey said tightly, "I was sound asleep in my home, in Jamaica. Everything was normal. I'd had a normal day, a normal evening, had a couple beers and shots with some friends, and went to bed around midnight there. I was tired and fell asleep just fine, and then suddenly, sometime later I woke up. I could have sworn Melly had shouted at me, and I knew something was wrong. I don't know how—I just knew it. I called Mom right away."

Tatiana took up the story. "As soon as I talked to Bailey, I called the security company that monitors Melly's neighborhood. It's a gated community, and they always have somebody on duty, twenty-four/seven. When they sent someone to check on Melly, they found her front door standing open."

Standing open, like the back door of Justine's house, the light from within throwing an illuminated rectangle on a well-tended lawn.

Julian's body went as taut as a drawn bowstring, while his mind began to race.

One door had been left carelessly standing open in Northern California. Another had been left open in Malibu, in Southern California.

The two incidents were hours away from each other, in completely different demesnes. There was no reason to make a connection between them, other than to note how similar the images were. No reason at all, and yet . . .

He considered it anyway.

Justine had been cultivating a relationship with Tatiana, and had made many friendly overtures to Melly. Julian had seen all of it as part of her political maneuvering—staying on friendly terms with the monarch of the neighboring demesne kept Justine in a strong position to create mischief. Also, it might garner Justine some outside support if she ever made a move against him in a way that would win Tatiana's sympathy and approval.

Could Justine have had anything to do with Melly's disappearance? Would she really destroy the friendly relationship with the Light Fae that she had worked so hard to cultivate? Tatiana made a deadly enemy.

Turning away from the others, he rubbed his eyes as he tried to put himself in Justine's shoes.

She had failed to kill Xavier, and she knew very well that Julian was actively hunting her down. And she had already shown how far she was willing to go when she had slaughtered her entire household.

Now, because the Nightkind demesne lay under martial law, not only were her movements hampered by the need to remain undetected, but those of her allies were as well. And while their hostilities had not yet become public knowledge, Julian was under no illusion. His demesne was caught in the middle of a civil war.

Justine would realize it too. She had to know that her life was at stake. She was a creature who only pretended to have a conscience. If she were threatened, she would sacrifice any relationship, any potential political advantage, in the fight for survival.

Tatiana turned to Graydon. "As soon as I realized Melly was missing, I had the area around her front door cordoned off. I wanted to keep it as clean as possible from too many contaminating—" Her voice broke, but almost immediately, she picked up her sentence and carried on. "From too many contaminating scents. There have been only two people inside the house, the original guard from the security company, and my own captain, Shane Mac Carthaigh. He's there now, making sure the perimeter is maintained. From the dust on Melly's car, it clearly hasn't been touched in a couple of days, which makes sense since she was just returning home from a skiing trip. Her luggage was stacked just inside the house. She hadn't unpacked yet."

Graydon said quietly, "Shane's a good man. You did all the right things. If Soren will take me, I can start investigating immediately."

She looked at the Djinn. "Would you do that?"

"Absolutely," Soren said. Julian noted the conspicuous lack of bargaining in the exchange. Djinn were notorious for striking bargains for an exchange of favors—which was their currency of choice—but clearly Soren had some affection for Tatiana, and perhaps even for Melly as well. "I also want to talk to the guard who was on duty at the gate yesterday evening. Did he notice anything unusual?"

Tatiana rubbed her forehead. "When Shane questioned

him, the guard said it had been a perfectly normal evening. Shane said he was telling the truth."

Julian shook his head. "You said the community is gated, yet Melly still disappeared. I know captain Shane is an experienced magic user, but I would examine the guard a lot more closely if I were you. Eyewitnesses are unreliable at the best of times, and memories can be tampered with. He could have been glamored or coerced. A strong Vampyre could do it, or a Powerful witch—even Dragos, so I'm told."

A silence fell, as everyone in the room considered him.

Soren said, "I'll be sure to examine him, myself."

Graydon pointed out, "There are also other ways a gated community can be breached. I could do it easily, and so could Soren."

"Shane said he hasn't sensed any residual magic," Tatiana said. "But he hasn't had time to comb the whole area."

Soren looked at Tatiana. "We have a lot to do, and we need to move fast, so we'd better leave now."

"Thank you so much."

Soren put his hand on Graydon's shoulder. In a whirlwind of Power, the two men disappeared.

As soon as they had left, Tatiana turned to Julian. With a restraint made painful by the amount of emotion behind her words, she said, "It was good of you to come."

It was the most genuine warmth Tatiana had shown him since he had cut things off with Melly.

Briefly, he considered mentioning his suspicions about Justine. However, he was under no illusions about his relationship with Tatiana either. She had reached out to him out of desperation, not from any newfound sense of affection or friendship. She wouldn't believe a word he said about Justine, not without proof, and he didn't have any. The only thing he had was a train of thought based on what could very well be a coincidence.

Gesturing with one hand, he said, "Of course."

"I was hoping you might help with increased patrols at the Nightkind border." She paused, rubbing her forehead. "I know your resources must be strained at present."

That was her way of referencing the trouble in his own

demesne. "Yes," he told her. "But I can still put out increased border patrols. I'll also issue a confidential demesne-wide alert for the Nightkind police to keep an eye out for any sign of Melly."

Her raw gaze dampened. "Thank you. Could you also make a list of places you think should be searched? Bailey and I have been writing down every place we can think of—if you could just take a look at the list and let us know if there's any place else you think we should add to it."

"Of course," he said again.

Bailey approached him, holding the notebook in one outstretched hand. From her rigid features, and tight mouth, he was willing to bet she hadn't agreed with her mother's decision to call him for help.

Ignoring her hostility, he took the pad of paper and turned away again as he scanned the places they had jotted down. It looked comprehensive to him. In fact, there were several places on the list he wouldn't have known to suggest, but then he and Melly hadn't been together in twenty years.

Had she taken lovers to these places? How many lovers had she had since Ferion? His mouth tightened at the thought, and the old resentful anger tried to resurface.

His skin prickled as a whirlwind of Power swept into the room again. A moment later, Soren reappeared. While the Djinn and the two women began to talk about search strategies, Julian jotted two places down on the paper.

One was a cabin at Lake Tahoe, where he and Melly had spent some time together. The winter that year had been so cold, the lake had turned into a sheet of ice, and he and Melly had made love over and over again in front of a roaring fire.

The other was a winery in Napa Valley. It had been a spur-of-the-moment trip.

That time had been much like the trip to Lake Tahoe. They couldn't keep their hands off each other. Her curves had felt like heated silk, and he had lost himself in voluptuous sensuality, drunk on the wine in her blood and a desire that burned away everything and left him feeling burnished and new again.

His lip curled at the memories. He shoved them aside. If he could burn them out of his head, he would.

Both places were so far-fetched as possibilities, he couldn't imagine they might still be relevant. But until they had a search strategy defined, they had no idea what might be relevant or not.

His phone buzzed. Pulling it out of his pocket, he checked the display.

It was a text message.

From Justine.

The old general in him roused, readying for battle. The waiting and strategizing was over. It was time to engage. He thumbed open the message.

If you want to see Melly alive again, meet me in one hour outside the de Young Museum in the Golden Gate Park. Say nothing to anyone. Come alone.

Well, that narrowed down the search considerably.

Rage and renewed fear roared inside as he stared at the text.

He was not surprised. He was not. Yet having the confirmation in writing felt like another blow to the stomach.

The Nightkind King did not negotiate with terrorists or kidnappers, but Julian the man was another matter entirely.

Thumbs flying over the tiny keyboard, he punched in a reply and hit send. I'm in Los Angeles. I can't make it to San Francisco in an hour. You've got to give me more time.

Her reply came swiftly. I am amused. Did Tatiana ask you for help?

Yes.

Behind him, Bailey said in a tight voice, "Can't you focus on something else besides yourself for once?"

"That's enough, Bailey," said Tatiana sharply.

He didn't bother to look at either Bailey or her mother. All of his focus strained on his silent phone, gripped so tightly between both hands.

Come on, Justine. Come on.

His phone vibrated as her text appeared on the display. You have three hours. Better get a move on.

Goddammit. The flight alone from LA to San Francisco took an hour and a half. Even with his authority to expedite his flight and commandeer a police cruiser to cut through city traffic in San Francisco, meeting her deadline was going to be close, very close.

He knew she kept the deadline tight in order to keep him from making some kind of countermove against her. And of course the whole thing was some kind of trap, but that was the least important part of their exchange.

In a clench, he forced himself to tap out the next words. I need proof of life or there's no deal.

Justine must have been waiting for that one, because almost immediately, her next text came, and it was a photo.

In the image, Melly stood in front of a man, looking both furious and terrified at once, her hands bound in front of her. The man's hands were sunk deep in her long, disheveled hair. Was he holding her hair back for the camera? Melly's face was tilted up at an uncomfortable angle, as if he had yanked her head back.

As Julian stared at the image, his emotions bled out—all the bitterness, resentment, regret, fear and rage—until he felt empty of everything, except the need to commit violence.

You, he thought at the unknown man restraining Melly. You are a dead man. You and Justine have just become my life's mission.

Soren said, "Julian?"

At the same moment, he received another text: That photo is from early this morning. Do we have a deal?

He replied, I'll be there in three hours.

Ticktock. Remember, not a word to anyone. I'll find out if you do.

He knew she could too. Justine was a talented liar. She also had a keenly developed truthsense. All she had to do was ask him a direct question and listen carefully to his reply.

A hand touched him on the bicep. Startling, he whirled to look into Tatiana's gaze. The Queen still looked frightened, but she was beginning to show signs of other emotions as well—worry and confusion, along with the beginnings of anger and distrust.

Distrust for him.

"Julian, are you paying attention at all?"

Not a word to anyone, Justine had said.

Staring at Tatiana's distrustful expression when he had done *not a goddamned thing in the world to earn it*, he decided to take Justine's admonishment literally.

Pivoting on one heel, he snatched his cloak off the back of a chair and strode for the hallway, ignoring the calls and questions that flew after him. With one slicing gesture, he pointed at his two guards then at the floor at their feet, ordering them wordlessly to stay where they were. They remained in place, immobile.

As he strode toward the front door, he slung the cloak over his shoulders and pulled the hood over his head, holding it in place with one fist. The two Light Fae guards stepped aside at his approach.

The last thing he heard before he left the house was Bailey, as she said bitterly, "I knew you should never have asked him to come."

Then he stepped out into the sunlight. Searing pain stabbed the skin on the back of his hand, and he broke into a lope that brought him to the car.

The keys were in the ignition. Lunging into the driver's seat, he slammed the door, started the car and gunned down the driveway. A glance in the rearview mirror showed

Tatiana, Bailey, Soren and the Light Fae guards, all standing on the front doorstep and staring in his direction.

He was fleetingly pleased to see that his two guards were nowhere in sight. They were following orders, at least for now.

The others had to have realized something was seriously off, but he couldn't count on them piecing things together in the right way. Even if they did, and they attempted to do something to help, they might just make matters worse.

If they didn't . . . well, fuck them.

He dismissed them from his mind. He had a plane to catch, and a deadline to keep.

Like Justine said, he better get a move on.

≈ FOUR ≈

Lying so far north of Los Angeles, San Francisco had a much cooler climate and entirely different weather patterns. As the Nightkind plane taxied into SFO, beads of moisture gathered on the outside of the windows from the dense, heavy fog that had rolled in some time earlier that day.

Julian welcomed the fog. It provided an effective cover from the deadly sunshine. From long years of experience with living in the Bay Area, he could tell that he would be able to walk outside freely without needing the cloak, at least for the next couple of hours, and the fog might actually linger until nightfall.

During his trip to LAX, and the subsequent flight, he had received several calls and texts. None of them were from Yolanthe or Xavier, the two people he would have actually chosen to talk to, in case they had discovered any leads on Justine's whereabouts, so he ignored all the messages and let the phone calls roll over to voicemail. Maybe if enough people took note of his prolonged silence, they would start talking to each other and figure out that something had gone wrong.

Once the airstair had been put into place, he exited the

plane, strode through the massive, overcrowded airport to the area allotted for pickups, and approached the first parked police car he saw.

Putting a hand on the edge of the roof, he leaned close to the window to look inside. No key in the ignition.

"I'm going to have to ask you to step away from the car, sir," a male said severely from behind him.

Straightening, Julian turned to face a young human, one eyebrow raised.

The cop's expression changed drastically. "S-sir," he stammered. "I mean, your majesty. No wait, that's English royalty. You're a–a–'your grace,' right? Or are you a 'my lord'?"

There was no way Julian could maintain silence after that. On the plus side, the cop would definitely remember every detail of their meeting. He said dryly, " 'Sir' or 'sire' will do just fine. I need your keys."

"Certainly, sir. Sire."

He was too preoccupied to be amused. "One or the other. I don't need both at once." He held out his hand peremptorily, and the cop dropped his keys into the palm of his hand.

"Where shall I go to pick up the vehicle, sire?" the cop asked.

Without replying, Julian climbed into the police car and, switching on the vehicle's siren, he drove off. He had very little time now to get to the Golden Gate Park, and the museum.

Cutting sharply across the highway, he settled into the fast lane and shot the car's speed to over a hundred miles an hour. In the heavy fog, it was a suicidal pace. What saved him were his preternatural reflexes.

The other vehicles on the road moved out of his way as drivers responded to the siren, but still there were times he had to slow as he waited for the traffic to shift to the right.

When he turned onto John F. Kennedy Drive, he had five minutes left.

Then four minutes, three.

Two.

He could tell by the line of red lights glowing up ahead that traffic was heavy at the intersection. He wasn't going to make it if he continued to the intersection to turn onto Hagi-wara Tea Garden Drive, the road upon which the museum was located.

He had no doubt Justine would kill Melly without a moment's hesitation if he were late. None at all.

Yanking hard on the steering wheel, he drove the car over the shoulder and onto the grounds of the park. He could feel the wheels of the car digging into the dirt, and he gunned the engine to compensate.

When the distinctive shape of the museum building loomed out of the fog, he opened the car door and leaped out while it was still running, leaving it to slow to a stop on its own. Blurring into his fastest sprint, he raced around the corner of the building just as the stopwatch on his phone started to chime.

He snatched the phone out of his pocket and texted, I'm at the front of the museum. Where are you?

Justine replied, Stop. Wait.

Coming to a standstill, he did as she ordered, studying his immediate surroundings with a soldier's sharp eye. Palm trees dotted the area, and despite the heavy fog, there were several people walking along the sidewalk. He focused on their conversations. All of them sounded innocuous enough.

A young girl came running toward him. Perhaps twelve years old, she wore a school uniform and she carried a laptop. He had dismissed her as harmless while she was standing in a crowd of schoolchildren several yards away, but as she came closer she caught his attention again.

Several dangerous creatures could masquerade as an innocuous school-age girl, and he tensed.

"Hi!" she called out as she ran up to him. "The lady from the museum said you left your laptop. She asked me to bring it to you."

Catching a hint of the girl's human scent, he relaxed somewhat. "Did she?" he asked, glancing behind her at the museum's entrance. "What did she look like?"

The girl gave him a bright smile. "Oh, she's very beautiful, and she has red hair. Is this yours?"

"I guess it is." He took it from her. "Thanks."

"Have a nice day!" She raced off again, heading for a yellow school bus where several other children in the same uniform were climbing aboard.

His phone vibrated. Did you get my present?

Tucking the laptop under one arm, he texted, Yes. Quit texting, dammit. Pick up your phone and call.

Oh, we'll talk, she sent back. Just not by phone. Open the laptop and click on the Skype window. It's logged into the museum's Wi-Fi. Don't move away from the building, or you'll lose your connection.

Furiously, he yanked open the laptop and clicked on the Skype window.

Even though he braced himself for what might come next, the image that appeared made him go more than a little insane.

The scene was the same as the photo Justine had sent him. The background looked like rough rock, as if it might be a cave, or perhaps an unfinished basement. There were no windows or other potentially identifying characteristics. The lighting was odd and inadequate, and very slanted, as if it came from a lamp set on the floor.

This time there was no sign of the unknown male. Justine stood with Melly in front of the camera. They were both near the same height and size, but Melly was no match for Justine's far superior strength and speed. Melly had a bunched cloth stuffed into her mouth in a simple, brutal gag. The Vampyre held the younger woman in a tight clench, and in one hand, she held a knife.

Julian ran his gaze compulsively over Melly. By some trick of nature, she was ridiculously photogenic. Even in such a horrible setting, with bad lighting, no makeup and a great deal of stress and danger, the camera loved her features and figure.

She looked disheveled, furious and scared. Her bare arms showed a few smudges that might be either dirt or bruises, but other than that, she didn't appear to be seriously injured or abused.

Yet.

Their gazes locked. Even through Skype he felt such a strong connection to her, for the tiniest moment nothing else mattered. All his anger and bitterness fell away. She looked at him like she used to with her beautiful eyes so full of emotion. Light glimmered in the wetness of her gaze, and in that moment, he would have given anything, anything at all, to be able to put his arms around her and tell her that everything would be okay.

Anything, just to feel her in his arms one more time.

"First things first," Justine said. She smiled into the camera. "I want you to tell me you didn't say a word to anyone."

He snapped, "I didn't tell anybody anything."

"Excellent. Put your phone in your pocket and leave it there. Remember—I have eyes on you right now, and I don't mean through our Skype session. If you try to do anything stupid, I'll carve off Melly's face and make it into a mask to wear to our next encounter."

His own truthsense told him that Justine wasn't making an idle threat. He hadn't targeted anyone suspicious when he'd studied the scene, but that didn't mean that watchers weren't there.

Hissing, he jammed his phone into his pocket. "I'm not going to try anything stupid."

Justine laid her cheek against Melly's golden hair and rocked her back and forth. "I guess we have an answer to our question, don't we, kitten? Apparently he does have some feeling left for you after all." Her smile widened. "Julian, you might want to compose yourself. Remember, the fog offers you some cover, but you're still in public. Those fangs and red eyes are sure to bring you more attention than you want right now."

He hadn't been aware that he had lost such control, and he struggled for some measure of composure. It was difficult, when the need for violence filled his mind with a red haze.

"You're going to be okay," he told Melly. "Remember that."

Briefly, she closed her eyes. When she looked at him

again, she did so with a steely calm. Good girl. Gods, she might be faithless, but she was damn brave.

Only then did he turn his attention back to the psychotic bitch holding her captive. "I'm here, just like you wanted," he said in a harsh voice. "Let's get on with this."

"Don't be so hasty," Justine said with evident relish. "I can't tell you how long I've looked forward to doing this—or something like this, anyway. This specific scenario is a surprise, but I'm excellent at improvising when I have to. I just want you to take a moment to really appreciate everything I've set up here."

He said between his teeth, "Believe me, nothing you've done in the last few days has escaped my notice."

She batted her eyelashes at him. "I'm so glad. This wasn't easy to do on short notice, you know. We're in a remote enough location I had to use a couple of relays just to establish a Wi-Fi connection. You can't imagine the hassle."

"You want me to tell you it's really fucking amazing?" he said flatly. "Okay. It's really fucking amazing. Justine, you've screwed up. Forget about me for a moment—take me out of the picture completely. If you do anything to hurt Melly, Tatiana will never rest until she has you hunted down and staked."

Justine pursed her lips into a moue. "I guess that means we'll have to make sure Tatiana never finds out I was involved. Maybe I should just kill her now. After all, it's not like I can let her go, because as soon as I do, Tatiana will know I was the one who kidnapped her."

She raised the knife to Melly's throat.

He started to talk fast, and desperately. "That's not true. You haven't gone too far yet. Tatiana will be pissed you kidnapped her, but no real harm has been done. She'll get over it—Justine, listen to me—"

Watching his face, Justine started to draw the knife slowly across Melly's neck. A red line appeared on the tawny skin of Melly's throat. With a hoarse, muffled scream, Melly fought against Justine's hold, but the other woman held her firmly captive.

Panic blew out Julian's mind. He roared into the camera, "Stop. *Justine, stop!* TELL ME WHAT THE FUCK YOU WANT ME TO DO, AND I'LL DO IT!"

Cocking her head, Justine pulled the knife away and licked the blade with evident relish.

As Julian stared while she tasted Melly's blood, he wanted nothing more than to punch his fist into Justine's chest, pull out her beating heart and crush it in one hand.

Justine said, "Or maybe I shouldn't kill her, since she seems to be an effective way to control you. Hm, what to do." She said to Melly, "Darling, you taste delicious. Stop struggling so hard, I barely scratched you."

Fixedly, he focused on the bleeding wound on Melly's neck. Even though the quality of the camera feed wasn't terrific, the cut didn't appear to be bleeding copiously. Justine was telling the truth. She hadn't cut deeply enough to sever the carotid artery.

He thought of all the expert slashes on the throats of her dead attendants. She knew what she was doing with a knife, down to the millimeter. Now that she had decided on her course of action, she would enjoy playing with them both, like a cat with captive mice.

He had to turn her attention away from Melly and back onto him. He snapped, "What do you want?"

All Justine's playfulness fell away, until her face turned cold and still. "It's so simple, Julian, I'm sure you already know the answer. I want you. Taking Melly, this whole set up—it was all for you. I hope you feel flattered. Now I want to know just one thing. If I agree to let Melly go, would you take her place? Would you trade her life for yours?"

"Yes," he said. Justine was right. He did already know she would ask that, because of course that was the trap.

Justine smiled. "That's what I was hoping you would say." Her gaze shifted to someone who stood behind the camera. "Now it's your turn."

A whirlwind of Power appeared in front of Julian. If that was Soren, his appearance on the scene could ruin everything.

Snapping the laptop shut, Julian faced the new arrival with a snarl, his fangs descending.

The figure of a Djinn formed, but it wasn't Soren.

It was a pariah Djinn named Malphas.

Like Soren, Malphas was a first-generation Djinn, and as such, he carried an intense concentration of Power. His physical form was that of an angelically handsome man with golden hair, but he was nothing like an angel.

Malphas smiled at him. "Hello, Julian."

He snarled, "What the fuck are you doing here?"

The Djinn lifted a shoulder in a casual-looking shrug. "When I heard Justine was looking to bargain with a Djinn, I decided to pay her a visit to see what she required. We had an interesting conversation, she and I."

"You can't bargain to help Justine," Julian growled. "Pariahs might not keep their word, but you can't afford to break the bargain you made with Tess and Soren. If you do anything to hurt anyone in the Nightkind demesne, or anyone Tess knows and cares about, Soren will open the envelope of information she gave him and distribute the contents to every gaming commission in the world."

Malphas's smile glittered with malice. "I can keep a bargain when it suits me, and I fully intend on keeping that one. However, there's nothing in that agreement to keep me from offering to give you a ride if you want it. After all, I wouldn't be hurting you. I would be helping you to get wherever you wanted to go. I can drop you off at the destination of your choice and be on my way. What happens to you after that is none of my business."

Julian's eyes narrowed. Clearly this was the Djinn's way of getting revenge for Julian's part in the confrontation that had trapped Malphas into making the bargain with Soren and Tess.

His mind raced as he tried to think of options, but Justine had planned too thoroughly and there weren't any. With Malphas's travel "assistance," Julian would have no way to trace their paths or to find out the location of the meeting.

"I know what you're trying to do," said Malphas. "You're

trying to think your way out of the situation. But this time all of the cards are in Justine's favor. You'd better hurry. From everything I've seen, I think she really likes to use that knife."

"All right," he bit out. Maybe he could think of something he could do once he came face-to-face with Justine.

Malphas raised an eyebrow. " 'All right' . . . what? Do you want me to do something for you?"

"Take me to where Justine and Melly are," Julian snarled.

Smiling, the Djinn crossed his arms. "Did you ask me a question in there somewhere? I didn't hear a request in that. I can't imagine why I would do anything for you when you haven't even said please."

His fangs sprang out. Lowering his head, Julian stared at the Djinn. "I might be trapped at the moment," he whispered. "But you don't want to push me too far."

"On the contrary." Malphas returned his stare with one as implacable and hostile. "That's precisely what I want to do—push you too far. Hurry up. I'm growing bored. You have no value to me if you stop being entertaining, and I couldn't care less whether or not Justine slits the Light Fae princess's throat."

Julian sucked in a breath. He said, "Will you please take me to where Justine and Melly are?"

"That's better." Malphas's smile returned. "Of course I will."

As the Djinn strolled toward him, Julian had time to consider a few things.

Every old Vampyre had talents that increased with age, and he was no exception. His talents were persuasion and also the ability to hold on to his prey. If he got his hands on Malphas, the Djinn wouldn't be able to dematerialize again until Julian either let him go or he was dead.

And he considered it.

He really considered it.

If he waited until after Malphas transported him to where Justine and Melly were, and he tried to call on Soren, he could force Malphas to stay until the other Djinn arrived.

But that was assuming Soren could hear him, or would choose to answer him if he did. Djinn made psychic connections to the people with whom they struck bargains. Those connections allowed them to hear when they were called, but Julian had always been careful to stay clear of Djinn obligations.

Witches were also able to put out calls to the Djinn with enough Power to make themselves heard, but Julian was no witch. Normally when he wanted to contact Soren, he did so in the most ordinary of ways, by phone.

Even if he were able to call Soren and the Djinn responded, the maneuver would kill him. Julian might be able to pin Malphas, but he couldn't defeat the Djinn on his own. Malphas was too Powerful.

A first-generation pariah could only be destroyed if several Powerful creatures teamed up to take him down. It had been done before, but it was a risky and dangerous proposition, which was why the Demonkind only went after a rogue Djinn when they had no other choice. At their essence, they were social creatures, and their preferred method of punishment was to ostracize a Djinn who went rogue.

And none of that took into account what would happen to Melly in the precious seconds it would take Soren to arrive and assess the situation. Justine would have her throat slit before Soren could do anything to stop it.

They really were well and truly trapped.

So Julian said nothing as Malphas stepped close enough to lay a hand on his shoulder.

And he did nothing, as the Djinn's whirlwind of Power rose up around him and carried him away.

Blood trickled down Melly's neck from the stinging cut Justine had given her. She thought, dear lords and ladies, all I want in the whole wide world is a bath, a piña colada, and the chance to stake this bitch in the heart.

And please, gods, a nap in a real bed is mighty high on my list too.

None of those things appeared to be in her near future. Not only was Justine's iron grip unbreakable, but Melly's makeshift stake lay several feet away, hidden in the pathetic little nest she had carefully arranged so that it hid the damage she had done to the frame of the cot.

When Justine and Vampyre Guy had shown up earlier, they had given her plenty of warning at their approach, although she hadn't understood what was happening until it was almost too late.

She had been hard at work staking ferals, which was a rotten, dangerous, tedious task, thank you very much. It was tough physical work, and her arm and shoulder tired quickly.

Horror was so much more fun on a movie set, where all the wounds were special effects applied by makeup artists, and there was a concession table with tasty snacks, and trailers with working plumbing, and weekend parties, and somebody else available to do her stunts whenever she didn't feel like doing them.

In real life . . . there weren't enough words to describe how much this sucked.

Also, the Vampyres were feral—that didn't necessarily make them stupid. It hadn't taken them long to learn to jerk back when she lunged for one of them.

Yet they wanted her . . . they really wanted her, so they stayed close, in case they might be able to grab her whenever she danced near. There were so many Vampyres, they crowded the ones at the front against the bars and hampered their movements, which was why she had been able to make as many kills as she had.

So far, she'd managed to stake five. Four of them had crumbled to dust, while the fifth one had gotten extra snarly and violent, and there were still so many left.

Then a high-pitched whistle sounded.

As she paused and tried to figure out what this new information meant, the ferals turned toward the sound and raced down the tunnel. A few lingered, including the one she had stabbed, but not for long. After a few moments they, too, raced out of sight.

At first she had been relieved but puzzled. What had made them run?

Moments later, she had heard Justine's and Vampyre

Guy's voices coming down the tunnel. That was when realization had struck.

They had conditioned the ferals to respond to a whistle.

Leaping into action, she had scrambled to get her nest arranged so she could hide her stake. She kept the cot propped on its side, the ends touching the walls in the corner, with the blanket and her food and water stacked inside the triangle.

The whole illusion was as risky as a house of cards. One good puff of wind and it would all fall down.

For example, if anybody chose to right the three-legged cot and sit on it, it would collapse under their weight, but she had bet that nobody would want to settle in for a relaxed visit.

So far she had been right.

"Relaxed" was definitely not what this visit was. Homicidal and psychopathic, but not relaxed.

She had watched them set up their technical operation, complete with camping lantern, a Wi-Fi router and a laptop. None of it had surprised her, except for the arrival of a Djinn named Malphas.

When Justine had stepped into the cell to take hold of her in a firm grip and turn to face the laptop, Melly had been braced to see her mom on the screen, or maybe Bailey, or even both of them together.

Not Julian.

Never in a million years would she have expected Julian.

He was such a bastard. He was two thousand years of mean streets rolled into a rough, foul-mouthed package. His best talents were making war, smoking cigars and wearing those god-awful, worn cowboy boots of his. Those were some of the things that had first attracted her to him, and they were what hurt so much now that she and Julian were estranged, because he knew all too well how to use words as a weapon.

But that look in his eyes when he had told her she would be okay . . .

The words he had roared echoed in her mind. TELL ME WHAT THE FUCK YOU WANT ME TO DO, AND I'LL DO IT!

In a daze, she thought, some part of him still cares for

me. Maybe it isn't the most important part. It certainly hasn't been enough for us to overcome all the damage, distrust and hurt that has built up between us over the years.

But it might be just enough to get him killed.

She wanted to scream at him, but Justine's hard hand clamped over her mouth and kept her from speaking. Even though he was too far away for her to connect to him telepathically, she still tried. *Justine isn't going to let me go! Don't throw your life away!*

He didn't show any evidence that he heard her, of course.

Then Malphas disappeared and Julian snapped his laptop shut, cutting off the Skype session. After a few moments, the maelstrom of Power that heralded a Djinn's impending arrival filled the area again.

Justine hugged her tight with every bit as much delighted affection as a child with a new pet. The Vampyre whispered in her ear, "Here we go, kitten. I wonder if this is how Christmas feels. Because of some blasted bargain, Malphas can't and won't take Julian against his will, so . . . did he agree to come, or didn't he?"

As the Djinn's Power coalesced, two male forms appeared in the cell across from Melly's. One of them was Malphas.

The other was the figure of a strong, powerful man wearing jeans, a plain gray T-shirt and scuffed cowboy boots. The man had hard, rough features, wolflike eyes and salt-and-pepper hair.

Julian was such an intense male presence, she couldn't fail to mistake him—she knew it was him before his body had fully formed.

He had come. He really had come for her.

Tears filled her eyes.

Telepathically, she said to him, *You idiot.*

His angry, red gaze met hers briefly. *Shut up.*

Malphas said in a cheerful voice, "Well, Julian, now that I've done you this favor, I believe it's time for me to leave." His diamond eyes seemed to sparkle. "Have a nice day."

The Djinn vanished, while Julian took in the scene with a single glance. His gaze focused on Justine, and despite all evidence of everything stacked up against him—the locked, secure cell where Justine held Melly, and the knife she held to Melly's throat—Melly had to swallow hard and shiver at his icy, deadly expression.

Trapped as he was, he was still one of the most dangerous men she had ever met. If she had been Justine and the true recipient of that look, she wouldn't stop running until she found a place to hide where nobody knew her name, and even then she would spend the rest of her life looking over her shoulder.

He said, "You said you'd let her go."

"You're not secured yet," Justine told him. "There are chains right behind you. Lock yourself in. Fix the manacles on your ankles first, because you're going to have to stretch up to get your wrists locked in."

Don't do it, Melly told him. *You know she's not going to honor any bargain she strikes with you. She's not going to let me go.*

I said shut up. Calmly, he stepped into position.

Since when do I listen to anything you say? she retorted, then desperately, *Julian, stop!*

Ignoring her, he snapped the manacles around his ankles and raised his arms to lock his wrists in the chains that dangled overhead.

Justine whispered, "That's the most damn perfect thing I've seen in decades. Maybe centuries."

Her punishingly tight hold on Melly loosened. Freeing herself with a jerk, Melly sprang several feet away and yanked the hem of her top into place angrily.

Neither Justine nor Julian paid any attention to her. They were wholly focused on each other as Justine strolled toward the bars of the cell.

Justine's lack of concern over letting her loose couldn't have been more insulting, but Melly was okay with that, since it meant the Vampyre wasn't paying any attention to her. Briefly tempted to slip over to her nest to retrieve her stake, she glanced at the corner, but as appealing as it was to make a try for staking Justine, the risk of getting caught was too great.

Now that Justine had Julian in chains, she had no reason to keep Melly alive any longer. If Melly attacked her and failed, even if Justine chose not to kill her, she would take everything out of Melly's cell, and they—yes, it was now time to say "they"—would need all the help they could get if they were going to escape from this alive.

Taking the key out of her pocket, Justine let herself out of the cell and locked Melly inside. Then the Vampyre strolled into Julian's cell while twirling her knife in between long, pale fingers.

Watching her, Melly's stomach clenched. Oh gods, this was going to get bad.

Maybe she could get Justine to focus on her instead of Julian.

She rushed to the bars, gripping them so tightly she bruised the palms of her hands. "Justine," she said in a sharp voice. "You promised to let me go. Locking me in the cell again isn't letting me go."

Justine gave her a glance filled with equal measures of contempt and amusement. "Poodles shouldn't try to think so hard. Everybody knew I wasn't going to let you go, except apparently for you."

"Julian was right." Melly spoke as fast as she could. "You're playing this all wrong. Stop and think for a moment. My mother considers you a friend, and that's a really valuable commodity. You don't want to jeopardize it."

"Tatiana will continue to consider me a friend." Justine's reply sounded almost lazy. She came to stand in front of Julian, who regarded her with the same contempt that she showed to Melly. "In fact, I'm going to be so sympathetic and helpful over your disappearance, our friendship will grow even stronger. That will be quite useful in the upcoming months, since Julian won't be the Nightkind King any longer. Now hush, Melly, and don't forget, you've just become a luxury mammal. You're no longer a necessity to me."

"Yeah, I figured that part out for myself," Melly muttered.

Justine dug into Julian's jeans to withdraw his cell phone. Dropping it on the floor, she ground it underneath one heel. Then, faster than Melly could track, Justine lashed out.

Ribbons of Julian's T-shirt drifted to the ground, revealing his heavily muscled, scarred chest and arms.

Justine told him in a quiet voice, "I like breaking things. It's always been my way, and I'm going to especially enjoy breaking you. You're dictatorial and arrogant, and inflexible, and you've been a pain in my ass for too many years. I'm going to tear you down until there's nothing of you left, and then I'm going to train you to be my pet."

Julian gave her a cold, bored look. "You're delusional."

Her voice gentled. "Just wait, you'll see. But before I destroy your mind, first I'm going to hurt you a lot. I want you to be fully aware, so you realize what's being done to you, and you know that it's me who is doing it. And you're going to let me, because if you don't, I'll carve something off of Melly while you watch. She's got lots of bits she can lose before she dies. A thumb, a breast, an ear or her nose. Even her hands and feet."

"Please," Melly whispered. "Don't do this. Justine, there has to be something you want more than this. What is it? Tell me what it is, and I'll see that you get it. I swear I will—I swear it."

The Vampyre didn't even glance at her. "There's nothing I want more than this."

Justine struck again, and Melly muffled a moan against the heel of one palm as long red cuts appeared on Julian's muscled arms and chest. A roil of nausea twisted in her gut. Leaning her head against the cold bars, she breathed evenly to make it go away. This leisurely sadism was so much worse than anything she could have imagined.

As Justine ran the tip of her knife along his abdomen, Julian's sharp, steady gaze met Melly's.

He said telepathically, *Don't watch.*

I have to, she whispered. *If it weren't for me, you wouldn't be here.*

Don't be stupid, he said. *Justine's the one who is responsible, not you. She's the reason why we're both here. Goddammit, Melly, turn the fuck away.*

I can't.

Justine cut him again and again, and Melly clapped her own hand over her mouth to muffle a sob. Each movement was drawn out, until the torture seemed to go on for hours.

"That ought to do it," Justine said finally. Taking a step back, she licked her knife clean. She made a sound of pleasure. "All the blood oaths you've taken as King have made your blood really potent. I hadn't realized just how Powerful you had become."

Dread pulsed a rapid tempo in Melly's veins. Ought to do what?

Julian must have been wondering the same thing, for he watched Justine with a sharp, wary expression. He said in a mocking voice, "Is that all you've got?"

Was he insane? Melly shouted at him, *Don't goad her!*

Justine laughed. "Oh, I'm not done with you, darling. I'm only just getting started. That was just to get the scent of your fresh blood in the air." Raising her voice, she called out, "Open up the gate!"

As Julian's frowning gaze met Melly's again, a metallic clang sounded from down the tunnel, and moments later, Vampyre Guy appeared. Julian's fangs sprang out, and he snarled at the other male.

Despite Julian being in chains, the sight of his full, naked aggression was so overpowering, Melly took a step back from the bars. Vampyre Guy pretended to be unaffected, but she noticed he was careful to keep Justine's body between him and Julian.

Followed closely by Vampyre Guy, Justine left Julian's cell and propped the door open wide. Then the two Vampyres walked into one of the empty cells. After Justine closed the door and locked it, she pulled something slender out of her pocket and put one end in her mouth.

A high-pitched, piercing whistle speared through the air.

"Oh gods, no," Melly whispered.

Snarling came from down the tunnel, along with the sound of running footsteps.

Many footsteps.

She flung herself against the bars, shouting, "*No!*"

Ferals flooded the tunnel. Some lunged toward her, forcing her to leap back again. Others found their way through the open cell door. Over the tops of the ferals' heads, Melly caught a glimpse of them on the inside of the bars in Julian's cell.

She couldn't see anything else, but she could hear things all too well.

An explosive snarling that gradually quieted.

Then that shuffling, or scraping sound she had first heard, as the Vampyres fed.

⇒ FIVE ⇒

After what seemed a hellish eternity, the whistle sounded. Melly had moved to crouch in her corner, behind the cot, where she rocked with her hands cupped over her ears, but even though it muffled the sounds somewhat, the whistle still penetrated. Pushing to her feet, she turned to watch the crowd of ferals.

This time, they were slow to respond. The whistle sounded again, sharp and piercing, and something cracked the air. It sounded like a whip.

Growling, the ferals retreated. As Justine appeared, Melly realized the other woman actually did have a whip. Once again, Justine cracked the whip across the ferals nearest to her, and they cowered away.

If Justine had really been the one to create the ferals, Melly could almost feel sorry for them.

Almost.

That was until she looked across to Julian's cell and sickened rage replaced all other emotion.

He hung limp in the chains, his head hanging forward

and his powerful body bloody and lax. Wiping at her wet cheeks, she said, *Julian? Please say something.*

He didn't answer.

Her eyes kept watering and obscuring her vision. He couldn't be dead. If he were dead, he would collapse into dust. There would be nothing left of him at all. Nobody to rage against. Nothing but the memory of the brief, bright warmth they had shared followed by years of bitterness.

Unable to maintain any anger toward him in the face of this horrible nightmare, she was left feeling a sharp pain and a sadness so dark it threatened to engulf her.

Justine and Vampyre Guy followed the ferals down the tunnel, and the sound of an iron clang rang against the stony walls. Moments later, they reappeared. They must have shut the gate to the tunnel again.

Fixing her gaze on Julian, Justine said to Vampyre Guy, "Clean up this mess."

Ducking his head, he got to work, packing up the laptop and various items.

As Justine went into Julian's cell, Melly said hoarsely, "Haven't you done enough for one visit?"

"Maybe I have. Maybe not."

"Leave him alone!"

Justine lifted Julian's head to look into his unconscious face. She let his head fall again. "Oh, very well. They drained him pretty deeply. He'll need time to recover enough so I can do it again."

In that moment, Melly had never hated anybody as much as she hated Justine.

She forced herself to take deep, even breaths and think more or less logically. The torture session was over, at least for now, and the sooner Justine and Vampyre Guy left, the sooner she could pick her way out of her own cell and help Julian.

But she was feeling shaky from lack of proper food, too much stress and not enough rest. How much blood could she give Julian when she was like this? While she did have a little of her food stash left, a candy bar and the small bag of nuts, this situation was desperately unstable, and she needed to hold on to as many of her meager resources as she could.

She said, "If you're going to keep me alive, I'm going to need more food and water."

Justine stepped out of Julian's cell, locked the door and swiveled to consider her. "I had forgotten about that. You have a point." As she paused thoughtfully, Melly held her breath. "And no, I don't want to get rid of you just yet. Not only have you proved useful for making Julian toe the line, but keeping you alive might prove useful in other ways as well."

What other ways? Melly's mind clicked into overdrive. Could Justine be planning on somehow using her against her mother?

Justine turned to Vampyre Guy. "Once you get this cleared up, see that you bring her more food and water."

"Real food," Melly interjected. "Not that useless gas station crap you brought the last time. And I need more batteries for the flashlight."

Raising one eyebrow, Justine gave her a sardonic look. "Listen to you, getting all demanding."

Lifting her chin, Melly stared back unwaveringly. "Do you want me alive or not? If you do, I need real food and water, not a candy bar here and there. And you know as well as I do that I don't need the flashlight to survive, but I would appreciate it. Please."

A long moment passed as the Vampyre considered her with a cold, assessing gaze. Then Justine smiled. "A 'please,' no less. It didn't take long for you to learn how to sit up and beg. Maybe you're not quite as stupid as I thought. Or at least you're trainable." She said to Vampyre Guy, "I think it will be so touching if she and Julian can gaze at each other from their prison cells. Be sure to bring her real food, water and more batteries. You and I have a lot to do, so make sure she has enough to last her for a couple of days. I'm not sure when we'll make it back down here."

"Yes, mistress," said Vampyre Guy.

"The dogs are sated for now, but Julian's blood will have made them faster and stronger," Justine told him. "Be careful when you return and make sure you bring them plenty of food to keep them busy."

So that was how she kept the feral Vampyres cooperative. As Melly thought of the people they had been feeding on when she had first discovered them, she felt sickened all over again.

Vampyre Guy glanced over his shoulder toward the gate. His eyes were wide, and he looked none too happy at the thought of returning alone. "Are you sure you won't come back with me? They're afraid of you, and they're easier to manage when you're here."

Justine gave him an impatient look. "Grow a pair and deal with it. Right now I have more important things to do than hold your hand."

He ducked his head. "Yes, mistress."

Justine strode away. Down the tunnel, the iron gate creaked and clanged again. Melly listened to her footsteps recede in the distance while she watched Vampyre Guy get back to work. It didn't take him long to finish packing up.

She glanced at Julian. He still hadn't stirred. Stifling her worry, she leaned a shoulder against one of the bars and said to Vampyre Guy, "She's not very nice to you, is she?"

He snapped, "She's my sire. She doesn't have to be nice."

She shrugged. "I get it. She tells you what to do, and you have to do it. Still, a little appreciation would be nice, wouldn't it? I mean, you're clearly carrying most of the load here, aren't you?"

Vampyre Guy gave her a scathing look. "What do you care?"

That was her cue to call on what acting skills she had. Melly turned her full attention onto him, met his gaze and gave him a slow smile. The Light Fae were a charismatic people, which was one of the reasons why they thrived so well in the entertainment industry, and Melly had more than her fair share of the attribute.

She watched him blink rapidly as the impact hit him. Yeah, she thought, I might never win no Oscars, but I still got something, babe.

She told him in a soft, sincere voice, "When I asked for more food and water, I didn't realize it might put you in danger. I'm awfully sorry."

With an obvious effort, he dragged his gaze away from hers. "You didn't know," he muttered. "It wasn't your fault."

"Still," she said, "It's really good of you to get it. I—I can't imagine how dangerous those Vampyres are, or how hard it is to deal with them."

He jerked a shoulder as if to shrug off her words, but after a moment, he said almost grudgingly, "You've got to keep on your toes with them, and know how to respond if they don't behave on command. If I didn't have such fast reflexes and upper body strength, I wouldn't be able to do it."

Melly widened her eyes and let the expression turn melting—just a little. Not too much, too soon. After all, they were on opposite sides of the cell bars, and she didn't want to lose his credulity.

She told him, "Well, I don't know how you do it. They scare me to death. I haven't been able to rest at all with them snarling and clawing at me between the bars. Can you leave the gate closed when you go?"

He finished collecting the gear in a pack and hoisted it onto his shoulder, picked up the camping lantern, then turned to her. "I'm supposed to let them loose in here while I'm gone, but it's not like you can break out of your cell anyway."

Quickly she switched her melting look into a more helpless expression as she shook her head. "No, I can't, can I?"

He tilted his head and jerked his chin toward the direction Justine had disappeared. "I'll lock the gate so they won't bother you too much."

"Thank you," she whispered, holding out a hand toward him—again, not too much, just a brief flutter of fingers before she dropped them again.

Vampyre Guy took a step toward her. She didn't think he was even aware of doing it. "So, I guess I'm out of the habit of buying food. Is there anything you want?"

Oh for crying out loud, now she had to go and wonder . . .

Is he one of Justine's victims too, or an asshole? Or is he

a victim who also happened to be an asshole? Or am I starting to suffer from a dose of Stockholm Syndrome?

The dial on her people-reading meter hovered somewhere in the uncertain zone.

"I'd kill for a chicken sandwich," she said, giving him a small smile. "And some cheese and fruit, please. Maybe some granola? Oh, and just so you know—I didn't mean to put down the candy you brought. The chocolate bars were really terrific. They just aren't enough sustenance."

Her sharp gaze picked up how he straightened under the praise.

"I can pick up more chocolate," he said. "It'll be a little while before I can get back. Not only do I have to go to the store, but I have to hunt down some people to throw to the wolves to keep them occupied while I come back down here."

The utter lack of remorse or any true feeling with which Vampyre Guy said it sent her dial swinging deeply into the red. Victim or not, he was an asshole. She lost all compunction for manipulating and/or staking him if the situation called for it.

Instantly, she clamped down on her self-control and kept her expression soft and sweet.

Possibly even, dare she say it, a touch poodle-like.

"I appreciate you telling me," she told him. "Be careful."

He swaggered a little. "No problem. I got it covered."

Melly's thoughts raced. Maybe she had accomplished enough in one conversation, and maybe anything else would be pushing too far, but—

Her gaze flicked to Julian. He was still so silent as he hung limp in his chains.

They were in a hot mess. Not only that, it felt deeply unstable, like their situation might change on a whim. On her next visit, Justine might decide it wasn't worth keeping either Melly or Julian alive, and she might kill them both.

So now was the time to push, even if Melly went too far, because they had nothing left to lose and potentially everything to gain.

And while Justine might not want anything more than

Melly locked up and Julian in chains, it was possible that Vampyre Guy might want any other number of things a lot more than his current situation.

Immunity from prosecution. Money. An easy life.

Freedom from Justine?

"What's your name?" she asked Vampyre Guy.

His eyes narrowed. "Why?"

Lifting one corner of her mouth in a lopsided smile, she told him, "Because I don't want to keep calling you Vampyre Guy."

He paused to search her face. "Anthony."

"Anthony," she said. "Okay listen, Anthony. You don't have a choice when your sire gives you a direct order, and I just want you to know, I don't hold any of this against you. In fact, I think that's even a viable legal defense, at least here in California, isn't it?"

Going still, he watched her with hooded eyes and an impassive expression. "What's your point?"

Melly raised an eyebrow. "I understand you have to do what you need to in order to survive, but while you're running errands, you might want to think about something. Did Justine ever give you a direct order to never call the Light Fae Queen? The fabulously rich, powerful Light Fae Queen, who would be incredibly grateful for any tips leading to the rescue of her daughter?"

Anthony's lip curled. "You think I would risk my life like that?"

While he tried to sound scoffing, Melly's people-reading meter said he ended up sounding uncertain instead.

"You have a rare opportunity right now," she told him. "Not many people get a chance like this in their lifetime. You could ask for anything, and my mom would gladly give it to you. The sky is the limit. One quick phone call from you, and this could all be over in a matter of hours. She could protect you from Justine, give you legal immunity and make you rich."

"You want me to betray my sire," he whispered. "My very dangerous sire."

"You know, my mom is really dangerous too," she pointed out. "Not only is she wealthy, but she also has strong political ties all over the world, especially with the Demonkind. She has her own private army, access to the best magical users, and I'm pretty sure she might have invented the word *vendetta*. I guarantee you—she's never going to give up trying to find out what happened to me. And the more time that passes, the greater the chances are that Justine's going to slip up and give something away. Either that or my mom will uncover evidence that will lead to her."

The problem was, of course, that Melly and Julian might not be alive when that happened.

From Anthony's expression, it was clear he hadn't thought of that. His eyes narrowed quickly on her.

She tried out another small smile on him. "On the flip side of the coin, right now, anything you ask for is yours if you want it. But if you do want to make that call, my mom will need time to act. You need to call her sometime when Justine isn't expecting to see you for a few hours. She can't get the opportunity to ask you what you've been doing, because you would have to tell her."

Anthony frowned and rubbed his mouth.

After a brief pause to let what she had said sink in, Melly shrugged and said, "For instance, you could walk out of here right now and make the call. Otherwise you'll have to wait for another window of opportunity." She met his gaze and held it. "Do you want her number?"

He jerked back and strode away. "I'm done listening to you. I got shit to do."

Dammit! She almost had him!

She called after his retreating figure, "Think about it, Anthony. You may not get very many chances."

The Vampyre didn't reply. As he took the lantern with him, the light faded.

She wasn't ready to go back into the deep well of blackness that existed in the tunnels without any light source. Darting to her nest, she dug out her flashlight and turned it on. After having gotten used to the greater illumination from the lantern, her small flashlight's thin, cold beam of light seemed terribly fragile, and all the surrounding shadows felt dense and heavy with an unseen malice.

Shoulders sagging, she listened as the gate opened and closed, and his footsteps faded into silence.

Out of the darkness came Julian's voice. He sounded ragged and more gravelly than ever. "I forgot how you could talk up a bitch when you wanted. I thought he was going to go for it."

Gladness and relief speared through her. She swung the flashlight beam around and trained it toward Julian. The illumination barely reached him. He still sagged in his chains, his head drooping, but the weak light caught and glimmered in his eyes.

"Julian," she whispered. "I am so sorry about what happened. . . ."

He must have shut his eyes, because that brief hint of a glimmer disappeared. He said, "How many times do I have to tell you to shut up?"

The words were as hostile as ever, but he sounded so unutterably weary as he said them. The combination twisted inside of her, until she felt angry and tearful at once.

Sniffing, she turned back to her nest and rummaged for the bag of nuts and the candy bar. While hoarding sounded good in theory, sometimes you just had to eat a little chocolate.

After swallowing a couple of mouthfuls, just enough calories to pick up her flagging energy, she forced herself to set the rest aside. While Anthony was supposed to bring more food, she couldn't trust anything good happening in this hellhole until she saw it for herself.

When she got to her feet again, she tucked her stake into the waist of her slacks at the small of her back and began to sweep the flashlight back and forth over the floor in a steady pattern.

After a moment, Julian asked, "What are you doing?"

"I'm looking for something." A small, gold metallic gleam caught her eye. It was the piece of hairpin that had bent in the lock earlier. She darted forward to pick it up and examine it.

The small slender piece had bent so sharply in the middle, it was almost at a ninety-degree angle. The hairpins were made out of cheap, soft metal, and she knew from experience that if she tried to bend it back into place, it would probably break.

Still, there might come a use for it. She slipped it into her hand and made a fist with one end of the pin poking between two fingers. If nothing else, it could add some damage if she threw a punch. If she aimed well enough, she could even possibly put out an eye with it.

Shoving it into her pocket, she turned her attention to the cell door, stuck the end of the flashlight between her teeth and pulled out her makeshift lock picks.

"What on earth are you doing now?" He sounded as grumpy as a bear with a sore head.

"I'm coming to rescue you, so you might want to dial your rudeness down a notch or two."

When the lock turned, she opened the door of her cell and walked out.

As Julian watched Melly pick the lock on his cell door, his emotions were almost indescribable. Not only was she alive, which was a miracle all on it's own, but she also looked relatively unscathed.

The cut on her neck had already crusted over. Her face was smudged with either dirt or bruises, and there were more bruises on the tawny skin of her arms. Something—or someone—had raked her forearm, but it looked like the wounds had scabbed over. That was all the damage he could detect. She even sounded more or less calm.

She had pulled her tangled hair back into a braid. He had almost forgotten how she could do that. Her hair was curly enough that it could stay in a braid without a tie for at least an hour, if it wasn't disturbed, but when they had been together, he had rarely been able to leave her alone for long enough to let that happen.

The relief that overcame him was more intense than any

other emotion he had felt in a very long time. He said hoarsely, "What are you using to pick the locks?"

She spoke around the butt of the flashlight she held between her teeth, and while the words were a bit distorted, they were also easily understandable. "Pieces of a hairpin."

A rusty, ragged sound came out of him like a cough, making the open wounds all over his body throb. With surprise, he recognized the sound. It was a laugh. "That might be the first mistake Justine has made since she took you."

Melly glanced at him, large eyes flashing, and then she focused on her work again. "Well, she got most of them, but they weren't handling me all that gently at the time, and a few slipped into my bra." She raised her eyebrows, and somehow, despite the flashlight between her teeth, managed to look quite regal. "I chose not to inform them of that fact."

They had manhandled her. Rage exploded in a supernova, but he didn't have the reserves to sustain it. As fast as it hit, it dissipated into a dull red glow. "Like I said, stupid of them."

She finished picking the lock, and pushed the door open while she took the flashlight out of her mouth. "I find it useful when people underestimate me."

Exhausted and in pain, he closed his eyes to avoid looking at her as she walked toward him. Disheveled as she was, she looked too beautiful, and his insides were in a riotous mess. Gladness, relief and anger—the old anger at Melly, and the new, hot rage at Justine—and something else that lay twisted into a knot deep in his heart. He chose not to examine that last bit too closely.

"Not a mistake I'd ever make with you," he heard himself saying. "I'd have done a body cavity search."

"Same old suave Julian. I never know when you're flirting." Her reply was acerbic, but her hands were gentle as she touched the wounds on his chest. Her intake of breath was all too audible in the dense silence. When she spoke next, her voice had turned small and tense. "Gods. They didn't just bite you. They tore at you, and you haven't healed."

"Too much blood loss," he muttered.

"Here." Something warm and soft nudged his lips. It smelled like her.

He opened his eyes.

She held her wrist to his mouth, her expression warm and concerned. While she was tall for a woman, because of the difference in their heights, she had to stand very close to him to hold her arm up at the correct angle to reach his mouth.

He could feel the heat from her body against his bruised and torn skin, and her scent twined around him in an invisible embrace.

He hadn't been so physically close to her since the last time they were together. Always afterward, whenever they had to see and interact with each other in public, he had kept at least a few feet of distance between them.

The sight, scent and sensation of her closeness pierced through him, right into the tangled knot lying deep in his heart. Sharp, raw pain flared up, as bewildered and jagged as it had been the day he had been given evidence of her infidelity, incontrovertible evidence that made a lie of every sincere-seeming glance from her, every affectionate gesture or quietly whispered words of love.

Reflexively he jerked his head away.

Silence stretched taut between them, so heavy and complete he could count the beats of her heart.

She said in a tight, brittle voice, "You have to feed, even if it's from me. If you don't, you won't heal. You'll stay weak, and that won't get either of us out of here."

He looked at her. Her expression had turned pinched, and her eyes glittered.

Much as he didn't want to bite her, she was right. "You startled me, that's all," he growled. "Come on, let's get it over with."

The curve of her full mouth drew tight, but she held her wrist up to his mouth again.

He didn't want to drink. He didn't want to need her in any way. Reluctantly, he forced his fangs to descend.

No matter how he tried, he could never let go of his anger at her. He could forget about it, sometimes for months at a time, but whenever he was confronted with the reality of her again, it all surged back in a hot, violent whirlpool that swept over his mind and clouded his thinking. Sometimes he wondered if he would ever be able to let it go. He was a mean, unforgiving bastard at the best of times.

But as angry as he was, he couldn't strike at her. Instead, he put his mouth against the tender flesh of her inner wrist and eased into the bite as gently as he could. As his fangs pierced her delicate skin, her fingers curled tight and the tiny intake of breath was clearly audible in the tomb-like silence.

Instinctively he paused, giving her the chance to adjust to the bite. There was etiquette to this sort of thing. At first the pain would be sharp, like an IV needle, but the properties in his saliva would ease that away within moments. Civilized Vampyres only began to draw from a bite once their participant began to feel pleasure.

In pain and as depleted as he was, he adamantly refused to allow Justine's abuses to drive him into behaving like the animals that had fed from him. So he waited until her fingers relaxed, unfurling like shy, slender flower petals. Only then did he begin to suck.

The rich, warm tang of her blood flowed into his mouth. Good Christ. He had thought he'd braced himself for the impact of her taste, but he hadn't. He couldn't. There was no way to brace for this.

Like the differences between types of wine and different wineries, each person's blood carried a taste that was unique to them.

Nothing else in the entire world tasted like Melisande. Nothing.

Before he had become a Vampyre, he had lived a rugged life in the Roman army. He had been almost constantly outdoors in all types of weather, yet that brief human experience had occurred two thousand years ago.

He had long since forgotten what warm sunlight felt like on his face, yet the warmth in Melly's blood reminded him. Like her smile, it was infectious. It stole into him and pushed back the icy darkness that had begun to take him over.

Her blood was unbelievably rich with the magic that came with her heritage, along with an ability she had never bothered to cultivate. She had never cared about any inherent magical talent and preferred to explore her other talents and attributes, but he could taste all of it on his tongue.

She tasted like home and hot sex, like laughter and intimacy.

She tasted like realization.

Before her, he hadn't known that he had been slowly expiring of thirst over the centuries. No matter how many people he tasted or how many lovers he had taken, he had been dying inside. Dying. Then she had lit everything up inside of him—only to snatch it all away again, leaving him bereft and alone as he approached the midnight of his life.

As he drew on her, he made a sound at the back of his throat, and she echoed it softly. Endorphins flooded her blood, and as he drank, her pleasure became his.

It was every bit as powerful as the first time the night of the Masque, when he had taken what a tipsy, mischievous goddess had offered him. The same kind of shock, the same intensity of connection.

Memory became entwined with the present.

Then, at the Masque, her breath had hissed in a sexy little catch, and she swayed as he sucked so gently at her delicate skin. Still feeding and hungry to feel her curvaceous body against his, he pulled her into his arms, and she came readily to nestle against him, the curve of her pelvis rubbing against his erection. Astonished intoxication bolted through him.

Her arousal fed his arousal, and his fed hers. The silken material of her white halter dress slipped under his calloused fingers, and when he forced himself to pull away from her wrist, he stared beyond the golden, elegant mask of a lioness into her wide, dilated green eyes and knew that his life would never be the same.

Now, the gift she gave him was necessary for life, and yet somehow crueler than any wound the ferals had inflicted on him. The Power in her blood slammed into him, and if he hadn't been chained in place, he might have fallen.

His body and his soul were so parched. He never knew he could be so hungry for another person—physically, emotionally hungry—and it had nothing to do with him drinking her blood and everything to do with how he needed to climb on top of her, sink into her soft, welcoming body, and feel her legs clasp him around his hips in welcome just like she used to.

Physically, strength and vitality flowed into him. His wounds closed over and healed seamlessly. Like that first time at the Masque, he needed to put his arms around her, but couldn't. Frustrated, he moved restlessly as much as his chains would allow.

She made another sound that was purely sexual, husky and needy, and the warmth of her body nestled against him. The soft curve of her breasts pressed against his bare chest, and her hips brushed against his painfully hardened cock.

Her heart rate picked up. He could taste her arousal on his tongue, scent it on the air.

The ravenous hunter in him took fierce note. All the signs were there. She could be his for the taking, all his again.

At least for a while, until their separate lifestyles pulled them apart.

Or until she chose to cheat again.

⟰ SIX ⟰

The thought made him recoil from her wrist. His chest moved, distracting him. Belatedly he realized he was breathing hard. Like all of his tangled emotions, it was an exercise in futility. Inwardly cursing, he made himself stop.

Melly lifted her head from his shoulder. Compulsively, he ran his gaze down her body. Her eyes were dazed, and her golden skin flushed with pleasure and arousal. He could just see a hint of the full curve of her breasts in the V-neck of her top, and his mouth watered as he thought of how he used to tongue her plump, erect nipples.

"Why did you stop? You didn't take nearly enough." She ran her tongue along her lower lip, moistening it, and he couldn't help but track the movement.

Feeling more trapped than ever and wild to get away from her, he snapped, "I took enough to heal. Get off of me."

Her eyes widened. Flushing darkly, she jerked away and put her back to him.

"I—I wasn't aware of what I was doing," she muttered. Raising her hand, she pushed her hair off her forehead.

Twin trickles of blood ran down her slender forearm,

intersecting her scabbed-over wounds. He hadn't taken the time with her that he should have to ensure she didn't continue to bleed after his bite.

Remorse struck, and he didn't welcome it. Reluctantly, he said, "I shouldn't have pulled away like that. You're still bleeding. Give me your wrist again, and I'll make it stop."

Now she was the one to recoil. "After your gracious attitude?" she snapped. "Not on your life."

Increased noise penetrated his awareness. The Vampyres, down by the gate, were snarling.

"Don't be stupid, Melly," he growled. "Can't you hear them? The ferals down by the gate can scent your fresh blood. It will make them even more focused on you as their prey."

Shoulders slumping, she tilted her head back and looked up at the shadowed ceiling of his cell. Then she pivoted to fix him with a narrowed, glittering gaze.

"I swear to all the gods," she said between her teeth. "If you say 'don't be stupid' to me one more time, I'm going to start using you as a punching bag. Because I've had a really rotten couple of days, and if you think I'm going to feel bad that you're chained up and can't do anything to stop me, you'd better think again, soldier. So you'd better rein in your asshole tendencies, because I'm in the mood to say hello, opportunity. You've been a long time coming."

Once he had liked it when she had called him "soldier." Halfway through her speech, he realized he was still hard as a rock and aching to bury himself in her. It infuriated him beyond all reason.

"Let's talk about stupid and those rotten days you've had," he snapped. "What did Justine do, show up on your doorstep out of the blue, wearing a big, friendly smile? And what did you do, Melisande—greet her with open arms and invite her in for a little girl talk? Are you really that naive?"

She blinked rapidly several times, and he saw that he had hit a nerve. Raising her hand, palm up, she crooked a couple of her fingers at him in a beckoning gesture. "Or feel free to go ahead and keep those sarcastic comments coming. Because it makes *so much sense* to piss off the chick with the lock pick. And besides, look who's talking about stupid—and look at where he's standing right now."

He had to focus on something besides her beautiful, angry face.

If it were possible for him to break free of his restraints, he would have done so already when the ferals had attacked him. Even so, because he couldn't bear to stand still without trying to do something, he spread his legs as wide as he could and strained against the chains imprisoning his wrists overhead.

As he fought to break free, he said between his teeth, "If I hadn't done what I did, she would have slit your throat and drained you dry while I watched." Glaring at her, he snarled, "Not that I'll get any thanks from you for doing it."

Folding her arms across her chest, she glared back. "She was playing you like a master musician with a tiny violin. You don't know that she would have slit my throat. She made it quite clear I'm a useful bargaining chip for more than one reason. Giving in to her demands wasn't just stupid of you—it was downright suicidal."

Instead of bothering to answer her, he heaved at the restraints again. While his joints popped audibly, the fastening in the ceiling never shifted. The restraints had been constructed with a Vampyre's strength in mind.

After watching him for a moment, Melly strode toward him. "Stop that. Julian, stop. You're tearing your wrists open for no good reason."

He grunted, "It's better than standing here and doing fuck all while you bitch at me."

When he glanced at her, she set the flashlight on the floor, angling the beam of light toward his right ankle, and knelt at his feet. "Well, you'd better not bring the whole thing down on my head. For God's sake, hold still, will you?"

The sight of her kneeling at his feet brought other erotic memories to mind, her sexy lips and tongue working on him as he pumped into her, fists buried in her hair. She had loved it when he fucked her mouth.

He had loved it too, had loved watching her enjoy what they had done more than his own pleasure. Orgasming was too simple a term for how he had felt at the time, but making love felt transcendent.

Had she been acting for any of it? How much of her pleasure had been real?

The brutal fact was, he would never know for sure. She could not only talk up a bitch when she wanted, but she could lie about virtually anything like it was the Gospel truth.

It was one of her strongest talents, and one of the reasons why she was such a popular actress. Not only did the camera love everything about her, but she could also convince audiences all over the world that she really had cared about the gigantic ape that had kidnapped her and climbed the Empire State Building, and she could sell zombies like they were the only true apocalypse.

Once they had laughed about that together.

Angling his jaw out, he averted his gaze. "What's taking you so long?"

Unable to resist, he glanced down at her again and saw that her shoulders had pinched together in an unhappy slump. He knew he was being a bastard, but he couldn't seem to stop himself. He had a devil riding him, and the devil wore worn cowboy boots, smoked a cigar and answered to Julian's name.

"I have pieces of two broken hairpins, not a magic bottle labeled 'miracles,'" she said tightly. "The locks on these manacles are a lot smaller than the ones on the doors. I'm having trouble getting at the tumblers inside." Angling her head up, she gave the chains over his head a grim look. "And not only are you taller than I am, but your wrists are locked above your head. God only knows how I'm going to get at those."

"You're going to climb up my body, that's how," he told

her. "If you have to, you can kneel on my shoulders. Hurry up. Justine's lackey isn't going to be gone for that much longer."

"I know that," she snapped. "Leave me alone, so I can work."

He bit back the retort that rose to his lips, and stood in clenched silence while she twisted to reach the lock of the manacle at the correct angle.

He muttered, "Your mom has called on a lot of help in searching for you, including Graydon from the Wyr demesne and Soren. I suppose if you could have called Soren by now, you would have."

She paused only for a moment. "Soren and my mom go way back, but he's her friend, not mine. I don't have a connection to him, although right now I sure wish I did."

How long had it been since Vampyre Guy had left? Like windowless casinos that deliberately masked all signs of time passing, it was impossible to calculate how long Julian had been in the heavy darkness of the caverns.

But it had been long enough for him to realize that Melly's nearness was just as excruciating as he had always known it would be. Certainly it had been long enough for them to argue and snipe at each other the way they always did whenever they saw each other these days.

It had also been long enough for him to realize he wanted her as much as he ever had. Perhaps even more so, as the long years without her had only served to make his hunger for her that much more urgent.

The thought that had been circling at the back of his mind came to the forefront again—he could take her. He could get his hunger slaked, at least for a time.

The prospect wasn't exactly a done deal. Apparently, to go by her angry responses to him, her emotions were just as complicated for him as his were for her, and the arousal he had sensed when he fed from her had no doubt been enhanced by the intoxicating properties in his bite.

But if he chose to go after her and set his mind to the

task, and if he got her, maybe he could make the infernal noise in his head and his heart quiet down for a little damn while.

This time, instead of recoiling from the idea, he actually considered it as he watched her work. His sensitive hearing picked up the miniscule sounds of the ends of the hairpins scraping on the metal of the manacle. Her fingers jerked as the makeshift pick slipped, and she swore.

His gaze ran down the shapely curve of her hourglass back and lingered at her round, sweet ass.

Mine, he thought. He had lost so much of what had passed for a soul that not even he could tell if the thought was cold-blooded or heated.

You will be mine again. I'll take you. I'll make you want it.

I'll make you want *me* again, at least for a while. Only this time I won't wait for our different lifestyles to pull us apart, or for you to cheat again.

I'll take you and make you mine, until I choose to walk away.

By sheer force of will, Melly forced her hands to remain steady as she tried again to pick the lock on the manacles.

On the one hand, this whole nightmare pretty much topped every other bad memory she'd ever had.

On the other hand, it was kind of a dream come true to have Julian hog-tied and at her mercy. She could get in his face and yell *what the fuck* until she got it all out of her system. Think of how cathartic that would be. Really, it could take her days.

The last occasion they had spent any significant time together was when he had broken up with her. She didn't want to think about that right now, but her mind went there anyway.

He had been so icy and terse. The lover who had known

her body and desires so intimately had vanished as if he had never existed, and the stranger who had taken his place had a face like a stone wall.

They had arranged to meet in Carmel, a charming coastal town in Monterey County. As she had spent the afternoon driving the scenic route through Big Sur, she had actually been daydreaming about leaving her life for him and living in that great, hulking pile of Machiavellian politics the Vampyres called Evenfall.

She had been amused by the idea, and optimistic, and not fifteen minutes later, he had accused her of cheating.

It had literally been a breathtaking experience. She had felt gut shot and utterly bereft. The confrontation devolved into a massive fight, while they hurled hurtful accusations at each other.

Funny. Looking back at it now, she couldn't even remember most of what they had said to each other.

Blah blah stop lying to me, he had said. Blah blah, I can't believe you won't believe me! she had said.

Along with more stuff along those lines. Now whenever she recalled that night, her memory was blanketed in a haze of shock and pain, although shards of clarity still stabbed at her, like the memory of how he had looked at her as if he hated her, and the cold, clipped tone of his voice.

Months later, she approached Xavier. Her pain had turned to outraged fury, and she had long since decided she didn't want to have anything to do with Julian. Anyone who could demonstrate such a lack of faith in her wasn't anybody she wanted to be with. By that point, all she wanted were some answers.

How had Julian become so convinced she had cheated on him? Somebody had to have told him so. But if so, who— and why? Whoever it was, it had to be somebody Julian had trusted a hell of a lot more than he had trusted her. . . .

If he had ever really trusted her.

Their liaison had only lasted a couple of months, but it had been unpopular to a lot of people. The Nightkind King together with the Light Fae heir heralded the possibility of a major shift in the balance in power in the North American Elder Races demesnes.

At the end of the day, what Melly really wanted was a name. She wanted to face her enemies, not have them in a position where they might be able to stab her in the back again.

But not even Xavier knew where Julian had gotten his information, and after that last terrible fight, she sure as hell wasn't about to go to Julian and ask, because she deserved so much better than what he had thrown at her, so really, screw him.

Justine was right, Melly thought. Sadistic and crazy, but right. Julian's dictatorial and arrogant, and inflexible doesn't even begin to cover it. He's the most infuriating son of a bitch I've ever known, and I don't even know why I'm fighting so hard to free him.

At that, she caught herself up. It was one thing to be angry at him—and she was extremely angry at him. But it was another thing entirely to indulge in such vindictive thoughts, especially when she didn't even believe them herself, anyway.

TELL ME WHAT THE FUCK YOU WANT ME TO DO, AND I'LL DO IT! he had roared.

He might still look and act like he hated her, but when Justine turned the screws on him, he hadn't even hesitated.

More than anything, she wanted to sniffle and lean against his jeans-clad leg. She wanted a hug.

She really did want to haul off and clip him as hard as she could with her best right hook.

Gritting her teeth, she thought, I've got to hand it to you, soldier. There isn't anybody else in the world who can tie me into such knots.

Meanwhile, her sense of urgency escalated. Justine might not be back for a day or two, and they had a long time to go until then, but Julian was right—it wouldn't take Anthony long to hunt down some prey and to pick up food and water.

The pieces of her pick slipped again. No matter how she tried, she couldn't get the damn pieces in the damn lock. Her core overheated, and she started to melt down.

"Julian," she said very low as she fought back tears. "I—I don't think I can get this. The lock is too small, and I can't hold the pick at the right angle and still get the other piece inside to trip the tumbler. I need thinner pieces of metal, and I don't have any."

Silence spun out. When he spoke, he sounded entirely calm. "That's all right. Melly, look at me."

All the antagonism was gone. This was the Julian who had looked into the camera and told her she would be okay.

Damn it, the bastard Julian didn't bring her to tears anymore, but the nice Julian did. Blinking the wetness out of her eyes, she sat back on her heels and looked up at him.

He regarded her with an expression that was every bit as calm as he sounded, that wolflike gaze of his trained on her face. He even gave her a small smile. "It's all right," he repeated. We're going to go to plan B."

"I didn't know we had a plan B," she said raggedly as she swiped at her nose with the back of one hand.

"We're going to make one up right now," he told her. "Along with a plan C if we have to."

Rising to her feet, she frowned. "What do you have in mind?"

"You need to get out of here," he said. "And Vampyre Guy is the way to do that."

"No." She started shaking her head and decided not to stop for a while. "I'm not leaving you."

"You have to. He knows the way out, and when he shows up here again, he'll have brought in enough prey to keep the ferals satisfied until he can get out again. Meanwhile, Justine is busy doing other things. We don't know if we'll ever get another chance like this again."

"I couldn't convince him to make one lousy phone call," she pointed out.

"You almost did," he told her. "You have him half-seduced already, and you didn't even put the full weight of those gorgeous green eyes of yours into the effort. If he walks away, he'll have time to talk himself out of calling Tatiana, but if you talk him into taking you with him, you can make the phone call yourself."

A small, feminine part of her perked up. He still thought her eyes were gorgeous?

Well, now she was just being pathetic.

Ducking her head to hide her expression, she rubbed the back of her neck. After a moment, she muttered, "I don't know; it sounds really risky."

"Can you take him, if you had to?"

The question brought her gaze back to his face. His expression remained calm and steady. This was the man who had become a Roman emperor's most successful and celebrated general, and he was assessing her, not judging, maybe for the first time in twenty years.

Just the simple connection of his eyes meeting hers without antagonism shouldn't feel so exhilarating, but it did. Resisting the emotional pull of it, she fought to become as analytical as he had.

"I think so," she told him. "I've had a lot more training than most people realize. And he's not only a young Vampyre, but he's also taking a lot of his cues from Justine's behavior, even if he's doing so subconsciously. He doesn't see me as a threat."

"You think so, but you're not sure," Julian said. "Is that what feels so risky?"

"Well, I don't know for sure how much training *he's* had, and I'm not one to make that kind of mistake about somebody else," she pointed out. "But no, that actually wasn't what I meant. If Justine decides to come back before help arrives, and she finds me gone, you realize she'll kill you. If she can't torture you, you'll have lost all value to her."

"You can't think about that." He shook his head.

He sounded remarkably calm about the prospect of being murdered. Even as one part of her took note, she snorted. "You can't tell me what to think, or not to think."

His expression turned impatient. "The risk to me only means you'll have to hurry." He paused. "I'm pretty sure we're underneath San Francisco."

"Yeah, I figured that out already."

"That means help is a lot closer than you realize," he told her. "When you get out, you shouldn't just call your mom. You need to call Xavier too—he'll be able to get trustworthy people to you much faster than Tatiana could."

She cast a leery glance over her shoulder at the empty cells. "Do you have any idea where we are in the tunnel system?"

"Nowhere I recognize." He angled his face up toward the chains overhead and braced his body to pull on them again. "If I had ever seen these cells or heard of them, I would have had them filled in with cement a long time ago."

As he strained to break free of his bindings, her gaze pulled back to him.

She didn't want to look. She didn't. But she also couldn't help herself.

Nothing about Julian was smooth or civilized. His powerful, heavily muscled body still retained a deep, burnished tan from when he had been human, and he still carried all the scars he had acquired throughout his years of waging war. The rough life he had lived showed on his hard face—while he had been turned in his midthirties, he looked more like a man who was in his midforties.

His looks might be rugged, but he didn't carry an ounce of extra fat anywhere on him. While certain parts of Roman society had been famous for its excesses, it was clear that Julian had not taken any part of it. His tastes ran to the simple, even Spartan.

That had been another thing that had attracted her to him. Given the many opportunities to indulge in excess that he must have encountered throughout the centuries, he still maintained an aura of mature, settled discipline.

She had tried before to imagine him as a young Gladiator in the arena. Back then he must have been as dangerous as a lean, half-starved alley cat. Now, the alley cat had long since vanished. What stood in his stead was a scarred and even more deadly lion who carried the weight of having lived for many years in his prime.

The muscles in his biceps, chest and flat abdomen bulged as he heaved again at the chains. He was an old Vampyre, on a par with Justine in terms of sheer age, and given the years of the blood oaths he had taken, Melly thought she had some kind of inkling just how Powerful he really was. Yet there wasn't an inch of give in his restraints.

Disquieted, she swallowed hard. "Justine built this place too well."

Spearing her with a sidelong glance, he said, "Yes, and none of it is new construction. She must have been using these cells for years."

Rubbing her arms against the chill, she looked around. "You never could fully eradicate the feral Vampyre problem."

"No, I couldn't. No matter how many times I burned out the tunnels, eventually they always came back. Whether it was fair or not for them to judge me on that, it's always been a black mark against me in the Nightkind council." He wiped his face on one bare arm. "This has got to be a completely separate tunnel system, or I would have found it before now."

Her body wasn't doing very well at warding off the deep underground chill any longer. Shivers ran through her muscles, and she felt too hollow, almost lightheaded. She forced herself to concentrate. "What happened to turn Justine rogue? Do you know?"

His attention focused on her. "That's right, you don't know any of the events from the last two days. She tried to have Xavier assassinated."

"*What*?!" She hadn't thought she had any room in her to be shocked at anything else, but she was wrong. "Please tell me he's all right."

He gave her a grim smile. "Luckily, Xavier is one tough son of a bitch to kill. He needs some recovery time, but he'll be fine." Telling the story in a few concise sentences, he filled her in on what had happened in the Nightkind demesne over the last forty-eight hours.

She grew more dazed as she listened. When he reached the part of exploring Justine's property, tears sprang into her eyes. "All of them," she echoed. "She murdered all ninety-two of them."

"Yes."

Some crimes were unfathomable. Dashing a hand over her eyes, she fought to steady her voice. "I knew some of those people. Not well, but still, I knew them. Sofia. Her majordomo, Peter. He was always so charming."

Julian's hard expression, normally so cold whenever he looked at her, seemed to soften. "I know." After a few moments, he said quietly, "Melly, I think you might be going in shock."

"I'm all right." Her voice sounded flat and dull, and she couldn't muster the energy to put any strength into the words.

"I don't think you are." He spoke the words carefully. The thin beam of the flashlight caught in his eyes and made them glow.

Ha. If Julian was taking care with her, then she really must be looking rough.

Her shivering had grown more pronounced. Much as she didn't want to, she was going to have to eat the last of her stash. She couldn't afford to be shaky and uncertain when Anthony returned.

"I need to get back to my cell while I still can," she muttered.

Keeping her head down, she left his cell. She had to fumble three times before she could get the door locked again, and then she had to do it all over again with her own cell door.

The beam of light that had been her lifeline flickered and was growing dim. The batteries in the flashlight were running low. She should probably turn it off to conserve the energy. After all, she didn't know for sure that Anthony was coming back.

At that thought, a flicker of rebellion stirred. There was thriftiness and being smart, and then there was needless paranoia. Justine had ordered him to come back with supplies, which meant he had to return. Leaving the light on, she wrapped herself in her rough blanket and sat in the corner, in the triangle of her little nest.

After that, her mind shut down, and she focused only on immediate necessities. While she tried not to eat her remaining supplies too quickly, once she had made the decision, she couldn't stop herself and practically inhaled the last of the nuts and the chocolate.

Afterward, she drank the last of her water, sparing only a little at the end to wash away the dried trickle of blood from the cut on her neck and the bite on her forearm. As she checked her wrist, she saw that the tiny puncture wounds had already scabbed over.

The food and water weren't enough. Her hollowed-out body clamored for more hydration and nutrition. In an effort to stop the discomfort, she pressed a fist into her abdomen, just under her rib cage, and huddled into a ball, but the pressure didn't help much.

The light had dimmed so that it only illuminated the area of her nest. She could sense Julian in the darkness, silently watching her, but instead of it bothering her, she almost found comfort in his regard.

She didn't care what he thought of her, and she was glad he remained silent, since usually when he opened his mouth it meant that sooner or later she would get infuriated with him, and she didn't have the energy for it right now. As long as he could watch her, it meant she wasn't alone in this horrible place.

Her gaze ran along the edge of the blanket, across the floor and followed the lines of the upended cot. Down, along and over. When she completed a circuit, she began all over again.

Julian's news had shaken her more than she liked to acknowledge. While she had known, of course, that Justine had jumped the rails, she hadn't realized just how far the Vampyre had gone.

There was no way that the details of such a significant massacre could be suppressed for long. How many people already knew about it?

Julian, of course, and the team he had taken to Justine's property, which must have been around ten or fifteen people. Then there was the human forensics team that Julian had sent in to investigate at daybreak. Xavier knew, along with whoever worked for him that he might have told. And probably a few more key people in Evenfall, like Dominic, knew what had happened.

That was too many to keep a secret. So the news of the massacre either had—or would—get out, and then what?

All the other members of the Nightkind council would have to decry what had happened, however they might feel about it in private.

In truth, some of the council members would be frankly indifferent. To them, attendants were inferior creatures, like pets, and no doubt they would view the killings as merely unfortunate, while others, Melly believed, were genuinely decent people, and she didn't think she was being naive.

But in public, none of them could afford any appearance of acceptance or indifference and hope to retain their seats, or maintain the successes of their businesses and the comfort of their lifestyles. The news of the massacre itself could ruin all of them, not only with the human population, but with the rest of the Elder demesnes as well.

And then what?

Melly's gaze completed another circuit. She started again.

Justine would be trying to do damage control. Maybe she could put the blame for the massacre on the one person who had gone missing—Julian. But wait, that couldn't hold, because Julian had been in the public eye virtually the entire time when the murders had occurred.

So Justine might not be able to pin it on him personally, but she might try to pin it on his soldiers, who would have been in the position to carry out such orders.

No, the timing of that wouldn't sit right. Melly didn't see how it could. And Justine couldn't spin the killings as retaliation for what she had tried to do to Xavier, because that would mean she would have to admit to trying to murder a member of the Nightkind government.

She had to be on thin ice with her allies right now. They would not thank her for the increased precariousness of their own positions.

And none of them would consider backing a bid for power from her. Not in the light of current events.

That meant Justine had miscalculated badly. If the Vampyre hadn't realized that yet, then she would very soon. By her own actions, she would have alienated herself from her allies, and martial law was still in effect throughout the demesne.

She was losing her power base, and she was isolated. That meant she had no anchor, no way to achieve any of her goals, and no reason to hold back from any of her excesses.

It also meant that Melly and Julian were in an even more precarious position than she had at first realized.

Or were they? She chewed a thumbnail.

What it really meant was that the value of Melly's life had increased, while the value of Julian's life had gone down. Right now, Julian had value to Justine only if she had the time and the interest to torture him, and Melly was willing to bet that Justine was rapidly running out of both time and interest.

And Julian knew it. That canny wartime general had already parsed the value of his life against the value of Melly's. He had been so calm earlier when he had argued for Melly to use Anthony to get out, because he already believed he was going to die.

Her gaze snagged on something and stopped running the circuit. She focused on the underside of the cot.

And cocked her head.

Maybe she did have a magic bottle labeled miracles after all.

The thin mattress was meant to rest on a piece of canvas stretched to the rectangular frame and held in place by metal springs that were roughly three-quarters of the length of her little finger.

The width of the metal springs looked like it might be thinner than her broken pieces of hairpin.

Snatching a hairpin piece out of her pocket, she held it to the cot to compare. The springs *were* thinner. Not by much, but she didn't need much.

Halle-fucking-lujah.

If she could flatten two of the springs out on one end, she might be able to get the ends into the locks of Julian's manacles.

Screw plan B.

It was time she came up with her own plan.

⇒ SEVEN ⇐

Rising up on her knees, she took her makeshift Vampyre stake and used the edge of one end to leverage prying off one of the springs. The task was frustrating and tedious. None of the pieces of what she had were meant to be used the way she wanted to use them, and her light source was getting dimmer by the minute.

She was concentrating so hard that Julian's voice, coming as it did out of the dark, made her jump. "What on earth are you doing now?"

If she told him, she could see all too well how that argument would go, and she didn't have the inclination or the time to waste on it.

"Never mind what I'm doing," she told him. "You focus on being held captive."

One spring popped loose and skittered across the floor. She retrieved it and started prying off another.

"Melly," said Julian. "You're cooking up something. What is it?"

"None of your business." A second spring popped loose. Feeling a real sense of hope for the first time since she'd been kidnapped, she jumped up and retrieved that one as well.

Now she needed to bend the ends at the correct angle. Sticking her tongue between her teeth, she used her stake to pin one end of a spring against the floor.

In the early 1990s, there had been a TV show, starring Richard Dean Anderson, about a genius that could make tools and bombs and shit out of ordinary, everyday items. What was the name of that show again?

Oh yeah. *MacGyver.*

Melly had loved that show. She whispered to herself, "I am a fucking genius."

The light grew even weaker. Her flashlight was going to give out at any moment. She worked at the spring until she had gotten one end bent out, then quickly started on the other.

"I don't feel good about this," Julian growled.

It annoyed her to no end that he sounded so damn sexy when he did that grumpy, growly thing. She used to love when he sounded grumpy-sexy.

The memory made her spine stiffen. She said, "Remind me, when did I start giving a shit about your feelings again?"

"That would imply that you gave a shit to begin with," he snapped.

Oh now, that one was too much to ignore. Her head came up, and she opened her mouth to blast him.

In the distance, a piercing, high-pitched whistle sounded, followed almost immediately by the sound of the ferals running away down the tunnel.

Real silence descended afterward, which was a major relief from all the nerve-wracking noises the ferals had been making in the background. The silence didn't last long. In the distance, a single set of footsteps sounded.

Quickly, Melly straightened everything up and draped the blanket over one end of the cot to hide what she'd done to the frame. When she was done, she tucked her stake into the waistband at the back of her trousers.

Julian told her in a quiet, clipped voice, "Whatever you're

thinking of doing, just drop it and stick to our plan. Everything will be okay."

"*Our* plan? I don't recall agreeing to any plan." Glancing over her shoulder in his direction, she arched one eyebrow. "Don't you mean your plan? Which, by the way, sucks."

Metallic sounds came from down the tunnel. Someone was unlocking the gate. Please gods, don't let it be Justine again.

Aloud, Julian snarled wordlessly, while telepathically, he exploded. *Goddammit, Melly!*

Feeling almost cheerful at her success in needling him, she told him, *I'm not listening to you.*

When I get my hands free again, I'm going to throttle you.

Once again, I have to point out—is that the smartest thing to say to the chick with the lock picks? Hush now, I'm ignoring you.

Light appeared in the tunnel and grew stronger. Despite her banter with Julian, her nerves were jumping and her stomach had tied itself up in knots. If the newcomer ended up being Justine, she thought she might throw up.

Julian must have been feeling the same kind of tension, because he finally fell silent.

She could have cried from relief when Anthony appeared. The Vampyre carried a full plastic grocery bag and a heavy-duty flashlight that was much more powerful than her cheap little one.

He glanced in Julian's direction. In the stronger light, Melly looked into the other cell as well. Julian had not only fallen silent. He hung limply in his chains, his head lowered, just as he had been before.

"I see he's still out of it," Anthony remarked. "He doesn't look very kingly now, does he?"

Fury tangled up her tongue, which was probably a good thing, as she was quite sure she wouldn't have said anything wise if she could have spoken.

After a moment, she managed to say, "Justine let the ferals feed on him too long."

Anthony directed his flashlight onto Julian. "I don't

know, it looks to me like he's healing really well. She might let them feed longer next time."

Before the Vampyre could pause to think about the implications of what he had just said and wonder why Julian hadn't yet regained consciousness, she asked quickly, "Did you bring me a chicken sandwich?"

Long seconds trickled past, and she held her breath. Then Anthony's attention turned to her. Unexpectedly, he trained his light full on her, catching her in the eyes. "Yes, I did," he said from behind the light. "A really nice one. And some more chocolate too."

Blinded, she threw up one hand to shield her gaze, while part of her took note that he sounded a little odd. Like maybe he was being thoughtful, or deliberating something.

Or something?

"Thank you," she told him. "Look, do you mind pointing your flashlight away? I can't see when you're pointing it at me."

There was a pause that went on too long. "Sure," he said. He directed the light away.

Toward her little nest, and the cot.

Well, damn it. That wasn't much of an improvement.

"How's the mattress on that?" Anthony asked. "Any good?"

He was definitely acting oddly. Her people-reading meter swung to point at an orange caution sign, while she made herself give a casual shrug. "Tell you the truth, I've been too stressed to really lie down on it. I've taken some catnaps, sitting up and leaning against the wall."

Anthony told her, "Why don't you try it out right now?"

At first she didn't understand what she had heard. When she did, her stomach tied itself into tighter knots. Quietly, she asked, "What do you mean?"

Melly, Julian whispered. *Be careful.*

She didn't have any room to respond. All her concentration stayed fixed on Anthony, who shrugged. "I was the one who bought you the cot. I just wanted to know how nice the mattress was."

This isn't a fucking hotel, asshole, and you didn't do me any favors. She wanted to say it so badly. Instead, she offered him a tentative smile. "Can I have my food and water now, please?"

Another pause that went on too long. It strung her nerves tight.

"Sure you can," said Anthony. "I'll be happy to give it to you, just as soon as you take off all your clothes and lie down on that mattress."

Braced as she was for something—what, she didn't know—that caught her completely off guard. Blinking, she said, "What did you just say to me?"

He took a step nearer to the bars. "I'll give you your food when you do what I want. I said, take off all your clothes and lie down on the mattress. I want your feet facing me with your legs spread apart."

She gaped at him. Nobody had ever spoken to her in such a way, not ever.

I'm going to kill him, Julian said in a soft telepathic voice that was so much more chilling than anything Anthony could produce. *I'm going to tear his head from his shoulders and shove it up his ass.*

You'll have to get through me first to do it, she told him.

She smiled at Vampyre Guy. "Now why would I want to do a thing like that? Don't you have a key? Can't you come in here and join me?"

Anthony's eyes narrowed. "My key works on the gate. Only Justine has a key to the cells. She ordered me to bring you food, and I have," he said. "I can leave it sitting out here in the hall for the next day or two, or I can give it to you. But you're going to have to work for it."

So much for your plan B, Melly said to Julian. *It's a good thing I already made up my own damn plan. But first I need to take a moment to marvel at how stupid he is.*

He may be stupid, Julian replied. *But he's still dangerous. Watch yourself.*

Aloud, she said, "I don't get it. You could have had so much more from my mom, and yet you're choosing to do this."

"Calling your mother is too much of a risk," Anthony said. "Being loyal to my mistress is the smartest thing for me to do. But I can still get something I want out of this, and I want to see the Light Fae princess strip down and give me a show."

She started to turn away. Just in time, she remembered her stake, tucked into her waistband, and jerked to a stop. "No. Go ahead and leave the food in the hall. When Justine gets here and sees what you've done, she'll take care of you."

There was a small, distinctive *snick*.

It sounded remarkably like the hammer on a pistol being cocked. Her heart kicked.

Melly! Julian shouted.

She was already whirling to face Anthony again, only to confront the wrong end of a revolver pointing at her between the bars. It was another in a series of first experiences. She had never faced the wrong end of a gun before. A massive dose of adrenaline dumped into her bloodstream, and she broke into a fine sweat.

With a toothy smile, Anthony said, "If we're going to go that far, and I'm already going to get punished, things won't get that much more worse for me if I put a hole in you somewhere. It doesn't have to be fatal to really fucking hurt a lot. You see, Justine's in a tight place right now. The stupid cow killed all her other attendants, and she needs me. Sure, when she punishes me, I might not be very comfortable for a while, but it definitely won't be as bad as it would be if I were to totally betray her by calling the Light Fae Queen. So what's it going to be, princess? You gonna do some work with your fingers and hips, or are you gonna insist on being shot?"

Yeah, I knew my people-reading meter got you pegged right, asshole. Lowering her head, she studied him for a moment.

Then she gave him a small, sad smile. She even threw in a quivering lip for good measure. "It didn't have to come to this," she whispered. "I liked you—I really liked you. If you had only asked me, I would have done so much better than a floor show."

The barrel of the gun lowered a notch.

"What do you mean?" he said shortly.

Wrapping her arms around her torso, she shivered and said pathetically, "Never mind. I don't care if I could touch you between the bars. I—I don't want to do it now."

The silence that greeted that statement sounded downright thunderous.

This is unbelievable, she thought she heard Julian whisper.

But she wasn't sure, because Anthony spoke at the same time. "That just opened up a whole world of possibilities, princess." Wiping his mouth, he ordered, "Come here."

"No. No, don't make me," she said, shaking her head as she hunched her shoulders. Meanwhile, she ran through her repertoire of moves. How far should she take the victim act? Would a sob be too much at this point?

She had just decided that yes, a sob would be too much, when—

The gun went off.

In the enclosed area, the report was deafening. She felt herself shriek rather than heard it, while at the same time she dropped into a crouch and threw her arms over her head.

The sound died, leaving a roaring echo behind.

Say something, Melly!

It took her a moment to realize that she hadn't actually been shot. Shakily, she said, *I'm okay.*

Julian said, *Jesus Christ. If I'd had a heartbeat, it would have stopped.*

"That's the only warning I'm going to give you," said Anthony. "Now, do what you're fucking told, and come here."

Numbly, she walked over to the bars, watching every move the Vampyre made. He strolled toward her and even licked his lips. The whole thing was almost like a scene from a really bad, bad—*bad*—movie, except it wasn't. It was horribly real.

"Unbutton your top," the Vampyre told her. "Press your breasts between the bars."

Watch the gun.

She did as she was told, slowly unbuttoning the front of her top until it hung free, revealing the lacy bra underneath.

She had to put her shoulders back to get her full, round breasts to jut between the bars.

As she did, she glanced up at the Vampyre's face. His gaze was fixed on her breasts. Slipping one hand to the stake at her back, she eased it free of her waistband and held it in a clenched grip.

The sound of frenzied snarling penetrated her ringing ears. When Anthony stepped in front of her, he laughed. "Guess who finally woke up? We're going to have an audience. That kind of makes me hot."

Easy, soldier, she whispered to Julian. *It's all going to be okay.*

Watch the gun and his hands, not his face.

"I wonder what you taste like," Anthony said. "I bet your blood is as rich as the rest of you, isn't it? I can't believe I didn't think of this before. The possibilities are almost endless. I could make you get on your knees to suck me off. Or if you turn around and bend over, I could—why I could fuck a princess through these bars. . . ."

She had to clamp down on the need to spit in his face. Every muscle in her body screamed for her to move. Not yet, Melly.

Not yet.

Anthony shot one of his hands between the bars and grabbed her by the throat. Then, confident and still laughing, he tucked the gun in the waist of his jeans.

Halle-fucking-lujah.

She exploded into movement. Grabbing him by the wrist, she tore free of his grip, braced herself and heaved as hard as she could, yanking him toward her.

She caught him completely off balance. As his body slammed into the bars, she lunged toward him and staked him in the chest. Rage lent her a delicious amount of strength. This time she didn't even wince as she felt the blunt end of her stake penetrate the tough barrier of his chest wall.

Please, don't let me miss his heart.

For one pulsing moment, the world froze. Anthony stared at her with an expression of shock and betrayal—what the hell—before crumbling into dust. The gun, which was not organic, clattered to the floor, along with a jangling bunch of keys, and a whistle.

"Jesus," Julian spat out again. "Are you all right?"

Was she? For one reason or another, her throat had taken a lot of abuse lately. She massaged the sore muscles with one hand.

"I'm okay," she croaked. Betrayal, bah. Life hadn't turned out to be quite how Anthony had imagined, had it? Angrily, she hitched a shoulder as she buttoned up her top again. "I only wish I could stake the bastard twice."

Julian watched Melly go through the tedious process of breaking out of her cell and into his again.

She gave him a wary look. "You've torn your wrists completely raw," she croaked. "You need to calm down, soldier. Everything's all right."

That was easier said than done. At the threat of Vampyre Guy raping Melly, he had gone berserk, and that didn't ease away in an instant, or because of a few soft-spoken words.

He knew he must look like a monster out of one of Melly's horror movies. His fangs had descended, and the structure of his face had changed. His eyes would be red and glowing, and all his fingernails had lengthened into talons.

His body had prepared itself for a life-and-death fight, only the fight had already been won. He was too far gone into his rage to do any more than snarl wordlessly at her.

She had collected everything Anthony had left in the hall and set it in a pile to one side before turning her attention back onto him. Then she did the most incredibly foolish thing.

She walked up to him, put a hand on his chest and whispered, "Hush."

Didn't she know she should never approach a Vampyre when he was in such a frenzied state?

He didn't want to hush. He wanted to tear and rend, and drink the blood of Melly's would-be attacker until he felt the man's body crumble to dust in his hands. He bared his fangs and hissed at her.

She just looked at him. "Now you're being pissy." Her voice was gentle as she said it. She patted his chest and raised her hand to his face. Because it was her, he fought to control his impulse to strike at her. As she cupped his cheek, her palm and fingers were warm. "Julian, I really need you to calm down. I'm starving and exhausted, and there are over a hundred ferals that are going to be back at the tunnel gate at any minute, let alone Justine who might show up earlier than she had planned if she decides to go looking for her missing attendant."

Her words began to penetrate the killing instincts that had flooded him. He ran his gaze over her. She did look exhausted. Dark circles shadowed her eyes, and her face was drawn with marks of stress.

He also noted that the other Vampyre hadn't been gentle when he had grabbed her. The slender, elegant line of her throat was already turning dark with bruises and swelling. The cut at the side of her neck had broken open again and was bleeding lightly.

The sight brought him back into himself.

"I hear you," he growled. Taking a strong mental grip on his self-control, he forced his fangs to withdraw. "I got it."

She searched his gaze, then gave him a small smile and a nod.

When she pulled her hand away, he missed her touch and grew angry at himself for it. Digging into her pocket, she pulled out two misshapen metal springs and knelt at his feet.

As she got to work again on the manacles at his ankles, he said, "That's what you were doing earlier. You were making another set of lock picks."

"Yep." She sounded as tired as she looked. "I told you I wasn't going to leave you. No matter what you might think of me, or what anybody else might have said, I always keep my promises."

He didn't know what to do with that, so instead of responding, he fell silent and watched her.

This time after a few minutes of trial and error, there was a *snick* and the lock fell open. She sat back on her heels and beamed up at him.

Triumph surged, along with a fierce sense of pride in her. He said in a soft voice, "Will you look at that. You're going to fucking break us out of jail after all. You are full of wow, lady."

"I don't know about that. I gave my bag of tricks a good shake a few minutes ago, and it's pretty much empty." She shifted and bent over the other manacle.

"That's all right," he told her. "If you can get me free, I can take care of the rest."

"That's my plan, soldier."

After a few moments, the second lock fell open with a *snick*. She put a hand at the small of her back as she straightened to look at the manacles overhead. "I know you said I would have to climb up your body, but I'm still not sure how I'm going to do that."

She sounded hoarse and listless, and he really didn't like how she looked. "First, check out what's in the bag," he told her. "It'll be a while before Justine starts to miss Anthony, and it won't take you more than a minute to take a few bites of food and a drink."

After a brief hesitation, she didn't waste time arguing. He watched in approval as she dug in the bag, pulled out a paper-wrapped sandwich and bolted a few bites. After she sucked down half a bottle of water, she held it to his lips so he could drink the rest.

While he needed a strong infusion of blood more than a drink of water, the hydration did help him to feel better too. When he had rinsed out his mouth and drank the rest of the bottle, she threw the empty container into the bag, squared her shoulders and turned back to him.

"Now, climb up on my leg and stand," he said. Bending one knee, he braced his foot on the inside of his other thigh and held steady for her to perch on him.

She squinted at his posture. "You can take my whole weight like that?"

"Yes. Use me to steady yourself."

"The strength you undead lot have is something else." Slipping off her delicate-looking flats, she stepped barefoot onto his thigh and held on to one of his arms as she straightened. Even though she clutched him in a tight grip, she still wobbled on her perch. "This isn't going to work. I need both hands to pick the locks."

"Don't just hold on to my arm," he said. "Use my torso as your support. Brace one foot at the top of my thigh and lean against me."

After a quick glance down at his expression, she gingerly eased against the length of his body. Their positions were odd and strained, yet the full curves of her body felt so incredibly delicious, he couldn't resist closing his eyes and turning his face into her warm, narrow abdomen.

She sucked in a breath and wobbled again, clutching at his shoulder to steady herself.

The whole maneuver had turned unexpectedly torturous.

She felt so good, smelled so fucking good. Her top had ridden up, baring her skin to his cheek. He wanted to lick her and bite—not to draw blood, but lightly, in sex play—and he tightened his jaw against the impulse. If he did nip at her, more likely than not, she would lose her balance entirely and fall off her perch, and until he was free, they were in no position to play games.

Clamping down on his self-control, he gritted, "Can you reach the manacles?"

"Yes, but they're too high and they aren't at the right angle." Her voice shook.

She was showing all the signs of being near the end of her rope, and it brought his attention into focus like nothing else could have.

"You're doing an amazing job," he said gently against her soft skin. "I knew they were underestimating you, but not even I could see how much you could accomplish on your own. I want you to hold on tight to me now."

"O-okay." She wrapped an arm around one of his biceps and gripped him by the shoulder again. "Like this?"

"Yes." As soon as he felt her weight stabilize, he flexed up as high as he could, gripped the chains and shook his hands so that the manacles slid down his wrists. There wasn't much give. After only a few inches, they were stopped by the thickness of his muscled forearms. His voice muffled against her, he asked, "Is that enough?"

"It might be. At least now I can turn the lock toward me." She twisted at the manacle, and he turned his wrist to help. "That's it—hold still!"

Obediently, he froze while she worked.

The lock snicked open just as she slipped and started to fall. "Oh shit!"

Shaking his wrist free, he snaked his arm around her and clenched her to him. "It's all right, sweetheart." He hefted her up a few more inches, and gods, even just that small freedom, just the ability to put that one arm around her, felt like bliss. "Only one more to go. Now you don't even need to balance."

"Piece of cake, right?" she said breathlessly. "Mmn, what I wouldn't give for a piece of cake right now."

It surprised a chuckle out of him. Never mind all the gourmet foods she had generous access to—she always had been a fiend for chocolate cake made from a box mix, with sour cream frosting.

"When we get out of here, I'll bake a cake for you, myself," he promised. "One with a file in it."

Her flat stomach flexed as she snorted. "Now, that I would have to see, although I don't know about eating any of it. You don't know the first thing about how to bake a cake, or for that matter, how to bake anything else."

"Don't be too sure," he murmured. "Baking is just chemistry, and the directions are printed on the box, right? Besides, I watched you do it a couple of times."

"Sure you did," she retorted. "You watched me all of twenty years ago, and you never had a vested interest in the process."

She was wrong. He'd had a vested interest in everything she did. What she wore, the way she moved, the things she loved. The times they had spent in the kitchen, as she fixed herself something to eat and he opened a bottle of wine for them to share, were some of his favorite memories of when they had been together.

He hadn't let himself think of those times in years, but he did so now, immersing himself in the memories. The way she had thrown back her head to laugh. The time she had teased him into dancing while her pasta water boiled away, forgotten, and the pan had burned.

After they had put out the small kitchen fire, he had growled, "To hell with it."

With one sweep of his arm, he had cleared the kitchen table and lifted her onto it. Laughing, she had lain back, her arms over her head, while he knelt between her legs to feast on her gorgeous, delicate flesh. When he had risen at last to sink his aching erection into her, she had clasped him tight in whole-hearted welcome, with her arms and legs, body and soul.

As he thought of how she had hugged him, his eyes grew damp.

The last manacle fell from his wrist.

"There," she whispered, her breath catching on another sob. "Oh thank God, there."

⟹ EIGHT ⟸

Finally free, he wrapped both arms around her and sank to his knees, only loosening his hold just enough so that she could slide onto his lap. Then he clenched her against his chest again. Her arms slid around his neck, and she held him just as tightly.

"I've got you, Melisande," he whispered.

Her quick, ragged breathing sounded in his ear. "I've been so, so scared."

"I know. I've been scared too." Without fully being aware of what he did, he sank one fist into the back of her curly, tangled hair and pulled her head back so that he could look deep into her eyes. He whispered, "Jesus, he was going to rape you, and I couldn't have done anything to prevent it."

"Don't think like that," she said, as she framed his face between her hands. "It didn't happen. I didn't let it happen. But oh God, Julian, when she was cutting you, I went half out of my mind. I thought it would never end—and when she let the ferals into your cell, I was so afraid they were going to kill you."

"Stop it." His voice turned harsh. "It was nothing, and it's over with now. It's all done."

She opened her eyes very wide. "*I. Can't. Stop. This.* And I'm not even going to try. I've been promising myself this meltdown for two damn hellish *hellish* HELLISH days, and nothing's going to keep me from it now."

He stared at her in utter perplexity. She looked terrible. She looked adorable.

She looked stripped down, totally raw, like she didn't have a single barrier left between her and the world, and he couldn't take it any longer.

He covered her shaking mouth with his, and when he felt the soft curve of her lips move in response to his, it felt *so damn good*, just as he had remembered it, just as he had always known it would.

No, it didn't feel just as he remembered—it felt better. It felt like a vital, necessary part of his life had come back to him. Ravenously he parted her lips with his tongue and conquered the private recesses of her luscious mouth.

And she kissed him back.

Her active, eager involvement, the sensation of her tongue colliding with his, set fire to all of his nerve endings. After having been so parched for so many years, he drowned himself in her.

She gripped him at the back of his head with both hands while she wrapped those long, slender legs around his waist, and in response, he growled low in his throat while his cock swelled to stiff attention, pushing at the restraints of his jeans.

He needed to lay her down on the floor, spread her legs and feast on her tender, private flesh again. He needed to hear her breath catch and sigh, while she stroked her fingers through his short hair. He needed to bury himself so deeply inside of her, he never truly came back out. He . . .

As he framed her face with both hands, he felt something wet slide over his calloused fingers. The sensation jolted his eyes open. She was leaking tears, and the muscles in her arms and legs trembled.

It brought him back to his senses. While he might be a bastard, and his soul might be incomplete, he wasn't completely heartless. He wrapped his arms around her again until he was simply hugging her, and rocked her in a gentle, soothing movement.

"It's all right now," he repeated. "Melly, I promise you, everything is going to be all right."

"I can believe you now." Pulling back slightly, she wiped at her eyes with the back of her hands.

After having gone so long without holding her, he was reluctant to let her go even that much, but fresh sounds came from the direction of the gate as the ferals began to return, reminding him of the challenges they had yet to face.

"You need to eat the rest of that sandwich," he told her. "And I need to clear out the feral infestation so we can get the fuck out of here."

Her expression calmed into resolve as she listened to him, and she nodded. "Before you do, you need to take more blood."

Immediately, he said, "Absolutely not. You're in no condition for me to take any more from you."

"That's not true." When he started to argue, she put her hand over his mouth. "Listen to me. You have to. You were hurt so badly, you weren't healing, and yet still, you barely took enough blood to close up your wounds. Not only are there too many ferals, but we really don't know when Justine is going to come back, and she's every bit as old as you are. You might be the Nightkind King with all the Power you've gained from taking blood oaths, but she hasn't been injured like you have." She searched his gaze. "It's not like you can safely feed from the other Vampyres, is it?"

Closing his fingers over her slender wrist, he removed her hand. "No. They're feral because they've had too much drug-contaminated blood. I can't risk it."

She shrugged. "There you go. You need to do it for both our sakes, because I'm counting on you to help me get out of here."

His mouth tightened, but her logic was inescapable, so

after a moment, he nodded. "Fine, I'll take more blood—but only a little, and only after you've eaten."

"Okay." Not meeting his gaze any longer, she pulled off his lap to explore the contents of the grocery bag.

Only then did he remember that he was supposed to hate her. It was a little late in the day to be recalling something as essential as that. Rolling to his feet, he rubbed his face and regarded her thoughtfully.

He thought about saying something dismissive about the kiss, but he couldn't help but note how studiously she avoided meeting his eyes.

All right, then. Message received. It looked like they were going to pretend it never happened.

Confused, he scowled at her. He didn't know if he felt relieved or not. The aggressive, predatory part of him wanted to push for any advantage he could get, but his hands were still damp from her tears.

He clenched them into fists. Then he went to complete the job she'd started on demolishing the frame of her cot.

Within a few moments, he had snapped off two of the remaining three legs to use as stakes. He paused to look around. Aside from the cot and the blanket, there was virtually nothing else in the bleak cell. She really had pulled off a couple of miracles, with very little to work with.

There was a fresh scar on the rock at the back wall, and he strode over to investigate the spot. It was where the bullet from Anthony's gun had struck. Julian rubbed the area with the ball of his thumb. She was so damn lucky the asshole had chosen to give her a warning and not shoot her outright, and doubly lucky that she hadn't been hit by the ricochet.

Turning away, he picked up the blanket and the thin mattress. After tearing a strip of cloth from the edge of the blanket, he rolled the bedding into a tight bundle and tied it with the strip.

Now it was Melly's turn to ask him, "What are you doing?"

He glanced at her. "We have no idea how big this tunnel

system is, or how complicated it might be. We also have no idea where we are in it, so we don't know how long it's going to take for us to find our way out. If we need to take a break and rest, it'll be a lot more comfortable to do it on a mat than on bare stone."

Her shoulders sagged. "I hadn't thought of that. When I first broke out of my cell, the tunnel system seemed pretty big."

"I'm not surprised." He walked back into the cell where he'd been chained. "If this is anything like the other tunnel system, some of it is natural, but Justine's definitely added to it over the years. This area and these cells are man-made."

"I hate her so much." She popped the last of the sandwich in her mouth and peeled a banana. "I'm not used to hating somebody that passionately. I hope I get to see her turn to dust."

The drawn, tight look to her features had eased, and a healthy flush of color banished the paleness from her golden skin. Squatting beside her, he opened the bag to look inside. There were more bottles of water, chocolate bars, a bag of granola mix, some single-portion packages of cheese, a couple more sandwiches wrapped in the distinctive paper of a well-known deli in San Francisco, another banana and a few apples.

"Look at that," he said. "He really brought you good food."

She said bitterly, "I guess this was supposed to be my reward for doing whatever he wanted."

Julian met her gaze. Letting go of the bag, he stroked her hair off her face and pressed his lips to her forehead.

"I have such extreme, conflicting urges," he murmured. "I still need to tear him limb from limb, but at the same, I also wish you could have gotten the chance to stake him twice. Because damn, Melly, now that I know you're all right and my heart isn't going to explode out of my chest, I can tell you, it was a mighty fine thing to witness what you did."

Leaning against him, she sniffed. "I done good, didn't I?"

"Yes, you did." He laid his cheek on top of her head, and

they rested together like that for a few minutes, without words of anger or pain spoiling the air between them.

There was, however, plenty of sexual tension. He would have to be truly dead not to notice the way her soft, plump breast felt as it pressed against his bare chest, or the way her fingers curled around his bicep as he stroked her hair.

But it was a tension he held under strong control. Not that long ago, she had been in tears, and he still had a pack of ferals to kill.

That left room for her words to come back to him.

I told you I wasn't going to leave you.

No matter what you might think of me, or what anybody else might have said, I always keep my promises.

She had made promises to him before. Not forever promises or formal vows—they hadn't gotten that far in their relationship—but still, she had said things that he had internalized and relied upon. And he had believed her when she had said them.

If keeping her promises meant so much to her, why hadn't she kept those promises she had made to him then?

It felt excruciating to have Julian hold her, to kiss her on the forehead, to stroke her hair. Melly felt as if she were the one who was being staked, as a heavy nail of pain drove into her heart. Worse, she welcomed the pain, just so that she could feel his arms around her again.

Any moment now, she was going to get a spine and reject his overtures, but not just yet, not when he held her with such evident, overabundance of care, as if she were a person who had incalculable value to him.

Then she did something dumb. She closed her eyes and pretended the last twenty years had never happened, and that all of the emotions she felt for Julian were strong, bright, shining and true.

But she couldn't maintain the pretense, because the twenty years had happened. She had become a different person. She was older, more cynical and guarded, and this powerful man who held her so gently, and treated her so kindly, was still the same bastard he had always been. A leopard did not change his spots. A battle-worn lion did not lose his scars.

Oh, soldier, how did we come to such a place?

With a shock, she realized she had murmured that aloud, as he whispered into her hair, "Damned if I know."

Well there, she had a spine after all, because suddenly it decided to start working again. She stiffened and pulled out of his arms. "You need to feed," she said abruptly. "Then while you go kill things, I'm going to eat a candy bar. After that, we're going to waltz out of here. Got it?"

He had lines on either side of his mouth that deepened as he almost smiled. "Got it."

She held out her wrist. He took her hand in his and held it, as he speared her with a hard, intent gaze.

"We need to get one thing straight, you and I," he said, his voice soft and ruthless. "And we're going to do it before I bite you, so we don't have the bloodlust interfering with either of our thinking. I have every intention of taking you again. And taking you. I'm going to make you want it so bad, when I finally sink my cock in you, you'll cry from the relief."

She felt her eyes widen from shock. Once again, he knocked her breathless. Senseless. Her mouth worked, as her brain tried to sputter out something pithy enough with which to lambast him.

She had to lambast him. She had to drown out the teeny, tiny part of her that had clapped its hands and squeaked *finally, yay!*

After a Herculean effort, she managed to whisper, "You're delusional if you think I would ever let you take me again, after the way you've treated me. You see this?" With her free hand, she waved her fingers in the air down the length of her torso as she shook her head. "I've said it before, and I'll say it again. You're neeevvver getting this goodness again."

At that he gave her a real smile, a slow one, full bore,

that creased his rough face. The impact hit her hard, in all her most vulnerable places. In desperation, she thought, how am I ever going to stand strong against him?

As his fangs descended and his eyes flashed red, he told her, "We'll see about that, princess. We'll see."

With that, he bit her wrist, not brutally, but with an elegant, lethal efficiency. Before the pleasure hit, she had room to wonder, *And I thought Anthony was remarkably stupid. How much more stupid is Justine, to make such an enemy out of this man?*

Then the sweetest, most delicious euphoria stole into her veins. She didn't welcome it. She was still angry. With her free hand, she slid her fingers through his short salt-and-pepper hair at the back of his head.

She whispered, "And you dare to accuse me of cheating. How many people have you seduced just like this?"

Anger flashed in his reddened eyes. He glared at her even as his mouth pulled on her with such knowledgeable care. Gods, she wanted to smack him.

Or kiss him.

No, definitely smack him . . .

As she tore off his jeans, straddled his prone body and took *him*.

After only a few sips, he eased his fangs out of her flesh and held still, his mouth resting in the place where he had bitten her. Even with the hostility that now radiated from him, he still took care this time to make sure the tiny wounds had stopped bleeding before he left her. She realized her hands were shaking and clenched them into fists to make them stop.

Then he lifted his head and snapped, "You did cheat."

She snapped back, "Like I said, you're delusional. I never cheated on you. I loved you with all of my heart, and you took that and trampled it into the ground. Even after the three months we spent together, you couldn't even give me the benefit of the doubt."

At that, strangely, all his hostility seemed to vanish. He

looked deathly tired, more tired than any other man she had ever seen. "Didn't you stop to think that I might have loved you with all of my heart once, too?"

With a single sentence, he wrenched her heart out of her body. She cried out, "Then why couldn't you have had a little faith in me?"

"I had faith in a lot of things once," he said. "Including you. Then reality came along and trampled that into the ground as well."

As she stared, his expression went blank, truly blank, as if he had become too empty to show even tiredness. He bent to scoop up his stakes.

More disturbed than she had been in a long time, she said, "Where are you going?"

"I'm going to kill things." He spoke without emotion, like an automaton. "It's the one thing I still remain good at."

He snatched Anthony's keys up as well, and strode out of the cell. Moments later, the snarling began. She covered her ears and buried her face against her raised knees, while inside, she remained frozen in a place of stricken realization.

TELL ME WHAT THE FUCK YOU WANT ME TO DO, AND I'LL DO IT! he had said.

You're going to be okay, he had told her. *You*, not *we*.

He had come down here in the tunnels, fully expecting to die. Calmly waiting for it. Possibly a part of him had been hoping for it?

He's broken, she thought. Something, or a combination of things, has broken him. In spite of everything he had done to her, she had room to feel a horrified sense of compassion.

He had also gone into the darkness to fight over a hundred ferals for her, just as he had given himself up to Justine, without complaint or hesitation.

She was so tired. This wasn't supposed to be her fight.

But she couldn't take it.

Leaping to her feet, she snatched up Anthony's big flashlight, her stake and the gun. She checked the gun over quickly. It was a large .357 revolver, with seven bullets left.

She should save two bullets in case Justine showed up. Unless she got incredibly lucky with a shot, those bullets wouldn't kill Justine, but they might help to slow her down if it came to a fight.

That meant Melly still had five. Five shots to the head or heart would mean there would be five less ferals that Julian would have to fight.

A glint of metal caught her eye. It was Anthony's whistle. After a second's hesitation, she snatched it up too.

Her heart rate revved up in preparation for battle. She strode out of the cell.

The scene at the gate was something out of a nightmare, dark and claustrophobia-inducing. Ferals upon ferals clawed over each other to get at Julian, who whirled, lunged and kicked so fast, she could barely track his movements.

Steadily and inexorably, he was taking them out, two by two. He was an unstoppable juggernaut, but there were too many of them for him to stake without taking some damage himself. They slashed and tore at him with fangs and talons, and blood flew everywhere.

It sickened and enraged her all over again.

She told him telepathically, *I'm right behind you.*

She caught a brief, piercing flash of his reddened gaze. He snapped, *Go back to the cell and lock the door!*

I can't do that. You're going to have to make sure they don't get through the gate. She set the flashlight on the floor and directed the beam toward the open gate where Julian fought. *What if we tried blowing Anthony's whistle? It might back them off.*

There are too many, he said. *They're not just trained to back away. They're trained to expect food, and we don't have any to give them. We can't risk confronting them outside the only shelter we've got—we've got to get rid of them.*

Sometimes she hated that he was right.

She told him, *Watch yourself. I'm firing to the right of you.*

Some of the ferals turned their attention away from Julian

and fixed on her. Taking careful aim at one, she pulled the trigger.

The revolver was a lot bigger than the trim semiautomatic pistols she used in target practice. Not only did it have quite a kick, but the report in the enclosed space was deafening.

The forehead of the feral she had shot exploded. More blood spurted everywhere, until the feral's body collapsed into dust. The noise made her ears hurt, but damn, making a feral disappear felt good.

Carefully, she took aim again. She couldn't afford to waste a single bullet. Refusing to let the emotional impact of the battle push her into shooting too quickly, she didn't pull the trigger until she felt confident of her shot.

Another feral vanished into dust.

Then a third. And a fourth.

After the fifth one vanished, she almost kept shooting. It was so difficult not to pull the trigger again when she saw how hard Julian was laboring. His broad, muscular chest and heavy, powerful arms were torn again with wounds. He was caught in the toughest kind of marathon, one that wouldn't come to an end until every one of his enemies was dead.

How many times throughout the years had he been forced to fight alone, without anyone to stand by him or guard his back? For so much of his long life, he had been a commodity to somebody—to his owner in the arena, to his emperor, and then for so many centuries to his sire, Carling. Even now, he was a commodity to the Nightkind council, useful and yet never fully trusted, no matter how much he did for the demesne.

Sometimes he would have had people at his back. Yolanthe was unswervingly loyal. So was Xavier, and Julian had once commanded entire armies.

But all too many times, he would have had nobody. Certainly there wouldn't have been anybody in that ancient Roman arena, not for the young, half-starved alley cat Julian had once been.

Fighting back tears, she tucked the gun into her waistband.

She might not be able to do anything for that long-ago young man, but she could by gods do something for him now.

When she had a good, strong grip on her stake, she strode forward.

⇒ NINE ⇐

The pack of ferals had thinned markedly. Now there were only thirty or so, but those would be the hardest thirty to kill. They were probably the strongest and the smartest of the pack, while she and Julian were at their most tired.

Standing to one side of the open gate, just out of reach, Melly watched them closely until one strained too far between the bars in an effort to grab her. She snatched its arm, hauled it hard against the bars and lunged forward to stake it.

At the same moment, one of the others darted forward to snatch at her. Fire exploded along her shoulder and upper arm, as it raked her with its talons. Shit, shit, shit. Clutching her shoulder, she stumbled back.

Goddammit, Melly—go back to the cell! Julian roared in her head. At the same moment, he lunged at the feral who had attacked her and tore its head from its shoulders. It vanished in a spray of dust.

Quickly, she inspected her new wounds. While they were painful, the deeper muscle underneath appeared to be undamaged. Experimentally, she flexed her arm. Ow, ow. It hurt like hell, but she could use it if she forced herself.

Don't be a wimp, Melly. Suck it up.

The good news was, the scent of her fresh blood had attracted more ferals away from Julian.

(That was good news? Man, their lives needed to get better fast.)

She told Julian, *I wonder when it's going to occur to you that I'm never going to take any of your orders.*

Turning his head briefly, his gaze fixed on her new injuries. He hissed at her before lunging into another whirlwind flurry of fighting.

The sight of him took her aback. Gods, he could be a scary-looking son of a bitch sometimes. Easily the most muscular and powerfully built of all the combatants, he looked every bit as feral as the Vampyres he fought. She was only glad he was on her side.

You're already hurt again, he snapped.

So are you, she pointed out, exasperated.

One of the ferals was trying to inch behind Julian, its red gaze fixed on her. Ew, it was salivating.

With a massive kick, Julian launched its body into the air. It slammed into a wall and hit the ground, rolled over and started to stalk her again.

Adrenaline tried to dump into her bloodstream, and her body sneered at the effort. Finally, she had to face facts—she was cooked. It took serious concentration for her to remain on her feet, and she didn't have the physical strength left to drive her stake into another Vampyre's heart.

Oh, hell. Pulling out the gun, she shot the feral between the eyes, and it collapsed into dust.

I wondered what you were saving those two bullets for, Julian said.

I was trying to hold them in reserve in case Justine returned before we got out.

He told her, *Better to use them now when we know we need them.*

There was a pause in the battle. Five ferals remained, along with Julian and Melly. Everybody was injured. They all took stock of each other.

Damn it, Melly said. She took the last shot, and another feral vanished in a sprinkle of dust.

The remaining four ferals were the smartest ones of all. They edged back down one of the tunnels, red gazes fixed on Julian's menacing figure.

"Oh, no you don't," he growled. He started after them.

Alarm pulsed. "Julian, no. Let them go."

"I'll be damned if I'll creep through these tunnels wondering when they might come at our backs." He tossed the keys at her. "Lock the gate."

Her hands were too unsteady to catch them, and they fell at her feet.

He ran after the ferals and disappeared into the darkness.

This time, she didn't have any choice but to obey him. She didn't have the energy to run after them. Nor did she feel capable of guarding the open gate by herself if more ferals appeared.

More ferals?

The thought caused her to sag where she stood. After fumbling with the keys, she found the right one and locked the gate. Then she slid into a heap against the wall while she waited for him to return.

In the normal course of events, she didn't have a single doubt that he could take all four of the ferals without breaking into a sweat. But he had been fighting for a long time. He was injured again, and before that he had been tortured and drained almost to death.

Closing her eyes, she huddled into herself and whispered, "He has to be okay. That's all there is to it."

The way he had kissed her earlier. She touched her lips with unsteady fingers, reliving the moment.

The world was full of beautiful, strong, wise women, but he had held her and kissed her like she was the only woman in the world. The only one. And she had kissed him back in just the same way, because for the last twenty years, he had been the only man.

Not for the first time, she thought to herself, I have to get over him and move on.

The thought didn't carry any weight. It never had.

Let's face it. I'm as much in love with him as I've ever been, maybe even more so, because after so many years, I sure don't look at him through rosy-tinted glasses anymore. I see every single one of his flaws all too well, and I love him anyway.

Now what am I going to do?

"Melly."

The sound of his voice, roughened and gravelly as it was, ran over her like a physical caress. Shivering, she opened her eyes and looked at him.

He stood with a hand holding one of the bars of the gate. In his other hand, he gripped his two stakes. His jeans were filthy, and so was the wide expanse of the bare skin on his chest. Only some of his wounds had healed, she noticed. Precious blood trickled from others. He was dangerously depleted again.

There was worry in his wolflike gaze as he watched her. He said, "Toss me the keys."

She made an immense effort and flung them at the gate. They skittered across the floor until he stopped them with the toe of one boot.

As he unlocked the gate, she asked, "Did you get them?"

"I got one. The others got away. Maybe I could have gotten them too, if I'd kept going after them, but I didn't want to get too far away from you." He knelt beside her. "I need to look at your shoulder."

"I'm not hurt as badly as you are. I'll live," she said, although she let him ease the edges of her top away from her skin. "I was sitting here thinking. You know, I was always the good twin. Bailey was the one who took risks and broke the rules. Now she's off having adventures in Jamaica."

"Not at the moment, she isn't. She's in LA, helping your mom look for you." He wore a fierce frown as he inspected her wounds.

With a wave of her hand, she dismissed his words. "Okay, but you know what I mean. Normally, she's the one who goes off to have adventures. Me, I always followed the rules. Bailey was the spare, but I was the heir. I had to look after things and be responsible. I'm even in the family business. Mom always wanted me to work in admin on the other side of the camera, but she never complained too much. At least my job has been fun."

"Come here." Easing one arm around her waist, he lifted her to her feet.

She tried to pull away from him, but he wouldn't let her. "You're hurt too. I don't want to lean on you."

"Tough," he told her. "I can take it."

Keeping his arm tight around her, he held her steady as they walked back to his cell and their meager supplies. Then he urged her to sit again.

"You think it's okay to take the time?" she asked.

"Yes," he said. "Our lives have changed for the better. Anthony's dead, I'm free to act, and most of the ferals are gone. Everything we do down here is a calculated risk, but we need to regroup before we set out."

"I can't argue with that," she muttered.

"Besides, Justine doesn't know most of her ferals have been staked," he told her. "If she comes, we'll hear her whistle long before she gets here, and we'll have time to get ready for her."

While he talked, he unbuttoned her top and pulled it open.

They both looked down at her lacy bra, which showcased the full curve and shape of her breasts. She was a C-cup, and she liked pretty underwear.

Now half the bra was streaked with blood. The Vampyre's talons had missed her bra strap, so structurally it was still functional, but the creamy, delicate material was ruined.

With the tip of one forefinger, he gently traced the skin at the top edge of the bra. "A pity," he said. "It was pretty."

"I have other pretty bras," she said with a small shrug.

He rose to his feet to get the grocery bag. Then he looked around the cell until he located pieces of the T-shirt Justine had torn off him. He picked through the bits of cloth until he finally decided on one. Opening one of the bottles of water, he soaked the rag and carefully sponged her wounds. "This isn't very clean, I'm afraid. The only other cloth we have is the blanket, and the wool would be too rough on your torn skin."

"Infection is pretty low on my list of concerns right now," she told him.

"It isn't low on my list. The ferals have filthy talons. Their bites are filthy too." She hissed as her wounds stung, and the skin around his eyes crinkled into a wince. "I'm sorry."

"It's all right." Grimacing, she turned her face away.

"Were you going somewhere?" he asked quietly.

"What do you mean?" She hissed again as he cleaned out the longest, deepest cut.

"With your story."

He was trying to distract her from what he was doing. Deciding to cooperate, she took hold of his thick wrist until his gaze lifted to hers.

"All my life, I was the good girl, the responsible one. You were my walk on the wild side, and I truly loved it. I loved you. I had so much damn fun with you. You were all I could think about, even when I had to go on site to Singapore to finish shooting that awful movie. Remember that?"

Reluctantly, one corner of his mouth pulled up. The half smile creased his lean cheek. "The movie wasn't that bad. Didn't it win an Academy Award for special effects?"

"It was *terrible*," she said with emphasis. "It took forever to film. I couldn't sleep without you, and the director was always mad at me because I kept forgetting my lines. If I could have gotten out of my contract, I would have, and to hell with my professional reputation. I hated every minute of it."

He finished washing her wounds, eased the edges of her top together and carefully buttoned it up again. "Where are you going with this?"

She took another fragment of his T-shirt and a fresh bottle of water and began to work on him, washing the dirt and the blood from his chest and shoulders and cleaning out the wounds that hadn't healed.

She gave him a crooked smile. "I was consumed with you.

The mere thought of going on a date with someone else was irritating and distasteful to me. Yes, I was asked out a couple of times, but I didn't have the time, not physically and not emotionally, and I certainly didn't have the interest. I don't know where you got your information from, Julian, but I didn't cheat on you. Not even with a kiss. Not from the moment you walked up to me at my mom's house, the night of the Masque."

He bowed his head, and while he didn't say anything, for once he wasn't rejecting her outright or snapping at her, but he was actually listening intently to everything she said.

She told him softly, "I just wanted to tell you all of that, and this time, I didn't want to make it about me or how you hurt my feelings. I wanted to make it about you. You deserve to know that I thought you were worth it. I can only imagine how I would have felt if someone had convinced me that you had cheated on me, and I'm sorry you had to go through that. That's all."

He took her hand with the washcloth and held it, as he studied it. Silence pounded in her ears with the rhythm of her own heartbeat. Then, with a gentle squeeze on her fingers, he eased her hand into her lap and turned away.

Okay, then. She hadn't really expected anything else.

It had taken twenty years and serious exhaustion and blood loss, but at least now she felt like she had said what she needed to say to him without shouting or fighting. Over the last several hours, the message had grown into something more generous and honest than she would have believed possible.

Maybe that could be cathartic for both of them.

Blinking tears out of her eyes, she tossed the used rag away. Maybe now she really could let go of her bitterness, figure out a way to get over him and move on.

Of course, that was provided they managed to survive getting out of here.

How much weight, Julian wondered, should you give to an old lie?

People lied all the time, and they did it for so many reasons. Self-protection, self-gain. Often it was with the best of intentions, to avoid hurting someone else's feelings. Hell, he lied without compunction whenever he needed to, or he spun the truth in such a way that it suited him, like he had done in the press conference about the multiple homicide on Justine's estate.

But this wasn't just any lie—it was a lie that had stabbed him to the core and had had a pivotal effect on his life.

And he simply didn't know anymore how much weight he should give to it. He felt adrift, confused again. He was tired of carrying his anger around. It felt heavy, cold and poisonous.

In the meantime, Melly was here in front of him, warm and vibrant, funny, sexy and as infuriating as ever, and man, could she ever sell something. Every word she had spoken felt like the God's honest truth.

In spite of knowing how well she could act, he still couldn't bring himself to believe that everything she had said was a lie. Clearly, her message mattered too much to her. It showed in the fragility of her expression, the dampness in her gaze—hell, even in the tenderness with which she had washed him.

Yet she still seemed incapable of admitting that she had cheated. Was it because she couldn't face confronting him with the truth, or because she couldn't face the mistake she had made?

Whatever the reason, his thinking had shifted. It wasn't that she wouldn't admit to the truth. It was that she couldn't look him in face and tell him.

After twenty years, you would think they could both let it go.

Maybe that's what he needed to do . . . just let it go.

Rubbing his face, he looked at the food. He said, "You never ate your candy bar."

"I couldn't stomach the thought," she said. "Not when you were down at the gate, fighting. I couldn't . . ." Her mouth worked. "I couldn't leave you to face them alone."

So, tired and depleted as she was, she had come down to fight with him, and had gotten herself injured because of it. Before they had gotten trapped together here in the tunnels, he would have said she wasn't capable of that kind of loyalty.

And he would have been dead wrong.

He had been fine with fighting the ferals on his own. After all, it was his responsibility as Nightkind King to clean them out. He hadn't been fine with watching her stumble back from the gate, soaked in her own blood.

Snatching up a bar of chocolate, he shoved it into her hands. "Eat it now," he told her. "As soon as you're steady on your feet, we're going."

She tore the wrapper open, snapped off a square and popped it in her mouth. "Speaking of getting steady on your feet," she said around the piece. "When we were together before, I gave enough blood to know just how little you've taken from me now. You've barely taken a thimbleful."

"I've taken more than that."

"What," she retorted, "*two* thimbles full?"

He thought he saw where she was going and started to shake his head. "No, Melly."

"Julian, you have to take more. Look at me."

Her voice was so firm that, reluctantly, he turned to glare at her.

For some reason, that caused her features to soften, and she gave him a remarkably sweet smile. There was so much simple affection in her expression, he lost his ability to keep up the strength in his glare.

She told him, "I've collected quite an array of scratches and bruises. They're colorful, but we both know I'm not badly hurt. Plus, now I have plenty of calories and hydration, which I didn't have before. The only thing I'm really lacking is proper rest. Since I'm healthy as a horse, none of that should prevent you from taking more of my blood, whereas you haven't healed again. You're dangerously depleted, and we're not out of the tunnels yet." She paused to search his gaze. "Come on, just a little, one more time."

It went against every instinct he had to take more blood from her when she was looking so vulnerable. He hated that she was right.

"All right," he said. "One more time."

She ate the last of the candy bar and downed half a bottle of water. Afterward, she turned to him and held out her wrist.

This time, when he took her hand, he didn't lift it to his mouth. Obeying a dark impulse, he pulled her toward him until he could put his arms around her. Her smiling expression turned serious and a little wary, but she came to rest against him readily enough.

He knew he shouldn't take from her this way. The base of the neck was an intensely sexual way to take blood, but he also knew he was going to do it anyway. Slowly, closing his eyes, he bowed his head to rest his mouth against the warm, soft skin in the hollow where her slender neck met her shoulder.

His body had a memory of this experience. How many times had they shared intimacy in just such a way? Without his conscious volition, his tight muscles relaxed, and he drew in a deep breath just so that he could inhale her scent. When her arms stole around him gently, the embrace felt like a rare, precious gift. She leaned her cheek against the side of his head.

He asked telepathically, *Okay?*

Yes, she whispered.

He brought his fangs down to her tender flesh and eased into the bite. The quiet hiss of her indrawn breath sounded in his ear, and he held himself rigid, waiting for her to relax. When she did, her body melted against his, and the warm, liquid evidence of her pleasure flooded his mouth.

He took sustenance from her with the greatest of care, cradling the back of her head in the palm of one hand. The pain from his wounds faded so effortlessly when he allowed himself to rely on her. Stirring, she muttered something, what, he didn't quite catch, but the soft, breathy sound was almost unbearably sexy and went straight to his cock.

Mindful of her shoulder wound, he eased her closer, until the graceful curve of her pelvis rubbed against his stiff, aching erection.

Stroking his short hair, she whispered, "Feeling better?"

He ran the fingers of one hand down her arched spine as he murmured, "Mmhm." Telepathically, he told her, *Thank you.*

I'm glad I could help, she told him.

Inside, he hovered at a crossroads. On the one side, sanity and caution, along with the ghost of the old, cold anger and pain, urged him to withdraw and erect all his barriers again.

On the other side lay the memory of warmth and laughter, and dancing in the kitchen to the rich smell of chocolate cake baking, and Melly saying to him with such transparent, inescapable sincerity, *I had so much damn fun with you.*

How much weight do you give all of that? How did that compare to the weight of one old, tired lie and a betrayal that was two decades in the past?

How much lighter would he feel if he—the meanest, most unforgiving bastard he knew—chose to forgive her and let it all go? How much warmer?

He had taken enough blood. Easing out of the bite, he rested his mouth against her skin, and in that moment, he truly didn't know which direction he might choose.

Then she made a sound. It was barely audible even to his sharp hearing, little more than a husky catch at the back of her throat.

That was when he realized he wasn't standing at a crossroads, but at a precipice, and with that tiny sigh of disappointment, she pushed him over the edge.

⇒ TEN ⇐

He went up in flames and everything inside of him spiraled out of control. His decades-long hunger and his need for her. Lifting his head, he drove his mouth down onto hers and slanted his lips. He felt the shock of it jolt through her body. Then she kissed him back with same kind of ravenous hunger as he kissed her.

She had never minded any of the earthier aspects of their time together, not the taste of his semen, or how her private, liquid arousal had tasted on his lips after he had licked her to climax, or the slight salty hint of blood. Mindlessly, he plunged his tongue into her, over and over, while she gasped and arched into him.

Driven by a hectic rush of need, he pulled back, reached for the bundle of bedding that lay nearby, and with a single yank, he untied the strip holding it all together and shook out the mattress. Even that brief moment away from her kiss felt insupportable.

He slid one arm underneath her hips. Lifting her, he twisted to lay her on the mattress and came over her prone body. Then, kneeling over her, he gazed down at her figure.

He loved her body with a greedy carnality that shocked even him. With round breasts and hips and long, muscled limbs, she was intensely feminine and graceful, strong yet welcoming. Her long, curly hair tumbled renegade over the mattress and spilled onto the rough cavern floor.

Even with her dirty clothes, smudged face and tangled hair, she looked burnished and vivid against the dinginess of the bleak cell, shining like a beacon of light. She watched him with a large gaze darkened by some unnamed emotion.

He hesitated. A part of him never forgot the slave pits he had fought his way out of, but she came from a finer, gentler life.

"Tell me no, Melly," he growled. "Just say the word, and I'll never approach you again."

As he paused to give her a chance to respond, he felt a pulse of unbearable suspense. If he had learned nothing else in his long, wicked life, he had learned one thing. "Never" is a heartbreaking amount of time.

Please don't tell me no.

She wasn't gentle with her reply. Reaching for the waistband of his jeans, she yanked the fastening open. "Like you said, we'll have plenty of warning—if she shows up, she'll blow the whistle. Come here."

Some kind of fierce, unnamed emotion roared through him. He replaced her hands with his own and yanked the fastening of his jeans open. While he did so, she lifted her hips to tear off her trousers and lacy underwear, and tossed them aside.

After twenty years of starvation, the drive to be inside of her was overwhelming. As he reached for her, she hooked one arm around his neck and lifted her mouth for his kiss.

He hadn't thought it was possible to be on fire for her any more than he already was, but her eagerness torched through him with the sudden intensity of a flash fire. His need turned aggressive, and he plunged into her mouth with his tongue, but that penetration only fed his hunger. Urging her back on the mat, he knelt between her legs, while he stroked at her soft, private petals of flesh.

She felt so good, so good, silken and so slick with moisture, he had to swallow a groan. As he stroked her, he lifted his head to watch her face. A shudder of pleasure rippled through her body, and he thought with fierce possessiveness, *I am doing this to her. She wants me right now, no one else.*

As he caressed her, she stroked her hands down his chest and abdomen, and reached greedily for the opening of his jeans. Underneath, he wore black boxers, and she yanked the thin material down so that his stiff penis jutted free.

When she closed her fingers around his cock, the pleasure of her touch was almost unbearable. He jerked in her grasp, hissing, and nearly spilled himself all over her inner thigh. Grabbing her by the wrist, he pulled her hand away.

"I can't take it," he muttered. "Right now I've got to get inside you."

He'd had so long to acquire finesse, literally centuries to discover how lovemaking can become a slow and sensual art. But she had reduced him to the most basic, and primal, of urges—the need to cover, protect and penetrate. To rut.

She lifted her head to hiss at him, "Get inside me now."

He had to pause for a moment to stare at her. Melly was not just photogenic. She was simply pretty, and her feminine looks were enhanced by a normally even temperament and easygoing nature.

Right now, her features were clenched and sharp. She looked as driven as he felt.

She reached again for his cock and urged him down to her. Bracing himself on one forearm, he drove his mouth over hers again, plunging his tongue deep to fuck her mouth while she rubbed the head of his penis against her velvety-soft, fluted opening.

As soon as he felt that he was slick enough with her arousal so that he wouldn't cause her discomfort, he pushed into her. She made an incoherent noise of pleasure and need. Panting, she kissed him back jerkily.

Melly knew how to finesse too. She knew how to make languid love, focusing on each pleasure point for its own sake, until the act of sex became like a voluptuous banquet. The knowledge of that, along with her urgency and lack of control, made him crazy.

Crazy.

Without fully intending to, he plunged all the way into her, and oh my God, she was so slick and welcoming. He felt as massive as an oak tree, and when she clenched on him, her inner muscles were tight as a fist.

He groaned, "Goddamn, you're so hot."

"I know," she whimpered as she moved restlessly under his weight. "I'm burning up."

At that, he had to lift his head and grin down at her. Her gaze was glazed with passion as she blinked up at him. "No, baby," he said gently, rocking his hips to begin moving in her. "That wasn't what I meant. I meant, *you're so hot.*"

Her eyebrows quirked, and dimples appeared in her cheeks as she suppressed a grin. "Yeah, I knew that."

He grinned back briefly, then they both lost their smiles.

They were dirty. The cell was abysmal, and the thin mattress from the cot was terrible. They hadn't even gotten fully undressed, but what drove them to couple overrode all of that.

She gripped him at the back of his head. He pinned her down, flexing to get deeper into her, moving faster and harder until he was pistoning into her. The pleasure was exquisite, the buildup of pressure intolerable.

She cried out something breathlessly as she dug her fingers into his bicep.

He needed to take all of her. Covering her mouth with his again, he mimicked the penetration of his penis with his tongue, thrusting into her with the same rhythm he used with his hips. She lifted up for each thrust, flexing as he flexed, matching his rhythm.

As he did so, belatedly, his mind caught up with what she had said.

That bitch better not blow her goddamn whistle.

A sharp convulsive wave of laughter shook through him again and was lost in a storm of sensation. His awareness splintered into fragments, each piece impossibly vivid and compelling.

The lean line of her thighs hugging his hips. The grit of dirt underneath the heel of his hand as he propped himself on one arm to stare down at her. The moisture glistening on her full lower lip. She was wet from his kisses, her mouth swollen.

The way she tightened on his cock as he slid back and forth in her passage. Holy shit, it was magnificent. She was his full partner in every way.

In a classic feline move, she clawed his back and ground against him. For a moment he held utterly still as he remembered another deeply intimate detail of their lovemaking from before.

Most of her climaxes came from her clitoris. They had laughed about it together whenever Julian went "deep sea diving" in the hopes of trying to coax her into a vaginal orgasm, or even more rare, an orgasm that blended both.

The memory jolted him out of his preoccupation with his own needs. Sliding one hand between their joined bodies, he located her stiff, delicate little bud and massaged it with the ball of his thumb.

"Come on, baby," he whispered, watching her face as he rocked into her.

Moving restlessly underneath him, she shook her head and gasped, "I—I don't know if I can. I need to, but . . ." She made a quick, frustrated gesture.

"Of course you can," he told her.

He was never above doing whatever it took to achieve his objective, including breaking his own rules.

As her wandering hand came back to grip his shoulder, he brought down his fangs to bite her neck again—not to drink any more of her blood, but to let her feel the pleasure that came from his bite.

They both stilled. Her heartbeat pulsed against his mouth. He had never felt so close to anyone before. Then a shaking moan escaped her lips on a puff of air that tickled his ear. Like a sexy ghost, the needy little sound shivered over his skin.

Oh my God, I love to fuck you, he said in her head.

That was her tipping point. Arching her back, her knees clamped on his hips. He could feel the ripples of her pleasure when they began. He never wanted to leave them. Rocking gently against her, he drew them out as long as he could. When he was sure she had finished, he withdrew his fangs and lifted his head again to look at her.

She looked dazed, broken wide open. It was the most honest expression he could ever remember seeing, from anyone.

Staring down at her shimmering gaze, he pumped hard into her, once, twice. His own climax, when it came, punched him like a sledgehammer, rolling up from the base of his spine. Swearing under his breath, his body arched from the savage strength of it.

She took his chin in slender fingers and turned his face down to her.

"That's my climax," she breathed. "I want to see every moment of it."

Even in the midst of the waves of convulsive pleasure that pulsed out of him, he found room to be surprised. Twenty years ago, she would never have done such a thing. She had grown. Meeting her gaze, he gave her everything he had.

When his climax finally began to ease, he stroked her hair off her face and pressed his lips to her forehead as he thought, It doesn't matter if I try to hold on to my old anger or not. I'll never be able to fully leave her.

As his lips pressed against her skin, Melly closed her eyes and thought, I'll never understand him. Never in a million years.

He has been so bitter and cold to me for so long. How can he show me such warmth and gentleness now? What happened to change his attitude—and when might it change back again?

When I open my eyes again, who will I be looking at—the bastard Julian, or the nice Julian?

But she already knew the answer to that. She could not look at one without the other, because they were both the same man. It was just that the bastard Julian was so much easier to live with when he wasn't so furious with her.

She felt exposed, euphoric. She felt disturbed at how easily she had given in to her desire for him, when just a short while ago, she had been so determined to never let him near her again.

And circumstances and surroundings be damned. She wanted to wrap her arms around his neck, pull him down to her and make love to him all over again. She wanted to tear off the rest of her clothes just to feel his calloused hands running over her bare skin.

When he lifted his mouth from her forehead, she said, "We shouldn't take any more time. We need to go."

A softer, more modern man might have frowned at her for being so abrupt, but Julian had spent his formative years owning nothing but his wits and his ability to kill, and he had lived too many centuries as a fighter.

"You're right," he said. Pulling away, he rolled off her and came to his feet. Matter-of-factly tucking himself inside of his boxers, he held out a broad, scarred hand to her.

She put her hand in his, and he lifted her effortlessly to her feet. While she found another rag from his shredded T-shirt and cleaned her inner thighs, he buttoned and zipped his jeans and collected her trousers and underwear.

She watched as he frowned down at the wadded-up feminine clothing in his hands, puzzling how to turn it right side out again for her. The slanted light from the heavy flashlight made flecks of silver in his salt-and-pepper hair shine.

He had an undeniably Roman profile with a nose that had been broken more than once, blunt, high cheekbones, and a strong jaw that more often than not revealed the determination of the man. Somehow he never managed to look quite civilized when he dressed in formal black tie. Now, standing shirtless in his battered jeans, he was the epitome of raw, lethal masculinity.

If his sire Carling hadn't seen his potential and turned him, he would have died almost two thousand years ago. Melly was under three hundred years old, and she would never have met him.

If she would have heard anything about him—highly doubtful—anything she might have learned would have been from human history books. And while she was well versed in the history of all the Elder Races, she hadn't studied much human history.

Chances are, she would have known nothing about his existence, nothing about his struggles or triumphs.

Or how he would have died.

Finding the thought deeply disturbing, she took her clothes from his outstretched hand without meeting his gaze. Quickly she pulled on her underwear and trousers, and slipped her feet into her ballet shoes.

"What's wrong?" he asked.

"Nothing," she muttered. His gaze was too penetrating at the best of times. The last thing she wanted was for him to dissect her right now.

Somehow he managed to make his answering grunt sound entirely skeptical, but he didn't push it.

She finished off another bottle of water and ate the second banana, which meant there were two less things they needed to carry. Working together, they gathered everything up within a matter of moments.

He hesitated only once, when he rolled up the cot mattress and blanket again and tied the bedding with the strip, then slung it onto his shoulder. She didn't have to ask why. Hopefully they wouldn't need the bedding and they would find their way out quickly enough.

As she tucked the revolver into the grocery bag along with the last two bottles of water and remaining food, Julian arched an eyebrow at her.

"Why hold on to the gun now?" he said. "We're out of bullets."

She lifted her chin. "I'm not letting go of a single potential resource until I know for sure it's no longer of any use to me. Maybe Anthony has a car outside the tunnels, and maybe he has a box of extra bullets in the car."

A quick smile creased his face. "Good point. Damn, I never thought of that. Are you ready?"

She cast a final glance around. Not that long ago, she had thought for certain she was going to die down here. "Oh, hell yeah."

"Come on." He tucked his stakes at the back of his waistband, took the large flashlight and led the way down to the gate. She carried the smaller flashlight, the grocery bag with the food and water, the gun, and her own stake in one hand.

After hearing so many ferals in the background for so long, the area seemed eerily empty. Looking quickly down both directions of the intersecting tunnel, he unlocked the gate, then paused to look at her.

"What?" she said.

Taking her chin in his hard fingers, he kissed her swiftly. "What happened back there—it wasn't a fluke, Melly. We didn't have sex because of the danger or because we got carried away by my bite. When we get out of here, we're going to do it again. And again."

Anger kindled at his words, and she jerked her chin out of his grasp. "You know what? You don't get to screw me when you want, *if* you want. I'll tell you if we're going to have sex again or not—and with that highhanded, primitive caveman attitude of yours, it's not looking very likely."

She meant every damn word. He shouldn't have smiled at that, but he did. As his lips slowly widened, his eyelids lowered and he gave her a look that was knowledgeable and full of intent.

"Oh, don't look at me like that," she snapped.

"Like what?" he asked, sounding almost lazy.

"Mister I'll-come-after-you-and-you'll-like-it. Fuck you."

His smile turned into an outright grin.

Gah, he looked so sexy. He made her crazy, and she still had a right hook with his name on it.

Then he snapped his head around and lost his smile, and at his hard, predatory expression, her stomach clenched.

She hadn't heard anything, but she had been preoccupied with being mad at him, and his senses were so much sharper than hers.

She switched to telepathy. *What is it?*

Someone's trying to be stealthy.

She strained to hear whatever it was that he heard. *Do you think it's one of the ferals?*

Yes. Justine would be more quiet. He wrapped a hand around her forearm.

Pushing the gate open, he stepped out. He kept a strong grip on her so that she nearly tripped on his heels. For once, she didn't mind his highhandedness. The tunnels seemed extra dark and menacing outside the protection of the locked gate.

Reluctantly, she said, *You have to let go. I can't use my stake when you're holding on to my arm like that.*

He frowned at her. *I'm taking point, but I still want you to stay as close to me as you can.*

Don't worry, she told him grimly. *I have no intention of lagging behind.*

When his fingers loosened, she missed the comfort of his touch immediately and grew annoyed with herself. As they came to the first intersection, she remembered her first foray out into the tunnels, before she had known anything about the ferals. It seemed like it had happened ages ago.

She told Julian, *When I first got out, I went exploring and I found a large, cavernous room. The ferals were there, feeding on a couple of people. They chased me back to my cell. I barely got it locked in time.*

He shook his head. *The thought makes me shudder.*

It was the worst few minutes of my life. She paused, thinking. *But here's the thing—if Justine and Anthony have been bringing victims in for the ferals to feed on, then doesn't it sound logical that one of the tunnels leading from that room can get us out?*

It does, indeed, he told her. *It might take us a while to find* the right tunnel, but if we keep the room as our reference point, sooner or later, we'll be able to find the right one. Can you get us back there?

She nodded. *I kept mental track of my turns.*

There was approval in his gaze when he glanced at her. *Good job.*

When he started forward again, he followed her directions. Right, right and across. At that latest one, he cocked his head. *Why didn't you go right again?*

She shook her head with a shrug. *I didn't realize at first how big the tunnel system was, so I was making decisions on instinct instead of some kind of well-thought-out plan. I was afraid if I took too many rights, it would lead me back to where I started.*

Fair enough. He shone the flashlight both ways down the intersecting tunnel.

What happened to the stealthy someone? she asked.

I don't know. There's an echo down here. It could have come from farther away than I thought. Or he might have stopped moving.

That sounded a lot more sinister than she would have liked. If the feral had stopped moving, that might mean he was lying in wait somewhere.

She glanced over her shoulder. Beyond the range of her flashlight, the darkness looked as solid as a curtain. It seemed to have personality, like it was watching her. She studied the darkness carefully but saw nothing.

For the first time, she realized the ferals had to exist in total darkness most of the time. The cavern where they had been feeding had been lit, but she suspected the torches had been more for Justine and Anthony's benefit, whereas the feral Vampyres would know every nook and cranny in the tunnels like the back of their hands.

After checking both ways, Julian stepped forward, and she followed.

Out of the corner of her eye, she caught a flash of movement. Even as she turned her head to look at the feral that had dropped from a shadowed hollow in the ceiling, Julian sprang forward to engage.

Another feral dropped down and leaped after Julian. They had coordinated an ambush.

As soon as the realization hit, she whirled in a complete circle, her stake out and ready as she looked for the third.

He rushed out of the darkness, not from behind her, but from the tunnel ahead. She had never faced one without the barrier of bars between them. Terror flared, followed by a surge of rage.

She was *done* with being scared of these things. *Done.*

He came at her so fast, she wasn't sure she could stake him accurately in the heart—and she didn't dare get into such close quarters with him and miss, or risk getting her stake caught in his chest.

Leaping and pivoting at the hip, she went into a roundhouse kick that clipped the feral in the chin and knocked him back against the tunnel wall. He rebounded immediately—but that time she was ready for him. Even as he reached for her, she grabbed him by the wrist and hauled him toward her while she drove the stake into his chest.

For a moment she stared into the feral's red gaze. She found herself searching for any sign of the personality he had once had, yet she saw nothing but madness in his eyes. As he bared his fangs at her, he collapsed into dust.

She turned just in time to see a snarling Julian in midlaunch toward her, easily two-hundred-plus pounds of deadly Vampyre male, complete with red eyes and fangs.

Flinching back against the wall, she gasped, "Holy shit."

He landed in front of her, slapping one hand against the wall, so close that his body pressed hers against the cold stone.

"Jesus," he said roughly. "I thought he had you. I thought I was going to be too late."

Any other time, she might have slapped him with a retort for thinking she couldn't take care of herself. But this time, she felt a shudder wrack his powerful frame as he sucked in an unsteady breath, and she realized he had been terrified for her sake.

Leaning forward, she put her head on his shoulder and wrapped her arms around his waist. "I'm all right," she told him in a soft voice as she rubbed his broad back. "Everything's okay."

Still breathing hard, he buried his face in her hair and held her tight.

An odd kind of peace stole over her.

Maybe they weren't going to have sex again. Or even if they did, maybe they wouldn't be together for long.

Maybe they would never get over what had happened before. Earlier, when she had given him her truth, he hadn't said whether or not he had believed her. Even now, after so long, their conversation remained unfinished.

But she did believe in one thing now.

Wherever she was, and whatever kind of trouble she might get into, he would always come for her to make sure she was all right.

Because he really did care for her at least that much.

⇒ ELEVEN ⇐

After a moment, she lifted her head.

He had calmed down enough so that he looked human again. She told him, "At least they're all gone now, and we don't have to watch over our shoulders for them."

He nodded. "And I know I don't have to come back to clean them out."

This time, instead of taking point, he took her hand, lacing his long fingers between hers. The gesture stole into her heart, damn him, and she couldn't make herself pull away. Instead, she fell into step beside him.

As they walked in silence for several minutes, she found herself thinking ahead. "Justine has to be local, doesn't she?" she said. "Somewhere in the city, so that she can get back and forth from the tunnels."

His attention sharpened on her. "Yes, unless she has come to some kind of agreement with Malphas. I wanted to ask you about that. Did you overhear them making plans or setting up some kind of arrangement?"

Biting her lip, she shook her head. "The only thing I heard them discuss was him getting you in the cell, and they weren't careful about what they said in front of me, so I think it's likely he's still helping her, but I can't say for sure."

"Fair enough." He frowned. "As soon as I can, I need to set up road barriers and search the city block by block if I have to. Maybe I can flush her out, unless she can fly."

She raised her eyebrows. She would love to hear he was making a joke about that, but he sounded dead serious. "What do you mean?"

His mouth tightened. "We have all her assets frozen, at least those assets that we could find, but she might still have the funds to hire a helicopter. Either that or one of her allies on the council might have agreed to help her."

Staring at his profile, she asked, "By now her allies must know what she did to her own household. Do you really think they would continue to support her?"

His expression turned cynical. "Anything is possible, including that."

She tried to keep her response as quiet and noncommittal as possible. "You sound pretty fed up."

He bit out, "I'm sick to death of the lot of them. Every year the council goes through the same damn arguments. Even Dominic is interested only in doing what is best for him."

Unsettled, she chewed her lip. After a moment, she said gently, "Since it makes you so unhappy, would you ever consider stepping down?"

"What makes you think I can?" The sharp bitterness in his look lanced through her. "My sire set me on this task, remember?"

Melly sucked in a breath. Carling, his sire, had once been Queen of the Nightkind demesne, but a long time ago, she had set Julian to be Nightkind King while she became a member of the Elder tribunal.

So very much had happened since that long-ago political maneuver. Melly was sure she had only heard a fraction of the entire story. When she and Julian had been together, he hadn't discussed it much, but even then she could tell there was tension between him and Carling.

Then last year, a series of fast-paced events had jolted through the demesnes of the Elder Races. Some of it had involved the Nightkind. Melly had heard the news from a distance.

All she really knew for certain was that Carling and Julian had had some kind of falling out, and he had banished Carling from the demesne. Carling had also lost her seat on the Elder tribunal, and she had even been incarcerated for several months, while Rune, one of the most Powerful sentinels from the Wyr demesne, had left his service and mated with her.

Since Carling was Julian's sire, the only way his banishment of her could be effective is if he never saw her again, because with one meeting and a single order, Carling could take control of him again.

That also meant that he would continue to carry out whatever orders Carling had already given him. He would never have any choice. He would never be able to walk away. He would work and work at those orders, until either somebody killed him, or Carling herself released him.

Horrified pity shook through Melly. She whispered, "Would you want to step down, if you could?"

His expression went blank, and for a moment, he looked utterly empty.

"I have no idea what I would want to do, if I could." His brows drew together. "But I think I would like to take a vacation and find out."

She tightened her hand on his. "What happened last year between you and Carling?"

"That's a long story, and neither one of us came out of it looking good."

"Whatever happened, it was a strong enough disagreement for you to banish her."

"I had to." His reply was as harsh as his expression. "Her behavior had gotten too erratic. Sometimes it happens with very old Vampyres, and she's one of the oldest. She kept giving me contradictory orders, and they were literally tearing me apart. At least by banishing her from the Nightkind demesne, I can keep her from telling me to do anything else."

She said, "Julian, I'm so sorry."

He shook his head. "Don't feel too sorry for me. When Carling's attendant Rhoswen came to me with stories of how dangerous she had become, I didn't question her very closely. Instead I went to the Elder tribunal, even though I knew they would probably issue a kill order. I was right, and they did."

Her hand tightened on his as she worked to absorb that. "Wait a minute. The tribunal doesn't issue kill orders for no reason."

"No, they don't," he said. "There was ample reason. There was also more going on underneath the surface. Long story short, Carling's attendant was acting out of spite and ended up getting herself killed, while Carling managed to convince the tribunal to put her in quarantine instead of enacting the kill order. Apparently she found some way to stabilize her condition. I don't know for certain. She and I don't talk. I don't dare risk it."

"Good gods," she whispered.

"Enough about that." His hard mouth twisted. "We're getting close to your cavern. Can you smell it?"

She could.

Before, when she had been exploring without any idea of what lay ahead, she had thought the stink might have come from a sewer line.

Now she had a different idea of what caused it, and her stomach rebelled. She had to breathe through her mouth to get past a wave of nausea.

"It's not my cavern," she said tightly. "And yeah, I can smell it. I would appreciate it if we could get through the next bit as fast as we can."

He gave her a sharp look. "Of course."

They finally came to the archway she remembered so well. This time there weren't any lit torches in the wall sconces, nor was there any other kind of illumination. The cavern looked black as a pit.

As she braced herself, Julian directed the beam from his flashlight into the open space.

There were corpses everywhere. In grim silence, Julian sent the light over the massive open space. Skeletal remains had been pushed to the edges of the cavern, against the walls, while fresher bodies littered the open expanse of the rocky floor.

She had never seen anything like it. Not in person, not right in front of her. For a brief, stricken moment, her gaze strained to find the body of a woman in a black pencil skirt, who was missing a shoe.

Then a low, shaking moan broke out of her. Pulling her hand from Julian's grasp, she let the things she had been carrying slide to the floor, and bent at the waist and wrapped her arms around her middle.

Julian's broad hand came to rest on her back. He didn't try to say anything or attempt to make things better, and she was glad for that. Sometimes things couldn't be made better.

Instead, he gave her what she needed, which was time. Rubbing her back, he waited until she was finally able to straighten up again. With the back of one hand she wiped at her wet eyes.

"Are you okay?" he murmured.

She would not let the gentleness in his voice break her down again. Gritting her teeth, she nodded. Her voice was hoarse as she said, "I'm fine."

"I count four other tunnel entrances that open into the cavern," he said. "And we know one thing for sure—the way out isn't going to be back the way we came."

She glanced at him. The slanted beam from the flashlight distorted how everything looked, including his face. The crags and the hollows of his face were accentuated, and he looked tired and angry.

He met her gaze. "We have to go through. We can't go around."

"I know." Bending, she snatched up the grocery bag, and when she straightened again, she stiffened her back. "Let's go."

He hesitated long enough that it brought her attention back to him. "What?"

With a quick shake of his head, he said, "Never mind, it will wait."

But he had caught her attention now, and she cocked her head. "You can't bring something up only to drop it again like that. Tell me quickly, and if we have to, we can discuss it in more depth later. What is it?"

At that, he shook his head and gave her a small not-quite smile. He told her, "No big discussion necessary. I just realized, there isn't anybody else I would have wanted at my back down here, aside from you."

Rough and outspoken as he was, his quiet statement hit her all the harder because of it. Despite the silent horror of what waited for them in the cavern, she felt her spirits lift, not a lot, but just enough.

She said softly, "I feel the same way. Julian, thank you so much for coming to get me. I'll be grateful to you for the rest of my life. Now, let's get the hell out of here."

Inclining his head, he strode forward. She followed as close as she could on his heels without actually treading on him.

In order to see where to walk, he had to keep the flashlight trained on the floor. She tried not to look down, but after she stumbled twice, she was forced to watch where she put her feet as well. The images burned into her brain.

The cavern was so large, filled with tragedy and implacably silent. It was the hardest walk she had ever taken, and she felt sick and saddened to the bottom of her soul.

Julian said gently, *Okay with you if we start with the left tunnel? If it doesn't lead to the way out, we can work our way around the cavern clockwise.*

For some reason he had asked it telepathically. Maybe he felt the weight of silence was what the dead deserved. If so, she couldn't argue with that. Breathing through her mouth, she nodded then realized he couldn't see her.

Yes, she said shortly.

He adjusted course, and she followed. After a moment, he held one hand behind him, fingers open in invitation.

"I told you I'm fine." She spoke out loud, but if she had known how thin and strained her voice would sound, she wouldn't have.

"Maybe I'm not," he said very quietly. "I've seen horrible things before, and some were just as bad if not worse than this. But none of them makes this any less horrible."

She grabbed his hand, and he squeezed hers so tightly she felt the blood pound in her fingers.

"It's not right that they've been thrown aside like this," she whispered. "They were people."

"I'll make sure each one gets identified so they can go home to their families." Like her, he kept his voice low. "If they don't have families, I'll see they get proper burials."

"Thank you."

After what seemed like forever, they finally came close to the opening of the first tunnel. Julian came to a stop, which meant she did too, but she didn't stop until she had walked right up to his back. Then she leaned against him, burying her face between his shoulder blades. She had no idea why they had stopped but trusted that Julian would let her know when they could move forward again.

"All right," he said. "We're moving on to the second tunnel now."

She lifted her head. "Why?"

"There are a couple of bodies across the mouth of that entrance," he told her. "They're pretty decayed. It looks like the passageway isn't used very often. We can come back to it if we have to."

"That makes sense. Maybe we can be quicker if we check out the entrances to all the tunnels." She tried to reclaim her hand, but his hold on her was like iron. "You can let go now. I'll work from the right, and you can work from the left."

He turned to face her, keeping his body close in front of hers. "As quickly as I want to get out of here, and I know you do too, I would rather we stay close. I don't want to have to get all the way across the cavern to you if something happens."

When she tilted her head back to look into his face, she found herself nose-to-nose with him. His proximity, along with the force of his personality, helped to push back the rest of the scene. Again, not much, but just enough.

"I didn't think of that," she muttered.

He put a hand on her shoulder, pressing down so she felt the heavy, solid weight of his touch.

"Only a few more moments," he told her. "We're very close now."

"I believe you," she said. And she did.

He looked calm, strong and steady. He looked nothing like how she felt, which was strung out and heartsick, and half-crazed to be anywhere else but standing where she was in a giant, delinquent tomb. Looking up at him, she saw another glimpse of why he would have been such a good general and leader in times of war.

He would have been a rock for people to look to when everything in their world went to hell. He would have been the person that people focused on when things had become unendurable, because somehow, they knew he would find a path to get them through.

He had become that person now, for her.

When he held out his hand to her again, she took it.

A very long time ago, when he had still been a young human, Julian had become experienced at putting certain barriers up between him and the rest of the world. Dealing with the constant realities of single combat, and then the more global consequences of war, meant keeping a tight rein on any impulse to empathize.

Even so, when crimes occurred, he never, ever blamed the victim. If you did bad shit, that was squarely on you, and you had better be running hard and watching over your shoulder if it was his job to bring you down.

The whole time he had been down here in the tunnels, he

had kept the blame squarely where he believed it belonged—on Justine. And he was determined to get her for it, with a wrath as righteous as any of the gods.

But in that moment, as they stood in the company of the rotting dead and he looked down into Melly's face, everything in his head and his heart underwent a complete reversal.

She wore a determined expression, her features set tight with endurance, but the shadows around her beautiful eyes were dark with hollows, and something grieving and fragile hovered underneath the surface.

Her expression filleted him.

He thought, this is my fault. All of these dead, all of the trauma that Melly has endured.

I should have known better. I knew Justine was creating some kind of trouble, but I didn't have any kind of proof that the Nightkind council would accept, so I did nothing. If it wasn't in my face, I could pretend that I didn't have to do anything about it.

So everything that Melly has endured and all the damage Justine has caused, it's all on me.

He had no words that could possibly make anything better. The only thing he could do was get Melly out as fast as he could, catch Justine and bury the dead.

Turning, he picked a path between the bodies to the next tunnel entrance. This time Melly joined him, and together they studied the floor around the entrance carefully.

He was about to suggest that they explore at least partway down the length of the tunnel when she released his hand, walked forward several feet past the entrance and knelt. Spitting on the tip of one forefinger, she ran it lightly across the middle of the floor and settled back on her heels to study the result.

Then she stood and showed him the filthy tip of her finger. "We can go down this way if you believe we should, but I think it hasn't been used very much. If it had been, the middle of the floor would be worn cleaner than this, don't you think?"

He did. Giving her an approving smile, he said, "I do, and I think we should move on too."

She gave him a crooked smile in reply and took his hand again when he offered it. They made their way to the third entrance.

This time, he knew immediately.

The scent of fresh air wafted against his cheek. He strode forward, tugging on her arm. "Come on. I think it's this way."

She increased her pace until she was almost running, and it was her turn to tug on his arm. He was more than happy to match her speed. They came to a few more forks, but now the current of fresh air was strong on both their faces.

He caught a hint of briny salt. "We're somewhere near the shoreline. Can you smell that?"

Her face brightened. "Yes. Oh gods, we're almost there."

They came to a curve that was so sharp it was almost a switchback, like a hairpin turn on a mountainside. Rounding the curve, he thought he saw something independent of the illumination from the flashlight.

"Hold up a second," he said.

With obvious reluctance, she pulled to a stop. He switched off the flashlight, and they waited.

Blackness so dense it was almost velvety pressed against his eyes, until . . .

Ahead, a lighter gray appeared as his eyes adjusted to the lack of light.

"There!" Melly exclaimed. She clutched his arm. "Do you see it?"

"I do." Jubilant, he swept her into his arms and hugged her tight.

As the light grew stronger, some of Julian's jubilation faded. The growing illumination was diffuse and pale, not the sharp halogen glow of streetlamps at night.

If it wasn't daylight outside, then it would be daylight soon—perhaps too soon for him to be able to leave the protection of the tunnel. He had no protective clothing with him and couldn't afford to be caught outside without it. Melly might have to go on without him.

From her excitement, he could tell that the thought hadn't occurred to her yet, so he said nothing. They would have to face the reality of it all too soon.

As they walked on, the tunnel began to shrink in size. The walls on either side of them narrowed, and Julian had to duck his head in order to continue.

"There's some kind of hole in the ceiling. That's the way out." Melly's voice shook.

She was right. As they got closer, the details became apparent. The hole was covered with a grate.

They came to stand directly underneath it. Thankfully, the light remained pale and gray. He guessed it was the light of predawn. The grate was rectangular and looked like it was made out of sturdy iron. It would be difficult, perhaps even impossible, for a human to move it without a crowbar.

He handed his flashlight to Melly, reached up to grasp the grate with both hands and pushed up. It was heavy to shift even for him. With a scraping sound, it popped out of place, and he pushed it to one side until they had a hole big enough to fit through.

He turned to Melly, laced the fingers of his hands together and bent to offer them to her. "Time to step up."

Setting the flashlight and her grocery bag aside, she placed one narrow foot in his grip and braced herself with both hands on his shoulders. Straightening, he lifted her until she could hoist herself out of the hole. Her weight left his hands. Tilting his head back, he watched her disappear.

Almost immediately her disheveled head popped into view again as she looked into the hole. Her expression had turned tense again, her gaze dark with worry. "Julian, it's almost dawn."

He nodded. "I know. Tell me what you can see."

She glanced around. "We're either in an alleyway, or a single-lane road. The area's deserted. There are buildings all around that look like warehouses." She bent over to peer into the hole at him again. "This spot is deep enough in shadow there won't be direct sunlight for at least fifteen minutes, maybe more, only I'm no good at judging that sort of thing. Please come out and judge for yourself."

"All right. Back up." When she disappeared from sight again, he leaped up, grabbed the edge of the hole and levered himself out to crouch warily beside her.

One quick glance around told him she was right, and he relaxed marginally. Their immediate surroundings were intensely industrial. Weeds sprouted in cracks in the asphalt, and there was a run-down quality to the buildings, giving the scene an air of desolation. If it had been a thriving warehouse district, the area would be bustling by now as businesses readied for the workday, but there was no movement in sight.

He straightened to a standing position, and she joined him. "I'm not sure, but I think I know where we are, at least in a general sense," he told her. "There's an area in southeastern San Francisco that's been marginalized for years. None of our attempts at revitalization have taken hold yet. If we're where I think we are, we're anywhere from six to ten miles away from Nob Hill."

She wiped her face. "On the one hand, that's not very far away. But on the other hand, that's much too far to travel when sunlight is going to appear overhead very soon now."

He turned to face her. "You can travel it. Direct daylight won't stop you."

At the first word out of his mouth, she started shaking her head. "No. I'm not going to leave you."

"You might not have a choice," he said. "If you go, you can at least get someone to come back with protective clothing, along with a vehicle that has tinted glass."

All the fragility and grief came to the surface in the look she gave him. "And leave you to do what?" she asked, her voice raw with exhaustion. "Climb back into that hellhole to wait for me?"

"I have more options than just the hellhole," he said, gesturing to the nearby buildings.

As she opened her mouth to reply, a quick movement of air brushed against the bare skin of his back.

It was all the warning he got.

Instinct made him spin on his heel. Even as he did, he felt a piercing pain in his lower back. It went very deep.

Arching, he grabbed at the pain while punching out with his other hand. He had no time to see his attacker or take aim. Instead, he struck out blindly. As his questing fingers curled around something short and hard that protruded from his lower back, he landed a glancing blow on something solid.

A gasped curse sounded in his ear. He yanked out the protrusion and glanced down at it. It was a knife. He'd been stabbed.

His attacker struck out again. This time, catching the movement out of the corner of his eye as a black blur, he had just enough time to leap back. Fire bloomed along the surface of his abdomen. He had been cut again, but this time it was a surface wound and the damage was minimal.

Another fighter might have continued to dance back so that he could parry while taking a minimum amount of damage. In another fight, he might have done the same.

But not this fight. He lunged toward his attacker, as hard and as fast as he possibly could. He connected in a body slam, sending them both to the ground.

Visual impressions came to him in almost instantaneous snapshots. His attacker wore all black from head to toe. The black hood and outfit were sun-protective clothing, and physically, she was shorter and slighter of build than he. But she was every bit as fast, and in his current weakened state, she was quite a bit stronger.

Justine had come to locate her errant assistant.

His existence narrowed until he had just one objective—grabbing hold of her and not letting go.

It was a vicious scramble. She flipped them both bodily, until he slammed into the pavement underneath their combined weights. He fought to get the chance to use the knife she had lost when she had stabbed him in the kidney, but he didn't dare loosen his hold long enough to accomplish a strike.

She feinted with her other knife, and he checked it with

one shoulder. The blade bit deep, slicing through muscle to scrape the bone. He headbutted her and heard cartilage crunch.

The entire struggle, he knew, would have been nothing more than a confusing blur to Melly.

Telepathically, he shouted at her, *We can't risk her getting hold of you, or she'll use you against me again.* RUN!

⟹ TWELVE ⟹

Melly knew Julian was right, so she whirled and ran. Leaving him was one of the hardest things she had ever done.

If Justine slipped out of Julian's hold and came after her, the Vampyre could move so much faster, she could catch Melly in a matter of moments. Melly tucked in her chin and sprinted as hard as she could.

Her delicate ballet shoes had never been meant for the kind of treatment she had put them through, and they offered almost no protection now. Stones and uneven pavement bruised the soles of her feet. She forced herself to ignore the pain.

Meanwhile the sky continued to lighten with brilliant, deadly streaks of sunshine. She had thought nothing could ever be as bad as her nightmarish run through the tunnels, chased by ferals, but she was wrong. With every second that passed, she expected to feel Justine's hands slam down onto her shoulders.

What was happening between Julian and Justine? The attack had occurred so fast, but Melly was almost positive she had seen Justine stab Julian at least once. Please gods, don't let her kill him.

Still surrounded by silent buildings, she came to a T-section, turned right and kept running.

Then another intersection. Right again. Keep track of your turns, Melly.

Ahead, a rocky hillside rose up, strewn with bits of trash, signaling the end of the warehouses. As she reached the end of the buildings, she paused only long enough to glance both ways.

When she saw what looked like the shoulder of a real road to her left, she bolted toward it.

Her breathing came hard now, and she was forced to strike a balance between pacing herself while still running as fast as she possibly could. When she reached the road, she looked around. Small houses dotted the unkempt landscape. Several of the houses had boarded-up windows.

Three blocks away, a glaring blue neon light shone at the front of a shabby one-story building.

The illuminated letters read:

ROADHOUSE OPE.

No *N*.

Even though dawn was breaking, at least a dozen motorcycles were parked underneath the sign.

Motorcycles. Not a single car was anywhere to be seen. Damn it.

She raced toward the building, slammed through the front door and didn't come to a stop until she was several feet into the main room of a bar.

Judas Priest rocked over the speakers. Bikers dotted the room. Some slouched at the bar, while a few played pool. Several were deep into some kind of card game that involved a pile of cash sitting in the middle of a table.

Most of the bikers were human, but there were a few ghouls as well. As she glanced around, she saw beards and black leather jackets everywhere.

Heads lifted at her precipitous entrance. As they all

turned to face her, silence fell over the room. The bartender reached under the bar, and the song cut off.

"Well, damn," somebody said. "That's unusual."

She could only guess what she looked like. She was wearing at least three days' worth of grime and blood. Her trouser outfit, originally a stylish cream color, had turned gray and was covered with streaks of brownish red. The bruises on her arms and throat had bloomed into full Technicolor, her cuts and scratches were covered in dark scabs, and while she had finger combed her hair, her attempt at keeping it tidy had only served to make each individual curl spiral out in every direction.

Chairs scraped as everyone in the room stood. Eyes wide, they began to advance on her.

She retreated a couple of steps, her chest heaving as she fought to catch her breath.

She said, "I'm Melisande Aindris, and I've been kidnapped. I'll pay someone thirty thousand dollars for a bike with gas in the tank, along with a jacket and a helmet, and a cell phone. . . ." She had to pause to suck more air. "And does anybody have a gun?"

There was a concerted rush toward her. The bartender leaped over the bar, joining the rest as they jostled and shoved each other. Disoriented and overwhelmed, Melly backed up.

When all the movement finally stopped, Melly found herself pressing back against a wall, and every biker in the place extended a gun toward her, handgrip forward. Two were sawed-off shotguns. As she stared at them, a bearded fellow extended his other hand, offering a switchblade as well.

One of them said, "I realize this might not be a good time, but sometime when you're having a better day, can I get your autograph?"

Another man snapped, "Seriously, George. Not appropriate right now."

The first one whispered, "I know, I know, just—when am I ever gonna get the chance to ask?"

Blinking rapidly, she told the man named George, "Sure.

You can have my autograph later." Focusing at random on a semiautomatic pistol, she grabbed for it. As the owner relinquished his hold on the weapon, she asked, "How many rounds?"

He said, "Twenty. It's fully loaded."

She asked, "Do you have a PayPal account?"

He nodded, his dark eyes intent.

She met his gaze. "I have no time right now. My friend is in big trouble, and I have to go help him. As soon as I know he's all right, I'll transfer the money into your account. Okay?"

Rolling one big shoulder in a laconic shrug, he reached inside his leather jacket and pulled out another gun. "I'll come with you. Gotta protect my investment."

Big and dangerous as he looked, he was still human. If he came up against Justine, he would be dead meat, but she wasn't about to waste precious moments arguing with him, not when Julian's life might be in danger.

She told him, "Fine, but we've got to go now."

As they strode out the door, they were followed by a stampede of the other bikers, including the bartender. Her biker led her to a late-model Harley. He tossed a helmet at her, and she jammed it on her head, while he mounted the bike, started it and revved the motor.

"Climb on," he said.

She leaped on behind him and grabbed handfuls of his jacket. "What are the others doing?"

He sent an amused glance over his shoulder. "Famous blond bombshell walks into a bar and mentions a shitload of money, guns and trouble all in the same breath. They would die before they stayed behind. Where are we going?"

Tucking in her chin, she told him. With a mechanical roar, he pulled onto the street, followed by the rest.

With transportation, it took only a few minutes to retrace her steps. When they neared the tunnel entrance, she looked around frantically. She knew it was the right place. She recognized it. The heavy iron grate was still pushed out of place, but neither Julian nor Justine were anywhere in sight.

Her biker pulled to a smooth stop several feet away from the hole. He had to raise his voice to be heard over the growl of all the motorcycles. "You sure this is it?"

"Yes," she snapped. Dismounting, she tore off the helmet and ran over to the tunnel entrance.

Inside, part of her screamed, *no, no, no.* Desperately, she searched the ground as several of the bikers joined her.

Would she be able to tell if Justine had staked Julian, and he had turned to dust? Had he been carrying anything metal on him?

With a quick glance upward, she noticed the bright, hot line of sunshine that bisected the nearby warehouse. When she had left, the wall had been entirely in shadow.

Taking in a deep breath, she shouted, "*Julian!*"

One agonized heartbeat. Two.

As the noise from the motorcycles died down, Julian's gravelly reply sounded clearly. "Here."

His voice came from below, down the open mouth of the tunnel. The relief that washed over her was inexpressible. Melly lunged toward the hole and leaped into it, ignoring the alarmed exclamations that followed her. She landed with a thud that jarred her teeth.

After being outside for so long, the shadows in the tunnel seemed impenetrable. Despite that, she stumbled forward blindly, until with a small *click*, Julian turned on the flashlight to light her way.

He sat several feet away from the daylight streaming in through the open hole, his long legs stretched in front of him. She fell to her knees at his side, and he hooked one arm around her neck, snatching her close. After hugging him, she sat back and ran her anxious gaze over his torso.

"What happened? I saw her knife you. How badly are you hurt?"

"I'll live," he said. "I broke both of her collarbones and tore up her clothes. She wasn't able to get any strength behind her blows, and without adequate sun protection, she decided she had an urgent appointment elsewhere." He looked behind her and coughed out a laugh. "I see you brought back reinforcements."

She glanced behind her in time to see her biker, along with two other men, drop into the hole. With the addition of three large males, the already tight quarters grew even more cramped. Julian's arm tensed, but he didn't move. She knew if he had been uninjured, at the very least, he would have placed himself between her and the other men. That alone told her how bad off he was. He certainly wouldn't have remained sitting.

Her biker took in an audible breath. He said to her, "When you said you had a friend in trouble, you didn't mention he was the Nightkind King."

She told him, "I was in a hurry."

Without preamble, Julian said, "I need blood. Are you, or any of your men, willing to donate? I'll pay."

Her biker came forward to kneel on one knee. "You're on the hunt for those responsible for killing all those people, aren't you?"

"Yes." Julian watched the other man with a guarded expression.

The biker held out his wrist. "I've given blood to a Vampyre before. No need to pay me. Ms. Aindris will be compensating me very well already. But if you need more than I can give, you might have to pay the others."

Julian took his wrist. "Do you take drugs? Don't bother lying. I'll know if you do."

The biker shook his head. "Never. I did indulge in too much Southern Comfort last night. Is that a problem?"

Julian gave him a faint smile. "Not at all."

Melly startled as one of the other men touched her shoulder. "Ms. Aindris, why don't you come outside now? It'll give us a little more room to maneuver down here."

He was one of the older bikers, with long gray hair pulled back into a ponytail. His simple kindness brought a flood of moisture to her eyes. Uncertainly, she turned back to Julian, who said in her head, *Go on, baby. I'll be out as soon as I can.*

Sniffing, she nodded and rose to her feet. After such a massive dump of adrenaline into her bloodstream, she felt suddenly bereft of energy and direction, and she stumbled. Taking her gently by the elbow, the gray-haired biker steadied her as they walked back to the tunnel opening.

Several faces peered down at them. "She's coming up," said the gray-haired man. "Help her out."

Two men reached down. She took their offered hands, and they hoisted her up. As her feet left the tunnel floor, she said, "I need my bag."

"Is it a purse?" The gray-haired man looked around.

"No, it's a grocery bag." Her voice wobbled.

"I'll hand it up to you," he promised.

Outside, she managed to stay mobile until she could collapse in a heap against the warehouse wall. Somebody handed her the grocery bag. Somebody else tucked a leather jacket around her shoulders. The interior lining was still warm from being worn, and she huddled into it gratefully, shivering while she dug into the bag for the two remaining bottles of water. She drank until she couldn't hold any more liquid.

Now that the most urgent of the drama had eased, the bikers gave her plenty of personal space. They grouped together nearby, looking her way often, several of them smoking cigarettes as they talked in low voices. A few left. Others climbed down into the tunnel to donate blood to Julian.

Melly searched the cloudless sky overhead. It was going to be a bright sunny day. She had never seen anything so beautiful in her life.

A shadow fell, and her biker squatted beside her. He asked, "You okay?"

"Yeah," she said. "I'm taking a moment."

He dropped something in her lap. She looked down. It was a smartphone. He told her, "It's unlocked and the bill's paid until the end of the month. No contract, unlimited phone and text. I think there's about half a gigabyte left on the web."

"Thank you." Her fingers closed over it too tightly. When her hand started to shake, she forced her grip to ease. The phone wasn't going to vanish into thin air.

His dark gaze lingered on her white-knuckled grip. He heaved a sigh. "Leonard is trying to convince me that I have a conscience."

Looking in the direction of his gesture, her gaze connected with that of the gray-haired man, who gave her a nod while he drew on a cigarette.

She asked her biker, "How's that working out for you?"

"It's inconvenient." He rubbed his face. "Look, I know you were in a bad way and desperate to find help. You don't have to pay me the thirty grand you promised."

She nodded and looked up at the sky again. After a moment, she said, "I made a deal with you, and I'm willing to stick by it. After all, you've lived up to your end of the bargain. I do have a phone and a loaded gun."

"You're also wearing my jacket," he pointed out.

She pulled the collar close. "It's my jacket now, right?"

"I guess it is." He exhaled in a silent snort and nodded toward the Harley. The helmet she had borrowed was perched on the saddle. "You know, at a generous estimate it's worth maybe fifteen grand. I've used it hard, but I've also kept it well maintained."

"Good to know. How much gas does it have?"

"Three quarters of a tank."

That was more than enough fuel. Riding the bike, she and Julian could be at his house in Nob Hill in twenty minutes or so, depending on traffic.

If it weren't for the cloudless, sunny morning.

She looked up at the sky again. "How about twenty instead of thirty? You'll still be making a good profit."

"Sounds good to me."

"What's your PayPal address?"

When he told her, she used the phone to log on to her PayPal account and went through the steps to pay him. His email address was simple and no-nonsense—his first and last name. She said, "Done. Thank you, Keenan."

He dropped the keys to the Harley into her lap and shook her hand. "It's yours. I'll sign the title over to you and messenger it to . . . Where do you want me to send it?"

"If you deliver it to Julian's house in San Francisco, he'll see that I get it."

"Fair enough." With a shrug, he stood and walked toward the other bikers.

Watching him walk away, she considered his laconic attitude and reluctant decency, and she thought she might be crushing on him just a little.

Two more men emerged from the tunnel, drawing her attention. Then Julian appeared in a catlike leap. He was every bit as filthy as she was and entirely healed, and he moved with an extraordinary, predatory grace. Aside from the sheer power of his physicality, he had a massive, forceful presence that made all the other men pale in comparison.

Watching him, she thought, so much for my little crush.

What she felt for Julian eclipsed everything else. Everything.

A pity her feelings couldn't tell her what she should do about them.

As she watched, he looked around the scene warily. The area where she sat was still in deep shadow, so he approached to crouch at her side.

"I bought a bike," she told him. Her voice was unsteady again. "And a helmet, and a jacket. But I didn't think about gloves, and your neck would be exposed. I think we're going to have to wait for a car after all, and there's no way I'm going to leave you again, so we're going to have to break into one of the buildings to either wait out the day or wait for a ride, because Julian, I cannot go back down into that hole or I will go insane."

Midway through her speech, he gripped her arms.

"Melly, stop." He pulled her against his chest, and she wrapped her arms around his waist, huddling against him. He pressed his lips to the top of her head and said into her hair, "You don't have to try to fix everything, damn it. You can rely on me. I'll handle this. And no, we're not going to wait for a ride or for daylight to fade. We have too much to do."

Too much to do. Hmm.

She'd been hoping for a croissant, and a cup of coffee with cream and sugar.

Resting her cheek against his pectoral, she nodded as if she knew what he was talking about. A part of her concentrated fiercely on soaking up the sensation of his closeness.

After a moment he eased away. He told her, "I'll be right back."

As he approached the other men, she took note of how they reacted to him. They had been so much more generous than she could have expected. They had fed Julian and brought him back to health, but when he neared, several of them also took a step back. They were rough men, all of them, ready and able to commit violence, but they all recognized the dominant predator in their midst.

After exchanging a few sentences, one of them handed a pair of black gloves over to him, while another shrugged out of a flannel shirt he had been wearing over a Metallica T-shirt. Julian shook their hands, pivoted and came back to her. Tearing the thick flannel material into strips, he wrapped it around his neck and donned the gloves.

She stood to shrug off the jacket and hand it to him. After slipping it on, he zipped it and turned the collar up. His gaze met hers. One corner of his mouth notched up. "It's not elegant, but I've gone most of my life not being elegant. It'll do."

"As long as you're sure." She fussed over him, pulling the flannel material as high as she could under his chin.

"I'm sure." He flattened a hand at the small of her back and pulled her forward to give her a hard kiss. "Do you know how to ride a Harley?"

She slapped the keys into the palm of his hand. "Nope, and this is not my morning to learn. Have at it, soldier."

His smile widened. Taking her hand, he hoisted her to her feet. "Ready to go?"

"Almost. Hold on a sec." It was her turn to walk over to the bikers. She met each man's gaze. "Thank you so much for everything. I don't know what we would have done without you."

Several of them ducked their heads. For scary, rough-looking dudes, some of them were quite adorable. Keenan offered her a faint smile.

Leonard said, "You're welcome. Go kick some ass."

Julian had followed her. He told them, "That's the plan."

She asked the group, "I have one more question for you. Does anybody have a pen?"

After a moment of surprise, they dug into their pockets, until one of them offered a blue ballpoint pen. Crooking her finger at the guy who had asked for her autograph, she gestured for him to roll up his sleeve. Then she signed *Melisande* on his forearm.

Staring at the signature, he breathed, "I'm never going to wash my arm again."

Leonard snorted. "That ain't much of a stretch. You don't wash much anyway."

"Wait, I can't sweat. I need a tattoo parlor, stat."

"Come on," Julian said. He led her to the bike, pausing just long enough to slip on the helmet. "It goes against all my instincts to wear this helmet while you don't have one."

She told him, "You'll live, which is the point. And you won't let us crash."

The dark faceplate of the helmet was blank, yet she got the impression he was frowning at her. He mounted the bike while she slipped her new phone into her pocket and tucked the gun into her waistband.

"If I have anything to say about it, we sure as hell won't crash. But I need you to be ready, just in case something happens. Is your gun loaded?"

She swung onto the bike behind him, and because this time it was Julian, she nestled close against his body, spooning him.

"I double-checked. It has a full clip. Why? You're not expecting trouble, are you?" She tensed at the thought.

"I don't know what to expect. Soon after Justine ran away, I heard the sound of a chopper nearby. It may have been unrelated, or she may have help, like we discussed."

"I didn't even notice," she said. Working as she did in LA, the sound of traffic helicopters was so frequent, she tended to block out the sound.

"We're not going to get complacent." Starting the bike, he told her telepathically, *Hold on tight. This is going to be a fast, rough ride.*

She tightened her arms around his waist. Briefly he squeezed her hand, and they took off.

Julian wasn't exaggerating. It was a wild ride. He drove aggressively, and on open stretches of road, their speed shot up until the world became a blur. Squinting, she peeked once over his shoulder at the speedometer, and saw they had hit over a hundred miles an hour.

The wind screamed in her ears, and it whipped her hair around. Tears streamed from her eyes so that she couldn't see. She didn't dare loosen her hold to wipe her face. Instead, she let go of everything—any worry that enemies might be tracking them, any fear at their high speed—and buried her face in Julian's back, putting all her trust in him. After being confined in the dark for so long and living in serious fear for her life, the release she felt at their speed was exhilarating.

As aggressive as he was, he was still forced to slow when they reached the congested city streets near Nob Hill. A couple of times, he avoided coming to a standstill by driving up onto the sidewalks, scattering pedestrians.

The sound of sirens wailed behind them.

She looked behind them, peering through her crazy mess of tangled hair. A police cruiser tried to follow in pursuit but was forced to plunge to a halt behind traffic blocking the street.

I'm rethinking our destination, Julian said. *If Justine has gotten help, it could get more dangerous the closer we get to my property.*

How likely is that? she asked.

His reply was grim. *I don't know. When she came to the tunnels, she wasn't expecting us to be free, but by this point, she's also had time to regroup and strategize, so anything's possible. Every time we've had an exchange, she's esca-lated. And I don't like how vulnerable and exposed you are.*

She had been so focused on finally reaching comfort and sanctuary, his comments shook her. After a brief internal struggle, she said, *The mansion's guarded, and you've been missing since yesterday, so they must be on high alert and watching the immediate vicinity. Screw it. Julian, just go for it.*

He hesitated only for a moment. Then the Harley leaped forward again, hurtling around street corners and racing the final blocks. Finally the mansion came into view. They fishtailed to a halt by the intercom box in front of the gates.

Warily studying their surroundings, Melly drew her gun and braced the heel of her hand against Julian's shoulder, while he punched a button and snapped, "Gregoire, open the damned gate."

The wrought iron whirred into motion immediately. As soon as a gap several feet wide appeared, Julian revved the engine and they shot through.

Hang on, he told her.

She clamped on him, clinging to his waist with all her strength.

Instead of slowing to a stop in the drive near the front doors, he sent the Harley rocketing up the front steps and onto the spacious portico.

"Whoa!" she shouted.

The front door opened as they plunged to a stop. Julian blurred into motion, sweeping her off the bike and into shelter before her feet had a chance to touch the ground.

As Gregoire slammed the door shut, Julian set her down. After such an intense finish to the ride, she was shaking wildly. He kept one arm tight around her while he pulled off the helmet.

Dropping the helmet, he brushed her long, tangled hair back from her face. His sharp gaze roamed her features.

"We made it," he said. "That's it. We're here. You're safe."

"Understood," she managed between gritted teeth. If he had let go of her, she would have fallen.

"Melly." He cupped the back of her head as he clenched her to him. She tried to clutch at his leather jacket, but her fingers wouldn't work properly.

"What can I do?" Gregoire asked in a quiet voice.

Vaguely she was aware of Julian plucking the gun out of her shaking grip and handing it over to the other man. "Increase security around the perimeter. Contact Xavier and Yolanthe. Tell them we're here and to expect a briefing shortly. Get hot tea and food up to my rooms. I need a new phone."

"Yes, sir."

"I'm o-okay," Melly told Julian.

"I know you are." His gaze was concerned.

Her teeth started to chatter. "I'm j-just reacting."

"Hell, I am too." Scooping her into his arms, he jogged up the main stairs.

She managed to hook an arm around his neck. "I w-w-wasn't expecting the t-trip to end like that."

"Your back was so unprotected, I couldn't stand it." Rapidly he walked down the hall.

She hadn't been in his San Francisco home in over twenty years. The décor had changed somewhat. It was still a sophisticated blend of creams and golds, with dark antiques, but the wallpaper and paints had been updated, giving the interior a combination of a traditional and a contemporary look.

The layout remained the same, and she knew where he was taking her—to his suite. For a brief moment she tried to decide if she cared, but she really didn't. She couldn't even scare up a ghost of pretense. Whenever she had visited, his suite had been a happy place, filled with safety and sensuality.

The future would take care of itself soon enough. Right now, she couldn't imagine anywhere else she would rather be.

Carrying her into his room, he set her in a worn leather armchair, set in a reading nook in one corner. A faint, comforting scent of cigar smoke surrounded her. A gold-inlaid humidor sat on a table beside the chair, along with a crystal ashtray and an old-fashioned metal torch lighter. This was where he sat to smoke and think.

She loved the smell of his cigars. Hand rolled and made of high-end, organic tobacco, they seemed clean and aromatic compared to the stink of so many modern cigarettes.

Steel shutters at the windows ran on an automatic timer. At the moment, they were all closed against direct sunshine. The room lay in deep shadow, with the only light streaming in from the hall, until he switched on the lamp beside the chair.

He knelt in front of her, gathering her close again. She threw her arms around him and hung on. He stroked her hair, and the silence that fell between them wasn't empty in the slightest. It was more full than any words could have made it.

When her arms loosened, his did too. He touched her cheek with the back of his fingers as he said reluctantly, "I have to go brief Yolanthe and Xavier."

She straightened in her seat. "I need to be there too."

"No." He shook his head. "Not two minutes ago you were shaking like a leaf, and you couldn't stand upright on your own. You need rest and good food."

She set her jaw. "I could sure as hell use a shower too, but Justine made me a part of this whole damn thing. Julian, I refuse to play the role of a helpless victim. I need to be a partner in bringing her to justice."

At that, he gave her a fierce frown, but she met his gaze steadily, and after a moment, he said, "I understand. How about a compromise? You stay up here and look after yourself. Let me brief Xavier and Yolanthe. I'm going to have them send investigators into the tunnels to start the process of extracting and identifying bodies. I'm also going to have them start a citywide search, and I want Xavier to investigate recent helicopter activity."

She frowned. "Helicopters don't have to file flight plans, do they?"

"No, but I'm hoping there'll be some kind of trail to follow.

If the helicopter was rented, there'll be a record of that. If either Xavier or Yolanthe has any news, I'll call you down to join the conversation. If not, after I'm done with the briefing, I'm going to come back up here and shower too." He searched her expression. "We need to rest while we can, so that we're ready for whatever happens next."

She rubbed her forehead and let out a sigh as the starch left her spine. He was right. She needed to be a partner, but she had to be a robust and reliable one.

She said, "Okay."

He kissed her forehead. "I don't have any women's clothes in here, but I can have Gregoire send out for some things. In the meantime, help yourself to whatever you need."

Was it wrong of her to be fiercely glad he didn't have anything feminine in his private rooms? If it was, she didn't want to be right.

"Go on, don't worry about me," she told him. "I'll be fine."

He looked deeply into her gaze. "We have a lot to discuss, you and I."

"It'll keep." Her eyes narrowed. "For now."

Nodding, he gave her a hard, quick kiss. "I'll be back as soon as I can."

When he strode out, he seemed to take all her remaining energy with him. She sagged in the chair while she stared into space. She had to call her mom and shower. Or shower and call her mom. They seemed to be insurmountable tasks, and she couldn't decide which one to tackle first.

The phone in her pocket rang, startling her. She pulled it out to look at the screen.

She knew the number from the incoming call like the back of her hand.

Huh.

She clicked the answer button. As she held the phone up to her ear, a woman's dangerous, icy voice said, "Keenan O'Sullivan, this is Tatiana Aindris. I will give you five million dollars for the safe return of my daughter. Or I can hunt for you forever, and if that happens, I promise you won't like what happens when I find you."

As she heard the Light Fae Queen's voice, decades of adulthood fell away until Melly felt like she was five years old again, happy and loved and utterly safe.

Her lips pulled into an incredulous smile. "Mommy?"

≈ THIRTEEN ≈

*M*elisande." The intensity in her mother's voice caused her to start shaking again, and her eyes to swim with tears.

"How on earth did you know to call this number?" She knew she was grinning like a fool, but she didn't care. Sluggishly her mind clicked into gear. "Wait. I made a PayPal payment."

"We started monitoring all your accounts within a few hours of finding out you'd disappeared. When the payment to Keenan O'Sullivan went through, we jumped on it. I have someone on the way to his house right now."

"Oh, *no*," she exclaimed in dismay. "Mom, you've got to call them off. Keenan and his friends helped me this morning."

"How do I know you aren't being coerced into saying that?"

"Because I'm not!" She heard how irrational that sounded and caught herself up. More calmly, she said, "Yes, I'm in San Francisco, but I'm at Julian's house."

"What?" The ice had come back, and it was sharp as a dagger.

"I just arrived—I literally sat down five minutes ago, and I'll tell you all about what happened. Just promise me you won't do anything to Keenan. He's totally innocent."

"If he's innocent, why did you pay him twenty thousand dollars? And why did you answer his phone?"

"Because I bought his motorcycle, gear and phone. And his gun." The silence that resulted from that was more dangerous than any ice. She took a deep breath and braced herself. Here we go. "Justine kidnapped me. She used me to trap Julian. She forced him to give himself up in exchange for my life, only when he surrendered to her, she didn't let me go. Julian and I got free, and I'm okay now. I've got some cuts and bruises, and I'm dirty and tired, but I'm safe. I'm fine."

Quickly, she sketched in the rest of the details. Another silence fell. This time she could hear her mother's breathing.

When Tatiana spoke next, she sounded ragged. "Julian acted so bizarrely when he left here, we knew something had to be wrong, but we didn't know what. Soren had come to help search for you, and so had Graydon, from New York."

"Julian told me they were involved in the investigation."

"While Soren stayed with me, Graydon tracked Julian to the de Young Museum, where his trail just stopped. Graydon's on his way to O'Sullivan's house now. Since Julian had vanished, we thought it would be better for him to go, instead of me sending Light Fae troops into the Nightkind demesne."

"Gods, what a mess," Melly muttered.

"Hang on." The phone went silent. When Tatiana came back on the line, her voice was steady, strong. "I got in touch with him. He hadn't found O'Sullivan yet."

"Oh, good."

"Cuts, you said," Tatiana said softly. "And bruises. I want to see you. I want to see your face."

Involuntarily she looked down herself. She couldn't remember looking like quite such a disaster before, not even for the worst of her disaster movies. A snort escaped her. "Trust me, you don't, not until after I've cleaned up. Listen, I'm going to help bring down Justine, and that includes any of her allies—if she has any left. The Nightkind demesne owes me that much. Julian has already agreed, so I don't know when I'm coming home."

"I don't know, Melly. . . ."

"Mother, I'm not asking you for permission," she interrupted. After her shake-fest a few minutes ago, she was surprised at how strong and focused she sounded. "I'm telling you what I'm going to do."

A very long pause greeted that statement.

Then Tatiana replied, "I'm sending you twenty troops. That's nonnegotiable. The Nightkind demesne owes *me* that much. What else do you need?"

A shower, rest, food. A resolution of some kind with Julian. None of it was anything her mother could give her. With an effort, she concentrated on practicalities. "Well, I don't have anything, so I could use clothes, my phone, credit cards, cash card. Cash."

"You'll have all of it by early afternoon, along with your own weapons and body armor."

"Okay, thanks." Depending on how the search went, Melly hoped to be sound asleep when it arrived. She asked, "Is Bailey there?"

"No, she's out, but I'll send her with the troops. I know she needs to see you."

"Sounds good. I love you."

"I love you too, darling." The gentleness in her mother's voice enfolded her like an invisible hug, but it was the Light Fae Queen who said in an iron voice, "And Melly—*make them pay.*"

After she disconnected the call, she stood to limp into Julian's bathroom. She couldn't take it any longer. If one more delay came between her and clean soap and water, she might get indiscriminately violent.

Along with the rest of the house, the bathroom had been updated too. While the fixtures—sink, toilet, tub—were physically in the same places they had been in before, the décor had changed. As with everything else, Julian's taste was simple. Dark cabinets and cream marble dominated, and the tub was now separate from a glass-fronted, walk-in shower.

She tore off her clothes, rolled them into a tight pile and set them on the floor by the door, hopefully to be burned later. Then she started hot water in the spacious tub and used a dollop of shampoo as bubble bath. While her bath ran, she dug around in the cabinets until she found spare toothbrushes.

She almost fell asleep leaning against the sink as she brushed her teeth, only coming awake with a start when she started to slide sideways.

Unh, Melly. Oh, no you don't.

Not even her own exhaustion was going to hold her back. With single-minded determination, she climbed into the tub, submerged in the water and lathered her hair twice. By that point, the water was so dark with dirt, she had to let it drain and run a new bath. She had been cold for so long, the warmth that sank into her bones felt glorious. After running a soapy washcloth all over her body, she curled on her side and fell asleep.

She woke up to Julian lifting her out of the bath. Blearily, she took in details of his appearance. He was still shirtless but he must have showered, because he was damp all over, his hair slicked back. It looked darker when it was wet, which in turn emphasized the faint crow's-feet fanning out from his eyes and the lines bracketing his hard mouth.

It felt so good to be in his arms, she curled against him and tucked her face into his damp neck. He carried her into his bedroom.

"How long was I in here?" A wide yawn cracked her jaw.

"Maybe forty-five minutes."

"Any news?"

"Nothing to speak of."

Reluctantly, she roused. "Put me down. I need to dry my hair at least partway. If I don't, it'll go crazy."

"Don't be so picky." He set her down, but on the bed, not on the floor. The covers had been pulled back. She rolled off the bed to avoid getting the sheets wet, only to have him scoop her up and put her on the bed again. "Nobody cares what your hair looks like."

"I don't recall you being this annoying when we spent nights together before," she told him grumpily, scowling. "It has nothing to do with what I look like. When my hair gets too tangled, it takes forever to get it brushed out again, and besides, I don't want to sleep on a wet pillow. Stop moving me around like that, damn it. I want a towel and a hair dryer."

He frowned at her. "Stay there. I'll be right back."

Yawning again, she watched him walk into the bathroom. He had wrapped a towel around his waist, and it rode low on his hip bones. She imagined licking his skin along the top edge of the terry cloth and looked around as she forced herself to think of something else. The door to the room was closed, and a covered food tray sat on the table beside the armchair.

She had a brief impulse to explore the contents of the tray, but he reappeared again almost immediately, carrying two thick towels, a hair dryer and a brush. Setting the hair dryer and brush aside, he slung one towel across her lap. Taking the other one, he scooped the long dripping weight of her hair up and draped the towel across her shoulders. Then he took each side of the fluffy cloth to her head, rubbing her scalp with strong, gentle fingers.

The sensation ran down the length of her body. All the starch left her spine, and she slouched forward until she found herself leaning against the tight muscles of his lean waist.

She mumbled, "I can do it."

"Sure you can," he told her. "But you're going to let me."

"Why?"

"Because I need to," he said quietly.

The words tugged her attention up to his face. Looking down at her, he caressed her cheek. His expression was introspective, brooding. Even though they were connected by the touch of his hand and by recent events, in that moment, there was something so alone and self-contained about him, she abandoned all impulse to argue and gave him an uncertain nod.

He plugged the dryer into an outlet by the bed and lifted long, curly strands of her hair with the brush, working out the tangles as he blow-dried them. More welcome warmth suffused her. She gave up trying to sit up straight and leaned forward to wrap her arms around his waist, pressing her cheek to his flat stomach. He stroked the back of her head, his long fingers pressing against the curve of her neck.

Maybe he couldn't let down his barriers for her. Maybe their past was too heavy for them to leave behind. Maybe he couldn't let his barriers down for anybody. He had spent such a very long time alone.

Unexpectedly, tears prickled at the back of her eyes. Pressing a kiss to his stomach, she whispered, "Tell me what the fuck you want me to do, and I'll do it."

He stood frozen and tense. When he clicked off the hair dryer, the resultant silence seemed shocking.

She had said it because she was remembering what he had said and done for her. Until she heard it out loud, it hadn't occurred to her that the statement could sound so erotic.

She rubbed her face against him, reveling in the vitality of his bare, scarred skin. The white that had begun to frost the dark hair on his head had not yet reached the sprinkle of hair on his chest that arrowed down his abdomen. He was caught forever between masculine strength and mortality, at the height of his power with just a hint of the death that would never take him.

"Melisande." Her name sounded wrenched out of him.

Glancing up, she saw that his expression had turned raw and open. He had hardened, and underneath the towel that cloaked him, his erection pressed against her collarbone.

Giving in to what she wanted to do felt like falling. Her own arousal pulsed as she pulled the towel from his waist and took him in both hands. As she touched him, he sucked in a breath. The long, heavy muscles of his thighs were taut and hard as steel.

The skin covering his penis felt silken. He was thick, the sensitive head broad, while veins traced the sides. His sac had pulled tight underneath. With one hand, she cupped his testicles, massaging gently as she rubbed his cock against her cheek.

She knew his body like an old, treasured companion. Verbally, they might have fought and caused each other pain, but physically, he had never given her anything but pleasure. She remembered and welcomed every detail about him, his clean, masculine scent, the warmth that radiated from him, the touch of his hands on her skin. Vampyres were supposed to run cooler than other races, but she had never found him cold.

She made a hungry, eager sound, parted her lips and took the tip of his cock in her mouth. Belatedly her mind caught up with what she had done.

Um, maybe she should have asked first. If somebody had grabbed her crotch and helped himself without so much as checking in with the rest of her, you can bet your ass she would react with a strategically aimed knee to the privates.

Just because he had an erection didn't mean he was willing or prepared to act on it. People were complicated. Bodies were complicated. God only knew, it was tough enough to try to balance what was in the head versus what was in the heart, let alone trying to figure out how to meet the rest of a body's needs as well.

Her face flooded with heat. Pulling back, she muttered, "Sorry."

Incredulity sharpened his gaze. "You're *sorry*?"

Her shoulders crept up to her ears. "I just grabbed hold and started sucking. Then I thought maybe I should have asked first."

Amusement bolted over his hard features, completely banishing his moody isolation.

Then, sobering—or at least appearing to—he said, "Melly, please suck me off. Fasten your sexy mouth around my cock and pull on me until I don't have anything left to give. My God, just looking at the erotic shape of your lips makes me want to spill all over your gorgeous face. . . ."

His blunt, raw language brought even greater heat to her cheeks, even as she pulsed in greater arousal at the images he evoked. She had always reveled in his earthy, unashamed sexuality.

Toward the end, though, she had to hold up both hands

as she started to giggle. "Okay, thank you for that exposition. You can stop now."

"But I'm not done," he said, his eyes glinting wickedly. "I need to tell you in great detail how much I want to sink my hands in your hair and fuck your mouth. Just so that we're clear."

A snort exploded out of her nose. She felt pretty sure her blush had extended to cover the whole of her upper body. Naked, his erection still quite stiff, he rested his hands on his hips and laughed down at her.

Then his laughter faded into something much more serious. Kneeling in front of her, he framed her face in both calloused hands while he searched her expression. He said, "You and I used to laugh a lot."

"Yes," she said softly. "We did."

"I'd almost forgotten what it was like to laugh out loud." His words were almost soundless. "I've gotten to a really dark place, Melly. The darkest place I've ever been."

"You don't have to be there anymore," she told him gently. "Don't you know what happens at the darkest point of the day?"

He stroked her soft lower lip with the ball of one thumb. "What?"

She rubbed her fingers soothingly along his muscled forearms. "A beautiful, brand-new day begins, and it's all fresh and full of promise." She smiled into his gaze. "That's why magic in the fairy tales happens at midnight, you know. When you reach that point, you have the power to change everything."

Closing his eyes, he turned his head to press his lips against her fingers as they rested on his arm. They held like that, unmoving, until she leaned forward to kiss his temple.

At that he wrapped his arms around her, and it wasn't just a mere hug. There was so much damn passion in it. He enfolded her. He held on to her like she was his lifeline and he was a drowning man, and he cradled her at the same time, showing her with his body how he considered her precious.

She had been exhausted before, but now she was wide awake and concentrating fiercely on every moment. How he cradled the back of her head. The expression in his eyes as he looked into hers. He was a man of violent tendencies and deep emotion. It had always amazed her that he could have such a tremendous capacity for tenderness.

When he covered her mouth with his, she met him gladly, and the concussion of arousal that blasted through her was deeper and more profound than anything she had ever experienced before.

Not even what they had shared twenty years ago came close. Things had been powerful before, but so much simpler, and even at times naive, at least on her part.

Now, complexity of emotion played through her like a symphony, the familiar juxtaposed with the new. She wasn't sure that her skin could contain it all, and she shook from the force of it, her mouth working under his.

In response, he muttered something against her lips. It sounded like a curse. Hooking one arm underneath her knees, he lifted her all the way onto the bed and climbed over her, while slanting his mouth over hers. He speared her with his tongue, hard and deep, while he supported his weight on one elbow and ran a hand down her torso.

His fingers were shaking. Or maybe she was shaking. Breaking away from his kiss, she plunged upward. She had so many competing impulses, she tried to do everything at once—rubbing her face against the sprinkle of hair on the wide expanse of his chest, reaching between his legs to cup him again.

He sank a fist in her hair and pulled her head back, wordlessly demanding she offer her neck to him. She loved—*loved*—his barbarism. Gasping, she let her head fall back, trusting to his hold, while she arched her body up to him.

Her gesture caused him to growl deep in his throat. He bit her neck—not as a Vampyre, not breaking the skin—but quick, erotic nips that shivered down the length of her body and escalated her growing need.

In response, she clenched her fist on his cock. Part of her knew she was being clumsy and rough, but she couldn't control herself. He didn't act like he minded in the slightest.

Instead, he hissed against her shoulder, bucking into her hand.

When he pulled away from her hold, it was her turn to growl in frustration, but he was only shifting down her body so that he could kiss and suckle at her breasts. As his tongue teased and flicked at her sensitive nipples, he ran his hand along the inside of her thighs, urging her to part her legs for him.

She did so gladly, anticipating the magic he could make with his fingers, the pressure and penetration, but then he teased her some more, barely stroking the surface of her private flesh, making her arousal spike so sharply, it became outright pain.

She felt his fingers grow slick with her response. He raised his fingers to his mouth to lick them with relish, then he went down even further to settle between her legs and tongue her most sensitive place.

His caress was knowledgeable, electric. It lifted her head off of the bed, while a shaking cry broke from her lips. The reaction inside her body was so volcanic, she had to hold on to something, somehow. She tried to grasp the back of his head, but his hair was too short. Tickling her clitoris with his tongue, he reached up to grab her hands and pin them at her sides.

She was trapped, exposed. The confinement made everything too intense. She tried to jerk her hands free, but he was much too strong for her. All the while, he feasted on her, flicking and sucking in turns at her delicate, stiff little bud, until she bucked in his hold and almost fought him.

Except she wasn't really fighting him. It was just that the pleasure was intolerable, and he knew, he knew what he was doing. He knew how she felt.

"I can't stand it," she managed to gasp.

"Mmm," he crooned against her. "You can."

"Seriously. Julian, please." She lifted her hips to his wise, wicked mouth. It was literally the only thing she could do. With every caress, he stripped her down until she was even more naked, more in need, and the pleasure built and built. . . .

Until the most glorious sensation flared up, blooming through her body like a glowing lotus flower.

A ragged cry broke out of her. She was not in control of it. She wasn't in control of anything. After the first wave of pleasure, her climax pulsed rhythmically. He found the secret of it, tonguing her in rhythm with the pulse, and oh my God, how did he know to do that, and she couldn't take any more.

"Holy shit," she said. Her voice was shaking badly, while tears spilled out the corners of her eyes. "Okay, okay— Julian, I can't do any more—"

Yes, you can, he said in her head.

He didn't let go of her hands.

He didn't lift his mouth from her, or stop.

Oh, God.

Her next climax didn't bloom like a flower. It cracked through her body like lightning. Lifting her head from the force of it, she would have screamed except she had lost her breath. All that came out of her mouth was a helpless, mewling cry. She tried to swear. Inside her head, she was going off like a sailor, but what came out of her mouth was begging.

"Please. Please."

Oh, baby, he said gently. *I'm not going to quit until you give me another one.*

"I c-can't!"

You can, he murmured. *You will. Tell me what you're feeling.*

He was the darkest of voices inside her head, the Night-kind King, and when he turned his gift of persuasion onto her, she wanted to take her soul out of her body and hand it to him.

Somehow she made her shaking mouth form words. She whispered, "I love you."

He stilled. The world stopped.

Then, while she lay totally open and shivering uncontrollably, he released her hands and lifted up to settle on her fully. The weight of his big body was such a relief, she wrapped her arms and legs around him.

Another, softer man might have stopped at that point.

But he wasn't a soft man, and he didn't stop.

Stroking her hair off her forehead, he played his lips over hers, with such light, ravishing voluptuousness, she lost even more of herself to him.

"Say it again," he said against her mouth.

That time, she couldn't articulate verbally and had to switch to telepathy. *I love you.*

He reached between them to bring the broad head of his cock to her opening, stroking her until she was ready for him. Then he pushed in and didn't stop rocking until he had planted himself, all the way to the root.

He felt so big and good, nestled inside. He pulled out and pushed in again. Pressing her face against his shoulder, lifting her hips for each thrust of his, she reveled in his penetration.

Gradually he picked up his pace until he was fucking her with long, sure strokes. At first she simply enjoyed it, but his pace was so relentless, so inescapable, it reached her deep inside, and the pleasure began to intensify again.

She couldn't reach another peak. She was spent. But then he reached between them again and found her clitoris.

"Look at me," he said.

She met the Vampyre's red, fierce gaze.

Baring his fangs, he said, *I told you. I'm not going to quit until you give me another one.*

She whimpered and gave it up to him. This third climax went bone deep, soul deep. It stamped itself onto her DNA. While she shook from it, he pistoned into her, hard and fast, until his back arched and he twisted with a gasp.

Inside, she felt his erection pulse, which was when she remembered how the whole thing had started.

Damn it, she was going to suck on that.

As quickly as the thought occurred to her, it ghosted away again. She was left watching him, feeling him climax. It was so beautiful to watch the power of what he experienced transform him. Greedy for every moment, she soaked it all in.

Afterward, he rested his forehead on the pillow beside her. She realized he was breathing heavily and smiled to herself.

That was when he whispered in her ear, "I love you too, Melly. Always have, you know."

All of her filters had been stripped away. At times, that could be a good thing.

Other times, it wasn't. The first thing that came to mind was what fell out of her mouth. "You have a hell of a way of showing it sometimes."

The silence that greeted that felt too charged and unpredictable. Inwardly cursing herself for shattering the moment, she turned her face away and covered her eyes with one hand.

Maybe they were going to have that talk right now, whether they were ready or not.

≈ FOURTEEN ≈

Julian stared down at Melly's averted face. She was hiding her eyes, but the rest of her was available for his perusal.

She looked so much better than she had when he had first laid eyes on her in the tunnel. Her skin glowed a warm, healthy color in the soft bedroom light, and her blond, curly hair glinted with gold highlights. The tip of one of her elegant, pointed ears peeked out of a curl. The healing properties from his bites were aiding her natural Light Fae ability to heal. Her bruises were fading, and her cuts and scratches already looked like they were several days old.

She was clearly upset. He rolled away from her, onto his back, and stared up at the ceiling.

He said in a controlled, even voice, "We're short on rest, and our emotions have been running at full throttle. Are you sure you want to have this conversation right now?"

"I don't know." She sounded frustrated. "Apparently the nap I took in the bathtub reenergized me. I'm sorry that fell out of my mouth, but I can't take it back. And I'm not even sure I want to."

"All right."

He watched as she left the bed, walked into the bathroom and reappeared a few moments later. She wore his dark blue silk bathrobe, and she had pulled her hair back into a loose braid. Not looking at him, she went to sit in the armchair where she lifted the lid off the covered food tray and inspected the contents.

After a moment, she picked up a cup of tea and cradled it in her fingers. Her expression was shuttered and unhappy.

He closed his eyes. Then he sat at the edge of the bed, pulled on a pair of dark gray boxers and put his head in his hands.

His old anger and pain had become such a toxic habit. He could feel the emotions begin to wrap around him again, like a familiar, restricting straitjacket. They felt as heavy as ever, only this time after the lightness of the sensuality and laughter that he and Melly had just shared, the weight felt intolerable and crushed his chest.

Intolerable.

No. No more.

Living with it was like living forever in the tunnels, or finding himself trapped back in the slave pits. It was a dirty, ugly place to exist. He might not have much of a soul, but those negative emotions were strangling whatever he had left.

He wanted her laughter. He needed her tenderness. He wanted her head resting on his chest in front of a winter fire, her fingers laced through his. He needed to embrace the possibility that he really could make different choices at the beginning of a new day.

"I want to let go of the past," he said quietly. "Can we do that? Let's draw a line right here and agree that whatever happened before is over and done. We make a pact to forgive each other and move on."

He could hear the stress in her breathing from across the room. "Why?"

"Because I love you more than anything we've done to each other," he told her. "Because I want to believe you're right, and that we can make different choices that redefine our lives. Because I believe in you now more than I was able to believe in you then."

He stood and walked over to kneel in front of her. She watched him with a damp, wary gaze, her expression closed in. Carefully easing the teacup away from her, he set it aside and took her hands.

"I want to tell you some things for your sake, not mine," he whispered. "Okay?"

Her mouth worked, then she pressed her lips together and nodded.

"You're a genuinely good person." His voice was gentle. "You are so much better than I am. You're kind, and you're funny, and you're ingenious and loyal to the point of stupidity."

"Hey," she said in warning.

In answer, he pulled the robe open and drew one finger lightly down the path of the scabs on her shoulder, where the feral had clawed her at the gate, and he raised his eyebrows pointedly at her. She scowled at him and yanked the robe closed.

Biting back a brief impulse to smile, he told her, "You are a beautiful woman, inside and out. I see you better now than I did when we were together before, and I love you more." He paused and shook his head. "Whereas, I'm still a bastard. I learned all the many ways there are to kill a person before I ever learned anything else, and I'm always going to be rough around the edges. I know where the spoons, knives and forks are supposed to go, and I just don't care."

A small snort escaped her, even as a tear spilled down her cheek.

Carefully, he wiped her face with a thumb as he told her, "When we were together, I wanted to believe all the things you said to me, but I think at my core, I never did believe I was worthy of you. So of course you would end up with someone else. It was inevitable, wasn't it? After you learned who I really was, there was no way you would ever want to be with me."

"Oh, Julian."

"Hush, I'm not finished." He tightened his hold on her slender fingers and brought them up to his mouth. He said against them, "For the longest time, all I wanted to do was strike out at you and hurt you the way I was hurting. And I don't want to live that way, or be that man anymore with you. I'm sorry I caused you so much pain, and I want very much to try again, if you will."

Sniffing, she tugged at her hands. When he released her, she picked up the napkin off the tray and blew her nose.

"I have so many reactions, I don't know where to start," she murmured. "Which is par for the course with you. So I'm going to tell them one at a time, okay?"

"Okay."

She met his gaze. "You're worthy of me. You're worth it. Spoons and knives and forks are the most unimportant things in the world. Even when you're at your lowest point, you have so much damn heart. You offered your life in exchange for mine when you were angry and full of bitterness. I think that's one of the finest things I've ever seen anybody do. So if you can be that man with me, and I mean if you can really let go of your bitterness and *trust me* when I say I want to be with you, and I love you, and I won't leave you, hurt or betray you—then yes, I want to try again."

He felt the smile begin to break over his face, and he opened his mouth to reply.

She put a hand over his mouth. "Hush, I'm the one who's not finished now. I listened very carefully to what you just said. It sounds like you still might think I cheated on you, even when I told you down by the tunnel gate that I didn't."

His smile vanished. "What happened in the past doesn't matter. All I want to do is draw the line between now and then, and let it all go."

"You want to forgive and forget, even that." She looked at him intently. "I'm not rehashing an old issue, Julian. That conversation just happened."

He felt his world start to slide away. She wasn't going to accept his proposition. This wasn't going to work.

There were only two choices in front of him, and both were impossible.

He couldn't say that he believed her, because she would hear the lie in his voice.

If he said he didn't believe her, they started the whole cycle over again.

He was trapped, here, in his darkest place. Trapped by the witch to live forever in the role of the Nightkind King. Never connecting with his princess, never winning the love of his life. There would be no transformative magic, no new day.

Looking at her, he did the only thing he could. He told her the truth.

"Is forgiveness such a bad thing?" he whispered. "I love you enough to forgive you anything."

Her expression was almost indescribable. Tender and exasperated, and with a deep, underlying well of concern.

Then she did a foolish thing.

The most completely unexpected thing.

She took his face in both hands and kissed him. Her lips were so soft, the caress so generous, it made everything clean and new again. It couldn't be the last kiss, the final touch he would ever receive from her, or he would lie down and die. When she pulled away, he snatched her out of the chair and held on to her.

"It's a hell of a thing to know, isn't it?" she said. "That somebody loves you enough to forgive you for anything. I have to tell you, soldier—right now it's a good thing I love you enough to forgive you anything too. So, yay for us, right?"

The same complexity that made her expression unreadable layered her voice. He muttered, "I don't understand."

"I don't either, but maybe we can finally get to the bottom of this." She hugged him, then pushed out of his arms and rose to her feet. He stood with her. "Something—or someone—has such a hold over you that you can't hear me when I say I didn't cheat." She faced him, hands on her hips. "I want to know who did this to us, and why. Tell me what happened."

He considered her with a frown. She clearly wasn't hurling accusations, or trying to start a fight. She looked like she was ready to go into battle, but while her words were determined her voice remained calm.

Rubbing the back of his neck, he turned away. "I don't know who did it. The why seems pretty obvious—a lot of people weren't happy that you and I were seeing each other. One day I received a packet of photographs." He looked over his shoulder at her. "They were of you having sex with Ferion."

She looked like he had slapped her. "Somebody sent you *photographs* of me and *Ferion*? Ferion, the new Elven Lord?"

He lifted a hand and let it fall, looking away.

She strode around to stand in front of him, planting her hands on her hips. "The photos were a lie. I have never been, nor have I ever wanted to be, with Ferion."

She looked so furious and determined.

And every word she said felt like the Gospel truth.

It threw him into chaos. Once he had thought she wouldn't tell him the truth. Then he thought she couldn't, but this was something else entirely. At this point, she had no stake in maintaining any lie, and his gut kept insisting that he believe her.

But . . .

"I couldn't accept what I was looking at, so I had the photos examined." He rubbed his face and looked at her over his hand. "Melly, the images weren't manipulated. They were real."

He tried to say it in as neutral a tone as possible, but her eyes dilated in quick reaction. She hissed, "*No, they weren't.*"

As he stared at her, the feeling in his gut worsened. Of all the ways he might have imagined this conversation going, this wasn't it.

"Once I verified the photos hadn't been doctored, I had to know when and how it could have happened. Remember when you were on location for that movie in Singapore? You told me you were too busy to take a break." He paused. He had to. Her distress was so palpable, he found himself reluctant to add to it. He added more softly, "But after a little research, I discovered you had gone to New York."

Her mouth tightened as her gaze turned inward and searching, looking back in time.

She said abruptly, "Yes, that's right. I did go for a quick visit. It was the only break I took, which is why I told you I didn't have any time. Bailey bought tickets to a Broadway show that she knew I'd been wanting to see. She insisted, and I felt like I couldn't say no. I'd been spending all my free time with you and I hadn't seen her in ages, so I got on a plane, flew in, saw the show with her and left again." Her voice shook. "What did you do with the photos?"

"I burned them," he said between his teeth. "Then I ground the ashes to dust. And I tried my damnedest to hunt down the motherfucker who had sent them to me, so I could break his face and fingers. Because clearly somebody was trying to start some shit—so I was going to give them shit."

Her eyes widened. "Did you find who sent them?"

"No. But I broke my fist on Ferion's face the next time I saw him, so there's that." He needed a minute, so he strode into his walk-in closet to pull on a pair of faded jeans.

When he walked back out, Melly was sitting in the armchair again, her arms wrapped around her middle. She looked shaken and a little ill. Quickly, he crossed the room to her. "What is it?"

She shook her head. Just when he thought she wasn't going to respond any more than that, she whispered, "The photos were real?"

As he gazed down at her, the bad feeling in his gut solidified into certainty. Before, he had followed the evidence until it had broken him down. Now, despite all the evidence to the contrary, he knew she was telling the truth.

He didn't know how any of it had happened, but he knew one thing.

She had always been telling the truth.

"I believe you," he breathed. "I don't know how any of it happened, but I believe you."

Her reddened gaze lifted to his. There was so much grief in her expression, he knelt in front of her. She put her arms around his neck. He scooped her out of the chair and sat with her on his lap, and she hid her face in him.

Could she have been drugged or coerced? His mind ran through a series of possibilities, each one more extreme than the last. His arms clamped around her while his emotions raged out of control.

"Melly, I'm so sorry," he said from the back of his throat.

She pushed upright to look into his eyes. She looked fierce and determined. "You forgave me, and I forgave you. We're drawing a line and moving on, remember?"

His jaw clenched. He couldn't have felt more cut up if Justine had taken her knife to his insides. "But I forgave you for something you didn't do."

"You didn't know that, which makes it all the more precious to me. You genuinely forgave me. In fact, it sounds to me like you tried everything you could do to prove it wasn't true." She scrubbed her face with the back of one hand, her mouth turned down in an unhappy bow. "Tell me what the woman in the photos looked like."

He didn't want to go there, but her words took him back to the moment he pulled them out of the manila envelope. The images were burned into his mind. Reluctantly, he said, "She looked like you."

Her chin shook. "How long was her hair?"

"It was the length of your hair. It fell down her back, just like . . ." His eyes narrowed suddenly. "Why would you ask that?"

She laid a hand against his cheek. "Because I'm about to accuse my sister of doing something, and I don't know if I can forgive her for it."

"Oh, fuck me," he growled. As much as he had obsessed over what had happened, he had never considered that. "Everything pointed to you."

"I know." Her eyes reddened again. "Someone put effort into making that happen, didn't they?"

Quiet footsteps sounded outside in the hall. Gregoire said telepathically, *Sir, I'm very sorry to bother you.*

Turning his head toward the door, he asked, *What is it?*

First sentinel Graydon is here. Should I tell him that you and Miss Melisande are unavailable?

While he was tempted to say yes, Graydon had done a great deal for them in the last two days. Julian pressed a kiss to Melly's forehead and told her, "Graydon's downstairs. I need to have a word with him. Would you like to come, or should I go down by myself?"

Her expression changed. "I'll absolutely come down too. I need to thank him in person for everything he did."

"Okay." Switching to telepathy, he said to Gregoire, *Please tell him we'll be down in ten minutes.*

Very good, sir. I've placed a few clothes for Miss Melisande in front of the door, along with a replacement phone for you.

Thank you.

As his attendant's quiet footsteps receded, he and Melly looked at each other. Her loose braid had slipped out a little, and gentle curls framed her face. He brushed one back, marveling at the softness of her hair.

"I think it was worth getting kidnapped," she told him.

He raised his eyebrows. "Really? In spite of everything? The fear, the danger, and if what you believe is true, finding out about your sister?"

"Well, I'm not going to deny it, some of it really hurts right now. I need to hear the truth directly from Bailey, and I need to find out if my mom was involved in any of it. But in the end, it's so much better to know the truth about something rather than living a lie." She tilted her head. "And then there's you and me."

You and me. Not that long ago, he never would have conceived of saying those words.

"You better be sure about this," he said. "Because I'm not going to let you go again. I'm never going to doubt you.

I may not know anything else about what's going to happen, but I know that much is true."

A slow, sweet smile broke over her face. It turned a touch wry, which was purely Melly. "You can hold on to me as tight as you need, because I'll be holding on to you just as tightly. I'm okay with the future being an uncertain place. We'll figure things out. Answers to questions always come with time. But I know one thing, and I have to tell you right now—I am not going to live in Evenfall. I considered it for a while before, but that ship has sailed, soldier. There is too much drama that comes out of that zip code."

A ghost of a laugh shook through him. "Don't I know it."

He pulled her close for a deep kiss. It quickly turned urgent. He fell into the dark intimacy of her mouth while she grasped the back of his neck and arched to get closer.

As her breath shuddered against his lips, he forced himself to pull back. "It's okay," he murmured. "We have time now. We're going to get all the time we didn't get before, and then some. And we will, by God, carve a niche for ourselves out of the universe somehow. I'll fight the world to see that it happens, and damn anybody who tries to get in our way."

She let out a deep sigh, and the tight grasp at the back of his head eased. "I'll be fighting right by your side," she whispered. She slipped her legs out of his lap and stood. "I need to freshen up before I go down."

He rose to his feet. "Want me to wait for you?"

"No, that's okay. I don't want to keep Graydon waiting any longer than necessary. You go ahead. I'll be right there."

"All right."

While she went into the bathroom, he opened the door to the hall. A Saks bag waited on the floor, along with a smartphone. He tucked the phone into his pocket, took the clothes in to her, then went to slip on a T-shirt, socks and boots and headed downstairs.

Gregoire had shown Graydon into the library, a large, comfortable room that faced the north of the house. As Julian strode in, he glanced out the open windows at the sunny day. While he might have to contend with sunshine, so did Justine, along with any other Vampyre.

He wondered where she was sheltering for the day. The citywide search would have begun by now, but San Francisco was a massive place and it would take time. Too much time.

The city was also bordered by water. If she grew desperate, all she needed to do was slip into the Bay and swim away. She would have the strength and the stamina to reach the East Bay, or even Marin County, to the north, or further down the coast. She had no need to breathe, so she could stay underwater and undetected for miles.

The trick would be emerging from the water, but she could do it, if she had managed to acquire more sun-protective clothing and knew where to take shelter.

Graydon stood near one of the windows, looking out at the grounds, his tall, burly figure outlined against a backdrop of the green tended lawn and colorful flowerbeds. He turned as Julian entered the room.

The sentinel was dressed much as Julian was in tough, practical clothes, in a T-shirt, jeans and boots. He wore a gun in a shoulder holster, and a battered jean jacket lay tossed over the arm of a nearby chair.

Julian strode over to shake his hand. "Thanks for stopping by."

"Julian, I'm glad to see you're all right," Graydon said. "I got worried there for a little while, when I lost your trail at the museum."

"Melly is on her way down—she wants to thank you too for everything that you've done."

"It's my pleasure. I was glad to help." Graydon paused. "I'm about to head back to New York, but first I wanted to ask you something."

"What's that?"

"At the museum, your scent stopped on the sidewalk right at the place where there was a distinctive magical residue." The other man's keen, gray gaze studied his expression. "It was Djinn magic, wasn't it?"

"Yes," he said. "It was, and that particular Djinn is a nasty, malicious fucker."

"Was it someone named Malphas?"

"Yes, as a matter of fact, it was." Julian raised his eyebrows. "How did you know?"

Graydon turned away, looking out the window again. "Malphas and I go way back," he said grimly. "I recognized his magical footprint."

Julian paused as he took that in. He'd had no idea that individual Djinn could be detected by their magical footprints, or that Graydon had the ability to track at such a sophisticated level. It was never a good idea to underestimate the abilities of one of the Wyr sentinels.

"If you've had dealings with Malphas before, you have my sympathies," Julian said. He walked over to a liquor cabinet and poured himself a glass of bloodwine. "I suppose it's too early to offer you a glass of scotch."

"Hell, no. I haven't been to bed. Man, it's late for me."

With a chuckle, he splashed some scotch into a tumbler and walked it over to the other man. "I don't know how much you know of what happened."

"Tatiana filled me in on the bare bones." Nodding his thanks, he sipped his scotch.

"So you know that Justine kidnapped Melly."

"Yeah. That's fucked up."

"Malphas agreed to help Justine without an exchange of favors. He transported me to where she was holding Melly captive. He did it to retaliate for some things that have happened here recently." Julian tossed back his bloodwine. "We forced him into a bargain with Soren as a witness, and I don't think he took too kindly to it."

"But Malphas is a pariah," Graydon said slowly. "How do you know he'll honor that?"

Julian's eyes narrowed. Graydon seemed to be listening intently for his reply. Something about Julian's answer mattered a great deal to the other man.

"He'll keep this bargain. Malphas believes that Soren is

in possession of information that could be damaging to his interests. Xavier has a new attendant who used to work for Malphas. Tess gave Soren a sealed envelope. If anything happens to her, or to anyone in the Nightkind demesne for sheltering her, Soren opens the envelope and distributes the contents to all the gaming commissions in the world."

Julian shook his head as he remembered how Tess had bluffed with both Djinn. With a sleight of hand and a little misdirection, she had slipped a blank sheet of paper in the envelope and sealed it, while retaining the real information on another piece of paper. It had been an insanely gutsy move.

Slowly, Graydon lowered his glass. The sentinel's normally good-humored expression had turned sharp and cold. He said, "I would very much like to know what that information was."

Julian cocked his head. Sometimes you had to work for years to get a little payback. And sometimes the opportunity for payback fell in your lap out of a bright blue sky.

"Tess can never talk about the contents of the envelope she gave to Soren," he told the other man. "That was her side of the bargain. But I might have in my possession some other information about him, if you're interested."

"I am very much interested."

He warned, "If I give it to you, it can't be traced back to the Nightkind demesne. Malphas can't get the idea that Tess betrayed her end of the bargain. The threat of exposure is the only thing keeping her alive."

"That's a weighty decision," Graydon said. "I can understand why it would make you pause. All I can say from my end is I would never betray a confidence that put someone else in danger of retaliation, especially from Malphas."

Julian smiled at the unmistakable ring of truth in the other man's voice. Graydon had a decency that went bone deep. "I know you wouldn't."

Quick, light footsteps sounded. Both men turned as Melly came into the room. She wore soft, fleecy clothes and slippers, the dove gray outfit loose and comfortable. As soon as she caught sight of Graydon, a smile wreathed her face. She walked over to hug him.

She told him, "Thank you so much for coming to help look for me."

As a smile lit his rugged features, the sentinel patted her back. "It was nothing. I'm just glad to see you're all right."

"It was so totally not *nothing*." Melly smiled up at him. "And if there is anything I can ever do for you, please let me know."

The Wyr's expression gentled. "I'm not like the Djinn. I didn't help to collect favors."

"I know." Melly touched the back of his hand. "But I still mean it anyway. If you ever need anything."

Graydon said, "Thank you."

"That goes for me too," Julian said. As Graydon's gaze touched on him, he added telepathically, *I'll get you the intel by the end of the day.*

Something hard, ruthless and eager flashed in the other man's eyes. It was there only for a moment. If Julian hadn't been looking directly at him, he would have missed it entirely. Within an eye blink, Graydon looked as affable and good-natured as he ever did.

Yeah, Julian thought. I bet people underestimate you a lot, yet there's a reason why Dragos made you his First among all his sentinels.

Gregoire appeared and unobtrusively added a few bottles of bloodwine to the liquor cabinet. Telepathically, he said, *Mister Xavier will be arriving within the half hour, sir.*

Will he? Displeased, Julian frowned. Xavier was supposed to be on his estate, recuperating from the effects of the brodifacoum poisoning.

He mentioned something about updating you on the city-wide search. As quietly as he had arrived, Gregoire slipped out again.

Melly said to Julian, "Bailey texted. She'll be here in about an hour." She paused. "Did I forget to tell you Mom is sending me twenty troops?"

At the mention of her twin, her smile had faded and the skin around her eyes had grown tense.

"You're both very busy, and that's my cue to leave." Graydon bent to kiss Melly's cheek, scooped up his jean jacket in one hand and nodded to Julian. "I'll look to hear from you later about what we discussed."

"Count on it," said Julian.

"Good hunting."

As he watched the other man leave, he said softly, "You can count on that too."

⇒ FIFTEEN ⇐

He turned his attention back to Melly. Her expression was calm and self-contained, but she had wrapped her arms around her middle again. Her stance was so defensive, it made his chest ache just to look at her.

He thought of the laughter and closeness they had achieved in the bedroom for such a brief time, and he ground his teeth.

"I can't believe I'm going to say this," he muttered.

She looked at him. "Say what?"

Walking over to her, he tilted up her chin and kissed her. "Come sit with me."

She followed him as he walked to one of the sofas and sprawled at one end. "You're not mad about the troops, are you?"

He snorted and pulled her down beside him. "No. We're lucky if that's all your mother chooses to do. Frankly, I'm a little surprised she hasn't bombed Northern California yet, but that's probably because you're still here."

She chuckled. The sound was wan.

Hungry to touch her and to feel her in his arms again, he

pulled her against his chest. With a big sigh, she laid her head on his chest. He put his face into her soft hair. She smelled like his shampoo, and he loved that so damn much.

He said, "You don't have to confront Bailey right away, do you?"

She lifted her head to consider him. Her expression had turned grim. "What do you mean?"

"You love your sister. I know you do." He looked at her steadily. "Would you say that she loves you?"

A series of emotions flashed across her face. Fury, hurt, puzzlement. Even calculation. Finally, she said, "Yes, she loves me."

"Here's the thing," he told her. "While we may have pieced together some information today, in reality, everything happened over twenty years ago. The truth is, we don't know exactly why Bailey did what she did or if she regrets it. We don't even know for sure that she did it."

"She did it," Melly said. "You know it, and I know it. It's the simplest, most obvious explanation."

He sighed. "Okay. But the only thing we really know for certain is that it's old news. You can take time to think about things and decide what you want to say, or how you want to act. The past isn't going anywhere."

As he spoke, he took a curl and wound it around his finger. He loved to touch her. He simply loved it.

"Why are you saying all this?"

He responded slowly, so he could feel out his words. "Because you do love her, and because she loves you. If you and I can draw a line between now and what has happened in the past, maybe you can do that with her too." He shrugged. "If you want to."

She rubbed his chest, an absentminded caress that soothed his soul. A sense of well-being stole into him. He was enchanted at the exotic sensation. He and well-being . . . They were not well acquainted with each other.

After a few minutes, she asked, "What would you do?"

I would grind her bones to dust.

He was quite proud that he did not say it.

"That doesn't calculate," he said. "I don't have a twin with whom I've been connected all my life. Relationships are breakable, Melly. It would be smart for you to be sure you know what you want to do before you break them."

One corner of her mouth lifted. She cocked her head. "You're so adorable when you're being openhearted and wise."

His eyebrows shot up. "I can honestly say nobody has ever said that to me before."

"It was worth it just for the look on your face." She grinned, but it faded again quickly. More soberly, she said, "Thank you."

"You're welcome." He brushed his lips on her forehead.

"You would totally destroy her, wouldn't you?"

"Absolutely," he said without hesitation. "Her, along with anybody else who might have been involved."

Groaning, she collapsed so that her full weight lay on him.

Hooking an arm around her neck, he murmured, "But I can see how things might be different for you. After all, she's family. You have a golden opportunity, baby. Don't do as I do."

She stretched to kiss him lingeringly.

"Mmm," she murmured against his lips. "I want to stop thinking about other people. We have . . . What do we have, forty minutes before Bailey and the troops show up? We could do an awful lot in forty minutes, soldier. Dirty, dirty things."

The tip of her tongue tickled his lower lip in invitation. Instantly, he grew hard as a rock. He groaned against her mouth. "We have something closer to fifteen minutes, I'm afraid. Gregoire told me telepathically that Xavier will arrive very soon."

"What?!" She collapsed on him again.

"I'm a guy. I could totally make it happen in five minutes." He cupped her breast. She wasn't wearing a bra underneath her fleecy top, and the full softness of her round flesh filled his hand. As he molded and caressed her curves, she let out a shaking moan. Wickedly, he whispered in her ear, "We could cut loose, you know. Every man for himself. I look after my orgasm, you look after yours. Right here, right now. Quick and dirty."

As he talked, her breathing deepened. With a sexy roll of her hips, she ground her pelvis against his erection. She groaned, "Quick and dirty. Oh God, I could almost do it. No, I can't. Not down here. Xavier's such a gentleman—I *know* he knows about sex, but if we happened to get carried away, I really don't want him to see me like that."

"Upstairs," he growled.

She raised her head. Her beautiful eyes had glazed, and a dark wash of color tinged her cheeks.

Suddenly, she moved. Rolling off him, she raced for the hall.

For a second, he held frozen. He had been teasing.

A crack of laughter snapped through him, and he leaped after her. Even when he was young, he hadn't felt this young. Their mischievousness made him feel buoyant and recharged.

He pursued her up the stairs and into his suite. Once they were both inside, he slammed the door. She was already tearing off her top and kicking out of her pants. The feminine hourglass of her body was magnificent. The tuft of private hair at the juncture of her thighs was a dark gold, and her plump nipples were rosy pink.

He lost the impulse to laugh, and his need became aggressive. He didn't think he could ever get enough of her. Yanking the fastening of his jeans open, he snaked an arm around her waist and carried her to the wall, flipping her so that she faced away from him. A breathless whine broke out of her.

Pulling her back against him, he spooned her and whispered in her ear, "Is this okay?"

Nodding, she wriggled back against him. "You've got

some catching up to do, soldier," she gasped. "I'm starting without you."

That was when he realized she was fingering herself, bracing herself against the wall with one arm.

A growl ripped through him. With a greedy, irrational sense of jealousy for those fingers, he sank to his knees to watch her pleasure herself. She had a heart-shaped ass that was begging to be bitten. He rubbed his teeth along her skin, hissing with frustration. He had bitten her too many times already in the past few days.

Her hand moved rhythmically between her thighs. "Not fair," she gasped. "I'm seriously aching here. Where are you? You better not be jerking off down there."

He burst out laughing. She paused to give him a glare. Rising to his feet, he spooned her again, took her by the hips and knocked her feet wider apart. She collapsed against the wall even as she groped between her legs for him.

Grasping his penis, she arched her hips back and guided him into place. He pushed in.

Entering her from behind made him feel more massive than ever. She was so tight, so hot, clenching on him like a wet, velvet fist. He pressed his face into her hair and started to swear through clenched teeth.

Then he was all the way in. She caressed the base of his cock and his testicles. Her fingers were soaking with her own arousal. Her inner muscles tightened on him as she pushed back, fucking him as he fucked her. He was ecstatic to be inside her, and furious at the world.

"Why can't we find any time, goddammit?" he growled against her shoulder.

"I know," she gasped.

Never any time. They wasted so much time.

He had wasted so much time. *He* had done this to them.

Grasping a fistful of her long, luxurious hair, he shoved in and in, while her gorgeous body moved and flexed with the onslaught. He needed to suck on her nipples and nuzzle her breasts. He needed to lose himself in the beautiful folds of her flesh, tease that tiny, exquisite clitoris of hers, listen to her gasp in his ear, and whisper things she would never dream of saying to anybody else.

He needed to be surprised into laughter by the next thing that fell out of her mouth, and to shelter her from all harm.

This was not the quick and dirty sex he had been expecting.

Something burning fell out of his eyes and splashed onto her shoulder. She twisted, staring.

"Stop," she said.

He reacted immediately, pulling out. She flipped in his arms until she faced him. Whatever she saw in his expression caused her to fling her arms around his neck and cling to him.

He couldn't speak. In her head, he whispered, *I want to take back every ugly thing that ever came out of my mouth. I'm so sorry, Melisande.*

He sank down to his knees. She came down with him.

I'm so sorry too, she told him. *I got pissy because my feelings were hurt, and my pride was wounded. I didn't fight for you, and I should have. I promise you now, I'll always fight for you. I'll never let you fight alone again. Never.*

He could barely comprehend what she was saying. It almost didn't matter. He would be happy to listen to her read the phonebook.

She straddled his hips and guided him back inside her. She whispered, "We have all the time in the world now. Nothing else matters."

He took her mouth, kissing her as deeply as he could. He was desperate for her. The power of what he felt for her eclipsed everything else. He was probably leaving bruises. Jesus, he needed to get a hold of himself and ease up. She was the light of his life. He couldn't continue to act like such an animal.

Then she ground against his pelvis and shook all over. She clawed at him and bit at his neck and jawline, and she was so gleefully savage about her own climax, he forgot everything that had just run through his mind, gripped her by the hips and exploded into her tight, welcoming sheath.

Afterward, he realized he was breathing heavily. Fine tremors shook through his muscles. She rubbed her cheek against his, nuzzling him with her eyes closed.

"You know what I miss?" she whispered. "Lake Tahoe. You remember how beautiful it was that winter? We closed out the world."

"I bought the cabin we stayed in," he confessed.

Her head snapped up, eyes flaring wide. "You *own* it?"

He nodded as he smoothed her hair off her forehead. "I never use it. I keep thinking I might go up there. Take some time off and see if I can remember how to fish. Then I've never gone. Why should I bother to learn how to fish? It's not like I can eat them. And something or other keeps cropping up. Truthfully, I didn't want to go back without you."

She took his hand and kissed the palm. "Let's go. Soon as we get done dealing with stupid Justine and all the stupid problems she's caused." She frowned. "Unless the cabin's a dilapidated mess by now. After all, it's been a long time."

He waved that away. "There's a caretaker that keeps up the property. I sank some money into some renovations not that long ago. Every once in a while they ask if I'll rent it out, but then I think again about going up there, so I always tell them no." He smiled into her eyes. "We'll go as soon as we can."

She smiled back. "You can relearn how to fish, and I'll eat them." She frowned. "Wait, let me revise that. You can relearn how to fish and clean them, and I'll cook and eat them. How's that?"

He laughed. "You've got a deal."

Then his smile faded. "This time we're going to do it right. We'll learn how to be with each other again, and we won't let anybody else come between us."

Leaning forward, she pressed a kiss on his shoulder. "And we'll make love in front of the fireplace all night long. I'll take a pile of books that I've been meaning to read forever."

"I'll watch sports on TV," he said.

They looked at each other. Grinning, she shook her head. "No, you won't."

Chuckling, he replied, "You're right. I probably won't."

Stroking her thigh, he thought ahead. He needed to contact the caretaker to make sure the cabin was cleaned. Maybe they would also stock the kitchen with food.

He knew that he and Melly were glossing over many challenges. The truth was, many people were going to dislike their liaison now—just as many as had disliked it before. Some people in the Nightkind demesne would be looking to take advantage of a closer relationship with the Light Fae in Southern California, but several would oppose it. Saboteurs were likely.

But they would make it work. They had to make it work. As he had said before, he would fight the world for her. He might not be able to leave the Nightkind demesne, but as long as Melly could tolerate that, they could make a life for themselves.

His new phone buzzed. Giving her a quick kiss, he eased away, and they both climbed to their feet. He dug into his pocket, pulled out the phone, and checked the screen. Xavier had texted him.

He told her, "Xavier's downstairs."

She nodded, looking unsurprised. Moving quickly, they both cleaned up. Julian straightened his clothes, while she dressed again. Just as he was about to open the door, she paused.

"You go ahead," she told him. "I have something I need to do first."

His mind had leaped ahead to the search, so he kissed her. "Join us when you can."

She nodded. He left, loping down the stairs. It was past time to locate and stake Justine, so they could get on with their lives.

As soon as Julian had left, Melly walked over to the armchair and collapsed into it. As she did so, the metal shutters on the bedroom windows quietly eased up, revealing the bright, sunny day outside. The shutters worked as discreetly as the rest of the household. Julian had a full house of attendants, but they were well trained and unobtrusive. The only attendant she had seen so far was Gregoire.

Now that she was alone, without the buffer of Julian's powerful presence to focus on, all the many emotions she had been avoiding came crashing in.

Desultorily, she inspected the food tray again and nibbled on cheese and a few grapes as she worked to collect her thoughts. While she appreciated everything Julian had said earlier, she honestly didn't know if she could look Bailey in the face without plunging into a heated confrontation.

And she didn't have time to reflect and settle on a course of action. Bailey was due to arrive within the next half hour.

At least, Melly could settle one question right away. Taking her phone, she tapped out her mother's number.

Tatiana answered on the first ring. "Melly. Are you all right? Has Bailey arrived?"

"No, not yet. She'll be here soon." Melly was gripping the phone too tightly again. "Mom, I have to ask you something. I know it's going to seem like it's coming out of nowhere, but . . . did you have anything to do with Julian's and my breakup?"

"Did I what? I would never do anything to hurt you like that. If I felt like you shouldn't have been with Julian, I would have told you so directly." Her voice hardened. "He isn't trying to claim such a thing, is he?"

"No, not at all." Tatiana was not above manipulation if it suited her purposes, which was why Melly had to ask her, but it was really good to hear the sincerity in her mom's voice. Relief made Melly feel lighter and more clearheaded. She rubbed her forehead. "We recently discovered some things, and I just needed to ask. I hope I didn't hurt your feelings."

"Don't concern yourself with that. What things did you discover?"

"I'll have to explain everything later. Right now I don't have time." She paused, thinking. "How did you feel about Julian when we were together? You never said anything at the time. I know you've been really angry with him."

"He hurt you badly, and I never forgot or forgave that. But when you originally got together, I was guarded yet willing to be open-minded about the prospect. As long as he treated you well, and you were happy, I could be happy for you." Her mother's voice turned dry. "And, of course, there were potential advantages."

Biting back a smile, she said, "Of course."

"Are you and he involved again? Because if you are, I have to tell you, he has got to work damn hard to make up for everything that happened."

"I'll make sure he knows that," she told her mother. "And yes, we are romantically involved again. Please try to keep an open mind. We were manipulated into breaking up. What happened before wasn't all his fault."

Tatiana's voice turned cold and crisp. "Not true. You are my daughter. I raised you, and I know better than anyone what a good and generous heart you have. He should have had faith in you, no matter what."

"Thank you," she murmured. It was clearly going to take some time to build some bridges.

"I will say this much." The reluctance in Tatiana's voice was clear. "When we discovered you were missing, and I called to ask him to come, he did so without hesitation. And as you said, he tried to exchange himself for you, so I'll grant him a small amount of leeway. Very small, Melly. Very, very small."

"Understood." She smiled. "Listen, I'd better go. I'll talk to you soon, okay?"

"All right, darling. Be safe."

"I will."

Disconnecting, she blew out a breath. At least her immediate family hadn't conspired together to take a wrecking ball to her love life, so there was that.

No, she was beginning to think that Bailey might have acted on her own. Hotheaded, impulsive Bailey who lived hard, broke the rules, and who had once called Julian a bloodsucking boneheaded bastard.

Had Ferion been a willing participant, or had he thought he was just playing a little sex game when Bailey whipped out a wig?

Oh, that was downright skeevy. Melly made a face. She was going to have to break her fist on his face too, the next time she saw him.

Slipping on the slender, new house shoes that Gregoire had purchased for her, she took one more bite of cheese and headed out of the suite.

Following the sound of voices, she made her way through the downstairs level to Julian's study. The room was darker than the rest of house, heavy on traditional décor, with wood paneling, oak floors, an imported Persian rug and a massive mahogany desk. A small sitting area with plain, cream furniture took up one end of the room.

As she entered, she found Julian and Xavier leaning over a street map that had been spread out on the surface of his desk. A young, dark-haired human woman with striking, angular features sat in the sitting area, listening to the men's conversation with an intent expression.

After giving the unknown woman a curious glance, Melly focused on Xavier and Julian.

Xavier was the perfect example of how looks could be deceiving. While he appeared to be a pleasant, somewhat nondescript young man in his early twenties, in reality he was a Powerful Vampyre at least four hundred years old, a gentleman to his core, and a deadly fighter.

Beside Julian's larger, more muscular build, Xavier appeared almost delicate to Melly's eyes. It was another deception. His slim build contained a steely strength.

The occupants in the room looked up as she entered.

She went straight to Xavier, who stepped forward to give her a hug. He told her, "Melly, I am so glad you're all right."

She took note of how stiffly he moved. Normally he did everything with a liquid, panther-like grace. She tightened her arms around him with care. "I feel the same way about you. Thank God you're all right."

He gave her a small, grave smile. "I'd like you to meet Tess. She is my . . ." His voice trailed off, and he looked at the woman in some consternation.

Tess raised an eyebrow at him. Her intelligent expression turned humorous. "Your girlfriend?"

He laughed. "Yes, she is my girlfriend."

Melly's gaze lingered on his expression. Despite the evident pain of his condition, and the serious reasons why he had come to Julian's house, he was lit with happiness.

She told Tess, "I'm delighted to meet you. Anyone who is important to Xavier is important to me."

The other woman gave her a shy smile. "Thank you. I'm delighted to meet you too."

"Tess saved my life," Xavier said. "If she hadn't known what to do and acted so quickly, the poison would have killed me."

"All the more reason to welcome you," Melly told her, returning her smile. Having finished with the pleasantries, she turned to Julian. "What do we know? How is the search going?"

His hard face was tight with frustration. "Too slowly," he growled. "The only thing we've achieved so far is keeping pressure on her—at least I hope so. The problem is, whenever I make a countermove against her, she escalates to doing something else. Each time it gets more extreme. The last time she kidnapped you."

"What about the helicopter you heard?" Melly asked as she looked from one male to the other.

Xavier shook his head. He said in his quiet, pleasant voice, "We've confirmed at least a dozen helicopter flights today alone. We're looking into each one, but that takes time."

Julian planted one fist on the top of his desk. "The one great advantage that any criminal has is that they can move quickly. Investigations take time. The fact is, we aren't going to get her with the citywide search. It's logical, methodical, and it's not moving fast enough. We have to get in front of this. We have to make an intuitive leap to where she is going next and be waiting for her when she gets there."

Closing her eyes, Melly pinched the bridge of her nose in an effort to think. Then she looked at Julian. "Justine said it, down in the tunnels. It's all about you. Everything she has done has been about you."

"Well," he replied dryly, "it might have sounded good in theory, but she said that to needle me, and it isn't exactly true."

Suddenly Tess spoke up. "What she really wants is power. Every time someone acts to check her behavior, she lashes out. Xavier was surveilling her, so she killed his operative and tried to get rid of him as well. Same thing with Julian. Even killing all of her attendants was a massive, monstrous *fuck you*." The human looked around the room. "I mean, come on. How likely was it that she let something slip that one of them would have overheard?"

"Can't argue with that," said Julian.

"Miss Melisande," said Gregoire from the doorway. "Your sister and the Light Fae troops have arrived."

Melly pivoted on one heel. Until that moment, she'd honestly had no idea how she was going to act, but maybe she'd only been fooling herself, because something switched in her brain, and everything became crystal clear, as if etched in ice.

"Thank you," she said to Gregoire. "Please show Bailey to the library. I'll be there momentarily."

Telepathically, Julian asked, *Want me to come?*

She glanced over her shoulder. *I've got this.*

He assessed her with that wolflike gaze of his, then gave her a nod. *If you need me, I'm here.*

At that, she had to smile. She told him, *I'll always need you.*

His face gentled, then Xavier called his attention back to the map.

Watching them, she came to an abrupt decision.

Come to think of it, she wasn't going to wait for Gregoire to show Bailey to the library. Melly would already be there, waiting for her sister to arrive.

≈ SIXTEEN ≈

When she reached the library, she headed straight for the liquor cabinet.

She had been fantasizing about having a piña colada for a long time. She might not get the chance to have one for a while, but for now, she could at least knock back something. Her days and nights were fucked up anyway, and you know it was five o'clock somewhere, baby.

Choosing a decanter at random, she splashed a finger of amber liquid into a tumbler and tossed it back.

Cognac. Unless she missed her guess, a high-end Courvoisier.

That would do nicely. She poured herself another.

Quick footsteps sounded in the doorway. She turned as Bailey entered the room. Bailey wore jeans, a short-sleeved T-shirt, a denim vest and a gun in a waist holster. Her short, curly hair was tousled as usual, and her face was etched with stress.

Even though they were identical twins, to Melly, looking at Bailey had never been like looking in a mirror. They, of all people, knew quite well the characteristics that made them unique.

Bailey was a touch leaner, her face more angular. Melly was fit and active, but Bailey was driven to athleticism. She exceled at using several different weapons, whereas Melly was perfectly content to be merely competent.

Melly's lips were fuller, her eyes a shade darker, and she had a dimple in one cheek that appeared whenever she laughed.

Still, when she looked at Bailey, she felt like she did when she looked at her mother. Whatever else had happened, Bailey had always been a fact of her existence. Melly had never known life without her. They had grown up together, had loved each other, played together and fought like cats and dogs.

As Melly regarded her twin now, pain and anger surged up so that she couldn't speak.

Bailey's expression lightened. She rushed forward to throw her arms around her.

Melly almost struck her in the breastbone with the flat of her hand to drive her back. Almost, but in spite of everything, she couldn't bring herself to raise her hand against her sister.

Melly couldn't return her hug either, so she stood stiffly in Bailey's embrace.

"Thank the gods," Bailey said in her ear. "I haven't been able to eat or sleep. I've felt sick to my stomach for three days."

Yes, Melly knew her sister loved her. That was why her emotions were in such a tangle.

Bailey pulled back and searched Melly's face with a frown. Melly knew her expression had to be as stiff as the rest of her body.

After a hesitation, Bailey asked, "Are you all right?"

Melly said abruptly, "You need to know Julian and I are back together."

All the confirmation she needed was there in her sister's face. A combination of dismay and guilt darkened Bailey's gaze. "How can you consider getting back with him? He treated you so badly when you broke up."

Melly gave her a steady, cold look. "Well, he had reasons, didn't he?"

Comprehension flashed across Bailey's expression. Her gaze fell. She muttered, "I—I don't know what to say."

"Admitting the truth would have been nice," said Melly, taking a step back. "Anytime, say, over the last twenty years. Of course it would have been so much better if you hadn't done anything to begin with, but that water is long under the bridge, isn't it?"

A dark flush of color washed over Bailey's cheekbones, and wetness glittered in her eyes. "I wanted to tell you. I thought about telling you so many times. If I could have taken it back, I would have. It was a stupid thing to do."

She bit out, "You think?"

"Ferion and I were hanging out, talking about all the shit that was going to happen if the Light Fae and the Nightkind demesnes came together. We cooked the whole thing up when we got drunk—and you wouldn't listen whenever I tried to point out what an asshole Julian was, and how you deserved so much better than him. . . . And I didn't realize how much it was going to hurt you. I didn't know how deeply you'd fallen in love with him. You'd only been together three months."

"Bailey," she interrupted sharply. The stream of words pouring out of Bailey's mouth cut off. "I didn't ask you for excuses or justification. The only thing I'm interested in hearing you say right now is *I am really so fucking sorry.* If you can't do at least that much, we have nothing more to say to each other."

They stared at each other.

Bailey whispered, "I am really so fucking sorry, Melly."

Now wetness dampened her gaze too. She pressed her lips tight.

After a moment, she nodded. "Okay," she said hoarsely. "I love you, and I promise, one day I'm going to forgive you, and you and I are going to be all right. But I'm not there today, and we're only going to be okay if you promise to get over how you feel about Julian and accept that he's in my life. You got that?" She stared at Bailey hard. "Because if you can't do that much, I don't want to see you again. And the thought of that really breaks my heart." Her face clenched. "Don't break my heart, Bailey. Not again."

"I wouldn't," Bailey said, very low. "I won't. I love you too."

She nodded again and wiped her eyes. "Okay," she said again. "We'll put this behind us. For now, go home. I'll get in touch when I'm ready to talk again. Don't expect to hear from me for a couple of months. I need some time."

Bailey took a quick step forward, her face crumpling. "Don't send me away. I've been in hell. I only just found out this morning that you were okay. Let me stay to help."

"Not this time, kiddo," she said quietly.

Bailey's obvious distress finally loosened Melly's limbs, and she felt able to pull her sister into a hug. Bailey clung to her.

"I really hate this," her twin muttered.

Yeah well, you should have considered that before you stabbed me in the back.

Melly thought it, but managed not to say it. As Julian had said, relationships are breakable.

She pulled away. "There's a reason why I need to take some time."

"Fine. Damn it. I understand. I'll be waiting to hear from you." Bailey swiped at her nose with the back of one hand. "Mom sent Shane, and he can captain the other troops. They have your gear with them."

"All right, thanks," she said.

Reluctantly, Bailey backed up. She whispered, "I really am sorry."

Melly had to turn away from the pleading in Bailey's gaze. Her emotions were too powerful and contradictory.

"I hear you," she said. It was the best reply she could offer.

"Melly," Julian said from the doorway.

He strode into the room, sweeping past Bailey without acknowledging her presence or giving her a second glance. Bailey hesitated only briefly before leaving.

Julian strode across the room toward Melly, his face and body tight with fury.

"What's happened?" Her heart kicked. She searched his face. "Justine's done something else, hasn't she?"

He shoved his phone into her hands. She looked at the screen.

There was a text message highlighted, from Gavin.

A single word.

Help.

Staring at it, she shook her head. Her thoughts felt slow moving, like a mudslide. "I don't understand. Gavin's the Nightkind government IT guy, right? Isn't he in Evenfall?"

"Exactly," Julian growled. "*He's in Evenfall.*"

He spun to go back the way he had come.

Shoving the meeting with her sister aside until she could think about it later, Melly followed on his heels. Back in Julian's office, Xavier paced stiffly as he spoke on his phone. Tess sat at Julian's desk, tapping furiously on the keyboard.

When Xavier caught sight of Julian, he clicked off his phone and pocketed it.

He said, "I can't confirm one way or another. One of the helicopters sighted this morning in the city could have been Dominic's, but it might not have been. And nobody's answering either of the secure lines at Evenfall."

As Tess stared at Julian's desktop screen, she spoke up. "The server appears to be down, which isn't exactly news with the blackout in place. Most likely, Gavin sent that text using a hotspot in his phone."

Xavier said quietly, "It's possible the telecommunications cables have been sabotaged."

Tess swiveled away. "The simplest way to create a blackout is to power down the servers. If they're turned off and unplugged, they can't be used or hacked, but that's an easy fix. If somebody has cut the cables, then it will take a couple of days and repairmen to bring them back online." She sounded frustrated. "Which is a shame, because if they were operational, I could try to patch into security footage to get some visuals from the camera feeds inside the castle."

Julian's expression turned violent. "And Gavin can't act independently to turn them on again without my express permission, because I gave him a direct order. He would have had to work against himself to get that one text out. I've texted him back to tell him to turn the servers back on, but now he's not answering. Goddammit."

The mudslide in Melly's head might be moving slowly, but it was as inevitable as a train wreck. She ran her fingers through her hair and scrubbed at her scalp. "If Dominic and Justine have teamed up, your people are in danger."

Xavier said, "Their main priority will be to take the IT and munitions area, which is separate from the rest of the castle. Once they have control over the technology and the weaponry, they can take care of everybody else at their leisure."

"Yolanthe is in there, along with troops who are loyal to me." Julian looked at Melly. "They won't surrender. They'll be fighting, and they'll be among the first casualties. I've got to go in to help them."

She moved close to him and touched his hand. "You're not going in without me."

His fingers curled around hers. He said telepathically, *This has turned into a much bigger issue than simply going after Justine. You don't have to do this. In a very real way, it's not your fight.*

She told him, *You can knock that shit right out of your head, soldier. If you're going to be in danger, then yes, it is too my fight. I know I'm not your equal as a fighter. I'm a relatively young Light Fae, and I would have to devote several hundred more years of my life to achieve that as a goal. But I can be your partner in other ways.*

I know you can. He squeezed her hand. *I saw that for myself, down in the tunnels. If it hadn't been for you, we wouldn't be free right now.*

Giving him a quick smile, she switched to speaking aloud. "How are we going to go in? They'll be watching the helipad, and they can shoot down anybody who tries to fly in and land."

Julian smiled back. As he still looked furious, the combination was chilling.

He told her, "Carling and I built Evenfall. I know ways in and out of that place that nobody else does. I'll get us in."

Xavier said, "We have to move fast. What kind of force can we put together quickly?"

Julian switched his attention to the younger man. "I have fifteen here at the house."

"Mom sent me twenty troops, including Shane," Melly told them. Shane alone was worth at least five other fighters in battle. "I haven't had a chance to inspect them, but I know they'll be some of our best. My sister would have been in that total. I just sent her home again, so I have nineteen."

"My estate is so close, I can get six to meet us," Xavier said.

"No." Julian pointed at Xavier. "You're no good in a fight right now. You're out. It's uncomfortable just to watch you move. It's one thing if you're forced to defend yourself, but that's different from choosing to go into active combat."

Xavier's face tightened in frustration, but Melly noted how Tess's tension eased.

The younger Vampyre said, "I'm not only close with Gavin and Yolanthe. I have other friends in Evenfall too."

"None of them would want you to risk your life, not when you're still recuperating. I rarely give you a direct order, but this isn't open for discussion, Xavier." Julian paused. "For this conflict, you may do anything you can to help, except go into battle yourself. Understood?"

The younger Vampyre bowed his head. "Yes, sir."

Julian turned incisive. "I count forty-two. That's Melly and her nineteen, me and my fifteen, and the six from Xavier. That's a good, fast strike force. Any more would be difficult to take on the route we're going to use to get in." He thought for a moment. "We'll leave in fifteen minutes. Do what you have to do to get ready. Xavier, get your six deployed. I want an advance scout to check out the grounds around Evenfall. If I were Dominic, I would set an outside guard around the perimeter. Make sure your people focus on the northeast side.

We'll be using a tunnel entrance in the forest. Tell them to get as close as they can for reconnaissance but not to take any unnecessary chances."

"Yes, sir," Xavier said again. Drawing out his cell phone, he walked out of the room.

Julian looked at Tess, who watched him with a fascinated gaze. "We need to make sure we have transportation for those we have here. Make it happen."

"Yes, sir." Tess bolted out of the room.

Once they were alone, Julian took Melly's hands and pulled her around to face him. "About your sister."

She shook her head. "It's not important right now."

He cupped her cheeks and turned her face up to him. "It *is* important. Tell me quickly if you're okay, and I'll let it go."

"I'm okay," she told him. She curled her hands around his thick wrists, drawing comfort from his touch. "I told her I needed space, and I would get in touch with her in a few months. I also said she needed to get over the fact that you and I are together again if she wants to continue to have a relationship with me."

"If she loves you, she'll get over it," he said. The gentleness in his hands belied the grim set to his mouth. He kissed her forehead. "She's not my favorite person right now, but so will I. Eventually."

"I think she will," she replied. "Get over it, I mean. For what it's worth, I also think she deeply regrets what she did."

"That's something."

His reply was so studiously neutral, she narrowed her eyes at him. "She also could have confessed at any damn time during the last twenty years, so that's the other thing."

His expression turned dry. "Well, yes."

She lifted up to kiss him, and his hard lips softened to caress hers. Pleasure stole into her, and like everything else good that had happened between them over the last couple of days, she grabbed onto it with all her might.

She murmured against his mouth, "I'm glad we got that quickie."

"Me too," he whispered.

Reluctantly, she drew back. "You have things to do, and I'd better brief Shane and the others so we can leave on time."

She watched the battle commander come to the fore in his expression. The intelligence in his gaze was sharp enough to cut steel.

Damn, that was hot.

He glanced at a clock on the mantel of the fireplace. "Ten minutes."

"We'll be ready."

She went to find out where Gregoire had stashed her troops. Even though the mansion was capacious, there were actually very few places where nineteen guards could wait comfortably.

She found them in the massive dining room. Gregoire and his staff had moved quickly. Large trays of sandwiches dotted the long, gleaming table. Most of the food was already gone.

As soon as the men and women saw her, they came to their feet. She knew all of them, and their relieved smiles lit her heart. She said, "Good morning. Thank you for coming."

Shane strode forward to hug her. "It's wonderful to see you."

He was a tall man, even for the Light Fae, with a muscular build and a strong, contained Power. He kept his tawny hair clipped short, which emphasized his lean jaw, high cheekbones and somewhat blunt, puckish nose.

In repose, he had a stern grace that was balanced with a bright, ready smile, and he was one of the most dangerous magic users she had ever met. One of Melly's favorite things to do as a child had been to ride on his shoulders, and she loved him like an uncle.

"It's so good to see you too," she told him. Her gaze swept the others in the room. "It's good to see all of you. Now, eat fast. We're about to go to war."

The atmosphere in the room sharpened, as if she had unsheathed a gigantic sword.

. . .

Once Julian was alone, he shut the office door. Then he leaned both hands on the door panel and hung his head. Days ago, he had reached some kind of breaking point, and shit still kept happening. It pushed him somewhere uncharted. He had to figure out how to navigate through the strange landscape he found himself in.

Yes, relationships were breakable.

He wasn't surprised that Dominic might have considered both sides of the Nightkind dispute. Dominic was, after all, primarily a mercenary and experienced at choosing the option that gained him the greatest advantage.

No, what surprised Julian was that he had believed Dominic would pick him.

Trust could be broken. So could faith.

At that, Julian's thoughts inevitably shifted to Melly. Inevitably, because he always thought of Melly now.

Somehow she had walked a line with her sister. Without trashing everything, she had stood up for herself and had made her needs clear. Bailey might choose to ignore them, but if she did, she would be the one who broke the relationship, not Melly. In spite of how angry and hurt Melly had been, she held true.

She had also shown him how to win free of an impossible situation. Just like down in the tunnels, when she had picked the locks and freed them both with almost nothing but ingenuity and perseverance.

In his bedroom, he had been faced with two impossible choices. Like a classic riddle, both led to failure, until Melly reached out past all self-protectiveness and kissed him.

She was a goddamn Houdini, was what she was.

He pinched the bridge of his nose. He had been born and bred to win, no matter what the cost. He fought dirty because he fought for survival, not for any moral code or sense of honor. He threw sand in the face, kicked his opponent in the balls and went for the jugular.

That didn't always gain him a victory.

The truth was, he was a dark creature in heart as well as in body. He was always standing at midnight.

He lifted his head. Maybe he could make different choices.

Maybe he could get in front of this and change his life, but in order to do so, he would need to make an intuitive leap.

He opened and closed his hands. What he needed to do lay right in front of him, waiting for him to get there.

Breathing hard, he pulled out his phone and punched out a number. He listened to ringing. A fine tremor ran through him. He felt sick with anticipation.

On the other end of the connection someone picked up. Carling said, "Hello?"

His sire's voice was as familiar to him as his own. They had, after all, known each other for centuries.

He sounded raw to his own ears. "You were tearing me apart with your contradictions. Ordering me to do this, then that. You weren't safe for anyone to be around. You made promises and you broke them. You were going to stay on your island where you couldn't do any more damage. Then you left."

Time passed. It felt like years, but it might have been mere moments.

Carling said, "Yes, I did. All of that is true."

His stomach clenched as he waited for her to take control of him. Not every sire could do so over a phone connection, but he was willing to bet Carling could.

Instead, she said in a soft, steely tone, "When I was fighting for my life, you tried to imprison me. You tried to have me killed. You banished me from the demesne I had created."

Looking up at the ceiling, he admitted, "Yes, I did."

Someone knocked on the door. He told whoever it was, "I need five minutes. Don't disturb me. I'll come out when I'm ready."

"No problem," said Xavier.

Julian listened to the younger Vampyre walk away.

"Why are you calling, Julian?" Carling sounded as cool and dark as an ancient river at twilight.

"I wanted to say I'm sorry." He was shocked to find that his eyes were stinging, and he rubbed them. He was too old for this touchy-feely shit. He gritted his teeth. "I heard you were doing well, and I wanted to tell you I'm glad. I learned a lot from you, and we worked well together for a long time. I trusted my sire to have my back, and to fight for me when I needed it. You did all of that, until toward the end when you couldn't anymore."

Her voice gentled. "You were my best, brightest progeny. I was proud of you."

"I need for you to set me free," he whispered. "I can't keep following the old orders you gave me. Once you asked if I wanted to become the Nightkind King. I said yes, and you set me to rule in your place, but that happened over two hundred years ago. Now . . . it's a leash on my soul that never goes away."

After a long pause, she sighed. "If I try to revoke an order that old over the phone, it might not take. Rune and I will have to come to you. Is that acceptable?"

Relief ran like sunshine through his body. "Yes," he told her. "But it's going to have to wait until after I kill Dominic and Justine."

"What?" The end of the word snapped like the tip of a whip. "Is that why you invoked martial law?"

In spite of everything, Julian had to smile.

"Justine tried to kill Xavier," he told Carling. "She slaughtered her household, kidnapped Melly, tried to kill me, and now she and Dominic are fighting to occupy Evenfall, but none of that is why I called you. Melly and I have gotten back together. She's helped me think of a lot of things in a different light, including you. And I need to be free to make real choices for a future with her. Maybe that includes ruling the Nightkind demesne, but maybe it doesn't." He shook his head. "I can make that decision after I turn the traitors to dust."

Their connection grew muffled, as if she had put her hand over the receiver. Still, Julian distinctly heard Carling say, "I made that demesne. I can bring it down if it misbehaves."

In the background, Rune said, "No, darling Carling."

"Damn it, Rune."

"We aren't going to storm a castle today. This isn't your fight."

"Oh fine," she snapped. The connection became clearer as she spoke into the phone again. "Call me when you're finished cleaning house. As soon as you're ready for us to come, I'll say these words in person. Until then, Julian Regillus, you are free of any obligation to the Nightkind demesne save those you choose for yourself. Your future will be what you make of it, and no longer what I order."

Did the leash on his soul lift, or did he just imagine it? It was impossible to tell for sure.

He said quietly, "Thank you."

"Melly's good people," Carling said. "She made you happy, and I'm glad you and she are together again. Give her my best."

"I will."

He disconnected, considering.

The conversation had gone so much better than he had expected. Almost, he thought, as if Carling had been waiting for him all this time to reach out to her.

Things could never be the same between them, and he wouldn't want them to be. There was only so much that could be done to repair something that became so broken.

Or maybe he was wrong. He'd been wrong a lot.

In the meantime, people who loved him despite all his shortcomings were waiting for him on the other side of the door.

Blurring into quick movement, he went to his weapons cabinet, hidden discreetly behind a wall panel. The cabinet also held sun-protective clothing and custom-fitted body armor.

He donned the clothing and armor, strapped his sword to

his back, and fastened on a gun belt with automatic weapons and extra ammo. Carrying gloves and a hood, he strode out.

Personal growth was damn hard work. It also took a lot of time, so it was going to have to take a backseat for a while.

Because right now, he had a battle to fight and Vampyre ass to kick.

⇒ SEVENTEEN ⇐

The woods that blanketed much of Marin County were some of the most beautiful in the world. Populated with massive redwoods and rich in land magic, the forest floor was dark and shaded enough so that the Vampyres in the group could pull off their hoods and walk in safety.

Julian stayed by Melly's side so he could spend as much time as he could with her. Like him, she wore fitted body armor and weapons. Despite carrying what he knew must be a good forty pounds in extra weight, she moved easily and with grace. She had braided her hair and rolled it into a tight bun at the base of her neck. It emphasized the graceful arch of her neck and the elegant bone structure of her face.

Much of the time, Melly greeted the world with a good-humored smile and a twinkle. Experienced at being in the public eye, she knew how to work the red carpet for movie premieres, and she made it easy for people to believe in her movie starlet persona.

Now as he looked at her, there could be no doubt—she was every bit Tatiana Aindris's daughter and the Light Fae heir.

They didn't have time to talk. Julian led them through the woods at a punishing pace. No matter how fast they deployed, every moment in a battle seemed to take forever, and he was all too conscious of what might be happening inside Evenfall.

Xavier's people joined them a few at a time. Led by Xavier's head of security, Raoul, the advance scout confirmed that while troops dotted the land close to Evenfall's walls, there was no sign of Dominic's forces this far into the woods.

Xavier himself had insisted on coming along. While Julian had forbade him from volunteering to go into battle, as he pointed out, accompanying the group through the woods was something else entirely, and Julian hadn't the heart to stop him. He had a challenging time keeping up with the rest of the force, but he did so with grim determination, and Tess never left his side.

Finally they reached the area that Julian had been looking for, a broken patch of high, rocky ground covered with moss and ferns.

He said telepathically to Melly, *This entrance has been secret ever since the castle was originally built. You can only use something like this effectively once.*

She looked around the area, her expression curious. *If there's any time to blow a secret, this is it.*

He nodded, turned to face the others and ordered, "Come in close."

The troops drew near, keeping their attention on his face.

He told them, "I have only one objective. I'm not going to let them take Evenfall. If I have to napalm the inside of those walls, I'm going to do it. That means we need to split into two groups. One will be with me. We'll be on the offensive. Another group needs to focus on evacuating noncombatants."

Melly said, "I'll lead that team. I'll take ten of my people to work on the evacuation." Her gaze told him she wasn't happy about the two of them splitting up, but she accepted the need for it.

His attention shifted to Shane. He said telepathically to

the other man, *As soon as Melly's presence becomes known, she could become a target again. Justine kidnapped her for a reason.*

The Light Fae captain replied, *The Queen's orders are that I'm to do anything Melly says, except leave her side. Today my goal in life is to make sure that the Light Fae heir remains safe.*

Relief lifted a weight off his shoulders. He told the other man, *That's more than acceptable to me.*

Aloud, he said to the group, "This tunnel leads to my suite. The passage is narrow, so my team will go first. Once we get inside, we're not going to wait, so the strongest fighters in the second team need to follow directly afterward."

The last person he looked at was Xavier, who told him, "Tess and I will come to the suite. Even if the cables were cut, the internal network might be operational. If it is, we'll be able to assess where the fighting is and communicate with people in the IT area." His mouth tightened. "If that's acceptable to you."

He considered the younger Vampyre with a narrowed gaze. Xavier was pushing right up to the edge of Julian's orders, but the reality was, not only would the suite be heavily protected, it shouldn't become the focus of any of the fighting. And Xavier and Tess could potentially do a lot of good from that position.

He said, "Excellent."

Turning to the broken, rocky rise, he located the door hidden deep underneath years of moss and ferns, and heaved it open.

Then, despite the fact they had forty witnesses, he stepped to Melly and pulled her close for a hard, deep kiss.

Honey, I'm going to war, he said in her head. *So put out, will you?*

She burst out laughing against his mouth. Throwing her arms around his neck, she kissed him back with all the passion and enthusiasm he could have hoped for, and much more than he had expected in front of their audience.

After spending so many years in the army, he had no shame.

What he had forgotten was, after her years of acting in front of cameras, she had no shame either.

Melly hadn't realized how hard it would be for her to step into the tunnels.

After all, this wasn't the same place where Justine had committed her atrocities. Melly was no longer imprisoned. There were no ferals, no piles of corpses, no would-be rapists. A team of experienced, deadly soldiers surrounded her and Julian, and everybody carried a flashlight, so the tunnel would be well lit for yards around.

None of those details made any difference. As soon as it was her turn to step below, the walls closed in on her, and she nearly hyperventilated.

Julian had already gone ahead. Shane gripped her elbow, his gaze concerned. "Are you all right?"

I'm dealing with a touch of PTSD, she told him telepathically, unwilling to admit it out loud in front of so many witnesses. *The tunnels where Justine held us . . . Shane, it was bad. After this, I don't know if I'll be able to tolerate even living in a house that has a basement.*

His face tightened in sympathy. Whispering something under his breath, a golden, calming energy spread out from his hand and enveloped her. While doing nothing to affect her reflexes or judgment, the spell loosened the tight band around her chest.

Does that help? he asked.

Giving him a grateful look, she nodded.

Others were waiting for her to go underground so they could follow behind. She plunged in, with Shane at her heels.

The tunnel was very long, perhaps as much as a quarter of a mile. It dipped down then gradually angled up again, until it came to rough steps hewn in stone.

They climbed for a long time. She imagined the staircase

cutting up through the hill on which Evenfall sprawled. It would need to ascend past the lower levels in the castle to reach Julian's suite.

The trek seemed to take forever when suddenly she arrived. Stepping out of the narrow staircase, she looked around.

She remembered Julian's suite as spacious yet streamlined, with large landscape paintings from European Old Masters and only enough furniture to make the living space comfortable.

Because of the artwork, the lack of windows had never bothered her before, but now she frowned. The castle had been built long before the technology for automatic shutters existed. While there were plenty of guest suites along the outer walls, the entire core of Evenfall was like this suite, window free and utterly secure from sunlight, with hallways running throughout the castle like a honeycomb, interconnecting everything.

The suite no longer felt spacious to her, but all the soldiers crowding the rooms might be influencing her perspective. The air felt electric with adrenaline. Energy jumped underneath her skin.

Julian and the rest of his group had already disappeared. A small part of her tried to panic. She might never see him again. Ruthlessly, she squashed it. She had seen firsthand what he could do when he had fought the ferals. He would win this fight.

Tess and Xavier were the last of the group to arrive. They strode immediately to the office area. Tess threw herself in front of Julian's computer.

Two Nightkind guards in black uniform stood just inside the suite's carved double doors, watching everyone with undisguised relief. One of them was a Vampyre unfamiliar to Melly, but the other was a ghoul whom she recognized.

She strode to him. "Herman?"

The ghoul fixed large, dark eyes on her. The long, downward lines of his gray face shifted into something that approximated a smile.

"Mum," he said. "You is a sight for sore eyes, you is."

"How are you?"

"Trootfully, mum, I seen better days," he told her.

Shane joined them. At that, he turned to face her and raised one eyebrow.

Telepathically, she said to him, *I love ghouls. They're the Eeyores of the Elder Races. He might have said the same thing on a perfectly wonderful day when the Nightkind demesne wasn't imploding and there was no attempted coup.*

Aloud, she asked the ghoul, "You've been guarding the suite?"

"Yes, mum," said Herman. "King's suite always haz a guard. Usually we stands outside no matter what, but shit happened dis morning. Mr. Dominic wanted in. We say no way, cuz he ain't no king of ours. Then we scarper inside, and we bin stuck here ever since." The ghoul rubbed the back of his bald head with long, skeletal fingers. "Whatta surprise when Mr. King himself walks outta that wall."

She told them, "We're going to start evacuating noncombatants. Don't let anybody through those doors if they aren't with us, do you understand?"

Herman's Vampyre partner said, "Yes, ma'am. The King told us what you would be doing and ordered us to help. We'll keep watch for you."

She glanced through the open doorway to the office area where Tess and Xavier were focused on the computer screen.

She told Shane, "Julian and his group will have gone down and north, toward the parking garage. The IT area is down there. I don't know where the munitions area is, but it has to be somewhere close to that."

He raised his eyebrows. "I thought the parking areas were aboveground."

"Those are the public parking areas. The garage is for private use, for Nightkind officials only. Julian took me through there a couple of times when we drove in." She paused. "We're going to go in the opposite direction—toward the public meeting halls. We'll do a sweep for people, and bring them back here. Anybody who might be barricaded in their rooms should be safe enough for now. Maybe by then, Tess will have some news for us."

Shane turned to their troops. "You heard the orders. Let's move out."

As Melly regarded her team, they drew weapons, their expressions calm and deadly.

Every one of them was Light Fae.

"*Hold*," she ordered.

Those closest to the door jerked to a halt. As one, they all turned to her. Pivoting, she strode into the office area.

When Xavier and Tess glanced up, she said, "We made a mistake. We sent some of the Light Fae troops to help Julian, but we didn't retain any Nightkind troops for my team. I can't take a Light Fae force out there and expect people to follow us to evacuate. They're going to be confused and scared. They won't be thinking rationally. For all they might know, they could believe we've invaded."

Comprehension flashed on their faces. Rubbing his face, Xavier swore in Spanish. He said to Tess, "I have to go with them."

Tess's gaze flared with alarm. "Julian ordered you not to go into battle."

"If it comes to a fight, I'll have to stay out of it," he said grimly.

Tess clenched her teeth. "But what if you're attacked?"

Xavier's voice gentled. "Remember *querida*, Julian left me an out. I'm free to defend myself if I need to. I simply can't choose to go into battle voluntarily."

"You shouldn't have to defend yourself." Tess gripped his wrist. "I should come with you. It's the whole reason I've been training so hard these last few months."

"I understand your frustration, but you can't come." He shook his head. "You have work here we need for you to do."

Hoping to offer reassurance, Melly told her, "I'll make sure he stays with me, in the core of the group."

The struggle in Tess's eyes was palpable. She whispered, "Keep him safe."

Melly's heart went out to the other woman. As difficult as it had been for her to see Julian go into battle, the feeling

for Tess right now must be a thousand times worse. "I promise you, we will."

Xavier bent to kiss Tess. The emotion between them was
so deep and evident, Melly felt like she was witnessing something meant to be private. Turning away, she went back to her
team waiting by the suite entrance.

Xavier joined them. The frustration and tenderness Melly
had witnessed so briefly had vanished. He looked sharp-
eyed, collected and calm.

He gave her a small smile. "Let's go save some people,
shall we?"

She turned to her team. "Now, we can go."

They headed out. Melly, Xavier and Shane led the way,
flanked on either side by guards. Moving quickly and quietly,
on high alert, they swept through ominously empty hallways
until they reached the castle's great hall.

Unlike the Nightkind council chambers and meeting
rooms, which were areas designed for smaller, more private
assemblies, the great hall was a large space used for public
gatherings. The design was classically simple and grand.
The hall had a high vaulted ceiling, huge support columns,
and a golden marble floor.

As they drew close, the sound of arguing voices echoed
off the walls. Slowing, Melly, Xavier and Shane eased up to
look into the large space. Four Vampyres wearing the black
uniform of the Nightkind guard stood in a semicircle around
a group of people who huddled back against one wall.

Swearing internally, Melly did a quick head count—there
were over thirty in the group of prisoners. Most of them
were Vampyres, but some were human, and a few were
ghouls.

". . . holding us here for hours without any kind of explanation," a Vampyre woman said icily. She stood at the forefront of the group and looked furious. "I demand to speak
to Dominic."

"As I've already told you, Dominic is busy at the
moment," one of the guards snapped. "He'll come as soon

as he can. Then you'll get all the explanations you want. Until then, you're all staying right here."

Melly recognized the woman. Her name was Annis, and she was a member of the Nightkind council. Melly exchanged a frown with Xavier and Shane.

Keeping his voice so soft it was a bare thread of sound, Shane whispered, "That guard speaking—who is it?"

"His name is Benet," Xavier replied just as quietly. His gaze had turned hard until his eyes glittered like bottle glass. "He's a captain who has apparently made some very unwise decisions. His three companions are from his unit. There's supposed to be another council member in residence, Leopold, but I don't see him in this group."

"He could be in his suite," Melly whispered. "If he is, he's probably being held there. Dominic and Justine would be working to control and suppress movement. They wouldn't want council members wandering about and possibly taking matters into their own hands."

"Agreed," said Xavier. "Neither Leopold nor Annis are warriors, but they have enough authority that people would listen to what they said."

Shane nudged Melly's arm. "I think I can take care of this without any of the prisoners being hurt. May I?"

She raised her eyebrows. "By all means, knock yourself out."

He hesitated and his eyes narrowed. "It necessitates stretching the Queen's orders a wee bit thin, so be sure you don't get hurt while I'm busy, you hear?"

Impatiently, she waved that away. "I'll be fine. Do it."

He closed his eyes, and a shimmer of magic rippled over his body. Suddenly Dominic stood in front of them, his scarred, handsome face cold and assessing. He asked Xavier, "Will this do?"

Staring, Xavier nodded. "You've nailed him exactly."

Melly stared too. She had heard of this kind of illusion spell before, but they were rare. They took a great deal of Power and training, and they were extremely difficult to maintain. They were risky too, as a strong wave of disbelief could dispel them.

She hissed, "Shane Mac Carthaigh, don't you dare get yourself shot, because I'm not going to be the one to tell Mom."

"This will only take a few minutes," said Shane/Dominic. He gave her a faint, reassuring smile. "Be ready to follow up."

He strode into the hall, conquering the distance to the group in a long, arrogant stride, while he held his semiautomatic in a loose, relaxed position at his side.

"Will you look at that," Xavier muttered. "He even moves like Dominic. How did he learn to do that?"

She whispered, "Shane watches everybody and everything. He could probably impersonate any one of the Nightkind council if he had to."

Xavier gave her a sidelong glance. He looked extremely thoughtful. "Good to know."

In the great hall, the four Nightkind guards, along with their hostages, all turned to Shane/Dominic.

"Benet," said Shane/Dominic as he approached. "Send your men to help keep guard over Leopold. You stay with me."

Everything Melly had ever heard about illusion spells unfolded now like a textbook case.

People tend to see what they're expecting to see, what fits the stories they know. They believe the evidence of their eyes, because it takes far too much effort for the brain to question every bit of information it accumulates. The more outlandish the illusion, the more difficult and fragile the spell became.

Shane was a clever, very dangerous man. This illusion apparently fit with the stories in the guards' minds.

"Yes, sir," said Benet. He snapped his fingers at the other three guards. "Go."

They shouldered their weapons and headed toward Melly, Xavier and the Light Fae guard. Whirling at the same time, Melly and Xavier waved the Light Fae back. They retreated back down the hallway several yards, weapons trained on the open space in front of them.

Moments later the three Nightkind guards walked around the corner. As they came face-to-face with ten soldiers pointing guns at them, they froze. One by one they raised their hands in a universal gesture of surrender.

From the great hall, a single shot rang out.

In the split second that followed, while the hostages in the great hall screamed or exclaimed, Xavier raised his gun and double-tapped each Nightkind guard in the head. They vanished into dust, their weapons clattering to the floor.

Recoiling, Melly stared at Xavier's hard expression.

He said, "Once a traitor, always a traitor."

The Nightkind was Xavier's demesne too. She didn't question his right to execute the soldiers. It wasn't her place to do so. Turning, she ran into the great hall, followed by the rest of her team.

Benet had disappeared, and so had the Dominic illusion. In his place, Shane stood with his hands up, his gun pointing to the ceiling. He was speaking calmly as he tried to de-escalate the group's panic.

Melly didn't bother trying to talk over the hostages' noisy reactions. Instead, she raced straight to Annis. The Vampyre gave her a wild-eyed look. "Melisande? What on earth are you doing here?"

Melly told the other woman, "I'm glad to see you're all right, Annis. Evenfall isn't secured, so we don't have time for extensive explanations. Julian's battling Dominic and Justine, and we're here to help you get to safety. Get your people under control and follow me."

Melly gestured her team back while Annis and Xavier worked to calm down the group. In short order, they headed back down the hallway toward Julian's suite.

Annis joined Melly, Xavier and Shane. Melly told her, "We're going to send you down a tunnel. There's no real shelter at the other end—the tunnel lets out into the woods—but it's shaded enough that it's safe for Vampyres, and it's a good distance from Evenfall. It's the most safety we can offer you on such short notice."

"It will do," Annis said. She was a tall, spare woman who looked to be in her late forties, with straight black hair, stern features and gray eyes. "I want to know if we'll be able to get cell reception."

"I tried when we were out earlier," Xavier told her. "It's patchy, but if you search around, you might be able to make a connection."

"I'll keep trying until I get word out." Annis's jaw set in a determined line. She sounded outraged. "People need to know what's going on in here."

"You should tell everybody you can," Xavier said to her, his tone solicitous. "In fact, our next objective will be to free Leopold too, so he can help you."

Behind her back, his dry gaze met Melly's. Before the hour was out, she knew the entire council would be informed, and she was willing to bet they would all descend upon Evenfall within the next few hours.

"Good," Annis said viciously.

They reached the outside of Julian's suite. Rapping on the doors, Xavier called out. Herman and his partner let the group in. As soon as everyone had stepped inside, they slammed and bolted the doors again.

If the suite had felt crowded before, now it was positively cramped. The Light Fae guard showed the former prisoners the opening in Julian's bedroom wall that led to the tunnel staircase, and one by one, they began to leave.

Melly blocked out the noise. She followed Xavier as he pushed his way through the crowd, and Shane joined them. When they reached the office area, Tess stood so fast, she knocked the chair back. She and Xavier came together in a tight clench.

Tess pulled back almost immediately. "Gavin didn't disconnect the server from Evenfall's internal network," she told them. Her face and voice were full of some kind of emotion that Melly didn't know how to identify. She met Melly's gaze. "He and I have been talking, and I have a visual feed from several cameras. I have to warn you, the feeds are hard to watch. I saw everything that happened in the great hall."

For Melly, everything else fell away. She rushed to kneel

in front of the computer and gripped the edge of the desk with both hands. Xavier, Tess and Shane joined her.

At first, Melly struggled to sort all the information. There were six camera feeds on the screen, and all of them showed different scenes.

The bottom right camera feed focused on Gavin and two other people. They huddled together, their expressions tense. The scene behind them looked like a typical busy office, with cubicles, workstations and electronics parts laid out on a nearby table. The trio appeared to be looking right out Julian's computer screen.

Gavin's voice sounded clearly over Julian's speakers. "Xavier, there you are—thank the gods."

Xavier said something in reply. Melly didn't pay attention. She tuned out their conversation as she searched the other camera feeds. The two others in the bottom row of images were of main thoroughfares in the castle. One was of the great hall, now standing silent and empty.

The top three feeds showed different scenes of a battle. Or maybe they were different battles.

The left feed focused on an image of an industrial-sized, reinforced steel door. The door looked battered and scarred with scorch marks. Two people knelt on the floor on either side of the door, using blowtorches along the edges. Others surrounded them, facing outward with weapons poised.

The middle feed showed the giant underground parking lot, but instead of peaceful rows of parked vehicles, Vampyres fought and shot at each other. A few cars burned. Billows of black smoke made it difficult to see details, and when she could, several of the Vampyres moved so fast, they were blurs.

The third feed focused on a wide stone stairwell and more fighting. She caught sight of a few Light Fae guards, along with Julian's salt-and-pepper hair and distinctive, powerful form in the middle of the undulating wave of people.

"These aren't all the same place, are they?" She clenched her hands into fists. "That stairwell is the one that leads into the parking garage, right?"

"Yes," Xavier said. He sounded as tense as she felt.

Someone took hold of her shoulder in a hard, steady grip. She jumped violently and whirled, but it was only Shane. His gaze was sober, even compassionate.

He said, "With your permission, I'll put together a small team to send after councilman Leopold. Annis hasn't left yet. Maybe she'll agree to go with the team to convince Leopold it's safe. Then they can evacuate together. You don't need to be involved."

"Good thinking. Thank you."

She had already turned back to the battle scenes before his hand left her shoulder.

Xavier told her, "There are several layers of barriers that were built into the lower levels. The first set of locked doors is at the head of the stairwell, where Julian and his team are fighting right now." He pointed to the feed on the battered door. "This is the munitions area. There's a door on the other side of the garage that leads down a hallway to this place. Both of those doors are made of reinforced steel."

"If this is a visual of the second door, you're saying they've already broken through the first," she said.

"Yes. Rocket launchers and other distance weapons are kept in there. If they break through and get into the munitions area, Julian will have no choice. He'll have to retreat."

Gavin leaned forward, until his worried face looked distorted in the feed, his forehead large and domelike. "Yolanthe and her group are just outside our doors. They were trapped, but now Julian's attacking from the rear. Justine and Dominic have to deal with a fight on two sides now."

Melly began to make sense of the feeds. Searching each scene, she muttered, "Where are they?"

Xavier knew exactly who she meant. He pointed to the top middle feed, showing the parking garage. "*There's Dominic.*"

Despite the chaos of the battle, Dominic's tall, athletic form, scarred features and blond hair were unmistakable. He wielded two swords with terrifying expertise. As Melly's attention focused on him, he staked one Vampyre in the chest and slashed at another.

Xavier asked Tess, "Can we get sound on this feed?"

Tess leaned forward to tap on the keyboard. The tumultuous sounds of battle blared over the speakers, and quickly she adjusted the volume.

Melly barely noticed Shane's return, even when he laid a hand on her shoulder again. Tension strung her muscles tight until her neck and shoulders ached.

An eddy of fast movement swirled through the battle. Suddenly Julian appeared, leaping over the heads of a cluster of fighters, sword in hand. While the feed was black and white, his fangs glinted long and wicked, and Melly knew his eyes would have turned hot red.

Landing, Julian moved toward Dominic, who focused on him and strode forward to engage.

Oh *gods*. Uselessly, she reached out to the screen. The blond Vampyre looked confident and lethal, while Julian was a juggernaut.

As they neared one another, Julian roared at him, "*KNEEL!*"

Even despite the physical distance and the all the noise from the rest of the battle, the savage Power in the command rocketed out of the speakers with such force, Xavier groaned and staggered.

All around Julian, every Vampyre fighter who heard the command reacted. Those visible in the feed slammed down onto his knees.

Except for Dominic.

He didn't kneel.

But his forward momentum hitched for a critical moment.

Julian lunged into a blur and struck. Dominic's blond head flew spinning from his shoulders, while his body froze in a posture of immense surprise before it vanished forever as it collapsed into dust.

⇒ EIGHTEEN ⇐

Using the Power of the blood oaths he had taken as Night-kind King was Julian's modern-day version of throwing sand in the face.

The Power command only bought him a few moments, and he doubted it would work again. He had felt the Power shoot out of him like a verbal bullet. It would take a while before he could pull that much together again.

Also, once Vampyres heard a Power command from some-one who was not their sire, they instinctively fought to throw it off and were more resistant to hearing it a second time. The older and stronger a Vampyre was, the less effective Power commands were, until they worked only minimally or not at all, which was why Dominic had been able to resist kneeling, yet he had not been able to contain his reaction.

Julian didn't pause to savor his victory over Dominic or wait for the Vampyres around him to recover. Instead, he spun to behead as many opponents as he could while they were still reeling and vulnerable.

He killed six before the command wore off. Out of the

corner of his eye, he saw that the Light Fae guards who had joined his team were doing the same.

It turned the tide of the fight. As the other Vampyres recovered, they scattered.

Quickly he scanned the scene. If any of his direct progeny had heard the command, they would remain on their knees until he released them.

Julian didn't personally turn many Vampyres. He didn't like to carry the responsibility for them. Aside from Xavier and Yolanthe, he had only four other surviving progeny. They were all in the Nightkind guard, but none of them had been close enough to hear him.

He beckoned to his team, and they gathered around him, facing outward, weapons ready. As they did so, he noticed how Xavier's humans and the Light Fae soldiers coughed. A few had tied cloths around their lower faces.

Rubbing his face with the back of one hand, he looked around. The air in the garage was hazy with black smoke from the burning vehicles. The quality of air, or lack of it, didn't matter to him or to any of the other Vampyres, but it did to the rest of his team.

He told them, "I'm grateful for what you've done, but you'll be no good to anyone if you pass out from smoke inhalation. Fall back. Go help Melly and her team."

They were good people, good fighters. Their reluctance to leave was obvious, but they followed orders.

As they pulled back, he did a quick head count. He had lost four of his own, and now after sending the humans and Light Fae away, his team was down to eleven. They needed to join up with Yolanthe and her troops.

To find Yolanthe, all he had to do was follow the noise.

The hallway that led to the munitions area was across the garage on his right, while the IT area lay to his left. The bulk of the fighting had been on the left, but now it had shifted.

Toward the munitions area.

Followed by his team, he strode to the conflict.

As they closed in, he saw that enemy forces had breached the first security door and gained entrance to the hallway inside. He raced from cover to cover, first hiding behind a concrete pillar, then behind a BMW riddled with bullet holes, while his team did the same.

Scanning the scene, he finally saw Yolanthe crouched behind an SUV. Lunging into a sprint, he joined her.

Her dark, short hair and hawkish features were smeared with soot.

When she saw him, she said, "Yo. Glad you're alive."

"Back at you." He slipped his sword into its shoulder sheath and braced one hand on a fender. "Dominic's dead."

"Witness my happy dance. Fucking fucker." Rolling up and around, she fired at the open doorway to the munitions hall. "We were pinned just outside IT until you got here. Dominic kept hammering at us, while Justine worked over here. I guess if she had already broken through the inner door, she would have fired a rocket launcher or two in here by now. So there's that."

He had to flush Justine and her fighters out of that hallway before they managed to break through the inner door. Justine couldn't gain the capacity to send a fireball through the garage.

A lot of times fighting took finesse, patience and strategy.

Sometimes it took a high body count and a bludgeoning force.

He said, "We need enough fire in that hallway to drive them out. I have two grenades. Do you have any?"

Her dark eyes flashed as she glanced at him. "No. Wait here. I'll see if any of the others do."

While he waited, he rubbed his dry eyes. He had so many things he wanted to tell Melly, but mostly he just wanted to know if she was all right.

Where was she? How had the evacuation gone? Had they run into any resistance?

He wanted to tell her, you're the light of my life. I had no idea how bright and open things could become with you.

Yolanthe reappeared, running so hard, her body slammed full tilt into the side of the SUV. When he looked at her, she opened her hands and showed him a grenade belt with three more grenades.

"Okay," he said. He gathered the belt out of her grasp and added his two to the belt. "Here's what we're going to do. I'll get these into the hallway. I need to get close enough and at the right angle to throw this in, so I need you to cover me."

"I love suicidal missions," Yolanthe said. She readied her automatic rifle and gave him a bright grin. "Let's go."

He gave a ghost of a chuckle and pulled the pins on the grenades. They pushed away from the SUV and raced toward the hallway. While Yolanthe laid down a hail of covering fire, he sprinted hard, spun like a discus thrower, and heaved the grenade belt. He put all the force he could into it, sending the belt shooting deep into the hallway.

He felt an invisible force punch his right shoulder and left thigh and knew he'd been hit, but his body armor blocked most of the damage. When he and Yolanthe had run past the hallway several yards, they spun around.

Fighters poured out, fleeing the impending blast.

One of them was Justine, her auburn hair flying out from her head like a flag.

She sprinted toward the staircase. She was one of the oldest, most Powerful Vampyres present, and she moved faster than almost anybody else in the garage.

Except for Yolanthe and Julian.

Everything in Julian narrowed down to the need to kill. He leaped forward, but his leg buckled underneath him. The hit he had taken in the thigh had done more damage than he had realized.

Yolanthe wasn't impaired. She shot forward, moving toward Justine like a linebacker. Leaping, she grabbed Justine by the hair with both hands, bodily lifted the other Vampyre, swung around and flung her through the air.

Justine's body slammed into a concrete pillar several feet off the ground. She dropped like a stone.

Yolanthe said in Julian's head, *Bitch wants to throw down with her lovely locks all loose and shiny? Okay then.*

Down the hallway, the grenades blew. The concussion blasted out through the garage. It knocked Julian to his knees.

He shoved up, drew his sword and launched toward Justine, ignoring the nearby fire and the fighting that had broken out all around.

Bitch hadn't turned to dust either. She wasn't dead yet.

As he neared, Justine rolled onto her stomach and came up on her hands and knees. Her teeth were bared in a rictus grin. She reached toward her waist and drew a gun.

And turned to level it at him.

Someone ran toward them from his right, aiming an automatic rifle at Justine and firing a constant spray of bullets.

The shooter was a tall woman with blond hair pulled into a tight bun at her neck. She had a cloth wrapped around her nose and mouth, and she was shadowed by a tall, powerfully built Light Fae male who threw combat spells like sparks of deadly fire.

Melly.

Justine's arm jerked back and her shots went wide.

Julian regarded the other Vampyre with some degree of incredulity. Bitch still wasn't dead. But her arm was sure shot to hell.

He limped forward the rest of the way to her, swung his sword, and Justine's head spun away from her body.

It flew straight toward Melly, as it happened, who flinched back and pulled a massive *ew* face that was obvious even through the masking cloth. Using the butt of her gun, she whacked at the head like it was a baseball, batting it away from her just as it crumbled to dust.

Meanwhile, bullets flew everywhere, and people still pounded the hell out of each other. Julian grabbed Melly by the waist and hauled her around the concrete pillar for cover.

He shouted at her, "What are you doing down here?"

Her eyes went very wide and she flung out her free hand.

She looked more than a little crazed as she shouted in reply, "*I couldn't keep watching this on TV!*"

Naturally, her Light Fae troops had returned to the garage with her. Their arrival turned the tide again. While pockets of fighting still raged in a few areas, he saw the battle was essentially over.

He turned back to Melly. "All those fantastic kill shots you made when you dusted the ferals, and you damn near shoot Justine's *arm* off?"

"All I could see was the gun she had pointed toward your head. I needed to stop it."

A fine tremor ran through her body. Her eyes were huge and dark. He snatched her close, hugging her with one arm hooked around her neck. With trembling fingers, she touched his face, his neck.

The scene around them was like something out of hell. It seemed fitting that hell might be found in Evenfall's basement garage. The last of the fighting came to an end.

Overhead, a fire sprinkler system tried to spurt water, but the system was a modernization that had been tacked onto the old, original stone ceiling. The grid of thin, exposed pipes had been too damaged from various explosions.

As a thin trickle of water dripped on his head, Julian looked up. "That's not going to be enough."

Yolanthe shouted, "Get fire extinguishers down here, people!"

Melly coughed. "Do you need to be down here anymore?"

"No. Let's go." He kept an arm around her shoulders and stayed watchful, just in case. He had seen too many tragedies occur when people let down their guard at the end of a battle. "It's over."

At that, she barked out a hoarse, rasping laugh and coughed harder.

"No," she told him. "It's not. Annis and Leopold are busily gathering the Nightkind council together. I predict they'll all be here inside of two hours."

He thought about that as they made for the staircase.

"Well," he offered after a few minutes. "At least Dominic and Justine are dead."

She put an arm around his waist. "At least there's that."

They made their way back to Julian's suite, where Xavier hugged them both and Tess gave Melly a wide, relieved smile.

Meanwhile, chaos reigned. Light Fae troops crowded in. People continued to pop into the stairway tunnel, until someone realized Julian and Melly had returned. Then instead of evacuating, they started pouring back through the tunnel entrance. A loud, excited babble of conversation filled the air.

"I'm never going to get my bedroom back again," Julian muttered, as he watched the influx of jubilant, relieved people.

Xavier told them, "Evenfall still isn't secure. We need to do a sweep."

"We also have to take care of Dominic's troops stationed outside." Taking Melly by the hand, he hauled her into his office, which was marginally quieter.

Xavier, Tess and Shane joined them. Melly watched as Julian picked up the receiver from the phone set on his desk. He slammed it back down immediately. "The phone's dead. Goddammit. They did cut the telecommunications cables."

Xavier said, "With your permission, I'll command the sweep. If there's any more fighting, it'll be minimal and the guards can take care of it. I'll also coordinate with Yolanthe to make sure the Nightkind troops are purged of traitors." Frowning, he paused to regard Tess.

Tess's expression turned determined. "You don't need me here anymore. I'm coming with you."

Purged of traitors. Melly swallowed hard.

"Good, go take care of it," Julian told the pair. He hadn't let go of Melly's hand, his fingers laced through hers.

Melly said to Shane, "It's still daylight. We can handle that much better than the Nightkind. Send fifteen troops to help with clearing Dominic's forces from the area around the castle. And we have to clear out some of the chaos in here. Would you make sure people are directed to go *out* of the suite, so they don't linger to chat? And close the tunnel entrance as soon as you can."

"Yes, ma'am." Following Xavier and Tess, Shane stepped out.

As soon as they had left, Melly released Julian's hand, stepped forward and slammed the door, shutting out the rest of the world. Julian followed her.

As she turned around, he pinned her back against the door panel with his body weight. Leaning both his arms on the door, he bowed his head next to hers.

Torn between holding on to him and running her hands over the surface of his scarred body armor, she tried to do both at once.

"You were hit," she whispered. "You were limping."

He shook his head, his cheek pressed against hers. "I'm all right," he muttered in her ear. "What about you? Did you take any hits?"

"Not a single one. I'm uninjured."

He touched her cheek, her hair, then gripped the back of her neck and kissed her with so much hunger, as if he hadn't seen her for years. It reflected exactly how Melly felt. She was starving for his mouth, his touch, and kissed him back wildly.

Someone gave a polite tap on the door. He lifted his head and bellowed, "*No.*"

Dismayed muttering sounded on the other side of the panel.

Dropping her forehead onto his shoulder, she started to laugh. Oh, this day.

She told him, "I don't remember when I last slept. Wait, it was in the bath, wasn't it? I feel like I've been on a runaway train for a week now."

"I know," he said. "We're going to put on the brakes. The council might be arriving, but that doesn't mean I'm going to see them right away. I'll convene a meeting tonight. As soon as the suite is cleared, I'll order some food for you. We can clean up and take a nap."

She didn't know if she could sleep. She felt strung out but clearheaded, and she was still running on adrenaline. Still, food and a shower sounded like incredible luxuries.

His body weight lifted as he finally eased back. He said, "I haven't had a chance to tell you. Back at the house, when you went to talk to your troops, I called Carling."

"What?!" Reaching for his face, she framed his cheeks with her hands. "Are you all right? She didn't try anything, did she?"

He shook his head and gave her a wry smile. "No, she didn't. We . . . talked. We just talked. It went better than I expected. I don't think it wiped away what happened last year, but it did clear the air. I asked her to release me from her old orders, and she said she would."

"And you believe her," she said.

"Yes, I do. She even said the words over the phone, although she warned she would need to say them in person to be sure it took." He smiled, took her hands and kissed them. "But I felt better immediately. That's all because of you."

She curled her fingers around his. "What do you think you'll want to do?"

The expression in his piercing gaze turned inward and reflective. "I honestly don't know. What I really want is to be able to make the choice."

"Let's take that vacation we discussed," she suggested gently. "I know Mom will help me clear my schedule if I ask her. You could have somebody in San Francisco deliver the Harley here. . . . I ought to get more than one ride out of that bike. It cost me enough. We can go to Tahoe. Or it doesn't have to be Tahoe. We could go someplace completely new. Hell, let's take a year off. What's a year, anyway?"

"What *is* a year, anyway?" He echoed her words softly, almost to himself, and started to smile. "As long as it's a year with you, it will be everything I need."

She closed her eyes for a moment. She loved him so much, so much.

Stepping away, he unbuckled the chest plate of his body armor and set it aside. Underneath, he wore a black, long-sleeved shirt that hugged his torso and arms. He dug into a pocket and pulled out his cell phone.

One corner of his lips lifted. "If you call your mom, I'll call mine."

She burst out laughing. "It's a deal."

With his help, she stripped out of her armor too. By the time Melly had finished talking to Tatiana, and Julian had called Carling to arrange for her and Rune to arrive that evening, the suite had finally been cleared and the tunnel entrance sealed.

When she and Julian emerged from the office, Shane, along with another Light Fae guard, joined the two Night-kind guards on duty outside the suite doors.

Only moments later, Xavier and Tess arrived. Xavier carried a tray of food. As soon as Melly smelled a hot, savory aroma coming from the tray, all thoughts of taking a shower and crawling into bed flew out of her head.

"Evenfall is secure," Xavier told them. "We even inspected the kitchens personally."

"And with great interest," Tess said. She smiled at Melly. "I wondered if you might be as hungry as I am."

"I'm starving," she confessed.

Xavier set the tray on the coffee table in the living room. "They have a lot of people to feed unexpectedly, so they went with pasta."

Melly uncovered her dish to discover a plate of steaming fettuccine Alfredo with slices of grilled chicken breast. Fresh shaved Romano cheese had melted on top, and the dish was even garnished with a sprig of parsley.

She moaned, "Oh my God, this is heaven."

A bottle of white wine had been included with the tray, but both Tess and Melly ignored the alcohol and concentrated on the food. Julian poured glasses of bloodwine for himself and Xavier, who briefed him on details as the women ate.

To Melly, everything sounded like blah blah, fine, blah blah, I'll take care of it, blah blah, sounds good.

She let it all wash over her as she concentrated on the excellent meal on her plate. Despite the high concentration of Nightkind occupants who never touched food, or perhaps because of it, the chefs in the Evenfall kitchens prided themselves on putting out some of the finest-quality meals in California.

Tess ate with as much enthusiasm as Melly, until Julian said to Xavier, "I need to ask if you would be willing to act as regent for a year."

Tess froze in midchew. Swallowing a bite of food, Melly shifted her gaze to Xavier, who raised his eyebrows. "Are you going somewhere?"

"Yes, as a matter of fact, I am." Julian sprawled back in his armchair. He had taken a few minutes to change into jeans and a dark blue sweater. For the first time in a very long time, he looked relaxed. "Melly and I are going to take a year off." He paused. "I can't promise I'll be back."

Xavier looked at Tess, who hadn't moved. Silence fell in the room and extended. They were talking telepathically. Sipping his bloodwine, Julian waited with every appearance of patience, while Melly concentrated on finishing her meal.

Once Julian had brought up the subject, she could see all the many reasons why it was the best possible idea. Already highly placed, Xavier knew the workings of the Nightkind government intimately, and he was utterly reliable.

But spending a whole year as regent was a huge commitment, especially with Xavier and Tess's relationship so new.

Melly said to Julian, *I love so much that you asked him, and you didn't make it an order.*

He gave her a faint smile that softened the edges of his hard mouth. *I couldn't do anything else.*

Judging by the increasing tension in both Xavier and Tess, it appeared their telepathic conversation might not be going very well.

Suddenly Tess burst out, "Okay Julian, I have to say this out loud. If Xavier agrees to do this, I want you to turn me. Would you do that, please?"

"*Querida*, no," Xavier said forcefully.

Tess turned to him. "I've already made up my mind. I want to be turned, and I don't want you to be the one to do it. Having you as my sire *and* my partner is far too much of a power imbalance."

Julian's sharp gaze dissected her expression. "Not that long ago, at the Vampyre's Ball, you had some serious problems with Vampyres."

"Yes, I did," Tess replied. Her attitude was unflinching. "But I have done a lot of growing since then." She said to Xavier, "Are you going to tell them, or shall I?"

Xavier's frustration eased somewhat. When he next spoke, his voice had softened. "I have asked Tess to marry me, and she has said yes." He told her, "But that doesn't mean you need to transform into a Vampyre overnight." He added gently, "It doesn't mean you need to transform into a Vampyre at all. I love you as you are, *querida*, and I don't want you to change because of me."

"First, thank you," Tess said. "But I'm not going to grow old while you don't. That's another imbalance that isn't going to happen. And if you become regent, the last thing you need is a frail human partner."

"I will thank you to remember that I know best what I need," Xavier told her. He said it with such old-world courtesy it took some of the sting out of the words. "What I need most is to know that you are fulfilled and happy. Again, I don't believe becoming a Vampyre has anything to do with that."

"I know I'm young, and I'm well aware it's is a huge decision," Tess said. "If you can trust me enough to plan on marrying me, you can trust me enough to know my own mind about this too."

Julian said in Melly's head, *She has a point there.*

Despite the obvious tension between the other two, he sounded amused. Melly rubbed her mouth to hide her smile.

Don't make my face do something inappropriate. This is serious stuff, Julian.

Look at him, Julian said. *Look underneath all his surface emotions. He's so stinking happy.*

Julian was right, Xavier was. His love for the young human woman came through in every word and gesture. The same could also be said of Tess. Even as Xavier and Tess exchanged a deeply exasperated glance, they both softened toward the other.

"Your argument has become irrelevant," said Julian. Quickly Xavier and Tess spun toward him. They both opened their mouths. Julian raised his hand. "Stop. As soon as Tess asked me to turn her, it became a conversation between her and me."

"I am part of that conversation," Xavier said furiously.

Julian speared him with a glance. "Yes, but you are not in control of it. She has to make decisions for herself. I make decisions for myself."

"Thank you," Tess said, sitting up straight.

"And," Julian added, "Xavier will make his own decisions too. Tess, there are so many reasons why Vampyres use a year as a probation period. As obvious as this might sound, becoming a Vampyre is irrevocable. If you still want this a year from now, I'll turn you myself whether you're still with Xavier or not. In the meantime, eat chocolate and steak. Get a suntan. Take the time to relish all the human things you'll leave behind." He said to Xavier, "If that affects whether or not you'll agree to be regent, so be it. Now, I'm finished with this discussion. Melly and I are dog tired, and I have to meet with the council this evening. All I need is your answer."

Xavier and Tess exchanged another quick glance.

Then Xavier told him firmly, "Yes. If you can talk the council into accepting a regency, I'll do it."

Oh, yay.

Melly was pretty sure relief lay on the other side of a great divide. She couldn't connect to the emotion—or to any emotion, for that matter. Her belly felt lovely and full, all the danger was gone, and suddenly her body demanded she go horizontal as soon as possible.

"I'm cooked," she said. "I'm out."

Vaguely she was aware that the other three came to their feet, but it all happened on the other side of that divide. She walked into Julian's bedroom, kicked off her boots and crawled fully clothed underneath the covers. The world began to spin away on formless clouds.

Suddenly Julian was there.

"Oh, baby." His voice was very gentle. "Not in your clothes. You deserve so much better than that."

With an immense effort, she managed to respond. "S'okay. I don't care."

"*I* care." He pulled back the covers and eased her clothes off.

She let him. "How much time do we have?"

He hesitated. "I've set the alarm for four hours. That will allow enough time to shower first and meet with Carling."

A four-hour nap sounded like heaven.

"You know, I have to say this," he said as he slid into the bed beside her. He had stripped out of his clothes too. "You don't have to come with me. You could sleep longer. God only knows you need the rest."

"Fuck you," she mumbled into her pillow. "Fuck that." *We've already discussed this.* "I'm good to go, soldier. Just lemme." *Take the nap first.*

"You're so tired, you're switching back and forth from telepathy." He pulled her into his arms, and she curled around his body.

She had been trying to figure out which method of speech took the least effort, but she couldn't decide. Meanwhile, the long, physical bulk of his presence was so soothing, and her head fit onto his shoulder so perfectly.

Yes, exactly there. That was home.

She plummeted to sleep.

Four and a half hours later, she and Julian walked hand-in-hand into the empty council assembly hall, accompanied by Xavier, Tess and Shane. Three more Light Fae guards stopped outside the doors.

The smaller assembly hall had been designed with classic simplicity, much like the great hall. Although Melly knew that chairs and tables were sometimes added for long meetings, currently it was devoid of furniture.

Melly had slept like the dead until Julian's alarm had gone off. Coming awake had been painful, but a hot shower had helped, along with gulping a cup of piping-hot coffee and eating a croissant.

Someone had left clothes for her in the living room, along with the food and coffee. They were simple, black trousers and a black sweater, but they fit well enough. After braiding her hair, she wound it into a knot at the nape of her neck again.

Julian had already risen and dressed by the time she got up, and he was meeting with various people. When she walked into the living room, his office door was closed. She had eaten while listening to the muffled sounds of his and Yolanthe's voices. There had been no more time to talk privately with him.

Now, nerves jumped underneath her skin again. She felt like she was about to go into another battle. Except what came next wasn't her battle. It was Julian's.

With a clang, the doors shut behind them. The next time they opened, it would be to let in the council.

She said in his head, *I'm okay with whatever you decide. When it comes down to it, if you feel like you need to stay, I'll support you no matter what. You get to have a real choice, Julian.*

He came to a stop. The expression in his eyes was so vulnerable, it made her want to throw her arms around him and never let go.

He said, *I don't deserve you.*

Well, that's true, she told him gently, smiling. *The important thing is that you recognize it.*

His hand tightened on hers. *I had the Harley delivered.*

It's waiting for us in the public parking lot, just inside the gate.

It took a moment for his words to sink in. Then she remembered their conversation from earlier in his office, and a burst of pure joy filled her chest.

He pulled out his phone and made a call. He said, "We're here."

Almost immediately the whirling Power of a Djinn filled the empty space. Three figures solidified. Melly recognized all of them.

One was a tall, imperious-looking male with long black hair and diamond-like eyes. He was Soren's son, Khalil.

The other two were a man and a woman. The man was Wyr, handsome and also tall, with tawny hair. He had once been Dragos's First sentinel, and now he was Carling's mate, Rune.

The woman was Carling. She was beautiful, with almond-shaped eyes, warm brown skin and short dark hair. The last time Melly had seen her, Carling's hair had been long and flowed down her back.

"Ah, Evenfall," said Carling. "It holds such memories." She murmured to Rune, "I could take it all back, you know."

"You love your new life too much," Rune said. He gave his mate a sleepy-looking smile.

Carling turned to Julian and Melly. "There, you see? I can't even tease him. Hello, Melly. Julian." She gave the others a nod.

While Carling appeared to be relaxed and Rune remained smiling, Melly noticed neither one stepped forward. Khalil didn't even pretend to smile. Instead the Djinn folded his arms and watched everyone with a raised eyebrow.

Melly didn't realize she was gripping Julian's hand so hard until he said telepathically to her, *It's all right. Broken trust can't be rebuilt in a day.* Aloud, he said, "Thank you for coming."

"You're welcome," said Carling. "Truth be told, while I'd love to stay and watch what happens next, I would be too tempted to get involved. As my Rune so wisely pointed out, I love my new life too much. So, Julian Regillus, I will say it again. You're free of any obligation to the Nightkind demesne save those you choose for yourself. Your future is no longer what I order."

"Unless you try to hurt my mate again," said Rune, still with that sleepy smile. In contrast to his lazy, handsome expression, his gaze was sharp as a drawn blade. "Then your future ass becomes mine." As Carling raised her eyebrows at him, he shrugged. "What? I had to say it."

At Carling's words, Melly had felt a tremor run through Julian's big body. She whispered, "Are you all right?"

Squeezing her fingers reassuringly, he nodded. He said to Carling, "I won't forget that you were willing to come here and do this." He looked at Rune. "Either of you."

"I hope you find the path that makes you happy, Julian." Carling paused. Then she nodded at Khalil, who put his hands on her and Rune's shoulders, and the Djinn's Power swept them away.

Did Carling's pause go on a heartbeat too long?

Melly spun around to face Julian. *What did she do? What did she say? She didn't take it back and order you to do something else, did she?*

He took hold of her arms reassuringly. *No. It's all right. She just advised me about something I already knew I needed to do.*

What's that? Melly searched his expression.

He said, *I have to kill Darius.*

Councilman Darius?

Yes. Dominic was a bad surprise, but we've known for a long time that Justine and Darius were co-conspirators. He said aloud to Xavier, "Open the doors."

It was hard to step away from Julian, but she forced herself to do it. Beckoning to Tess and Shane, Melly led them to one side, while she murmured in Shane's head, *This meeting may get a little touchy.*

It's a good thing you warned me. Shane's mental voice sounded comfortably dry. *I was in danger of relaxing.*

She rolled her eyes at him. *If things go the way I think they will, you can take the troops home afterward.*

He nodded in acknowledgement. *This was a good outing. It's been a good day.*

As Xavier opened the doors, the surviving ten members of the Nightkind council poured in. Although she wasn't acquainted with any of them very well, Melly knew all their names.

Marged, Connor and Nicholas. Dylan, Leopold and Annis.

Trey, Jaylinn and Gustave.

And of course Darius.

Danger entered the hall on quiet cat feet along with the council. These Vampyres were some of the most deadly of the Nightkind.

Julian strode to the center of the room. The other Vampyres grouped loosely around him. After the last one had entered, Xavier closed the doors again. With his customary erect posture and quiet dignity, he made his way around the edge of the room to Tess, Melly and Shane.

Melly noticed how Leopold and Annis positioned themselves in front of her, Shane and Tess. She didn't know who had prompted that, whether it had been Julian or Xavier, or if Leopold and Annis had volunteered to do it on their own, but she knew it hadn't happened by accident.

As Leopold glanced over his shoulder at Melly, he inclined his head. *Thank you for what you did earlier.*

She returned his nod with a smile. *You're welcome.*

Other council members took in the trio's presence with less equanimity.

Darius said, "Really, Julian, a human and two Light Fae? This is an emergency *council meeting*. Not even Xavier should be present."

"Shut up," Julian said. His icy voice cracked like a whip.

Reaction rippled through the council. Gustave and Jaylinn looked outraged, while Marged, of all people, appeared unsurprised.

Darius snapped, "You dare talk to us like that? After slamming martial law down on this demesne then disappear-

ing into thin air—And now you've killed two members of
this very council—"

Julian had stood in such a neutral posture that when he
exploded, Melly startled violently.

Oh, shit.

He had said he needed to kill Darius. He didn't say he
needed to do it right now.

Julian body slammed Darius into the wall. Both Vampyres
blurred into vicious movement. Snarling filled the air.

Shane shoved Melly back into a corner and covered her
body with his, facing outward. Xavier did the same with
Tess.

Julian and Darius tumbled along the length of the room,
striking blows at each other. Like an avalanche or some
other natural disaster, they seemed utterly unstoppable, until
Julian slammed Darius's head into the floor so hard, the
crack resounded through the hall.

The blow would have killed any number of other creatures, including younger Vampyres. Darius struggled to get
to his hands and knees.

Some of the council members had stepped forward, as
if they might plunge into the fight as well, while others
moved to block them. Tension held everyone at some kind
of brink. They stared at Julian and Darius with shocked
faces and reddened eyes.

Before Darius could fully rise up, Julian kicked him. The
blow flipped him onto his back. Coming down hard with
both knees on the other Vampyre's stomach, Julian drove
one fist into Darius's chest wall, pulled out his beating heart
and crushed it in his fist.

Darius's body collapsed. Julian stood. He looked around
the rest of the group. His face was so savage, several council
members took a step back.

"I just executed Darius for crimes of treason," he growled.
"Just like I executed Dominic and Justine earlier today. For
the record, Justine tried to kill Xavier. She slaughtered her
household, kidnapped the Light Fae heir and tried to kill

me more than once over the last few days. Dominic tried to take Evenfall and murdered several innocent people in the process, and Darius colluded with them both. Now, do I need to execute anybody else today?"

The resulting silence was so profound, Melly swore she could have heard a pin drop from across the hall. Several council members looked at her, their expressions appalled. She gave them a grim nod, silently confirming the story.

Julian took a step forward. Death covered him in an invisible mantle, present in his aggressive posture and his transformed features.

To a person, all the council members took a step back.

"Now, this is also for the record," snapped the King. "You are not here tonight to debate by committee. I am not your servant. I do not ask for your permission when I take action, and I do not owe you explanations. I am done with your petty shit. I'm done with working to hold this demesne together while you all indulge in self-serving attitudes. Do you hear me? *I am done.*"

Annis made a placating gesture with both hands. "Tempers are running hot right now," she said. "Why don't we all take a day? We can talk tomorrow night, when we've had a chance to cool down."

"I won't be here tomorrow," Julian said. "Melly and I are leaving."

"What?" said Marged. "You've been gone for several days already." Julian hissed at her. Marged took another step back and muttered, "I recognize that wasn't your fault."

"Here's what's going to happen," said Julian. "I'm taking a vacation. I'll be gone for a year. Frankly, I don't know if I'm coming back. Xavier will act as regent, and you will either finally commit to this demesne and work toward something bigger than yourselves, or you won't. If you do, I might return. If you don't, I'll wash my hands of you, and you can each go to hell in your own way."

The council erupted.

"You can't just leave!"

"—an entire *year*? You've got to be kidding—"

"—some of us have businesses to run—"

Blah blah protest, blah blah, dismay, blah blah what about me?

Melly let it all wash over her while she watched Julian. Only Julian.

He turned to her and said telepathically, *That's our cue to leave.*

Halle-fucking-lujah.

She wiggled out from behind Shane and kissed him on the cheek. Then she hugged Tess and Xavier quickly. She told Xavier, "Keep in touch."

Wry amusement showed in Xavier's gaze. "Oh, you know I will."

Then she left them to walk to toward Julian, who held out his hand. The murderous fury in his expression had faded, to be replaced with a look that made her pulse pound and her heart sing.

The assembly hall fell silent as she reached him and took his hand. It remained silent as they walked out the door.

Julian set a fast pace. Melly passed down hallways without registering details, her mind in a daze. Part of her couldn't believe what was happening.

But part of her could too.

Midnight had passed. They were starting a new day.

Outside, the night was crisp and clear, with a luminous canopy of stars overhead. A ghoul waited by the Harley. It was Herman. Giving them a mournful smile, he handed them jackets and a helmet. "We packed tings in dose saddlebags, just like you ordered, Mr. King."

"You don't have a helmet?" Melly asked Julian as she shrugged into her jacket and helmet.

"I don't need one." He zipped his jacket. His gaze met hers. "You don't either. Yours is just to keep your hair from getting so tangled. I won't let you crash."

He wouldn't either. Smiling, she buckled her helmet into place.

He straddled the Harley and started it. She climbed on behind and snuggled close, wrapping her arms around his waist. The growl of the machine vibrated between her legs as he pulled away. As they left the lights of Evenfall, the night wrapped them in its embrace.

Julian took the winding roads at a leisurely pace. Laying her head on his shoulder, Melly watched the countryside pass.

Are you tired? he asked.

No, she told him. She felt glorious. She never wanted this ride to end.

His head turned sideways. She caught a glimpse of his hard, sexy profile. *So, we can ride for a while.*

Yes, please. She laid a hand over his heart.

They came to the winding entrance that would take them onto the interstate. She asked, *Where are we going first?*

I don't know. Are you okay with that?

Oh, hell yeah.

Briefly he covered her hand with his.

Then he punched the gas.

The Harley shot forward, like a thoroughbred bursting out of a gate.

⇒ NINETEEN ⇐

Julian came indoors after spending a couple of hours fishing in the cold, quiet predawn. It felt delicious to relax in front of a roaring fire. Lazily, he watched the leaping flames in the fireplace while he listened to Melly move around in the kitchen.

A metallic clang ruptured the peace in the cabin, and she swore so colorfully, he had to chuckle.

"What happened?" he called out.

"I dropped the flour canister, and now there's flour everywhere." She appeared by the sofa and grumpily nudged him. He shifted so she could lie down and curl against his side. "Yes, I'm running away from the problem. I put the trout in the fridge. I can always cook it later."

"I'll help you clean it up in a bit." Stretching, he wrapped his arms around her, and she laid her head on his shoulder and snuggled into him.

A month had passed since he had killed Dominic, Darius, and Justine and walked away from the Nightkind council. Every day, he felt like he was going to wake up from a dream. Even though Melly felt solid and real when he held her, he couldn't internalize the beauty of her smile, or the peace he saw all around him when he took the boat out onto the lake.

It was going to take some time, she kept telling him. One month could not wipe out years of isolation or stress. He was okay with that. The one thing he had learned over his long life was that worthwhile things could take time.

Stirring, she turned away from him, curling on her side while resting her head on his arm. He turned with her, spooning her from behind. Together they looked out the picture window at the serene water.

While they called the property a "cabin," the term was a bit of a misnomer. In actuality, it was a three-bedroom house tucked into a tiny cove, with a spacious family room, a living room with a picture window that covered an entire wall facing the lake, and three fireplaces. Through clever landscaping and the position of the building, they couldn't see any other houses.

The house sat at the edge of the waterline, while below, instead of a basement there was a compact boathouse that held a rowboat, a small, sleek motorboat, and a variety of water toys, including Jet Skis and paddle boards.

They also had their own pier, and over the last four weeks, they had replaced all the older, outdated furniture with new, quality pieces, like the chaise lounge by the living room window where Melly loved to read, and the spacious couch that offered plenty of room for cuddling.

"We did a good job when we picked this place before," she said. "I'm glad all the trees have survived and have grown to be so big. It's nice to go through the day without direct sunlight coming in any of the windows."

"Even if we do lose a tree to an ice storm, the shutters are installed if I need them," he replied. "For now, I'm glad I don't need them. It feels good to look out."

They fell silent for a time and watched the sunrise together.

He and well-being . . .

They were beginning to know each other, just as he and happiness were getting acquainted.

What do you know. Sometimes an old dog really could learn new tricks.

"Do you miss it?" she asked finally. She twisted around to look into his eyes. "All the intrigue, politics and power. I could imagine they would be addicting."

Various members of the council had begun to email Melly, asking after her well-being and attempting to solicit her help in persuading Julian to return. She told him about each email with great satisfaction, although he wouldn't let her read them to him.

"Not at all," he replied. Honesty forced him to add, "At least, not yet." He played with her hair. It was one of his favorite pastimes. "Do you miss the fast pace of the movie set?"

She smiled. "Absolutely not. At least not just yet."

He stroked down her body gently, taking his time so that he touched every hollow and curve. The clothes she wore at the cabin were soft and pretty—silks and sometimes fleeces, all in jewel tones that complemented her golden skin, green eyes and tawny curls. She left her hair loose, just the way he liked it.

She was not only beautiful to look at, but also a pleasure to touch, and he could talk to her for hours.

They played conversational games with each other. He would ask her a question, then she would ask one in return. The intricate, winding discussions unlocked barriers in his mind that he hadn't realized he'd had.

He fell into enchantment, exploring possibilities like walking a green maze drenched in afternoon sunlight, turning countless corners and discovering new treasures, always working to go further in and discover the heart of the place.

The center of it all. Melly.

She said quietly, "I'd like to confess something, if you don't mind."

He lifted his head off the couch pillow, immediately fascinated. "Of course."

Taking his hand, she played with his fingers. "Over the past five years, I've toyed off and on with the idea of in vitro fertilization." She peeked at him over her shoulder, her expression tentative and self-conscious. "Keep in mind—it doesn't bother me in the slightest that Vampyres can't father children. When I started thinking about this, I wasn't in a relationship. I think I just want to be a mother. How would you feel about that?"

The strength of his response astonished him. All kinds of powerful reactions resonated through his body. His imagination ran wild. Melly, round with pregnancy, the baby kicking under his hands as he stroked her belly.

As he held still, stricken with the images that unfolded in his imagination, she searched his face anxiously.

He whispered, "I would love that. Really fucking love it."

Her expression lit up. "We could keep talking about it then. We don't have to do anything right away. Hell, I'm okay if we discuss it for a couple of years before we come to any decision. I don't want to rush into anything before we're ready."

He rolled onto his back and stared at the ceiling. "I have no idea how to be a father."

"I don't believe it," she told him. "All I have to do is look at how you are with Xavier." As he glanced at her sidelong, she amended, "You might not know how to be a father to a baby or a young toddler, but Julian, none of those things come instantly to anybody, anyway. You have to learn them."

Draping one wrist on his forehead, he frowned. "True."

"As long as you're not opposed," she whispered, then paused. "If I need to, I can also give up the idea."

At that, he lifted his head to scowl at her. "I won't have you give up a single thing to be with me."

Searching his gaze, she chuckled. "Well, I don't want you to agree to have a baby just to make me happy. That wouldn't work out very well for the baby, would it? I think the subject is a little like facing battle—we both need to be all in, or we need to be all out."

"Good analogy," he told her.

She added, "And there's always the possibility that in vitro wouldn't take. After all, it's very difficult for the Light Fae to conceive and bear a child, just like it is for the rest of the Elder Races."

They could always adopt. He thought it but didn't say it. They could explore that conversation at a different time. For now, he simply listened to what she had to say, watching the play of expressions on her face.

She paused, then added, "If we do decide to go ahead with trying, we would have to be prepared for one other thing."

He nuzzled her ear. "What's that?"

She told him, "When the women in my family conceive, we tend to have twins."

His mind leaped from Bailey to her mother Tatiana, and her aunt Isabeau, the Seelie Light Fae Queen in Ireland.

"Of course you do," he said with a chuckle. "I hadn't connected." He cupped the back of her neck, rubbing her soft skin with the ball of his thumb. "Everything you're saying is very sensible. We'll take all the time we need in order to be sure. And I realize I have no idea what I'm really talking about. I've smiled at babies. I've held one or two. But I have no real concept of what it would be like to raise a small child. Even with all those qualifiers in mind, I'm drawn to this, Melly."

Her expression softened. "I guess a lot will depend on the next year and what we end up deciding to do. If you truly want to go back to rule the Nightkind demesne, and I'm committed to going back to making movies, we might end up with too much of a commuter lifestyle."

He shook his head. "Now you're coming up with obstacles that don't need to be there. If we want to have children, we should try to have children, and we'll work out the rest. You could take a break from making movies for a couple of years, and I don't need to go back into a situation that has danger lurking around every corner. I may not know much about children, but I do know one thing—they don't stay young and small for long."

"That's true." As he massaged her neck, her head drooped and her eyelids grew heavy.

Watching her beautiful face, he whispered, "Do you want to go clean up the kitchen now?"

Languidly, she shook her head. "No. But I am hungry."

He started to smile.

She wiggled down his body until she came to the fastening of his jeans. As she unzipped him, he drawled, "Are you going to grab on and start sucking again?"

She snickered, her expression filling with mischief. "Yep. You got a problem with that, soldier?"

He was already so hard for her, his cock ached. "I can't imagine ever having a problem with that," he growled. "Just so we're clear."

He lifted his hips so she could tug off his jeans. Earlier, when he had slipped out to go fishing, he hadn't bothered to pull on boxers, and as he kicked off his pants, his full erection bounced on his abdomen. Sitting, he pulled off his T-shirt and tossed it after the jeans. Then he propped one foot on the floor, parting his legs.

"Mmm," she murmured as she looked up the length of his nude body. It was such a satisfied little sound, he had to grin. Spreading her flattened hands against his abdomen, she rubbed up and out in a wide, sweeping caress that encompassed his torso.

Then she entwined her fingers with his, urging his arms down by his side. Intrigued and aroused, he complied, watching her ravenously as she shackled his wrists with her hands.

The silent reference was unmistakable. His mind flashed back to pinning her on his bed while he sucked and licked between her legs. The memory caused him to growl underneath his breath even as he angled his hips so that she had better access to him.

It was the gentlest of sex games, getting inside his head and playing off his memories. She couldn't hold him in place if he didn't let her.

He let her.

Lowering her head, she began to lick, kiss and nibble at the skin of his flat abdomen. His muscles tightened as the sensation ran all over the surface of his body. She moved all around his cock, which lay distended and aching on his stomach, but she never focused on it. Instead she focused everywhere else.

Because of the angle and movement of her body, she still ended up touching him. Her cheek came into contact with the hypersensitive skin at the head of his erection. Then her jaw brushed against the shaft. A lock of her hair fell forward over her shoulder and tickled at his balls, which had drawn up tight in anticipation.

Every glancing caress made him hotter, harder. When she rubbed her nose affectionately in the dark hair that sprinkled his torso, he hissed, "Come on, get on with it, damn it."

"Hold your horses," she said against his skin.

Tension vibrated through his arms as he fought conflicting urges. He needed to break free of her hold, sink his hands into her hair and demand that she take him in her mouth.

But he also needed to subject himself to her desires. She gave him the gift of her compliance when his need for dominance took control. He would do no less for her.

She felt his struggle in his body's response to her. Angling her head, the dimple in her cheek appeared as she gave him a naughty smile. "You're still such a sexy beast, your majesty. Sexy and beast—two of my favorite things."

The sight of her pulled him out of his preoccupation with his growing urgency.

She looked so happy. The sight fed all the dark places inside him. Tugging gently with one hand, he silently asked to be freed, and her fingers loosened.

He ran his fingers along her cheek and stroked her soft, smiling lips. "I adore you, you know," he told her quietly. "Just so that we're clear."

Adore. What an exotic, extravagant word. He couldn't remember ever saying it to anyone before.

Her smile deepened. She pressed a kiss against his erection, and it flexed in reaction. She whispered, "I adore you too."

Lowering her head, she licked around the sensitive edge of the broad tip. His indrawn breath was clearly audible in the peaceful silence of the cabin. With a small, contented sound, much like a purr, she grasped him at the base and took him in her mouth.

She still held one of his wrists. Turning it in her grasp, he took her hand and rubbed her fingers. With his free hand, he stroked her hair.

Liquid fire cascaded along his nerve endings as she worked him. Opening her throat, she took him all the way in. She was such a generous lover. She used her lips and tongue with single-mindedness, creating a wet, tight suction and rhythm that made him crazy. Gasping, he gave up on control, fisted his hands in her hair and raised his head to stare at her as he pumped into her mouth.

The pleasure quickly became too intense. He pulled her head up.

She made a disappointed moue. "Hey, I was busy with that."

But he had lost his sense of humor.

"Come here," he muttered. As she changed course and readily shifted up to him, he drove his mouth onto hers, plunging as deep as he could with his tongue. The fire she had lit in his veins wouldn't let him slow down.

With a heave, he flipped them so that she landed on the couch while he sprawled on top of her. She gasped at the drastic change, her hair flying in her face. While she shoved the curls out of the way, he stripped off her soft, loose pants.

Lifting her torso, she pulled off her fleecy top. Underneath, she wore one of her pretty, lacy bras. He managed to rein himself in so he didn't rip the delicate material as he unhooked it and slipped it off. When she was completely nude, he hauled her up and around until she knelt on the floor, her upper body braced on the couch cushions.

"One of these days, I really am going to stop acting like such an animal," he said between his teeth as he ran his hands greedily over her curves.

"Please don't do it on my account." She braced herself with one arm against the back of the couch and spread her knees wide, baring herself to him in invitation.

He might be an animal, but he wasn't totally inconsiderate.

Fingering her gently, he drew out moisture so that she was ready for him. With a breathless moan, she shifted restlessly underneath his touch.

He enjoyed her reaction so much, he eased two fingers inside. She was velvety soft, tight and wet. Her inner muscles clung to his fingers as he fucked her, making him growl under his breath.

"I could come just by watching you," he muttered. He loved everything she did during sex. He loved everything about her.

"Come on," she whispered, moving back against his hand as he worked her. "Bite me."

Pausing, he tried to think. "How long has it been since the last time?"

"It's been a while. Long enough." Reaching behind her, she stroked and squeezed his cock.

He covered her fingers as she grasped him, otherwise he might explode. "Are you sure?"

"I'm sure. It was the day you baked that awful chocolate cake, remember?"

Her shoulders shook, and he realized she was laughing. He told her darkly, "We don't talk about that cake."

"*You* might not talk about it," she retorted. "But it happens to be one of my very favorite subjects. When you started, you were so—annoyingly confident. . . . *Ohh.*"

She gasped the last as he pulled away his hand, positioned himself at her entrance and pushed in. He flexed in and out until he was able to plant himself all the way inside. Then, obeying a primitive instinct, he lowered down until his chest covered her shapely back. In that position, he could only fuck her in shallow thrusts. Physically titillating, it satisfied some deep-seated emotion.

Lifting her head back so that it nestled in the crook of his shoulder, her breath came hard at each quick thrust.

Putting his lips to her ear, he whispered, "Let's get another thing clear. We might decide to do in vitro. You might get pregnant. If you do, it will be my child. No one else's. Mine. Just like you're mine. Understood?"

Her face twisted. She nodded.

"Say it," he said. He reached around her hip to finger where they joined, and found her pleasure point.

"I'm yours."

He believed her. He had faith in her.

His fangs descended, and he bit.

The sharp, sweet pain of his bite pierced the tender flesh where her neck met her shoulder. They both stopped and waited.

Tremors ran through the muscles of her arms and legs. His weight pinned her against the cushions, his hard, muscled arms enfolding her. He felt so good inside her, both silken and hard at once. With his fingers pressing on her clit *yet he was still not moving*, she felt like she was going to fly apart.

The momentary sting from his bite disappeared. Pleasure stole into her, so much pleasure, and oh my God, something had to give.

She whimpered, "Julian, please."

The gentle draw of his mouth intensified everything. The rasp of the couch cushion against her bare skin. The tickle of his chest hair. The pressure that built from inside. He could climb inside her head like nobody else she had ever known.

She needed to move so damn badly, yet he held still, and he held still, until she couldn't hold back a muffled scream.

At that, a deep, quiet growl vibrated against her back, and he moved.

Just his fingers.

The sensation that rocketed through her was so extreme, she exploded. She bucked in his arms, sobbing. He clamped down on her and held her in place effortlessly, stroking and stroking, while she rode the waves of her climax. He took her to a place beyond words, until finally she had to pull his hand away.

Only then did he ease out of the bite and rise up. Grasping

her by the hips, he began to pump into her in long, powerful strokes. She didn't know what was more devastating—when he focused on giving her more pleasure than she had ever experienced in her life, or when he focused on taking his own.

Helpless tears leaked out of her eyes. All she knew was that making love to Julian stripped her of every barrier, until she felt totally open and exposed.

Then he went rigid. She could feel his tension pouring through the tight grip on her hips.

He whispered, "Melisande."

There was so much yearning in his deep voice, she lifted her head. Twisting, she reached back to him with one hand. He grasped it. Their eyes met.

His thick, muscular body was in silhouette against the backdrop of the lake. The diffuse, early morning sunshine highlighted the flecks of white in his hair and the power in his piercing gaze.

And oh God, the look on his face.

To be loved like that . . . it was so much more than she could ever have hoped for.

His head and shoulders bowed, and his face clenched. She watched him orgasm while she felt the pulse of it inside, and she helped prolong his pleasure by rocking gently back against him.

"You're mine too," she whispered. "Don't you ever forget it."

"Yes," he whispered. "I never will."

Afterward, when he finally pulled his softening penis out, she sighed in resignation. "I always hate that part. I want you to stay inside."

"I do too," he said, stroking her buttocks and thighs.

He took his T-shirt and gently cleaned her, while she yawned and a heavy lassitude crept over her. "The fire's so lovely," she murmured as she crawled onto the couch. "I want to curl up here for a while. We can go to bed later, okay?"

"Okay." Grabbing a soft chenille throw, he joined her. She laid her head on his chest, while he wrapped them in the blanket.

Held in his arms, a deep, peaceful sleep took her.

When she next opened her eyes, the light had changed and she was alone. Yawning, she stretched and looked around. In the fireplace, the flames had died down. What remained of the logs glowed a deep, gorgeous red.

Her clothes had been folded and set on the floor near her head, and a familiar rich, appetizing smell filled the house.

Smiling, she dressed and padded into the kitchen.

He had cleaned up the flour. She was sorry to have missed the sight of the Nightkind King wielding a broom and dustpan.

Barefoot and shirtless, and dressed in his jeans, he stood at the counter in front of a pan of chocolate cake. Evidently, she had slept hard for a couple of hours, for the cake was not only baked, it also appeared to be cool. He had opened a container of store-bought, cream cheese frosting.

His head bent, he focused on spreading the frosting evenly. He took such care with the task, gently working the knife so that he didn't damage the delicate surface.

For some reason the sight brought fullness to her chest. Tears sprang to her eyes.

"What did you do?" she asked.

It was a stupid thing to say. She could see very well what he had done.

He looked up to give her a smile that creased his face.

"I baked you another cake," he said. "I hope I did it right this time."

Turn the page for a sneak peek at
Thea Harrison's next novel
of the Elder Races

SHADOW'S
END

Coming soon from Berkley Sensation!

W ith one blunt forefinger, Graydon tapped out a text on his smartphone.

We can't put off meeting any longer. We're running out of time. I need . . .

He paused as an onslaught of emotion cascaded through him.
I need to see you.
I need to touch your cheek, clasp your hand.
I need to look into your eyes. Your beautiful eyes. I need to know the precious light inside you has not died.
That was when the vision hit him.
He was used to having visions. He'd had them his entire, very long life. The Gaelic had many words and terms for such a thing. *An Da Shealladh* or 'the two sights' was one of the most famous of them.
When he was tired to the point of distraction, or hungry to the point of feeling hollow, he saw images of places he had not yet seen or things he had not yet done, and he knew

he would see those places, and he would do those things. Eventually.

The scene rolled over him as inescapably as if he had plunged into a vast ocean and water closed over his head.

Over the last two hundred years, the vision had become familiar. He had seen it so many times. It held a scent of danger, smoky like gunpowder and sharp as a stiletto.

White, like snowfall, blanketed the ground near a dark, tempestuous shore. The white was broken by rocks as black as midnight. Nearby, a behemoth of a building crouched atop a sprawling bluff like a huge predator. When he looked down, he saw bright scarlet blooming on the white ground, like roses opening to the sun.

Only the scarlet wasn't flowers, but blood.

His blood, dripping between his fingers.

"A dark, compelling world. I'm hooked!"

— J. R. Ward, #1 *New York Times* bestselling author

FROM *USA TODAY* BESTSELLING AUTHOR

THEA HARRISON

The Elder Race Novels

DRAGON BOUND

STORM'S HEART

SERPENT'S KISS

ORACLE'S MOON

LORD'S FALL

KINKED

NIGHT'S HONOR

TheaHarrison.com
facebook.com/TheaHarrison
facebook.com/ProjectParanormalBooks
penguin.com

M1122AS0314

*Centuries ago, two lovers were torn apart by forces
beyond their control. Now they have been reunited by
destiny and are willing to sacrifice everything again
to save a world on the brink of extinction.*

FROM *USA TODAY* BESTSELLING AUTHOR

THEA HARRISON

The Game of Shadows Novels

Rising Darkness

Falling Light

AVAILABLE NOW

TheaHarrison.com
facebook.com/TheaHarrison
penguin.com

M1605AS1214